USA TODAY bestselling and RITA® Award–nominated author **Caitlin Crews** loves writing romance. She teaches her favourite romance novels in creative writing classes at places like UCLA Extension's prestigious Writers' Programme, where she finally gets to utilise the MA and PhD in English Literature she received from the University of York in England. She currently lives in the Pacific Northwest, with her very own hero and too many pets. Visit her at caitlincrews.com.

Clare Connelly was raised in small-town Australia among a family of avid readers. She spent much of her childhood up a tree, Mills & Boon book in hand. Clare is married to her own real-life hero, and they live in a bungalow near the sea with their two children. She is frequently found staring into space—a surefire sign that she's in the world of her characters. She has a penchant for French food and ice-cold champagne, and Mills & Boon novels continue to be her favourite ever books. Writing for Modern is a long-held dream. Clare can be contacted via clareconnelly.com or at her Facebook page.

Also by Caitlin Crews

Unwrapping the Innocent's Secret
Secrets of His Forbidden Cinderella
The Italian's Pregnant Cinderella

Once Upon a Temptation collection

Claimed in the Italian's Castle

The Combe Family Scandals miniseries

The Italian's Twin Consequences
Untamed Billionaire's Innocent Bride
His Two Royal Secrets

Also by Clare Connelly

Spaniard's Baby of Revenge
Shock Heir for the King
Redemption of the Untamed Italian
The Secret Kept from the King
Hired by the Impossible Greek

Crazy Rich Greek Weddings miniseries

The Greek's Billion-Dollar Baby
Bride Behind the Billion-Dollar Veil

CHRISTMAS IN THE KING'S BED

CAITLIN CREWS

THEIR IMPOSSIBLE DESERT MATCH

CLARE CONNELLY

MILLS & BOON

First Published in Great Britain 2020
by Mills & Boon, an imprint of HarperCollins*Publishers*
1 London Bridge Street, London, SE1 9GF

ISBN: 978-0-263-27835-4

MIX
Paper from
responsible sources
FSC C007454

This book is produced from independently certified FSC™ paper
to ensure responsible forest management.
For more information visit www.harpercollins.co.uk/green.

Printed and bound in Spain
by CPI, Barcelona

CHRISTMAS IN THE KING'S BED

CAITLIN CREWS

CHAPTER ONE

"YOUR BETROTHED IS waiting for you, sire," came the diffident voice of King Orion's personal steward from behind him. "In your private salon, as requested."

Orion murmured his thanks, but didn't turn around. He kept his brooding gaze on his beloved country, laid out before him in the November sun. This view from the heights of the palace took in the largest town on the main island that made up the kingdom of Idylla, a sweep of stark-white buildings with the blue Aegean beyond. He had always loved this view. In the long, dark days of his father's tumultuous, dissolute reign—meaning, the whole of Orion's life until a few months ago—he had often stood here. He had gazed out on the splendor of the tiny kingdom that had endured so many wars, regime changes, and horrors in its time, yet still stood.

He had told himself that Idylla would survive his father, too.

And he had spent long hours imagining what he would do differently when it was his turn to rule. How best he could honor and serve his people, who deserved so much better than what they'd had in King Max.

Orion had vowed he would do whatever it took to erase his people's memories of his father's excesses and scandals. Whatever it took to restore peace and serenity to the island kingdom.

But now the time had come to do just that.

And he did not want any part of it.

"'Your betrothed,'" echoed his brother, Prince Griffin, in the lazily sardonic tone that matched the way he lounged in his preferred armchair, there before the fireplace that took up the better part of one wall. "You do know that you're the king now, Orion—don't you? I was there when they put the crown on your head."

"Do you mean when you swore an oath of fealty to me?" Orion asked mildly, without turning around. "Feel free to enact it."

"Yes, yes, my entire life is an act of homage to my liege," Griffin murmured in the same tone. He paused a moment. "You could also choose *not* to be betrothed. Then make it law. Again—you are the king. You can do as you like. I would have thought that was the main benefit of the whole thing."

Orion could do just that. Of course he could. But there were factors at play that Griffin didn't know about and, more important, Orion had given his word. Their father had gone back on his word habitually. Constantly. King Max's word had been meaningless.

Orion had no intention of being anything like his father.

"If I did such a thing I would be no better than him," he said quietly, to the only other person alive who knew how seriously he took these things.

"You were born better than him," Griffin retorted, a familiar harshness in his voice that always accompanied any discussion of their late, unlamented father.

Because King Max had not simply been a bad monarch, though he was that. In spades. He had been a far worse father than he'd been a king, and a terrible husband to their mother to boot.

But this was not the time to compare scars.

The future Orion had promised his people was here. He was that future. And he had no intention of breaking his promises. His earliest memories were of the vows his father had broken, one after the next, as if it was a game to him. He had betrayed his family and his country with the same carelessness. Orion would do neither.

No matter how little he liked what he needed to do next.

When he'd been sixteen, he had made a vow to the pack of reporters who had followed him about, clamoring for the crown prince's take on his father's every scandal. He had told them with all the ringing intensity of youth that *he* would live a blameless, honorable, scandal-free life.

Orion had gone to extraordinary lengths to keep that promise.

He saw no reason to stop now.

"Then I will leave you to your martyrdom," his younger brother said. "I know how you love it."

Orion turned, then. Griffin grinned at him, then rose—as wholly unrepentant as ever. He stretched like a cat instead of a prince, because he had always taken great pleasure in flaunting his physicality at every turn.

The spare could do as he liked. The heir, on the other hand, had always to think first of the kingdom.

Their father had apparently missed that lesson, but Orion had stamped it deep into his bones.

"Duty comes for us all, brother," he said lightly.

Or lightly for him, in any case.

"I haven't forgotten what I promised you," Griffin replied. "Even though, obviously, you could wave your autocratic pinkie and save us both from our fates." He let out a long, delighted laugh when Orion only frowned at him. "Please spare me another lecture on what we owe our subjects. Or your subjects, more like. I've heard it all before. I, too, will commit myself to blamelessness. Soon."

"It becomes no less true in the retelling," Orion said with what he hoped was quiet dignity. Instead of what he actually felt. That being the lowering realization that if he could, he would shirk this betrothal in a heartbeat, no matter what destruction that might cause. He would wave the royal pinkie—

But he did not break vows. To himself, to others, or to his people.

That had to be the beginning and the end of it, or who was he?

Griffin rolled his eyes at his older brother and king as if he could read Orion's mind. He likely could. He lifted a hand, then prowled his way out of Orion's private office. No doubt off to despoil virgins, carouse, and enjoy the last days of the scandalous reputation he'd built for himself as possibly the most unrepentant playboy in the history of Europe.

Orion stood where he was, a muscle in his jaw flexing with a tension and fury he couldn't control.

You are *controlling it,* he told himself stoutly. *Because, unlike your father, you are always in control. Always.*

And always, always would be. That was one more promise he'd made himself.

He blew out a breath, there where even Griffin couldn't see him.

And then there was nothing for it. Putting off his unpleasant duty wasn't going to make it any better. It wasn't going to save him from the unwelcome task he had no choice but to perform.

Like everything else in his life, he was simply going to have to do what must be done, no matter what.

His personal feelings were irrelevant and always had been.

He had learned that beyond any reasonable doubt when, at seventeen, he'd been the one to discover his mother, the queen, after she'd taken her own life. And when his father had proved unequal to the task of handling her funeral—preferring to decamp to the Caribbean with a brace of starlets on each arm—Orion had stepped in to handle it.

Not because he'd wanted to handle it. He'd been seventeen. Still considered a child by some. But despite his feelings and his youth, he'd handled it because it needed to be handled.

As the years passed, his father had increased his vile behavior, made ever more unhinged demands, and had shirked more and more of his royal duties. Orion had stepped in and shouldered the load, each and every time.

He'd been doing the lion's share of the monarch's actual work for a decade, but always with the knowledge that at any moment, on the slightest whim, his father could and likely would sweep in and undo all his work.

Today was an example of the old king's machinations from beyond the grave, in point of fact, and it was the same as it ever had been. As if he was still alive to ruin lives. Orion would have to do what needed doing, not because he *wanted* to do it. But because it was for the good of Idylla.

He pushed away from the window and headed for his door, automatically checking his appearance in one of the mirrors as he passed. Not because he was vain, but because he was the crown. And in contrast to his father's visible, heedless decline, he wished to look above reproach—and as much like the official photographs of himself—as possible.

Because that helped his people feel secure.

Everything Orion did was to make Idylla better. To convince his people that all was well, that he could be trusted, that the years of shame and scandal were behind them all. Part of that was presenting them with an image of a king they could believe in.

One that was as opposite his father's slovenly appearance in his last years as possible.

Orion looked presentable enough, and left his office, moving swiftly now that he'd stopped stalling the inevitable.

He might not wish to be betrothed, but he was. And that meant he was getting married, because a broken betrothal was a broken promise—a scandal in the making—and he would allow neither.

No matter what happened.

The palace corridor outside his office was quieter than it had been while his father was alive, when Orion's staff had always rushed to and fro, always in one crisis or another as they'd all done their best to anticipate and/or manage the king's mercurial decisions. Becoming king had actually eased Orion's duties in many ways, because he no longer had to spend 89 percent of his time conjuring up ways to handle the fallout of each and every one of King Max's contradictory decrees.

Competent, reserved, and sane. Those were Orion's goals as king.

Idylla had been the world's punch line for far too long. It ended now.

His betrothed might not know it yet, she might have her own agenda, for all he knew—but despite who she was and what she represented, she would fall in line with the goals of his new regime.

One way or the other.

Or she would pay the price.

He headed toward his private salon, nodding at courtiers and staff as he went. No one approached him, which told him he probably ought to do something about his expression.

But he didn't.

Because he was not his brother, who could produce a smile from the ether on command, then wield it like a weapon. Orion had not spent years perfecting a *smile*, thank you, when he'd had a kingdom to run and a rogue monarch to manage. His face did what it would.

He opened the door to his private salon briskly, prepared to lay out his plans and his expectations—

But the room was empty.

Orion blinked. He prided himself on being approachable, and no particular stickler for courtly etiquette, but he was still the king. Even as the crown prince, there was only one person who had ever dared keep him waiting—and his father was dead.

This was not an auspicious beginning to matrimonial life.

A moment later he realized the French doors that opened out onto one of the balconies was ajar. He frowned, because this was not part of his plan. Moreover, he would have laid odds—not that he ever gambled the way his father had—that his betrothed would have been eager for this meeting he'd been putting off for the better part of two years. He wouldn't have been surprised if she'd stood just inside the door, waving one of her father's tabloids in his face while crowing about her victory and his capitulation.

He'd expected as much, in fact.

And perhaps that wasn't fair, he thought, because he prided himself on fairness, too. Or tried. The truth was, he knew very little about Lady Calista Skyros, the woman he was meant to marry. Because no matter what he liked to thunder at his brother, he too had been holding out hope that he wouldn't have to do this.

Lady Calista was the eldest daughter of perhaps the single most vile citizen of the kingdom of Idylla, now the old king was dead. Aristotle Skyros had been born into Idyllian nobility, had ponced about in between various universities—getting sent down from each in turn—and had blown through his own fortune by the age of twenty-three. Luckily for him, his appalled father had died shortly thereafter, with no choice but to leave his considerable estate in his disappointing son's hands. According to the many interviews he gave on his favorite topic—himself—Aristotle had disliked the seven months of so-called destitution he'd experienced and had thus vowed to do better with his second fortune.

Annoyingly, he had. He now owned a sprawling media empire, almost entirely made up of the kind of tabloid filth that made anyone who looked at it dirty. And those who were featured against their will in his snide, insinuating columns and slickly produced shows could never make themselves clean again.

As Orion knew personally.

When his father had announced, three years ago, that he had arranged Orion's eventual marriage, Orion had not bothered to argue about it. There was no point fighting his father, especially not when the old king was deep in his cups, which was where he'd preferred to live. Orion had assumed that if he waited it out, his father would reverse himself. Possibly within the hour—another thing that happened with alarming regularity.

But instead, his father had died. In the squalid circumstances the country and the world had come to expect from him, naturally, with unfortunate women and mood-altering substances all around. Because why change in death what he had so exulted in during his life?

Aristotle Skyros had slithered out of his hellhole and into the palace almost before *"The king is dead, long live the king"* finished echoing through the halls. And he had made it known that as far as he was concerned, the betrothal the old king had made between the new King of Idylla and his daughter was set in stone.

"Surely I decide what is stone and what is nothing more than a bad dream we have now happily woken up from," Orion had said.

With perhaps more menace than was wise.

Aristotle, an unpleasantly dissipated-looking man whose bald head gleamed with the same malevolence that was apparent in his gaze, had smiled. Oily and insincere.

"You can do anything you please, Your Majesty," he had replied unctuously. He'd bowed his head as if in deference. "As will I, if necessary."

Orion had been tempted to pretend he didn't recognize the threat in the other man's words. He had been king for a matter of hours at that point, and had been naive enough to imagine there might be some kind of grace period. Some allowance while he found his feet—but no. Of course not.

But he had tamped down on his temper and had not, sadly, strangled the other man where he sat. "If you wish to threaten me, Skyros, I suggest you do it. I detest pretense."

Aristotle had not bothered with another show of false

obeisance. "You will marry my daughter, Majesty. Because if you do not, I will have no choice but to release a selection of photographs I have in my possession that were in a private collection for years. Photographs so shocking and potentially explosive that your father offered you as collateral to keep them hidden."

Orion had scoffed at that. "My father would have cheerfully offered me as collateral in a game of checkers. And likely did." He'd shaken his head. "What could possibly be worse than the things he already felt comfortable foisting upon the entire world?"

"I thought you might ask that," the other man had said, with entirely too much satisfaction in his voice.

That had been Orion's first inkling that this was all worse than he'd thought.

Aristotle pulled out a file and placed it on the table between them. A low coffee table where he could, with what seemed to Orion to be great relish, flip through the photographs he'd brought with him.

It took three pictures.

Orion sat back, feeling faintly sick.

And with those images in his head that he knew he would never be able to wash clean.

The man across from him hadn't laughed, though there was a look about him that suggested he would, later.

"Tempting, isn't it, to imagine that with the old man dead and buried, all his scandalous acts are swept away. But I think you see, now, that there are some things that can never go away. And more important, that you too will find yourself tainted if they are exposed." Aristotle had smiled again. "Your Majesty."

For a moment, Orion hadn't been sure that he could speak. And he had been closer to indulging the tidal wave of fury inside him than he ever had been before.

It took everything he had not to launch himself at the other man. Everything he had and the sure knowledge that Aristotle would love it if he did.

But everything in him had rebelled. Giving in to blackmail was never the right answer. He knew that. It had been impressed upon him from a young age that he must never allow another person to have that kind of hold over him, not when he would one day rule—except, what choice did he have?

Idylla could not stand another scandal.

And certainly not one that was, though it beggared belief, worse than all that had come before.

Aristotle had waited, the very picture of corpulent malice.

And, as ever, Orion had shoved his personal feelings aside and thought of the kingdom.

"I do not know what bargain you made with my father," he had said eventually, though every word was like poison on his tongue. "Therefore, I cannot honor it. If you want your daughter to be my queen, you must agree to my terms."

Aristotle had chuckled. "That's not how this works."

But the longer Orion gazed at him, expressionless, the less he laughed.

And when he stopped, Orion continued. "You will sign a binding legal document that will ensure two things. One, that you will be imprisoned for life if you violate any of the terms in said document, all of which, of course, will insist upon your silence regarding these photos. And two, in addition to your jail time, you will be fined. To the point of insolvency and beyond, if you are ever responsible for any of this coming to light. Do you understand me?"

Aristotle sputtered. "I don't think—"

But Orion had spent his whole life dealing with a man

just like Aristotle. A man who was even worse, in fact, because his every word had been law, like it or not. Once the red edge of his temper had faded, he'd understood that like it or not, he was in his element.

He would be handling his father unto eternity, it seemed.

But at least he was good at that.

"In return," he said coldly, "I will elevate your vile, polluted bloodline. I will marry your daughter. I will do this because unlike my father, I am a man of my word." He'd watched Aristotle's face grow mottled. "But because I am my father's son, I will also put the betrothal agreement in writing." He'd taken out his mobile and fired off a series of texts to his staff. "I will have my attorneys deliver the appropriate documents while we wait for the search on your properties to be finished."

And Aristotle hadn't liked it but he'd nodded, anyway, and made the deal.

There were worse things, Orion told himself now as he opened the French doors and stepped out onto the balcony. Men in his position had been marrying for reasons like this, or worse, as long as there had been kings. So it went. His own parents' marriage had been arranged and if he knew nothing else it was that without even trying, he would be a better husband than his father had been.

No matter if Calista Skyros was a carbon copy of her repellant father.

He was sure that the woman who stood at the balcony rail, her gaze somewhere in the distance where the Aegean met the sky, heard his approach. But she didn't turn.

And whether she had a sense of the dramatic, was deliberately being rude, or was girding her loins for this confrontation, he didn't know. But he took the opportunity to do the same.

Orion had seen pictures of her, of course. His staff had presented him with an exhaustive portfolio on Lady Calista within hours of his father's initial announcement. He knew she'd been educated at the Sorbonne, not at an Idyllian university. That she had been bred to make an aristocratic marriage, regardless of her father's filthy trade, because that was how Idyllian nobility worked. Its purpose was to continue itself.

He knew that after the Sorbonne, Calista had come back to Idylla and started work at the lowest level of her father's company, which he was sure was meant to counteract suggestions of nepotism when it was clearly the opposite. These days, she had clawed her way much higher in the company. She was now the vice president of a media conglomerate that trafficked in lies.

His betrothed was a liar by blood and by choice, in other words.

She was in no way an appropriate choice to be his queen. If he'd been permitted to choose for himself, he would have looked for someone who worked with charities. Someone whose calling in life was service to others, not…revolting tabloid speculation.

But Orion was a practical, rational man. He'd had to be, whether he wanted to be or not. The truth was, he had never expected that he might get the opportunity to fall in love like a regular person. Because he wasn't one.

In a way, this was no different from any arrangement that might have been made for him.

And all that mattered was that he would protect Idylla, come what may. Even if it meant marrying this creature and linking her detestable family to his.

He had placed the Crown of Idylla upon his head and he had sworn to do his duty, and so he would.

She turned then, and for a moment, Orion didn't think of duty at all.

His betrothed was not the least bit photogenic, he understood in a searing, unexpected flash of what he was appalled to understand was desire.

Electric and near overwhelming.

Every photograph he'd seen of his intended had led him to expect that she would be pretty. In that way that so many slender blonde women were pretty. Not quite interchangeable, but then again, the world was filled with them. One blended into the next.

But Calista Skyros was not the blandly pretty blonde she'd appeared in photographs.

There was something about her. Something about the way she held herself, maybe. Or the surprising, sparkling intelligence in her aquamarine gaze. She was blonde, yes. And pretty, inarguably.

But something in him pulled tight and seemed to *hum* as he gazed at her, and he had not been prepared for that.

For what seemed like an eternity, their eyes caught and held, out there on the windswept balcony.

And Orion was uncomfortably aware of himself as a man, not a king. Flesh and blood and need, to his horror.

"Your Majesty," she said in quiet greeting, and he was sure some kind of shadow moved over her face.

It only made her prettier. And more interesting. She straightened from the rail as she faced him, then sank before him in the expected deep curtsy, exhibiting both an easy grace and the kind of excellent manners that would have told him of her years of comportment classes if he hadn't already known.

He would have said such displays were fussy, old-fashioned window dressing he could do without, but the sight of Calista Skyros genuflecting before him made everything inside him tighten, then shift.

She rose with the same ease and he studied her, this woman who would be his queen. His wife. The mother of his heirs.

It seemed an odd thing indeed to stand on this familiar balcony while cool November air came in off the ocean, with an edge to it despite the sun, and think so dispassionately about *his wife*. About the sex he would have with this stranger to ensure his line of succession. About the relationship they would be forced to cobble together because of those things, one way or another. Toward the end of his mother's life his parents had been separated by as many layers of staff and physical distance inside this palace as possible, but Orion had always hoped he could create some kind of harmony in something so cold-blooded.

And yet what he thought when he looked at her was… not harmonious.

Not precisely.

He forced himself to remember who she was.

"Lady Calista," he said coolly by way of greeting, inclining his head.

He could not fault her appearance in any way, though he wanted to find nothing but faults in her. That would be easier, somehow, but unlike her father, she was flawless. She wore a long-sleeved dress in a soft dove-gray color that flattered her features and was both modest and modern at once. She wore pearls at her ears, and though the brisk sea air rushed around them, her hair stayed put in its sleek chignon.

He felt his jaw tighten, because, of course, she was auditioning for the role of queen. A role she knew she'd already won, perhaps. But that being the case, she could have rolled into this meeting like a publicity disaster waiting to happen—simply to show him how little control he had, as he suspected her father would have if he was her—and she hadn't.

Orion would take his triumphs where he could.

"Perhaps we can step inside," he said, because maybe it was the sea air and the view that was getting to him. Maybe the usual Idyllian sun was making her appear lovelier and less patently evil than she was. Inside the palace, surely, reality would reassert itself. "We have much to discuss."

She smiled in a quick sort of way that made him imagine she felt awkward, though that was unlikely.

Beware the urge to consider her a pawn in this, he growled at himself. *She is the vice president of her father's company, not a sacrificial virgin he's offered up in tribute.*

Whatever she was, he ushered her indoors with exaggerated courtesy, then sat across from her on a set of antique sofas that dated from the fifteenth century.

And then instantly regretted it.

Because it was quieter in here. More intimate, and the last thing in the world he wanted was intimacy with a member of the Skyros family.

If his parents' twisted relationship had been any indication, intimacy was not a prerequisite for the royal marriage. Or even particularly desirable, for that matter.

He didn't know how long he sat there, studying her as if the force of his attention could render her as bland as he'd expected her to be. But when he realized they were sitting in silence, and would continue to do so because he was the king and should speak first, he cleared his throat.

"Thank you for coming today," he said, sounding stiff and formal and pompous, which struck him as far more appropriate than standing about on balconies, confusing himself. "I thought it was best for the two of us to meet before our official engagement announcement."

He paused, and she seemed to startle, as if she'd never heard of such a thing. "Of course. Yes. The official announcement."

That struck him as disingenuous, but he wrestled his temper into place, locked up tight inside him.

"It will take place in two days' time, at the first holiday ball of the season." She didn't react to that, so he carried on with his talking points. "We will discuss our whirlwind relationship and how it was a bright light during the dark days before and after my father's death. We will talk about hope, and a new dawn, not only for ourselves, but for Idylla. As is tradition, we will be married six weeks from the first ball, on Christmas Eve, captivating the hearts and minds of not only the kingdom, but the world. Yet as spectacular as our wedding will be, as is customary, our marriage will be reserved. Competent."

"And sane," she chimed in. And smiled when he lifted a brow at her, though he rather thought the curve of her lips had an edge to it. That was unexpected. "Forgive me, Your Majesty. But I have heard your speeches."

Was that a slap at him? He shoved it aside. "Excellent. Then you already know how things will go."

"I admire your..." She paused. *"...certainty."*

"I am certain," Orion said quietly. "Because I will make it so."

"How...monocratic."

"Indeed. As I am the monarch." He waited for her to swallow, hard. "I will marry you, Lady Calista, because I gave my word that I would. I will make you my queen and consort, because that is the bargain your father made with mine. But hear me."

And this time, she only stared back at him mutely. No clever comments at the ready.

"I will tolerate no scandals," he told her. "And I understand that this might be hard for you, as scandals are your stock in trade." He saw something flash in her eyes like the sea, but she only pressed her lips into a firm line. "But there will be no anonymous stories from this palace. There will be no salacious insider exposés. If you cannot comply with this requirement, I am sorry to tell you that you will find our marriage…challenging."

"'Challenging?'" Her voice was huskier than before. "What, precisely, does 'challenging' mean?"

He allowed himself a faint smile. "I will take a page from kings of old," he told her, the vow of it in his voice. He felt certain she could hear it. "If you defy me I will install you in Castle Crag."

"Castle Crag." She blinked. "You don't mean *Castle Crag.*"

"I have never meant anything more."

"Castle Crag is in the middle of the Aegean." She stared at him, her eyes widening at whatever she saw. "It's a slab of rock with an ancient fortress on it. I don't think it has electricity. It's a *prison.*"

"That is precisely why any number of my ancestors preferred to keep their wives and assorted other dissidents there," Orion said, his voice even and his gaze hard on hers. "I plan to rule as a progressive king, Lady Calista. But when it comes to the queen I was blackmailed into accepting, know this. Where you are concerned, you can expect me to be purely medieval."

CHAPTER TWO

CALISTA SKYROS COULD have gone her whole life without ever meeting the King of Idylla.

That would have been her preference, in fact, because she liked the royal family well enough—but only in a distant sense. As pomp, circumstance, and background noise to the real work that went on in the island kingdom.

But since when had her father ever taken her preferences into account?

She stared at the man before her. Because he was a man, she reminded herself. A man who happened to be a king, sure. But no matter how her mother fluttered around her—insisting that she dress like Idylla's answer to one of those overexposed British princesses—or her father growled at her about his *agenda*, Calista's goals did not involve palace intrigue. Or calling herself queen of anything, for that matter, no matter how many fancy dresses might be involved.

Her goals had always been simple.

Protect her sister. Neutralize her parents. And while she was at it, take over Skyros Media, oust her father from the board, and control her own destiny, at last.

It was all very simple indeed, if not as easy as she'd hoped when she'd started down this path years ago. Regardless, she was so close now. So close she could taste it. She had every reason to believe Skyros Media would be hers by the end of the year.

At last.

Her father had come to her when the news of evil old King Max's death had reached him, puffed up with malicious joy that he would be installing his eldest daughter in the palace at last.

Not that Aristotle Skyros called her his *eldest* daughter. He liked to refer to her as his *only* daughter, which made Melody laugh but was one more reason Calista loathed him.

For a moment, she'd forgotten to pretend that she wanted the things he did, her usual gambit when dealing with him. For a moment, she'd forgotten that she wasn't out of the woods just yet.

"Not this betrothal nonsense again," she'd said, blinking at him over a mountain of paperwork on her desk in Skyros Media headquarters, there in the center of the royal city that spread out in a crescent below the palace and reminded her daily that she could endure as it had. "You can't be serious."

That had been a mistake. She hadn't been thinking, too focused on how close she was to the end result she'd been pushing for all this time. Her entire life, it seemed—but she hadn't made it there yet.

"Don't you dare take that tone with me," her father had snarled, that dangerous note in his voice. The one Calista had gone out of her way to avoid hearing for years now—and had been mostly successful. Because she'd convinced him that she was obedient. His protégé, desperate for his approval. His successor who followed his every command. As close as it was possible to get to the son he'd always wanted but had never had.

But she knew in that moment that if she'd been within reach, he would have slapped her soundly.

Don't go and ruin everything now, she'd warned herself.

"I'm sorry," she'd said at once, the conciliatory tone bitter on her tongue. She'd tried to shift her body language where she sat, hunching her shoulders and making herself small, the way she'd used to do. Back when she'd been a girl, and her father's rages had been a daily, inescapable trial there'd been no hope of escaping. "I just... Me as a queen? I can't imagine it, Papa."

She hated that word. *Papa.* As if there was some affection between them. As if her father was capable of such a thing as a paternal feeling. Or feelings at all.

But long ago, she'd learned how to soothe him, and calling him *papa* as if she admired and revered him was one method. Sometimes the only way to make it through life in her father's fist was to bow and scrape a little and tell him only things he wished to hear. As she'd grown, she'd learned that what a man like her father truly wanted from her was accomplishments he could claim as his own. So she'd thrown herself headfirst into making them happen.

She hadn't gotten herself in a situation where she needed to be *quite so* conciliatory in a long while. She couldn't say she liked the feeling.

Calista had been relieved to discover that she still had the knack for calming him when he settled himself in the chair on the other side of her desk, looking less furious and more...avid. She'd had to fight to conceal her shudder of distaste.

"I paid a great deal of money to secure your betrothal to Max's royal spawn," he'd told her, the remnants of his infamous temper still a little too obvious in his voice. "I expect you to honor that investment with a formal engagement and wedding."

"Of course, Papa," she'd murmured, aiming for *sweet* and *humble*. "Have I ever let you down?"

Calista was able to make herself say such things because she knew full well that the takeover she'd been planning for years was close. The annual board meeting was December 23. That gave her what was left of the year to make sure all her ducks were in a row. Everything she wanted was *so close* within her grasp she could almost reach out and touch it with her fingertips—

But if she got ahead of herself, she'd ruin everything. Overconfidence would lead straight to a loss. She knew that. Just as she knew she needed to win.

So despite her feelings on the subject, Calista had agreed to go ahead with this ridiculous engagement. And the wedding, she understood, theoretically would follow it. She had no other choice. Or, more accurately, her father had assumed she was fully on board because she knew better than to argue with him. It was pointless. Aristotle was obsessed with marrying her off to the brand-new king, and fighting with him about it would only get in the way of her true aims.

But she certainly hadn't expected it to take so long to get her first audience with King Orion. His father had died in the summer and here it was November. She'd had to spend months acting as if she was not only interested in marrying the man, but devastated that he was ignoring their betrothal. She'd had to listen to her father complain endlessly about the situation and about how it was a personal insult to him.

Worse, she'd had to suffer her sister's unapologetic cackling about her upcoming *royal wedding.*

Still, Calista had come here today prepared to do what

she needed to do. Pretend anything, act any part to hasten this along—not because she wanted to marry anyone, much less the king, but because it would give her father something to focus on while she gutted his company and made it her own. And the more her father focused on himself, the less he was likely to turn his attention to Melody.

Calista was determined to keep him from concentrating on her younger sister, no matter what.

But as she stared back at the new, young king, having acquitted herself marvelously—if she said so herself—with a little of those noble manners her teachers in boarding school had claimed she would never learn, she found herself revising her thinking on this whole big mess.

Because if what her father had ranted repeatedly was true, King Orion *had* to marry her.

He didn't have a choice in the matter.

And that meant Calista didn't have to fall all over him. She didn't have to pander to him, or try to smooth things over with him the way she did with her father. Unless she was very much mistaken, it meant she had to do nothing at all but show up.

"I'm not interested in any scandals either, actually," she said now, with images of remote Castle Crag still spinning around in her head. She folded her hands in her lap, presenting him with the perfect posture she liked to roll out in the boardroom, where no one expected much from the blonde, pretty daughter of such a hateful man. They looked at her and saw a bimbo. Which was usually right about when she whipped around and sank her teeth into their jugulars. "But I'm also not interested in being threatened with fortresses on rocks a million miles from shore."

He…froze. "I beg your pardon?"

Slipping back into her familiar corporate mode was

comforting. Because there was something about King Orion that made Calista…edgy. He wasn't what she'd expected, maybe. For one thing, the approximately seven trillion photographs she'd seen of him in her lifetime didn't really capture him. He looked like the images she'd seen, with his close-cropped chestnut hair, grave hazel eyes, and that stern mouth. It was just that, put all together, he was a lot more than a novelty tea towel sold to tourists in all the shops.

A *lot* more.

Her chest felt a bit tight and her pulse was a bit dramatic, if she was honest.

Part of it was that he was so shockingly fit. Rangy muscle, surprisingly solid, and packaged into a dark suit that should have made him look stuffy. But instead, it was cut so well that she found herself feeling remarkably patriotic about the way the fabric clung to his wide shoulders.

Even as he sat there and made pronouncements about what she would or wouldn't do, all she *wanted* to do was move a little closer to see whether or not his abdomen was as hard and ridged as she suspected it was.

But more than all of that, it was that air around him. As if he emitted his own electrical charge. There was a sense of leashed power in him, in the way he held himself and *waited*, almost, that she had not been expecting.

The same way she hadn't been expecting a hollow, hungry thing deep in her belly to hum at the sight of him.

You need to get your act together, Calista, she snapped at herself. Because she had far too much riding on all of this to lose her head over a handsome man.

Even if the handsome man in question was her king.

And, more, thought she was going to marry him and produce babies on command.

"It seems to me that you're under the impression that you have control here." She smiled, that little curve of her lips that business associates liked to claim was enigmatic. Usually after she'd pummeled them into dust. "But my understanding is that you actually *have to* marry me. Whether you want to or not."

He stared at her, that same frozen and arrested expression on his face. "Am I to understand that you know about the—ah—*leverage* your father has used against me?"

Aristotle had ranted excessively about the fact he had something on the old king that the new king would kill to conceal. He had not shared what that leverage was.

Something Calista saw no reason to share with the man staring her down.

"The point is that the leverage exists," she said, because she had always been good at playing these little power games. "And it exists on you, not me. So I'll thank you to stop making threats about Castle Crag. I have no interest in playing Knights of the Crusades, or whatever your threats of going medieval are supposed to mean. As far as I'm concerned, this is a business proposition between our two families, nothing more. Which is medieval enough, I'd think."

She thought she'd startled him. Or maybe she only wanted to. An expression she couldn't name and certainly couldn't read flashed through his eyes, then disappeared into a flash of grave hazel.

"How refreshing," he said after a long moment, though she doubted very much he found her the least bit refreshing. "I was led to expect the usual princess fantasies."

Calista laughed. "I can't think of anything I would like to be less than a princess. Luckily, what we're talking about is my becoming a queen, not a princess. I can get my head around that."

"Am I to understand you see yourself as one already? Metaphorically speaking, of course."

"I'm a businesswoman, not a queen," she replied, her heart beating a little faster because he'd challenged her, however obliquely. "And let me set the mood here, to save us some time. I don't care what your relationship is with my father."

"I would never describe the interactions I have been forced to have with your father as a 'relationship.'"

King Orion's voice was so frigid she was faintly surprised icicles didn't sprout into being round the room. Suddenly, it felt like November in a more northern, snow-covered place, instead of the typically mild Novembers here in Idylla's balmy Mediterranean climate.

She told herself she was immune to the cold. "Whatever you want to call it, I'm not interested in it. I'm sure you have your reasons for bowing to my father's whims and accepting this ridiculous betrothal. But whatever those reasons might be, it means only that you, like so many others, have surrendered to his blackmail."

"Again, I would dispute those terms."

She waved a hand. "Dispute them all you like. It doesn't change the facts. You're in his pocket, which means you're now in mine. And who knows? I've never had my own king before. Maybe it will be fun."

And she watched, fascinated despite herself, as King Orion Augustus Pax looked at her as if his head was exploding. Internally, of course.

Externally, all she could see was a muscle flexing in his lean jaw. And that fire that turned his hazel gaze to gold.

Despite herself, her breath caught. She suddenly wondered what it would be like if the most controlled creature in the history of the world—something that had been apparent when King Orion was no more than a princeling, especially when stood next to his disaster of a father—let go.

Could he let go?

She felt goose bumps shiver down the length of her spine.

Orion's eyes were volcanic. But his voice was calm. "I will remind you, Lady Calista, that I am your king."

"I do know that, Your Majesty. That's why I curtsied."

She made her voice careless, but the seething heat that was blasting her way was more uncomfortable than she wanted to admit. She got to her feet as if this was her meeting. Her darling little room tucked away in the royal palace, and the man before her nothing but…some guy.

Though no one could possibly confuse King Orion for *some guy.*

Just as, no matter what she'd said, it was hard to imagine a man so electric and indisputably regal in anyone's pocket, either. Even if she knew that he was. Her father had made certain to brag excessively that he was the architect of this betrothal, as if she wouldn't have figured that out on her own.

"This must be hard for you," she said, moving to look at the pictures scattered on the dreadfully elegant sideboard. Pictures of the two princes. The former queen. And not a one of King Max, which she supposed was only to be expected. She had yet to meet a soul who missed him, except possibly her father. And not because he'd had any affection for the dissipated late king. But because he'd been so easy to manipulate.

"Which part?" Orion's question was crisp. A bit like a slap. "The part where, for my father's sins, I am forced to contend with a base, repulsive reptile like Aristotle Skyros? Or the part where, having accepted that I must do my duty to my country even in the face of such an insult, I am confronted with a craven display of overweening self-importance that I must crown and call my queen?"

Ouch.

But she laughed and she couldn't have said why. "*Overweening* is quite a word, Your Majesty. Though I think you'll find that what men consider self-importance in women is usually the sort of confidence they consider par for the course in a man."

"On the contrary, Lady Calista." And that light in his hard gaze made her want to shiver. "Were any man to dare speak to me as you have just now I would lay him out flat."

Her curse was that some part of her longed to see it.

She made a tsking sound, and found herself leaning back against the sideboard in what was, she could admit, a bit of a show. How could she help herself? She was being forced into an arranged marriage against her will. That was the long and the short of it, and no matter her intentions where that was concerned or her reasons for going along with it, a girl had to make her own fun.

And you're in no way trying to cover up your response to the man, a voice inside her that sounded a lot like her sister's chimed in.

"Violence is something we expect from your brother, King Orion," she said, ignoring that voice. "Never you. Never the desperately responsible crown prince and possible savior of our dissipated country, a man so excruciatingly polite and correct that no one has ever been able to dig up the names of his lovers."

The king did not rise. He did not lounge back in his seat. He did not fidget, adjust his clothing, or shift his weight—and yet she still had the impression that he gathered himself. And changed, somehow, the very composition of his body. Right there before her eyes.

She told herself she was being foolish. But all the while, that gaze of his grew ever more molten.

"I imagine that must be a favorite pursuit in a media enterprise of such journalistic integrity as Skyros Media." His voice was a sardonic lash and it cost Calista something not to wince. "Rifling about in the trash for private information that is none of your concern."

She lifted her chin. "I think the word you're looking for is *news*."

"There is nothing newsworthy in someone's personal life. It is private and personal, by definition."

"I was under the impression that you were the king of this country," she shot back, lifting her brows at him. "Can a king have a personal life? I rather thought that what you do with the life your subjects support is our business. Either way, the choices you make personally affect us all. Or did you miss out on the entirety of your father's reign?"

Something blazed in his gaze then, and she expected him to erupt. To shoot to his feet. To hit something.

Or even raise his voice.

But instead, King Orion stayed where he was.

Locked down, she found herself thinking. Frozen solid.

And she didn't know why she had the sudden, sharp urge to see if she could melt him, by any means necessary.

When he spoke, she couldn't repress a shiver, because his voice was perfectly even. Measured. As if there had been nothing the least bit volcanic here when she was sure she could still taste the ash in the elegant room all around them.

"If your aim was to impress upon me that you will do as you like, consider it done." He studied her, and to her surprise, she almost felt as if she might…blush. Something she didn't think she'd done in her entire life—not when she'd grown up under Aristotle's thumb. Thankfully, the odd, prickling feeling passed. "I appreciate you coming into this meeting prepared to show me exactly who you are, Lady Calista. I assure you I won't forget it."

That, too, was a threat. And a more effective one, perhaps, because he said it so calmly.

"If you think I'm going to curl up in a ball and cry because you don't approve of me, think again," she told him, striving for the same tone, and refusing to duck her head or make herself smaller. There was only one man she pretended to cower before, and it wasn't this one. No matter if, deep inside, there was that *humming*. "I've agreed to marry you, Your Majesty. I'm fully aware of what that means."

"Are you?" He tilted his head slightly to one side. "I wonder. For example, can I expect this same aggression in bed?"

Again, a prickling heat swept over her, and horrified her. Worse, there was a gleam in the midst of all that stern hazel that told her he knew it. He *knew* he affected her.

When Calista had spent all these years learning how to conceal her feelings so well she sometimes wondered if she had any left.

She met his gaze as if he didn't trouble her in the least. "If you had the slightest idea how to be aggressive in bed or anywhere else, Your Majesty, I feel certain we would have found evidence of that by now." Calista allowed herself a smirk. "And run it in our tabloids, of course."

To her surprise, he laughed. "Is that how you measure

things, then? Whether or not it shows up in one of your sick, sad little magazines?"

"I believe in a free press. Was that the question?"

Orion looked entirely too satisfied, and she hated that something deep in her belly *quivered.* "I'll take that to mean you haven't the slightest idea what you're getting into with me, Lady Calista. How delightful to find we have something in common."

She felt breathless again, and had to remind herself that no matter what happened here in the battle for control over their dreary arranged marriage, it didn't change reality. And the reality was that he could talk a big game, but he had no power here. He could go on all he liked about his reserved, competent, sane rule, but he had no control over her or what she did or if she was any of those things.

She would go along with this betrothal because it served her ends, not his. And because it did, she would go to these balls, announce their engagement in front of the whole world, and if necessary, even marry him on Christmas Eve in accordance with tradition. Who cared?

Because as soon as she made her move and took over her father's company, it didn't matter whether she was a queen or not. She would be the owner of Skyros Media and she would finally be in the power position over her father, and able to make sure that no matter what happened, Melody would be safe.

She'd worked her whole life to get to this place.

What did she care where King Orion was in all of that?

"Since we're speaking so frankly," he said, and she got the strangest sensation, then. It was almost as if he could read her every last thought. But that was impossible. He was a stranger and she'd been told a thousand times that she was unreadable. "I should tell you that I will insist on fidelity."

"Of course you will." She rolled her eyes and got the distinct impression that no one else had dared do such a thing in his exalted presence. So she did it again. "That must be one of those king things."

"It's one of those funny little *king things*, yes. The royal bloodline determines the line of succession and the throne of Idylla, which has been in my family for centuries." His stern mouth almost curved. Calista almost shivered. "You will find, I think, that most people in my position feel strongly about such things."

"Let me tell you how I see my role as queen," Calista replied, in a brighter tone than strictly necessary. "I can dress the part. But if you expect me to look adoring or fold my hands awkwardly while standing obediently behind you, that's not going to work."

"You are of noble blood, Lady Calista. Surely you are aware that there are certain rules of etiquette. One of them, I am very much afraid, is that you cannot precede your king."

She sighed. "I understand etiquette, thank you. But you need to know, right now, that I have no intention of pretending I'm subservient to any man. King or otherwise."

"Of course not." His voice was soothing. Too soothing, she realized. "That is why you have agreed to marry a total stranger. Because you are in no way subject to your father's demands."

"For all you know I agitated for this job."

She should not have said that. It had been a reaction, not strategic at all, and she regretted it at once. And then regretted it even more when those eyes of his glowed gold, and she knew beyond a shadow of a doubt that he was somehow aware he'd scored points.

"I am delighted that you understand that it is, in fact,

a job." He nodded toward the windows, somehow incorporating the whole of the island with a single peremptory gesture. "Idylla is an ancient kingdom. Small but independent. An independence that historically came with a price."

"Are you…telling me the history of my own country?"

"The history of this country is the history of my family, Lady Calista. Yours, I believe, was elevated to nobility a great many centuries after the first in my line took the throne."

"Oh, I see," she said after a moment. After that sunk in. "You don't have the power in this interaction that you think you should, so you need to turn it into a measure of your manhood. In this case, a *purer blood than thou* contest. Too bad blood isn't actually blue. Or we could each open up a vein and see whose better matches the sky."

"You missed my meaning entirely," Orion said calmly. She decided she hated that tone he took. Its very calmness was offensive. "The fact is, with a few notable exceptions like my own father, my line has held the throne throughout the ages because members of my family have always been aware that a king can only be as effective as he is loved."

"Loved by whom?" she asked, with a laugh.

And she ignored the fact that the laugh felt a great deal more brittle than it should have.

"I do not require your love, never fear," Orion said coolly. And, once again, he made her imagine for a terrible moment that she might actually flush beet red. Like some silly girl, when she was anything but. "I require you to do your job. And no, that does not involve making cow's eyes at me before the cameras, though I would prefer it if you did not scowl. That is not good optics, as

I believe someone in your profession should know. But all of that is window dressing."

"Window dressing? I would have assumed you had staff for such things."

"Your actual job is really very simple, Lady Calista," he told her in the same cool, intense way. "All you need to do is provide me with an heir."

Something fairly sizzled between them at that. Much as Calista wanted to deny it.

She felt her breath punch out of her lungs. She felt her body change, growing hot and heavy.

Though she would die before she let him know that he had that effect on her.

She would die before she admitted that the idea of making heirs with him suddenly seemed a lot more interesting to her than wresting control of her father's company—because it was a betrayal of everything she'd worked for.

It was a betrayal of her sister, herself, and the things they'd held dear their whole lives.

It was a betrayal, plain and simple, and she loathed herself for even a moment's lapse from her primary goal, even if only in her own head.

She made herself laugh instead. As insultingly as possible.

"You don't have to dress it up, Your Majesty," she drawled, and smirked at him. Edgy and tight. "You could have just said you want to have sex with me. You don't have to pretend it's for the greater good."

CHAPTER THREE

TWO DAYS LATER, like it or not, Orion found himself getting ready for the first of the traditional Idylla Christmas balls he would share with his betrothed—soon to be his fiancée.

And if he wasn't mistaken, he was actually…filled with a kind of anticipation.

Though he told himself it was not as simple as that.

He'd assumed that their initial meeting would sort things out between them and make their respective roles clear. He'd expected Lady Calista would be like any of the typical Idyllian nobility he'd contended with in his time. She'd been meant to fawn all over him and tremble and agree with his every utterance, pretending she was a vestal virgin instead of the usual party girl. His staff had assured him that while, yes, she had a place in her father's company, it was only for show.

But she hadn't done any of the things he'd expected she would.

To say that their first meeting had not gone according to plan was vastly understating things.

She'd underscored that by continuing to do nothing but laugh, at him, clearly and boldly—and then leaving. Without waiting to be dismissed from his presence.

And more to the point, without agreeing to a single one of his terms. Or even pretending to consider them.

He had no idea what to expect from her now.

Orion had spent entirely too much time since then trying to reconcile who he'd imagined she was based on the depth of her curtsy and the demure outfit she'd worn with who she'd proved herself to be thereafter.

He was appalled at himself, actually.

If he thought about it, he should have assumed that a man like Aristotle Skyros could, naturally, bring into the world only creatures of selfish greed and astonishingly bad behavior just like himself. There was nothing surprising about it.

What Orion couldn't countenance was his reaction to her.

Everything she'd said and done had horrified him on every level, obviously. But his body had taken a different tack despite that. His body—which he had long treated with a monastic fervor Griffin liked to tell him took zealotry to a new level—did not seem to care that Lady Calista was nothing at all like the queen he'd imagined would rule at his side. His body had not been overly concerned with her disrespect, her flippant responses, her outright rudeness to both her king and her future husband.

His body had gone rogue.

Orion had woken in the night, hard and aching. And no amount of exercise, cold showers, or sheer fury at his own flesh had helped. The only thing that had was a detailed fantasy about what it would be like to feel that sharp tongue of hers on that place where he was hardest of all.

Damn her.

Orion prided himself on being in control. Of himself, his body and his mind, in every regard. It was another decision he had made a long, long time ago, faced with the knowledge that one of the great many ways his father was weak was King Max's inability to deny his appetites. Particularly those of the flesh.

Orion had decided that he would be master of his own body in the same way that he had learned to master his emotions. He stayed in control, always, no matter the provocation.

Calista Skyros tested him. She tested his control.

And he hated it.

But he hadn't lost a test yet.

Grimly, Orion allowed his fussy, demanding valet to finish dressing him in the exquisite black-tie ensemble appropriate for the occasion of the first ball of the Idyllian holiday season. The ball that happened to also be the place where the newly crowned king would announce his engagement, God help him. Once he was suitably regal, he walked through the palace to meet the woman he would never have chosen to be his bride, especially now that he'd met her. There in the same private salon where he'd faced the unpleasant fact that he was not as immune to a blackmailer's daughter as he should have been.

Perhaps the truth was that he was still trying to face that fact.

This time, when he opened the door and stepped inside, the room was not empty.

It was, in fact, rather more full than he had been anticipating. He was displeased to note that Calista had come with her father and mother in tow. Something he was sure he ought to have been horrified by.

But for the moment, a very long moment that seemed to drag out for an eternity, all he could see was her.

Just her, as if there was a separate sun that was all hers and it shined on only her, even at night.

He dismissed the strange, almost poetic notion and focused on this woman he was bound to marry, but that was no better. Because she was even prettier than the last time he'd seen her, which should not have been possible. And even though he knew now that the *something* about her he'd been unable to name on the balcony two days ago was the same sort of malice her father wore visibly on his skin, his body didn't know the difference. Tonight she wore a dramatic gown, a dress that sparkled and made her look exactly like a girl with a princess fantasy only he could make come true, when he now knew she was nothing of the kind.

Did he want that kind of woman? Wrapped up in some kind of a fairy tale when the reality of royal life was far less shiny and sweet? Before meeting Calista, Orion would have sworn he did not. But that was before she had haunted him, simply by looking at him as if *she* was in control of things.

She smirked at him again now, which he already both detested and found sent a heat spiraling deep into him.

Making him ache anew.

"I take it that when you're a king, you don't have to observe typical first-date protocols. Like picking a girl up at her own house, rather than forcing her to traipse all the way to the palace to act overawed and under-royal."

That was her greeting to her future husband, lord and king.

Orion could not have said why it was he wanted to smile.

"Kings do not go on first dates, Lady Calista," he said. Forbiddingly. "Nor do they dance attendance at the front doors of their lessers. The nation would revolt at the very idea."

And he enjoyed that too much, maybe. Because judging by their reactions, neither Skyros nor his daughter considered themselves *less than* anything—and particularly not less than their king.

But it was Skyros's wife who surprised Orion the most. She was the one who'd dropped into a spine-crackingly low curtsy at the sight of him. She rose now, long after she'd descended, her carriage painfully erect. And she glared at her husband and daughter in turn.

"We do not treat the King of Idylla with disrespect," she hissed. "*We* know our duty."

"Spare me the royalist rantings, Appollonia," Aristotle growled. But even so, he performed a perfunctory bow, almost as if he worried someone might be hid behind the paintings, recording the meeting. Then, to Orion's astonishment, Calista curtsied, too.

But when she rose, she fixed Orion with her own fierce glare. As if she was daring him to comment on the fact that her mother still held sway over her behavior. At least in public.

He tucked that away like a small, handy knife in his boot—the kind Griffin carried about with him ever since his time in the military.

"I hope you're both prepared for this tonight," Aristotle said then, puffing himself up with his usual self-importance, his beady eyes all over Orion as if he was not a king, but a piece of meat for the carving. "Everybody loves a royal love story and the two of you need to sell it."

Orion did not dignify that with a response. Particularly when the response he had in mind involved the Royal Guard.

"Papa." To his surprise, the smirk on Calista's lips changed to a far more engaging smile when she aimed it at her father, though Orion found he believed it less. "This isn't a love story. You know that."

"It doesn't matter what it *is*," Aristotle retorted, with

a laugh that made him seem even oilier than before. "No one cares about what's real, Calista. What matters is what I can sell."

And he kept his gaze fixed on Orion on the off chance he was confused as to who was the greater commodity here.

Odious, appalling man.

Soon to be your father-in-law, a dark voice in him intoned.

It was unbearable.

"Thank you," Orion said. With all the authority in him. "I would now like a few moments alone with Lady Calista, please."

And he inclined his head in a manner that made it clear he was not making a request.

Aristotle grumbled, but his wife managed to somehow genuflect while removing herself from the room, backward. A feat that would have impressed Orion, but then the door closed behind Aristotle and Appollonia Skyros.

Leaving just the two of them in the room. Orion and Calista.

He should not have let that simple fact work its way beneath his skin, all heat and need.

The way she did, too, doing nothing more than standing there looking like a proper royal princess, save for the smirk on her clever mouth and the challenge in her aquamarine gaze.

He reminded himself that he was meant to be deeply appalled, but she was wearing a sweeping, romantic gown and he wanted to put his hands on her more than he should have wanted anything that in no way benefited his kingdom, and he couldn't quite make himself believe that he was *appalled* at all.

"Do you have more demands for me to refuse?" Calista

asked. And Orion really should have found himself sickened by the tone she used. So disrespectful. So patently challenging. So invigorating, if he was honest, after a day crammed full of deadly dull policy advisers and pompous cabinet ministers. "That sounds like fun to me."

"Not quite," he said.

He reached into his pocket and withdrew the small, velvet pouch he'd slipped in there earlier, despite his valet's protestations that it *murdered the line* of his suit. He pretended he did not notice the way she watched him, or the way she stood there before him, stiffly, as if she didn't know how to anticipate what he might do next.

Orion sensed he had the advantage, and he knew he should seize it, utilize it—

But first he had to do this. It was tradition, no matter the circumstances of their betrothal, and he was nothing if not a slave to tradition.

He upended the pouch and shook out the ring inside it. And he knew he didn't imagine the quick indrawn breath he heard from Calista when it landed on his palm.

"This is the foremost crown jewel of Idylla," he told her, though he expected she already knew it. He held the ring there where it had landed, gleaming in the lamplight and seeming to take on a life of its own—as if all the legends that had ever been told about it were there in its stones and shimmer. "It is always worn by the Queen of Idylla whether she is ruler or consort. So it has been for generations."

"I—" For the first time since he'd met her, Calista Skyros actually looked…rattled. "I can't wear that."

"You must," he said, simply enough. "It is a symbol. It is meaningful to our people. And it matters to me that it grace the left hand of my bride, as custom and tradition requires."

He watched her swallow, as if her throat hurt. "I think you should save it," she said in a low voice, after a moment. "For someone more appropriate."

"We are far past the point of debating what is *appropriate*." He held the ring in his hand, admiring, as he always did, the ancient workmanship. The pile of diamonds and sapphires, seemingly haphazard, yet all together a monument to sea and sky that captured the essence of his island kingdom. "I do not plan to have a selection of queens, Calista. Only the one."

Her gaze had dropped to the ring he held while he spoke, but she jerked it up to his face then.

"Of course you don't think…" She blinked, and for the first time since they'd met, looked…uncertain. Off balance. "This can't be…"

His head tipped to one side. "Do you know something about my marriage that I do not, Lady Calista?"

And he watched as she took a deep, shaky breath. Then another.

"You are being bullied into this whole thing by my father," she said after a moment. "I assumed the moment you found yourself free of whatever he held over you, you would divorce me or annul this, or whatever it is kings do to rearrange reality to suit themselves."

"Henry VIII preferred execution. Is that what you mean?"

"Surely you don't think this is anything but temporary. You can't."

Orion should rejoice in that, surely. He should have felt relief pouring through him, because their first interaction had been so fraught and this, at last, was some sense. Some acknowledgment of what was happening and even the faintest hint that they might share a bit in this thing that they must do.

But instead, he was caught somewhere between her clever mouth and that odd, arrested expression in her gaze.

And when he shook himself out of that, he reminded himself sternly that it didn't matter if Calista had a modern sensibility about the situation they found themselves in. It couldn't. It changed nothing.

"There will be no divorce," he told her. "No annulment. My father's reign was too tumultuous. Too humiliating and upsetting, for this family and the country. There will be no scandal if I can help it."

If anything, that seemed to agitate her more.

"Your Majesty. Really." She moistened her lip and he found himself drawn to that, too. What was the matter with him? "You can't possibly think that we would suit for anything more than a temporary arrangement to appease my father's worst impulses."

He had been horrified by her earlier. And now he wanted to argue with her about their suitability?

"I need to marry, Lady Calista. I need to produce heirs, and quickly, to prove to my people the kingdom is at last in safe hands. There will be no divorce." He smiled more than he should have, perhaps, when she looked stricken. "We are stuck. In each other's pockets, it seems."

She blanched at that, but he had no pity for her. Or nothing so simple as pity, anyway.

He moved toward her, taking stock of the way she lifted her head too quickly—very much as if she was beating back the urge to leap backward. To scramble away from him, as if he was some kind of predator.

The truth was, something in him roared its approval at that notion. He, who had always prided himself on how civilized he was, did not dislike the idea that here, with her, he was as much a man as any other.

Surely that had to be a good sign for their marriage.

Whether it was or wasn't, he stopped when he reached her. Then he stood before her and took her hand in his.

And the contact, skin on skin, floored him.

It was so...*tactile.*

It made him remember the images that had been dancing in his head ever since he'd brought up sex in her presence. It made him imagine it all in intricate detail.

It made him hard and needy, but better yet, it made her tremble.

Very solemnly, he took the ring—the glorious ring that in many ways was Idylla's standard to wave proudly before the world—and slid it onto one of her slender fingers.

And because he was a gentleman and a king, did not point out that she was shaking while he did it.

"And now," he said, in a low voice that should have been smooth, or less harshly possessive, but wasn't, "you are truly my betrothed. The woman who will be my bride. My queen. Your name will be bound to mine for eternity."

"I understand what it means."

But her voice, too, wasn't as sharp as usual. He expected her to yank back her hand, but she didn't. He had the odd notion that she couldn't.

The funny thing was, though he had never imagined that he would be blackmailed into marriage, it was no hardship at all to admit that Lady Calista looked a great deal like the woman he'd always vaguely imagined would be his. She was prettier than the last time he'd seen her, he was sure. There was something ethereal about her tonight, with her hair arranged on top of her head in something that looked effortlessly chic and complicated. It called attention to the beauty of her bone structure, from her high cheekbones to her elegant nose.

She looked like the queen she would become, and soon.

Orion dropped her hand, and was pleased to see that for a moment, she held hers where it was. Right there in midair, staring at the astounding ring on her hand as if she couldn't quite believe it was real.

When she finally dropped it to her side, she looked almost lost. He told himself that was why he offered her his arm.

And when he led her from the salon, then down through the grand halls of the palace to the car that waited to take them from the palace, she seemed…almost subdued. Uncharacteristically, he would have said.

Though in truth he knew very little about her character—other than the fact she was happy to participate in his blackmail, that was.

"Where are my parents?" she asked when they were both inside the car, and his driver had pulled away from the palace.

"I sent them in a separate vehicle," Orion said coolly. "Is that a problem? You will understand, I think, if I would prefer to do without your father's company at present."

"My father can be difficult," she agreed, with a small laugh. And something in her gaze that he might have mistaken for dislike, had she been anyone else. Someone who didn't work so closely with Aristotle, for a start.

Orion settled himself in his seat, wishing for perhaps the first time in his life that it was a tighter, smaller car. So that he would have the opportunity to touch her more. To enjoy the fact she was sitting there beside him, smiling faintly of something he could only describe as sparkling vanilla.

"Why do you do his bidding if you find him as difficult as the rest of us do?" he asked, because the seat was vast and it was the only way of touching her available to him.

And he didn't want to investigate why it was he wanted that so much.

It seemed to take her a long moment to lift her gaze from where it rested on her hand in her lap. On the ring she wore. His ring, claiming her.

Something roared in him at that, too.

When her eyes met his, she looked far less dazed than before. And Orion found, to his surprise, that he liked the sharpness. The challenge.

That intensity that was only Calista.

She shook her head. "Of all people to ask me that question."

"I don't follow."

Calista didn't quite laugh. "Don't you? My mistake. Or are you not the man who followed the dictates of a mad king for the better part of his life?"

That was a direct hit, but a part of him enjoyed that she swung at him like that. A part of him wanted more—because whatever else it was, unlike so much else in his life, it was real.

"The difference being that my father was indeed the king. Yours is…what? A businessman with a family title?"

"As if a hereditary king is any different."

"You could leave at any time," Orion pointed out. "You could have stayed in France, for example. Or gone off to America, as so many do. Instead, you chose to stay. Here, on the island. And to involve yourself in his schemes."

She pressed her lips together. "You wouldn't understand."

"Perhaps not. But I do know that I would never participate in blackmail."

But if he expected to shame her, he was disappointed. She only shrugged, then smirked a bit, as if pleased with her own insolence. "That doesn't keep me up at night, Your Majesty. Did you think it would?"

"Orion."

Her smirk faltered. "I beg your pardon?"

It was his turn to shrug, then. "You're my betrothed. And, apparently, intend to continue to treat me in as cavalier a fashion as possible. You might as well use the correct name, don't you think?"

And he could see, somehow, that didn't sit well with her. That there was something about the request that made her shift, then sit even more stiffly beside him.

"That wouldn't be right," she said, glaring down at the ring on her finger. "That would make everything… messier."

"Would it?" He found himself smiling, and his heart was beating too fast in his chest. "Or is it instead fear? Once you succumb to familiarity, will it be harder and harder to do your father's bidding?"

She let out a breath that was not quite a laugh. "Don't be silly."

"Familiarity. Intimacy. These things take their own toll. What will become of you, Calista, do you think?"

"I didn't give you permission to use *my* name," she pointed out, but there was no heat in it.

They were in the back of a car, winding their way down the hill into the city proper. They were as alone as they could get.

Maybe that was why he reached over and picked up

her hand, the hand that wore the ring that was the symbol of his kingdom.

"I am your king," he reminded her. "I do not require your permission. And in any case, using your name is the very least of the intimacies I plan to share with you tonight."

Her gaze flew to his, alarmed. "Tonight? What intimacies?"

"It is customary to seal the announcement of a royal engagement with a kiss, Calista. Surely you know this."

"How would I have the slightest idea?" she asked, her voice sharp again. But not, he rather thought, in quite the same way it had been. Instead, it felt connected to all that heat in him. "I wasn't alive when your father and mother were betrothed, was I? How could I possibly know how they did it?"

"I thought all Idyllian girls were raised on dreams of marrying into the royal family."

Her hand in his flexed, as if she wanted to curl it into a fist. "Not this Idyllian girl."

"My father was more traditional back then," Orion told her. "He was still the crown prince, for one thing, and my grandfather would have taken a dim view of any deviation from tradition. So at the first of the holiday balls, my father presented my mother to the kingdom, as the Kings of Idylla have always done. He showed them all that the ring of Idylla sat on her hand, claiming her for the people as well as himself. And he kissed her on the balcony of the opera house, then danced with her as a grateful nation cheered."

"That sounds ghastly. My teeth hurt just thinking about all that forced sweetness."

"Nevertheless, we will follow the same script. Your dental trauma notwithstanding."

"Will we?" She glared at him. "I have no desire to kiss you, on an opera balcony or anywhere else, and I don't dance."

"Whether you choose to dance or not, in your private life, is your business, Calista." She tried to tug her hand from his, but he held on. "But tonight, your dancing is my business, and I regret to inform you that I'm already well aware that you know how. Like every other girl of noble birth, you were trained in such things at a very young age. Did you think I would not check?"

"You can't make me dance with you."

"I don't have to," Orion said, almost idly. "You appear to be more afraid of your father than you are of me. Feel free to tell him that you intend to buck tradition entirely tonight. I'm sure he will be fully supportive of this choice."

She was silent for a moment. The car was making its way down one of the city's wide boulevards, done up with holiday lights. Flags waved from the hood while people lined the street, the holiday decorations that went up this first week of November making them look red and green and gold, and cheered.

"If you kiss me, I will bite you," Calista promised him.

"Another empty threat, I think." And suddenly, it occurred to Orion that he was enjoying himself. He hardly knew where to put that, so unexpected was it. "But never fear, my surprisingly bashful betrothed. It cannot be a real kiss. That would be inappropriate."

She wrinkled up her nose. "What a relief."

And Orion never surrendered to his demons. He never let feelings control him. Urges were anathema to him and strong emotion was his enemy.

Still, what moved in him then proved too strong to deny.

He reached over and took hold of her, sliding his hand along the curve of her cheek and then guiding her face to his.

"What—? What are you—?"

She sounded breathless. But she didn't pull away.

"This is a real kiss, Calista," he heard himself say.

And then he demonstrated.

CHAPTER FOUR

THE KING WAS kissing her.

And, worse, he was kissing her *well.*

Everything inside Calista went haywire. Alarms kicked off other alarms, each shrieking so loud it should have deafened her completely, but he kept going.

And despite herself, she felt herself…softening.

His lips coaxed hers. His mouth, so stern from a distance, was firm against hers, and it made her stomach dance.

Butterflies, something in her whispered.

She pulled back slightly, perhaps to consider the horror of that thought—

But that was when he angled his head and took the kiss deeper.

And everything inside Calista burst into flame.

It went on and on. She burned, and she kissed him back, moving closer to him as if that would make the fire in her better. Or hotter. She couldn't tell which.

There was a song in her, louder and louder, and it took her a moment to realize when he pulled away. And worse, that her hands were clenched on the fine fabric of his jacket.

For one breath, two, she could only cling to him. And stare back at him, astonished.

But then reality reasserted itself and she hitched in a breath.

"We won't be doing that again," she said, hoping she sounded more outraged and faintly disgusted than what she was. Knocked off balance. At sea, even.

But the way Orion very nearly smiled at her suggested otherwise. He looked far too male. Too smug. She told herself that was redundant and he was a king who was the worst of men anyway, and tried her best to make herself furious—

All while terribly afraid that she was trembling with all that leftover sensation. Visibly.

"If you say so," he murmured. In a dark, rich tone that should not have had anything to do with the sensation of sparks cascading down her spine. She managed not to shudder. Somehow.

And it took the concentrated force of all her willpower, far more than it should have, but she managed to keep from pressing her fingers to her lips. Because it suddenly seemed to her like an act of sheer survival to prevent him from knowing how much he'd affected her.

No matter how much of a lost cause that might have been. It was one thing for him to suspect. But if he knew…

Well. She didn't intend to let that happen.

And no matter that she could still taste him in her mouth.

Orion reached into his jacket pocket and pulled out his mobile, more evidence that his royal blood did not prevent him from being a mortal man like anyone else. Like everyone else, even. She pretended not to watch him scrolling through whatever messages waited him with an expression that was entirely too calm for her tastes.

Surely if she felt wrecked, torn inside out and made

new despite herself, he should feel the same. And it should show.

But Calista had turned biting her tongue into an art, or she never would have survived her childhood, and she did it now. She jerked her gaze away from Orion. She folded her hands in her lap, maneuvering around the unfamiliar ring that sat on her hand, so beautiful she didn't dare look at directly. And yet heavy enough to feel like a portable dungeon.

She directed her gaze out the window instead, at the royal city that slipped by as the car took them toward this destiny of hers that she had never wanted.

This destiny she had felt fairly smug about until tonight, if she was honest. Before he'd kissed her. Before he'd taken her mouth with such raw, consuming mastery that she still felt fluttery, knocked off balance, and a little silly.

And Calista had no experience whatsoever with *silly*. She hardly knew what to do with herself.

Especially when Orion appeared to expect this union of theirs to be permanent.

"I hope you're prepared," Orion said from beside her, surprising her. Once again, his voice went off inside her like a tuning fork and everything in her yearned toward him, like a song.

She would cut out her own tongue before she gave in and actually sang, thank you very much. She promised herself that no matter what, she would ignore that odd urge.

Calista cleared her throat. She felt almost misshapen, as if he'd kissed her so thoroughly that if she were to look in a mirror just now, she wouldn't recognize her own face. She didn't test that theory.

"What sort of preparation do you mean?" she asked,

as smoothly as she could, and congratulated herself on sounding anything but shaken up. "I'm the vice president at a multinational corporation, but thank you. I don't normally need to be reminded to prepare for a party."

"I cannot speak to corporate wrangling, of course," Orion said. With a glint in those grave eyes of his that she was tempted to consider evidence of a heretofore unknown sense of humor in the new, stern king. Surely not, she thought. Her head must still be spinning. "Or party planning, for that matter. But you must know that the moment you emerge from this vehicle on my arm, your life will change."

She waited for him to laugh. Or even smirk.

He didn't.

And she felt herself go cold. "What do you mean by that? I don't want my life to change. I like my life." Or she would soon enough, anyway. "I've worked hard on the life I have."

With single-minded focus, in fact. All pushing toward the finish line she could finally—*finally*—see before her.

But the cheers from outside the car seemed to press in on her, then. The way the city slid by as if it, too, danced attendance on this man. Then again, maybe it was the way he studied her expression, the look on his face a bit too close to pity for her liking.

"Surely you cannot be so naive," Orion said, and the fact that his tone was gentle kept her still.

So still it prevented her from snapping at him, or even getting her back up in the first place. Both of which she would have preferred, because the alternative was staring back at him, feeling awfully close to stricken.

"Every time I escort a woman to an event, it is like a feeding frenzy," he told her in the same way. Kind enough. Gentle, too. But certain all the same. "No matter how many times I tell them that the women in question are my poor cousins, the result is the same. A complete and utter circus."

She knew all about that circus. She'd seen enough of it without even looking for it—on the television, in all the newsagents. She'd even known, the way everyone did, that if Orion had ever dated, he'd managed to keep it quiet.

She'd known all of that in the way she knew what month Christmas was. Or that snow was cold, little though it fell in Idylla. It wasn't anything personal, it was just a fact.

Her heart squeezed tight in her chest, then began to beat like a drum.

He continued to eye her with that mix of pity and patience. "But I have never before arrived at one of the holiday balls with a woman I was not related to, Calista. You should prepare yourself, at the very least, for the reaction the crowd will have when you exit the car."

"But… But I…"

But Orion wasn't finished. And worse, he seemed inclined to keep sounding kind, which was the last thing Calista wanted. It made everything so much harder.

It made her feel so much weaker.

"All of that will pale in comparison to the fervor that will grip the nation, the press, and a good part of the world once we announce that our engagement is finally going ahead tonight, all these years after my father arranged it." His voice was as grave as his expression, then. And the small gleam she saw in his eyes had nothing to do with amusement, she was sure. "I do hope you know what you've gotten yourself into."

For a moment she didn't know what he meant. Then she remembered. Blackmail. Her vile, grasping father and this thing she'd become to counter him. To fight him—all while appearing to have surrendered to him long ago. All to save her sister no matter the cost to herself.

Her throat was so dry she thought it might catch fire.

"I'll be fine," she replied, though her lips still felt stung and stained from his. Her pulse had taken on a hectic life of its own, and the noise from outside the car as it began to slow in its final approach to the opera house seemed to batter against her.

Like real blows.

Orion reached over and took her hand. For a moment her heart seemed to seize inside her chest. But instead of lacing his fingers with hers or caressing her in some way—which she assured herself she would have shaken off at once—he fiddled with the ring he'd put there instead. It was the ring of the Queens of Idylla, after all. Every school-aged child knew that and could identify it on sight.

What they didn't, couldn't know was that the ring itself was warm against her skin. Or that the stones caught the light from the street outside, sending fragments and patches of illumination dancing about in a shimmering splendor.

The light caught his profile, too. The same profile that would soon grace the Idyllian currency, slowly taking his father's place. He looked like precisely what and who he was, the product of centuries of royal blood. As if the throne of Idylla was superimposed on his skin.

That should have horrified her, surely.

But it didn't.

And when he didn't speak, his fingers on that ring as if that was all the statement necessary, Calista felt as if the bottom of the car fell out from underneath her. As if she was suddenly tossed out into the cobbled streets, unable to gain purchase or find her feet or even *breathe.*

The chanting and cheering outside grew louder. And she knew no one could see her inside the car, with its tinted, no doubt armored windows. But even so, she couldn't seem to make her lungs work the way they were supposed to. And she felt dizzy all over again, but this time it was from nothing so pleasant as a kiss.

Because it hadn't occurred to her until this very moment that as fake as she wanted to treat their engagement, or even their marriage, that was the private reality. That was what was between them because they knew the truth of things.

But there was going to be a huge public reality she couldn't control.

Calista had been so busy focusing on how best to ignore the whole marriage thing while she pursued her own ends that she'd neglected to think about what it was going to mean to announce herself engaged or even adjacent to… Orion Augustus Pax. The bloody king.

Her attitude in that private salon the day she'd first met him struck her, then, as hilariously idiotic. If not activcly suicidal.

The truth was, she wasn't a public person. Her father was notorious, and that was about as much public attention as she'd ever wanted. It had led to snide comments at school. The odd sharp word. But mostly, the many people her father offended went after him, not her.

Unlike many of her peers, Calista wasn't the sort who constantly had her picture in the society pages. Nor did she parade about Europe, from yacht to club to charity ball. She had always been too busy working. And the irony wasn't lost on her that her life's work was in a media company that existed almost entirely because it procured pictures of others and made them public whether they wanted those moments shared or not.

Maybe because of the things Skyros Media had done, Calista had always preferred to stay behind the scenes.

She felt herself begin to sweat as the car rolled to a stop.

Outside, there was a loud, endless roll of noise, like the wall-sized swells at sea. She tried to make herself breathe, but she couldn't seem to get any air much deeper than the back of her throat.

"Is it always like this?" she managed to ask.

Faintly.

"I am the king," Orion replied, mildly enough, though she had the feeling those grave hazel eyes saw far too much of her internal battle. "Better they should greet me with expressions of joy than the howls of hatred they used to greet my father. Don't you think?"

"I was never the sort of person who chased around after the royal motorcade," she made herself say in a sharper sort of voice, though she was still but a shadow of her usual self. "So I can't say I ever paid much attention to the cacophony one way or another."

He only looked at her. Until she couldn't tell whether the noise outside was the crowd or if it was inside her, somehow. As if it was part of that singing thing that seemed to connect them, heating as it sang, until she felt scalded straight through. Or maybe she had already been scalded, her skin stripped away so she *felt* too much, despite her best efforts. Maybe one royal kiss had rewired her brain—by burning it up into ash and need and noise.

Or maybe you need to get a hold of yourself, she told herself sharply. *This whole thing is nothing but a distraction.*

"Isn't this where you tell me I don't have to do this if I don't want to?" she asked before she thought better of it.

His mouth firmed then, forming a hard, stern line. And she couldn't decide if she found that comforting or insulting, but it didn't matter.

Because the look in his eyes matched the shape of his mouth and pinned her to her seat.

"But that is the rub, is it not? You do have to do this. As do I. That is the nature of blackmail, I think you'll find. So tawdry and revolting. One is ever forced to do detestable things."

Pull yourself together now, Calista ordered herself. *It's only a crowd. And he's only a man. A very powerful, very pampered man.*

Though this close to Orion, Calista couldn't help but think he didn't feel like *only* anything.

Maybe it was nerves that kept her mouth going. "At the very least I would have thought you'd have sage advice to offer. That I should imagine them all naked, or something."

"I can't imagine I would find the prospect of a heaving mass of nudity particularly comforting," King Orion said, his voice dark and sardonic. And possibly *satisfied*, too. "But if that helps you, Calista, then by all means. Imagine whatever sea of flesh you think will make you calm."

She stared out the window for another moment, still feeling stricken and breathless. And hopelessly out of her depth. Then she blinked. "You're right. That's not better at all."

Orion fixed her with another long, dark stare. He didn't say another word, but still, she could feel the weight of the way he regarded her. As if it had its own heft and heavy, booted feet.

He rapped on his window, and a moment later, the

door was opened. The roar from outside shoved in, even louder and wilder. He flicked Calista a look, indicating that she should slide after him to exit behind him.

Then he stepped out—into the noise, the lights, and the howls as they greeted him—with an innate athleticism that made her blink.

This was a fine moment indeed to rethink her choices. A fine moment to ask herself why she hadn't pushed back a bit harder against her father. It was hard to remember why she'd chosen to go along with all this nonsense as she sat here in the back of a royal vehicle, her last moments as a private citizen spiraling away from her. It was hard to remember anything, really—much less all the reasons she'd had for allowing her father to think he was still in control of her.

The one very good reason in particular.

She could hear a strange little sound, high-pitched and plainly terrified, and realized she was panting.

And as she didn't wish her big moment in the spotlight to coincide with the first time she fainted, she made herself take a deep breath. Then another.

Outside the car, in the wedge between door and vehicle, she could see Orion waving at the crowd. At his subjects. And what was left of her time was ticking away, second by second.

She reminded herself this was a distraction from her plan, not the plan itself.

And she reminded herself that none of this mattered. What mattered was surviving it intact so she could do what *she* wanted to do. Orion was being blackmailed. Calista was simply doing what was expedient.

Orion turned slightly, extending his hand back into the vehicle.

She didn't lie and tell herself that wasn't a sovereign command, because she knew it was.

God help her, but she wasn't ready. She hadn't thought this through. It had been one thing to sit in a private room in the palace and shoot off her mouth, but this was something else. This was terrifying.

She was *terrified.*

Orion waited with a kind of brooding, intense patience, his hand extended.

Calista found herself mute, frozen, and lost all the same in that grave gaze he settled on her.

Every inch of him a king. Her king. There was no doubt that the way he looked at her was an order from on high.

And on some distant level, she was astonished to find that it worked. She couldn't seem to grasp onto a full thought in her head, but her body obeyed him anyway. She was moving automatically, reaching out to grasp his hand, like a deep, blooming flame when his strong fingers closed around hers.

For an eternity, there was only that. The flame and the bloom of it, eating her whole. His hand in hers. And the way their eyes caught, her still in the shadows of the car and him outside.

Her heart seemed to wallop her inside her own chest, like it was a weapon, and worse, he wielded it.

And then everything sped up.

Orion helped her alight from the car in another smooth, easy show of strength, though Calista rather thought it looked like nothing more than good manners. She tucked that away, because the fact the king was built like a god felt like a burst of sunshine deep inside her.

There was a smile on his face as he greeted her, though

perhaps only she could see it didn't match the intensity of the way he looked at her.

"Optics, my lady," he murmured near her ear as he brushed a cool kiss across her cheek, and then he turned.

Presenting her to the crowd.

And sealing her fate, which felt a lot like drowning.

For a long while, possibly an intertwined string of forevers, there was nothing but the endless noise. Bright lights, popping flashbulbs, disorienting and overwhelming.

But Orion never let go of her. And Calista held on to her smile and his strong hand as if her life depended on it.

She rather thought it did.

And by the time they made it up the red-carpeted aisle to the ornate front doors of the Royal Opera House, where the inaugural holiday ball was always held, Calista felt as if she'd run back-to-back marathons. She, who had never deliberately run more than a few feet in her life.

If this was what it felt like, panicked and distraught down to her very bones, she had no plans to start.

Inside the first vestibule of the opera house, it was shockingly quiet. So quiet that it almost hurt.

Except, of course, for the ragged sound of her breathing.

"Try not to hyperventilate," Orion advised her, in that same mild way of his that was simultaneously enraging and comforting. "This is the opera, I grant you. But even so, best to avoid the fainting couch. It will only raise unfortunate questions."

"I'm perfectly fine," she managed to say, though she wasn't. She really, really wasn't. But as she didn't plan to collapse on the floor and cry, what was the point of saying so?

"I'm delighted to hear it."

Orion nodded past her. That was when it occurred to

Calista to look around, too. Beneath the dramatic gargoyles up high and statuary littered about the marble foyer, there were liveried servants standing at the ready.

And she realized what she should already have known. Most people did not get a moment to collect themselves before entering the ball proper. This was an indulgence granted the king, no doubt so he could make an appropriately pageant-like entrance.

So that *they* could make an entrance, she corrected herself. Together.

Because this was what she'd signed up for. Or her father had signed her up for, which amounted to the same thing. And it was no one's fault but hers that she'd failed to think it through.

Calista blew out a breath, found her smile again, and took the arm he offered her.

And then, like it or not, she allowed the King of Idylla to walk her into the first holiday ball of the season.

Worse still, she allowed him to claim her as his with a perfect, romantic kiss from the balcony that would have swept her off her feet entirely. That would have made her forget the crowd, and the astonishment from all quarters, and the cruel satisfaction on her father's face.

It would have broken her heart and sewed it back together, she was sure, if only she hadn't been faking.

And if she had to remind herself, repeatedly, that she was faking, that Orion was performing under duress, that none of this was real nor ever could be—

Well.

Calista had learned a long time ago how to keep a smile on her face and pretend like her life depended on it. Like Melody's life depended on it, too.

Because it always had.

CHAPTER FIVE

"THE STAFF IS in disarray," Griffin declared, letting himself into Orion's study.

"Do come in, Griffin," Orion murmured sardonically as his brother prowled over to fling himself in his favorite chair, without even pretending to wait for an invitation. "Make yourself right at home. No need to worry I might be tending to delicate matters of state."

He wasn't, just at the moment. But he certainly could have been.

Griffin looked notably unbothered at the possibility. "It's an uproar out there. The palace halls are alive with speculation now that everything has been made official and all the rumors are at an end. You may have kicked off a revolution after all."

Orion sighed and stopped attempting to make sense of the latest lengthy, meandering tome that his least favorite minister had presented him, expecting Orion would have it read and annotated with cogent commentary already. He rubbed at his temples, suddenly aware that he'd been at his desk reading stacks upon stacks of documents since early that morning. Because like it or not, he was playing catch-up on the past twenty years. The whole of his father's reign.

"What is it I've done to provoke the revolutionary

forces today?" He eyed his younger brother with the usual mix of baffled affection, no little hint of jealousy at the antics Griffin as spare rather than heir was permitted to get up to, and a rush of gratitude that all the same, they were who they were.

"Your fiancée, my liege," Griffin drawled, stretching out his legs. He was dressed for appointments, though he preferred a rather more carefree and rumpled approach to his sartorial choices. Then again, no one expected any different from a man not expected to ever take the throne. "Or are you unaware that she has refused to submit herself to the tender ministrations of your fleet of private secretaries?"

"What do they want from Calista?" Orion asked, and couldn't help but think that it was an excellent question. One he asked himself nightly, come to that.

He kept waiting for familiarity to breed contempt, as it was meant to do. But instead, the more time he spent with the woman he was to marry, the more feverish his nights became. Because the more he saw her, the more he wanted her.

It hadn't helped that he'd seen beneath that sharp, edgy surface she wore so comfortably. He could have done without the vulnerability she'd shown before their first ball. Just like he could have happily stayed ignorant of the way she tasted.

It would have made things easier, surely.

During the long nights when all he did was ache for her, he reminded himself that finding himself sexually attracted to a woman he was forced to marry anyway was a gift. That he should celebrate it, no matter how the marriage itself came to be. Because that attraction could only make what lay ahead of the pair of them easier. More pleasant, certainly.

During the day, however, he reminded himself whose daughter she was. And he was horrified that he was allowing the chemistry between them to poison him, when he knew better.

Of course he knew better.

Every week, he collected her from the same salon. She wore a series of exquisite ensembles, all of which were gushed over and picked apart the following day in all the papers, much the way their engagement kiss had been. And not only in the ones her family owned.

There had been no more kissing. No more fraught conversations laced with need. And no more flashes of vulnerability, for that matter.

Instead, they danced.

And it did not help Orion in the slightest to discover that Calista Skyros—blackmailer's daughter, insolent and disrespectful by nature and inclination alike—fit him like all those steamy dreams he had. Graceful. Lithe. Something like ethereal.

As if she had been specifically created to fit right there in his arms.

When that could not possibly be true. He knew it wasn't true.

And in case he thought he was imagining such things, no. He'd seen the pictures of the two of them. He could hardly have avoided them if he'd wanted to. And worse, the videos that made it clear their chemistry was not only in his head.

God help him.

"They want Calista to act the way the king's betrothed ought to act," Griffin was saying. He shook his head at his older brother, and Orion opted not to let himself notice the speculative gleam in Griffin's gaze. "It is all so irregular, after all. She has refused to present herself for the proper… How shall I put it? Molding."

"She dances as a girl of noble blood ought to have learned as a child. She wears appropriate clothing and has yet to embarrass the palace. What else should she be doing?"

"Come now, brother." Griffin laughed. "Surely you have not already forgotten the greatest joy of our formative years? Day after day after day of royal etiquette pounded into our heads by battalions of grandfather's private secretaries?"

Orion opted not to mention that he had enjoyed those sessions rather more than Griffin had. "Again, Lady Calista is of noble blood, born and raised right here in Idylla. I have it on the greatest authority that she has already suffered through comportment classes. At length."

Griffin only shrugged. "I'm not the one who needs convincing. I don't much care. It's your staff, Orion. They believe your chosen bride is…" He paused, then, in a manner that Orion might have called *delicate* had he not been able to see the smirk on his brother's face. "…too well versed in playing to the press. While ignorant of the duties that await her once she marries you."

Orion accepted the fact that he did not particularly want to deal with the endlessly thorny problem that was Calista. But when he glanced down at the sheaves upon sheaves of papers on his desk, it seemed less overwhelming a task than it might have otherwise.

Liar, something in him whispered. *You* want *to deal with her. You want to see her when you know you shouldn't.*

He stood, inclining his head grandly at Griffin—who only grinned back, sprawled out with every appearance of idleness. "Thank you for bringing this to my attention. I am forced to wonder why I employ a staff at all when they are more comfortable gossiping to my younger brother than bringing their concerns straight to me."

"It is more that I like to gossip, as I think you know," Griffin said mildly. "What else is Idylla's favorite playboy to do with his fortune and time?"

Orion smoothed a hand down the pristine front of the suit he wore. "About that."

"Yes, yes," Griffin said, rolling his eyes. "I haven't forgotten what I promised you."

"If you do not choose a bride for yourself, brother," Orion said quietly, "you may force me into a position where I must choose for you. Is that what you want?"

Griffin didn't look remotely concerned. "Father chose your bride. You seem to be holding up well."

"If by that you mean I am acquitting myself with all magnificence of my station, yes. That is my job."

"You don't look at her like she's a *job*, Orion." Griffin flashed another grin when Orion glared at him, and shrugged. "You don't. And who on this planet knows more about carrying the sins of the fathers than you and me? Perhaps this girl—"

"I understand my duty, Griffin." Orion sounded harsher than he meant to, especially where his brother was involved. Given Griffin only ever looked delighted that he'd provoked a reaction—any reaction. Today was no different. "And I will do my duty, as always. You may recall you promised me that you would do the same."

"My problem isn't finding one woman to marry, Orion," Griffin said then, his grin so bright it almost concealed the darker gleam in his gaze that Orion sometimes thought only he ever saw. "It's that there are far too many to wade through, all with their own particular demands."

"I'm happy to do it for you, then, if you find the task too onerous."

"Perhaps you should deal with your recalcitrant bride-to-be," Griffin suggested, laughing. "I'll find my own, don't you worry."

Orion did worry. He worried about everything, the way he always had—because there was no one else to do it. But he knew there was no pressing Griffin when he was in one of his languid moods, so Orion left him in his office and marched out to find his staff, half expecting to find that Griffin had misread the situation. More than half. Because sometimes it was hard to tell what was actually gossip swirling about the palace, and what Griffin decided to make gossip.

But when he astonished his staff by presenting himself in their offices, everyone leaped to their feet and began bowing dramatically. And in the resulting chaos, he quickly understood that for once, his brother had not been exaggerating.

"Her behavior is quite extraordinary," his head secretary confided once they'd left the bowing and scraping behind and repaired to the man's office, where he looked ill at the sight of his sovereign sitting in a regular chair in front of the desk. But he pressed on. "In the history of the throne, there has never been a queen who…" He blinked, as if he could hardly bring himself to say the word. "Your Majesty, Lady Calista *works*."

"In her family firm, yes. I believe she's quite proud of this."

His secretary managed to radiate severe disapproval while looking faintly obsequious. A skill Orion doubted he could master. But he was too busy wondering when he'd appointed himself Calista's champion to study how the other man did it.

"The wedding will be on Christmas Eve, sire," his secretary pointed out.

"I have not forgotten."

His secretary bent his head. "And your fiancée has yet to present herself at the palace so that we can begin to instruct her in the duties of her new role. She cannot… simply *appear* overnight and hope to acquit herself as queen. That would be disastrous."

Orion did not need his secretary to remind him that there had been enough disasters in the kingdom already. His staff had been forced to help him through his father's rule, where they'd spent their days attempting to smooth everything out, fix what was fixable, and do their best to present the public with a vision of a better, calmer, more competent king than the one they had.

Of course they were all concerned that his fiancée represented a kind of throwback to those chaotic years.

Still.

"It is not as if she's a stranger we picked up off the streets," Orion pointed out, a bit drily. "She is the daughter of Idyllian nobility."

"Which has no doubt prepared her adequately for a robust role as a socialite, Your Majesty, but can in no way substitute for proper training in how to represent the kingdom as its queen. That is, as they say, a different kettle of fish entirely."

Despite himself, Orion found himself thinking about his own mother. She had received all that same instruction, presumably. But she'd been so young. And no one could have been instructed in what it took to handle his father. Especially given what Orion knew now, it was perhaps unsurprising that his mother had taken her own life in the end.

He thought of the stark terror he'd seen on Calista's

face in the car that first night. That hint that she was something more than simply her odious father's daughter, sent to enact his squalid little games.

And the thought that another queen—*his* queen—might end up in such despair that she followed in his mother's sad footsteps one day made something in him shift. Hard. As if the notion might take him from his feet.

"Leave it with me," he told his secretary.

And then he decided to indulge himself while he was off putting out fires.

His father had dearly loved the pageant of monarchy. Always a motorcade. A parade, if possible. Armed guards wherever he went and as much pomp and circumstance as every engagement could hold.

And pageantry had its place, certainly. Orion tried to be careful not to eschew things simply because his father had enjoyed them—like the glorious history of the throne of Idylla, and of his family.

But today, Orion changed into regular clothes and slipped out a side door of the palace where reporters were never allowed to camp out and wait. He would have loved to have gone alone, but he was a king, and well aware of his responsibilities—even when he was shirking them. And so two bodyguards came with him, also dressed down, though they fanned out enough to give him the illusion of living a normal enough life that he could simply…take a walk in the royal city if he liked.

And he did like. Every now and again, he liked to go out from the palace and away from his usual concerns and blend in. Sometimes his subjects recognized him, but they were usually so delighted to see the king out there engaging in normal pursuits—instead of making embarrassing headlines like his father had—that they rarely caused a fuss.

Today, it was a brisk morning. Cool, by Mediterranean standards. Orion followed a meandering sort of path down the hill where the palace sat, a beacon of depravity or hope, depending on how well he was doing his job. He found his way into the affluent part of the city, where the better part of Idyllian nobility lived while in town. He knew they all had their ancestral estates either out in the rural parts of the main island, or on the smaller, supplementary islands that made up the rest of the kingdom.

As he drew close to the street where Calista lived in her father's grand old house, he slowed, because he could see the scrum of paparazzi from a distance. They heaved about outside Aristotle Skyros's house, even though, as far as Orion could see, there was no one there to take pictures of.

He didn't turn down the street. Why give the vultures more to pick apart? He kept walking, flipping up his collar against the damp as he made his way into the central business district.

And once again, he saw paparazzi six deep, milling around outside Skyros Media's flagship building.

After a brief consultation with his bodyguards, he let them lead him around to the back, down an alley where he slipped in a heavy door that was marked Exit Only.

He jogged up the stairs to the third floor, where he'd been told Calista's office was, thinking he would drop in on his lovely fiancée for a little chat she wouldn't have had time to prepare for. He was imagining her reaction to that, sharp and exhilarating, when he stepped into the hallway. And then stopped, because he heard raised voices from around the corner.

"This is not a request, Calista. Have you looked out in the street lately? It's a zoo!"

Orion knew that voice. Aristotle, sounding more vicious and bombastic than usual.

"Papa. Please." Her voice was strained. "I can't abandon my work!"

"Vice presidents grow on trees like olives, girl. You're going to marry the king. That is far more important."

He could have revealed himself, then. He could have marched around the corner and let them know he was there, eavesdropping.

But Orion stayed where he was. Which was how he knew, beyond a shadow of a doubt, that he was not as upright and honorable as he'd always like to imagine he was. Because if he was, he would never stand there and listen as they discussed him and his upcoming marriage. If he was truly a man of honor he would let them know that he could hear their conversation.

He and his bodyguards exchanged a long glance, but none of them moved.

Orion was as surprised as anyone that it turned out he was human, after all.

"That's not a career, is it?" Calista snapped. "That's a vanity project. *Your* vanity project, not mine."

And the sound of the slap Skyros delivered was still resounding in the air as Orion moved. Without meaning to.

But he had to see it with his own eyes. That red handprint on Calista's cheek and her wide eyes.

Both father and daughter looked stunned to see him as he rounded the corner, but he couldn't take any particular pleasure in that.

Not when he was too busy trying to keep his hands from bunching into fists.

"You do know, Skyros," he managed to say, with what he felt was admirable calm, "that there are penalties for striking a member of the royal family? It's an ancient law, handed down across centuries. But whether or not the nation still likes a hanging, it is illegal to put your hands on any one of us. Treasonous, in point of fact."

So was blackmailing kings, of course, which hadn't given Skyros a moment's pause.

"Where the hell did you come from?" Aristotle barked.

But Calista, Orion noted as he bore down on them, only held a palm to her bright red cheek, and glared.

At him, not her father.

"Do not put your hands on my fiancée," Orion growled at Skyros. "Or I swear to you, I will see you in chains."

"You wouldn't like the consequences," Aristotle sneered at him. "Mark my words."

"Shall we try it and see?" Orion retorted.

Aristotle only sneered again, then curled his lip at Calista. "My decision stands, girl. You're fired and that's final."

And even though she made a strangled kind of sound at that, as if he'd truly hurt her, Aristotle ignored her. He stormed away, heading toward what Orion assumed was the rest of the Skyros Media offices.

"Did he hurt you?" Orion asked, aware only then that his heart was kicking at him, as if he'd been sprinting for time.

"He slapped me," Calista said brusquely. She dropped her hands from her face—her pretty, lovely face—one red, angry cheek with Aristotle's handprint all too visible. Orion felt something roll over in him, like a fault line about to blow. "He's never shy to dole out a slap or two, if that's what you're asking. I'm just out of practice. I've managed to avoid getting smacked for a long while now. And you turning up here like this doesn't help anything."

"Calista." There were so many things he wanted to

say. Too many things, and he could see her stiffening, as if she knew what they might be. So he looked down his nose at her instead. "You forget yourself. I am your sovereign. I go where I like."

"The balls, the dresses, all that king and queen malarkey—" She shook her head, a hectic kind of light in the gaze she trained on him. "None of that has any place here. This is a corporation. People *work* here."

"But not you," Orion pointed out, perhaps not as kindly as he could have. "Or did I misinterpret the fact that your father just fired you?"

He saw something wash over her, some strong emotion that wasn't as simple as her temper. "He's overwrought. He'll come around."

"As it happens, I don't want him to come around." He inclined his head as if he was inviting comment, when he wasn't. "I would prefer it if you didn't work."

She blinked, then scowled at him. "What is that supposed to mean? Did you plan this with him?"

"I do not 'make plans' with a man like your father, Calista. His plans hijacked my own. But as it happens, my staff has been agitating—"

"All your staff does is agitate," she snapped at him. Interrupting him, which made his bodyguards bristle, but at this point he rather thought that was an endearment on her part. Or as close as he would get. "They've been harassing me for weeks."

"It's their job to prepare you for your new role. A job they cannot do if you are here, doing your old one."

Now that his temper was cooling a little, and he was no longer tempted to take a swing at Aristotle, he was able to take in everything else. The way she looked, cool and blonde and untouchable, there in the stark-white hallway. He did not spend a great deal of time surrounded by corporate fashions, but it was instantly clear to him that Calista was dressed to send a specific message.

A message he quite liked.

The high, dangerously sharp heels. The miles of her legs exposed beneath the tailored skirt she wore. Her blouse that managed to hint at her figure while showing none of it, and the soft wrap at her shoulders he shied away from calling a cardigan when it looked far more like an elegant piece of feminine armor. Her hair, as usual, was caught back in something sleek—and his enduring trial was that he liked it. He liked all of it. He liked the way Calista vibrated with tension and intelligence. He liked how tough she looked, if a man knew where to look.

He did.

Corporate life clearly suited her. He felt a pang of regret that she was going to have to step away from it—and then reminded himself that she was the one who had crowed over the fact that he was supposedly in her pocket.

She was still a blackmailer's daughter, sent to do his nefarious bidding.

Why did he struggle to remember that?

"I agreed to marry you," she said, looking as dangerous as her shoes. She folded her arms over her chest and glared at him. "I didn't agree to be hounded by your staff. Or to be fired from my job. Or to have packs of reporters hounding me day and night, while we're on the topic."

"What did you imagine marrying a king would entail?" he asked quietly. Not exactly roughly. "Did you truly believe that the Queen of Idylla would have a day job, Calista? Punch a time card and live for Fridays?"

Her mouth fell open. Orion had the distinct impression that he'd shocked her, and he was reminded, somehow, of her panic the night of their first ball.

"Explain to me how that would work," he suggested, mildly enough. "Your colleagues would be going home as usual while you head to the palace."

"But…"

"It is obvious that it cannot be," he said, when she only gaped at him. "I must tell you, Calista, I don't think you really thought this through. That is a pity, and I do feel for your predicament, but I'm afraid it will not help you any."

"That sounds like a threat."

"Only if you wish it to be."

He wanted to touch her. He didn't know how he didn't. How he kept from running his fingers over her over-bright, faintly swollen cheek. How he had managed to convince himself that he was coming here to help when the truth was, he'd only wanted the excuse to be near her again. Who was he fooling?

"I wish my father had never…"

She was wise enough not to finish that sentence. And Orion's smile felt strange on his face. Misshapen, perhaps.

"I wish the same thing," he told her, aware as he said it that it was no longer quite as true as it had been. No longer as true as it *should have* been. He would have to deal with that at some point, too. But her eyes were the color of the sea in summer, and it turned out he was far weaker than he'd ever imagined. "Still, we are here despite our wishes. And I will be moving you into the palace where you belong. Today."

CHAPTER SIX

"I DON'T KNOW what you're going on about," Calista's younger sister, Melody, said in her usually practical, matter-of-fact way. "Not only would I very much like to live in a palace, I would consider it a lovely holiday away from our father."

Most of Calista's things were packed. Her mother had overseen that personally—mostly so she could veto anything she didn't feel was appropriate for the next Queen of Idylla—and Calista had left her to it. There was no arguing with Appollonia when she was in what Melody called her *royalist fugue*.

All that was left was the library. Calista had to content herself with sneaking a few of her favorite books into a satchel, muttering angrily about her fate all the while.

As ever, Melody was unsympathetic.

Calista glared at her, hoping that Melody really could feel other people's gazes on her skin like knives as she liked to claim. Sure enough, her sister smiled. She was sitting cross-legged in her favorite armchair, over near the great fire that Calista had personally made certain was lit each day. It wasn't as if their parents spent any time in this library. Aristotle and Appollonia Skyros didn't have time to *read* when there were worlds to ruin and monarchies to worship.

This library had been installed in the house because libraries were expected in the stately houses of Idylla. Calista and Melody had claimed it ages ago and it had been theirs alone, the two of them.

Calista had hated her time in her father's house, and she and Melody had told each other their complicated, glorious daydreams about getting out of this house. Getting away from him. Getting to live as they liked, far away from here.

But now that it was happening, notably not as planned, she felt hollow inside.

"I don't understand any of this, to be honest," Melody continued, clearly choosing to ignore Calista's mood the way she often did. "I'd love to be a queen. Who wouldn't? Mother was carrying on about all the dresses and the jewels, but I think I'd enjoy the power."

"The Queen of Idylla is a consort, not a ruler," Calista snapped.

And she curled her hand tight over the jewel she wore. The astonishing jewel King Orion had placed there himself that she should have wrenched off and tossed back at him at the first opportunity.

Instead, to her great shame, she had yet to take it off. Not even once.

"The consort of the ruler is still closer to being the ruler than we are," Melody pointed out. "I'd take it in a heartbeat."

She did not add: *But I've never been asked.* She didn't have to add it. They both knew full well how their father felt about the daughter he seemed to think had been born blind purely to spite him.

"You should come with me," Calista said fiercely. "I don't feel right about leaving you here. We both know what could happen. It's already bad enough with the minders he keeps hiring to bully you."

But when Melody shrugged, Calista wasn't surprised.

"Then it happens. Of the two of us, Calista, I'm a little more at peace with my fate. And my prospects, such as they are. You don't understand that there's a freedom in being ignored and underestimated."

"You shouldn't have to be at peace with anything. You shouldn't have to be stuck here, either, constantly under threat of being shipped off to some institution if you displease our father—"

"You went to university," Melody said, though she was grinning. "Really, if you think about it, what's the difference?"

Calista tossed her favorite Jane Austen collection into her bag, which was already pushing her capacity to lift, much less carry. There was no point arguing with Melody when she was in this mood. She knew that. Her sister was the last person on this earth who would ever think of herself as a victim, and there was no use trying to convince her otherwise. Still, she couldn't quite get her head around what it would mean for her sister to live here unsupervised with their parents and the questionable aides he insisted loom about the place to "help" with Melody.

Nothing good.

And if her parents made good on the threats they liked to make about shipping Melody away—*To find her true potential,* Aristotle sometimes said, when what he meant was, *Where her existence can no longer plague and shame me*—it would break Calista's heart. Because she knew, even if Melody pretended not to, that the three years Calista had spent in Paris pretending she'd never heard of Idylla or Skyros Media bore no resemblance to the life Melody would lead if their parents succeeded in institutionalizing her.

But it was as if Melody could read all of Calista's thoughts and feelings in the air between them. She stood up from her chair, then came over. She took Calista's shoulders in her hands and held them there. Tightly.

And it was a good thing to remember that Melody was no wilting violet. Her hands were tough. Strong.

So is she, Calista told herself. *And if you don't trust her to take care of herself, are you any better than our parents?*

"Go," Melody said, gently but firmly. "You could even try enjoying yourself, for a change."

Calista blew out a breath, fighting to steady herself against a wave of emotion she couldn't afford. And shouldn't have had in the first place, as this was all a great farce. She wasn't *really* leaving her childhood home to go live with her husband-to-be, who happened to be the king. This wasn't a real engagement and it wouldn't be a real marriage. Why should she suffer real emotions?

She was still on the board. Her plan was still in place whether she went to the office or not. Her revenge—and Melody's freedom—was within reach.

"Enjoy myself?" She tried to laugh. She tried to stop *feeling.* "You do know where I'm going, don't you? I've been fired from my job and now I have to go play pretty princesses." She wanted to make an immature gagging sound, but restrained herself. "I will likely die, Melody, stifled to death by boredom and inactivity."

"You've been working feverishly, day and night, since you were eighteen. I don't think that learning how to be a queen sounds particularly boring, if I'm honest, but even if it is—it has to be more entertaining than spending the whole of your life figuring out ways to thwart Father."

"I don't want to thwart Father," Calista said softly. "I want to destroy him."

And that was just a start.

Melody smiled. "And you will. But I don't see why you wouldn't look at all the avenues available to you now. Instead of the one you decided on when you thought it was the only one around."

Wouldn't that be lovely? Calista entertained a quick, beautiful fantasy of throwing her problems straight at the feet of the king, who could surely help her when no one else could....

But her father had something on him, too. Her father was the poison in everything.

You could try... something in her whispered.

Calista pulled away from her sister, then, and threw a couple more books into the satchel that already felt like a ton of bricks. And she tried very, very hard to keep her little surge of hope out of her voice. "All this royal nonsense is nothing but a distraction. It's not an avenue toward anything."

Melody sighed. "Once again, Calista. You will be the consort of the king. Any way you look at it, that's a more powerful position than vice president to a pig. If I were you, I would stop viewing the palace as an obstacle and start looking at it as an opportunity."

Calista couldn't believe that anyone could help her. But she had been willing to try—or think about trying—when the car the king had sent arrived to deliver her to the palace a few hours later.

"You remember what we're doing here," her father told her right before she left his house, pulling her aside as the palace staff loaded up the last of her things. He gripped her arm in that way she particularly didn't like, because it hurt. Though it had been years since she'd given him the satisfaction of wincing.

She didn't now, either.

"By *here*, I assume you mean the palace," she replied, not quite airily. "Not here as in right here in my childhood home."

It was a mark of how intense her father was about all this that he didn't sneer or slap her. He only gripped her a little harder and moved her closer.

"It's your job to find something we can use against him, Calista," he growled at her, his face in hers. "Don't get your head turned by that fancy ring he gave you. That's window dressing and nothing more."

But she remembered Orion storming around that corner in the Skyros Media offices, as if he'd fully intended to charge her father and take him down. She remembered that look of dark fury on his royal face when he'd seen her father's handprint on her cheek. Maybe she really could ask him to help her. Maybe he was the only one who *could* help…

"What are you talking about?" she asked, no longer pretending to be the least bit *airy*. "I'm marrying him because you want me to. A total stranger, who I have nothing in common with, because he's the king. I thought that was what you wanted. I thought that was all you wanted."

"What I want is leverage over the palace," Aristotle told her harshly. "It was easy enough to find some on King Max. King Orion is harder—but we're not wasting prime positioning like this. You'll find something. You won't rest until you do. Do you understand me, girl? Because if you don't, it won't be you who suffers. I'll have your sister put away."

He had danced around that threat for years, but he'd never come out and said it like that before. So flat and matter-of-fact. So ugly and unmistakable.

Her head spun.

"You don't mean that," she said, though she knew better to argue.

"I will have her sanctioned and committed, girl," her father growled at her. "Her only use to me is the power it gives me over you, and believe me, I have every intention of using it. Test me, Calista. I dare you."

She thought her stomach might betray her, and swallowed, hard, to keep the panic down. To keep any further arguments to herself, because there was no point antagonizing him. There never was. But it was as if she couldn't help herself.

Because she couldn't allow anything to happen to Melody. But she just didn't see how she would do what her father wanted her to do. She didn't see how she could possibly find leverage on a man like Orion, so stalwart and *good*, damn him.

Of course he can't help you, she told herself. *No one can help you.*

Her father must have sensed a counterargument brewing, or worse, an appeal to the better nature he didn't have. He pinched her to stop it before it happened, hard enough to bring tears to her eyes. That was his farewell gift to the daughter he'd sold.

She had the whole ride over from her father's house to wait for the stinging to subside. And she had that little gift with her—bruising up nicely—when the palace staff ushered her, with no little pomp and circumstance, to the rooms she was told had been set aside for her use in the family wing.

"Quite an honor, madam, I don't mind saying," the

stuffy butler had intoned down the length of his impressive nose.

Inside, alone, Calista had sat there in one of the sitting rooms. It was easily the most elegantly appointed room she'd ever beheld. And it made her feel lonelier than she ever had in her life.

She had no reason to imagine that would ever change.

Not when none of this was real, or hers. And when her brief was to gather incriminating information on the king while she was here so her father could continue to wield his repulsive influence. Or *thought* he could continue—until she took his company out from under him, which might be more difficult to pull off than she'd anticipated if she was locked up in the palace…

But her own self-pity was too much for her to bear. She wiped at her face, annoyed to find she'd actually let a few tears fall. She wandered through her suite until she found the bathroom and splashed water on her face until she felt a bit more like herself.

Feeling sufficiently pulled together, she went back out into the main hallway, and stopped. Because she came face-to-face with three officious-looking men.

"My goodness," she said mildly. "Have I already run afoul of the palace guard?"

"The palace guard would be armed, madam," said the one in the middle, with a bristling mustache. "We are His Majesty's private secretarial staff."

"Thank you," she murmured sweetly. "But I don't need any dictation at present."

And the three of them managed to look as if they might have swooned from horror, died from it and been resurrected, all without actually moving a muscle.

"We are here to see to your education, Lady Calista," intoned the mustache. "You will be married to His Majesty in only a matter of weeks. And unless I'm mistaken, you know very little indeed about palace life, royal etiquette, or any number of other things that will fall under your purview as queen and consort."

"Funnily enough," Calista said, glaring straight back at him, "the job was sold to me as a pretty simple one. Make an heir and go about my business. And as far as I'm aware, the making of heirs, even royal ones, doesn't involve a crowd."

But the mustache only smiled.

Pityingly.

And that was how, a week later, Calista found herself actually looking forward to the first of the December holiday balls.

Her parents had practically had to throw her in the car and drag her to the palace before, but now she was already here in the palace. And she was so sick and tired of being followed around by the Trinity of Doom that she'd claimed she needed significantly more time to get ready than she actually did, and more, had actually taken that time. Because it turned out that the only thing better than a week at the spa—something she'd dreamed about but never done—was taking advantage of all palace life had to offer when it came to preparing for grand occasions.

A lovely, lengthy massage until the shoulders that were usually in her ears felt like butter. Her hair styled theatrically and her makeup applied just so. And a set of attendants to help her into a sumptuous gown that made her look like she belonged in a Disney movie.

It was almost enough to lull her into a false sense of security and well-being. It was almost enough to make her imagine this all might be real…

Almost.

She waited for Orion the way she always did, in that private salon of his that was now down the long hall instead of across town. She stood where she usually did, though it felt oddly intimate that she'd simply…walked here. Without a wrap, as she hadn't gone outside. She knew that the palace was a huge, sprawling complex, and yet the fact they now shared a roof seemed to lodge beneath her skin like its own pop of heat.

Don't be ridiculous, she chided herself.

But when Orion entered the room, at last, in all his kingly splendor, their eyes seemed to meet as if tugged together by magnetic forces. And then they held.

Calista told herself that she needed to hold on to her panic and fury about what was happening. That if she didn't, she would have no choice but to let go and lose herself in all that grave hazel.

"I'm told you're making progress," he said after the moment had long since turned awkward, and that made it easier.

"How patronizing." She scowled at him. "I didn't realize that I was a remedial case. Or that progress reports were being issued."

But he didn't take the bait. He never took the bait.

"I feel certain that my secretaries impressed upon you that there was much you need to learn in a short period of time, Calista. And you cannot truly be surprised that they have let me know how the process has been unfolding, can you?"

That he sounded perfectly reasonable only made it worse. It made her want to hunker down and feed the fury in her whatever it needed to explode.

"I have learned many important things, Your Majesty." Her voice was clipped and not exactly polite, and she decided on the spot that she would rather die than tell

Orion that she'd enjoyed much of it. Not the endless corrections, but the scope of a queen's role—and all of it to be performed with grace and wit.

Assuming such attributes are at your disposal, the mustache had sniffed.

If she'd been planning to remain his queen, she might have found it a challenge in the best way to rise to the levels expected of the king's consort. The deft ability to influence ministers without appearing to do so. The political machinations hidden behind an easy smile. She would have loved getting to do those things—

But she wasn't going to be queen.

And she could be just as patronizing as he was. "I have heard a great many lectures on state dinners, for example. I have been informed that I must learn a certain fluency in the language of flowers, which is apparently very important, even though I have the blackest thumb imaginable. I have been forced to attempt every possible iteration of a curtsy, which should really be its own workout craze. *Royal Squats and Noble Lunges* has a nice ring to it, doesn't it? I have spent untold hours dissecting where, how, and to whom I may or may not incline my neck. All of this has been riveting." There was a gleam in his hazel eyes that made that fury inside her seem to melt. And caramelize. "Absolutely riveting."

"Yes, well. Not everything can be as exciting as prying into the personal lives of strangers with an eye to ripping their lives apart. It will no doubt be an adjustment."

Was it her imagination or was Orion rather more testy than usual tonight? Edgy, she might have said. If he was someone else.

"Is something the matter?" she asked, and it was only after she'd asked it that she realized she would have been better served pretending not to notice.

Because she certainly shouldn't care.

"Not at all," Orion said. "Or nothing more than usual. Sometimes it is not possible to rule a country. You must rule yourself and hope the country follows afterward. Eventually."

Calista had the urge to upend the nearest incidental table, scattering figurines and precious objects to and fro. She refrained. Barely.

She made herself breathe into the fury. "Self-control is admirable, I'm sure. Though I'm not certain it takes the place of, I don't know, basic human rights."

"Human rights?" He looked amazed then, and inarguably royal. As if he'd turned into a bust of himself. "Have human rights been violated in some fashion that I am unaware of, here on the quiet streets of Idylla?"

"Perhaps not on a wide scale. Not in Idylla, anyway." Admitting that felt like a surrender, and she didn't want to give up so much as a centimeter. "But I'm feeling rather concerned about my own rights at the moment."

"Yes." Orion eyed her. "I can see how you suffer."

"There's no need for sarcasm," she shot back at him. "You don't have the slightest idea what it's like to have your whole life taken away from you at a whim."

"Calista. I must beg of you." He shook his head. "Do you really think that I'm likely to lend a sympathetic ear to my blackmailer?"

"I'm not the one who blackmailed you."

"No, worse, you are my blackmailer's instrument."

There was something in his gaze, then. She didn't understand it. It was a glittering, dark sort of thing, and it made her skin prickle. Everywhere. It made that melting, caramelized mess she wanted to call fury…very distinctly something else, especially as it sank lower.

"Now you live beneath my roof. I receive daily reports

of the ways you challenge my staff. You treat me with rampant disrespect, so I am not particularly shocked that you are not the biddable girl they might wish you were. And none of it matters. I will marry you all the same, come Christmas Eve, because that is the tradition. You may not have been my choice, but you are my betrothed, and I do not break my promises." Orion's eyes gleamed, while his voice seemed to get tangled up in all that fire and fury within her. "But by all means, stand before me and tell me what it is like to have the life you'd planned snatched out of your fingers."

She blinked. Then again. "I suppose you have a point."

And to her surprise, he smiled. "You are the one who decided we must be enemies, Calista."

"Perhaps I was hasty."

Suddenly, it was as if she couldn't think what to do with her hands. Or her neck. She felt…outsized and awkward, and she knew, now, in no uncertain terms, that it would be inappropriate for her to sit until he did. That royal etiquette decreed that unless and until they sorted something else out for the two of them in private, she must continue to treat him with the courtesy due his station no matter how she felt about it.

The trouble isn't that you know, a voice in her whispered. *It's that you care.*

She rather thought she'd preferred it when she didn't.

"Did your parents get along?" she asked. He stared at her, and this time, there was no hoping she didn't flush. She did, and rather brightly, she feared. "I don't mean at the end. Everyone knows how…sad she became, of course. But surely they could not have begun at the place they ended." She swallowed, her throat suddenly dry. What had made her think bringing up the queen's death—officially called an accident but widely regarded as the suicide it was—was a good idea? No matter how the old queen was pitied because who *wouldn't* wish to escape from King Max? "Could they?"

Orion stalked over to the sideboard, and she watched as he fixed himself a drink with decisive, peremptory movements of his hands that made her feel a bit…fluttery.

He turned back, swirling liquid in a crystal tumbler, and eyed her rather darkly over the top of it.

"What is it exactly you are asking?"

"According to what I've learned in the past week, your mother was bred for the job," Calista said, still standing there feeling foolish with her hands folded in front of her and her back pin straight. Not because she felt in control, the way she did in a boardroom. But because she felt ripped into a million little pieces and she didn't have the slightest idea how to start putting them back together. So perfect posture it was. "She and your father were promised since the day of her birth. She was trained not only in how to be a queen, or how to be Queen of Idylla, for that matter, but how to be your father's specific queen. His likes and dislikes, his strengths and weaknesses. Other girls learned about history, but your mother? She studied your father."

"So I'm told, for her sins," Orion said darkly.

"Well? Did it work?"

Orion tossed back his drink. "To a point. Yes."

Calista wanted to fire questions at him, particularly because the look on his face then was troubled. But she bit her tongue. And though it was more difficult than it should have been to a seasoned negotiator, she waited.

Not at all sure he would reply until he did.

"While my grandfather was alive, it was different," he said. "My parents were newlyweds and from all I have ever been able to ascertain, they got along well enough.

This was no love match, but then, no one expected it should have been. My mother was an excellent support for a crown prince. She provided the heir and the spare in short order. She maintained a full slate of complementary interests. She took great care to create a certain image—elegant, yet approachable. But then my grandfather died. My father became king."

"'Heavy is the head…'?"

"Heavy was the ego," Orion growled. "This is all documented history. It's not personal. My father was spectacularly ill suited to be the king of anything. He surrounded himself with the worst people. Sycophantic courtiers who told him only what he wished to hear. He'd already secured the bloodline, so why not indulge himself as he pleased? He began to throw parties. He began to neglect his duties. And my mother, always trained to think first and only of my father, went with him wherever he led. How could she not?"

"She was a grown woman," Calista pointed out. Carefully. "A grown woman and a queen, in fact. With her own courtiers, advisers, and so on. Or so I am informed."

His mouth twisted. "If you already know, why are you asking me?"

"I want to know how you see this role I am to take in a few weeks." She lifted her chin and tried to understand why that severe look on his stark face made her want to do dangerous things. Like move closer. Or worse, touch him. "That's really what matters, isn't it? What do *you* want from a queen, Orion?"

She didn't understand why the tension in the room was so intense. But she also didn't move when he slapped his tumbler down on the sideboard with a decisive click, and then started for her.

Calista stood her ground. Somehow, she stood her

ground, when he seemed to her like some kind of avenging angel as he bore down upon her.

And then his fingers were on her shoulders, pulling her close.

As if he wanted to flirt with the same dangers she did.

Because her secret shame was that there was not one single shred of resistance inside her. Not one, when she knew that this wasn't real. That none of this was anything but elaborate staging.

No matter how it felt.

"I've already told you what I want," he growled at her.

"Sex," she threw at him, because challenging him was the closest thing she had to a wall and she needed a wall. She needed *something* between them. "That's what you wanted from the start. You do know that you're the king, don't you? You can snap your fingers and have as much sex as you want with whoever you want. You don't have to marry unwilling women to get it."

She thought he ought to have been gripping her hard, as if he wanted to hurt her. The way her father would have done. But instead, his thumbs moved restlessly against the exposed skin of her clavicle. And she could feel the fire of it, the rhythm, the deep, drugging song as it spooled out inside her.

"I could snap my fingers, yes," he agreed, and if there was a wall between them it was made of need. "And then before I know it, I could also have a collection of tabloid articles to my name, one for each new scandal that would rip this kingdom apart. I prefer to keep my private life private. And all scandals in the past."

There was something in the way he said that. She tilted her head slightly to one side, trying to work it out. Something inside her longed to simply reach out her hand. To lay her palm against his cheek and feel the heat of him.

Another part of her wanted to bury her head against his chest, because she knew, somehow, that if she did, he would gather her against him and hold her tight.

But she could feel that song inside her, the pitch growing higher and more insistent.

And she thought of his mother, bred since her birth to play the supporting role. To disappear while standing in plain sight, there next to her husband. A woman created for the sole purpose of bearing children and smiling prettily beneath the weight of a crown that was never hers.

Calista understood something terrible about herself then. She understood exactly how she'd been lying to herself all this time.

She'd worked so hard, and sacrificed everything, but not only because she wanted to save her sister from her parents. Not only because she wanted to put her father in his place at last.

She'd been doing it for those reasons, yes. But more than that, she'd wanted her own power. She'd wanted to prove that she *could* do it. She alone. She'd wanted the life she knew she could have had if she'd been born the son her father had always wanted.

She had never trusted anyone.

She didn't see herself starting now.

And it had all happened too quickly, hadn't it? She'd been removed from Skyros Media. She'd been shunted off to the palace. She'd spent a week learning about all the ways she could better serve and support the king.

Calista didn't know if it was galling or pathetic that she'd already drowned, had disappeared in her own mirror, and was the last to know.

"I've already said this to you once," she said now, swaying closer to him because it felt like danger, and that felt like resistance. "You don't have to go to all these lengths to have sex with me, Your Majesty. You could do it right now, if you wanted. All you have to do is ask."

"We have a ball to get to," he gritted out at her, but his thumbs brushed against her skin. And he didn't let her go.

"My bad," she replied, smiling because that felt meaner. Edgier and therefore safer. "I should have known. You only want me if it's a challenge. If there's some kind of hunt. Even kings are mere men, after all."

"Hardly," Orion growled. "I just want you, damn you."

And then he slammed his mouth to hers.

CHAPTER SEVEN

ORION SHOULDN'T HAVE let her goad him. He should have been better than that.

More controlled. More in command of himself—and her.

But as Calista's taste exploded in his mouth—far better than he remembered, far darker and wilder and more addictive—he found he didn't much care.

He wasn't the fool she thought he was.

Orion knew that she was acting out. That despite her performance that first day, she was in many ways a victim of her father the same as he was.

He knew all that. He simply couldn't care about it the way he ought to have. Not just then.

Because she tasted like all the dreams he'd been having, one hotter than the last. Intense and demanding and astonishingly perfect.

She was every fire he'd ever known and denied himself, burning hot within him. Making him think she was something he could not possibly survive intact—

But immolation sounded good to him just then. And tasted better.

He knew that they had a schedule to keep. He knew that their car was waiting to take them to the ball, and more important, all the people who had bought tickets would be waiting for them, too. He knew that this particular holiday tradition, with or without a royal engagement in the mix, was beloved by his people. They looked forward to it all year, and it was part of their national character to note, with pride, that Idylla boasted a season for commoners and kings to dance and make merry together.

His father had started blowing off the holiday balls years ago, to no one's great surprise. But Orion never had. In fact, as crown prince, he'd never missed one.

Orion was always where he said he would be. He was always on time and prepared. If his schedule decreed that he would set foot on a certain flagstone at 6:37 p.m., that was precisely when his foot struck the earth.

"It's easy to be a monk when you rid your life of any temptation," Griffin had told him, years ago.

Orion had ignored him back then. He'd assumed that was no more than Griffin being provocative, as ever.

But tonight, Calista was in his arms, her mouth was open beneath his as she kissed him back, and Orion understood at last that he had never been tested before.

He had never come close to a test.

That should have appalled him, but it didn't. It couldn't. Because he was kissing her, and that was all he could manage to care about.

He kissed her like a dying man. He kissed her as if she alone could quench the great thirst he hadn't known he had. He kissed her and he kissed her, moving closer and pulling her even tighter in against him. He angled his head, kissing her hungrily. Hotly.

He wanted to sink his hands into her hair. He wanted to throw her down on the nearest flat surface and truly indulge himself at last.

He *wanted.*

And that meant he was as weak as his father had ever been.

It was that thought that penetrated, dousing him like sheets of ice.

He thrust her away from him, taking in the fact that she looked as wrecked he was. That her eyes were glassy, her mouth soft.

But he couldn't process any of that.

All he could think was that after all this, after everything he'd done, after the years and years of keeping himself separate from the things that tempted other men because he wanted to be something better, something more, something worthy of the crown he now wore—in the end, it all came down to this.

Petty sins of the flesh.

A lifetime of control and commitment and all it took was one woman to ruin him. He almost laughed, though nothing was funny.

"Is this why your father sent you here?" His voice was rough and thick, two signs that he was already too far gone. "Is this the game you're playing? Just like every other honey trap that has ever been set for me?"

For a moment, she seemed to vibrate. Her aquamarine eyes were wide and glued to his, but the look in them was haunting.

Because it was the same one he'd seen on her face in that hallway in Skyros Media. Right after her father had literally slapped her cheek.

Orion had now done the same himself, with his mouth.

Did he really need any further evidence that at the slightest provocation, at the first temptation, he became his father?

He remembered his mother, then, though he preferred

not to think of her outside of a few stray, happy memories when he was small. But now he remembered those later years. How she would cry and wail, literally crumbling if King Max so much as glanced in her direction. Cringing and sobbing, until Griffin and Orion, though only boys themselves, had been forced to act as her protectors.

Deep down, Orion's secret shame was that he'd grown impatient with her. His own mother.

You can't cry in front of him, he'd told her once, furiously, with all the conviction of the overly serious child he'd been. *You can't show him that he's hurt you.*

But she had only done it more.

This time, he assured himself, he would do no such thing, no matter the provocation tonight. It surely wasn't *her* fault that he was so tempted by her. He waited for Calista to cringe away from him, assuring himself that he would understand her. He would support her. He would do whatever was necessary to—

But instead, she laughed.

It was scornful, bracing laughter, as much a relief as it was an assault.

Her hands found her hips, and she scowled at him, and all of that was better than cringing, certainly. Though Orion couldn't say that it was *comfortable*, exactly. Or that he liked it much. Only that it was better than the alternative.

"Honey trap," she repeated, as if he'd called her a filthy name. "You must be joking."

"Your father could have used the leverage he had on my father to do any number of things," Orion said, perhaps a bit gruffly. "He chose to force our marriage. You tell me why a honey trap isn't the first thing that would come to mind under the circumstances."

"First I'll point out the distinct lack of honey in the

trap," she retorted, her voice arch. "Who knew that the King of Idylla himself could be lured in with this much vinegar? I don't really know what that says about you, Orion. But I don't think it's good."

He wanted to kiss her again. He wanted to peel her out of those clothes and keep his mouth on her until she melted against him. And then he wanted to taste every last inch of her skin, until both of them were immolated. Until there was no telling the difference between spark and flame, fire and heat.

Him and her.

He was so hard it hurt.

But the hurt was a good thing. It was like a hair shirt, to carry on with his brother's favorite monk analogy. It reminded him who he was.

"We have a ball to attend," he told her, taking a deep pleasure in the fact he could sound so mild. So unbothered. He could see temper flash over her, and enjoyed that even more. "I don't say this to stop you taunting me. Carry on all you like. You'll just need to do it in the car."

When he beckoned for her to precede him out of the room, he thought she might balk. He waited, oddly primed and charged, as she stared back at him, her hands in markedly unladylike fists at her sides.

Inside, he *wanted*. He ached with it.

And what was the matter with him that there was a very large part of him that wanted nothing more than for her to launch herself in his direction? For her to take a swing at him, even—the way no one else would dare?

Because one way or another, that would allow him to put his hands on her?

Instead, Calista lifted her chin, gathered the skirts of her dress in those fists of hers, and swept out of the room.

And he was a little too aware of the tension between

them as they sat in the car, building up their defenses again, brick by brick. He consulted his mobile. He took calls that could have waited, had he wanted them to wait. All the while, Calista pointedly repaired her makeup and hair. He wondered if she knew how it felt to him—like she was easing those iron bars between them back into place. And locking them up, separately, in their original prisons.

He told himself he ought to have been grateful.

Tonight's event was at the Royal Botanical Gardens, with portable heaters everywhere to ward off what passed for the chill in this first week of December. The gardens were lit up, with little lights sprinkled everywhere, so that more than one person remarked that it was as if they'd been set down in their very own Christmas ball. The sort that one could hang on a tree, and build traditions around—

Not that Orion, raised as he was by wolves in royal form, had ever had anything of the kind. Trees festooned about the palace, bristling with decorations, certainly. But their only family traditions involved making themselves scarce while King Max raged, then collapsed in a drunken stupor.

He spent a long while circulating through the crowd, doing his best to mimic the sort of man who was filled with Christmas cheer.

Still, when the first waltz started, he knew his duty as king and therefore, always, the guest of honor. He wanted to touch Calista just then about as much as he wanted to punch himself in the face, but he swept her into his arms anyway, because it was expected.

And for a few moments, they danced in pointed silence.

But only for a few moments.

"This is really taking your martyr act a step too far," she said when she could clearly take the quiet no longer, though she smiled joyfully up at him while she said it.

"I don't know what you mean."

"You do." Her smile widened. "It really is so boring, Orion. It's one thing to crucify yourself on every stray piece of wood that crosses your path in the palace. But it's something else again, I think, to fling yourself upon the altar of your own self-importance *in public*."

He took his time looking down at her, and if he held her a shade too close, well. The crowds would have to deal with it. He was the bloody king.

"I will repeat. I don't know what you mean."

The spark of challenge lit up those eyes of hers, and suddenly, he could think of nothing but her fists at her side in that private parlor. And how surprised he'd been that she didn't swing then.

He should have known that, of course, she'd waited.

"Don't you?" she asked, still looking—to someone not quite as close to her as he was—happy and filled with appropriate seasonal delight. "I thought you prided yourself on being such a rational man. Such a reasonable king after all our dark years with your father." She made a tutting sound. "How tragic not to know yourself at all."

"Perhaps a better conversation would be to investigate what it is you know about yourself, Calista," he replied, and it was like a song inside him, almost as good as his mouth on hers. "As far as I can tell, you've made yourself your father's handmaid. You prance around in your corporate costume. You shout at anyone who will listen about your importance. But at the end of the day, the first moment he could sell you, he did. Even pawns are treated better than that, surely."

"You are the reigning expert on pawns, of course," she replied coolly.

"Whose pawn am I?"

"My father's, for one thing." She smirked at him. "Look at that. We have something in common after all."

He thought it wise, then, to finish off the dance with less talking. Because for the first time in his life, in as long as he could remember, he wasn't entirely certain that he remained as in control of himself as he ought to have been.

And he wasn't even kissing her.

That notion was so astounding—so hideous, really—that when the waltz ended he executed a stark, stiff sort of bow, and stalked away from her.

Better to leave his fiancée on the dance floor abruptly than to descend into...whatever it was that moved in him, dark and dangerous, that had everything to do with the taste of her, still there on his tongue.

Far more potent than wine or spirits.

The night wore on. Nobility and dignitaries danced attendance on him, as ever. He posed for a thousand pictures, trying to exude calm. Quiet certainty. As if his very presence was a happy ending. One the whole country had been waiting for, all this time.

Not that he knew much about such things. Still, he tried.

Toward the end of the night, conscious that it was impolite for anyone to leave until he did, Orion once again sought out Calista. The gardens looked mysterious at night. All the sparkling lights and the glow from the heaters gave the winding paths an almost unearthly glow. Orion walked with no apparent haste, as if he was out for a stroll, enjoying that even he could find a measure of anonymity in the shadows. And when he was seen, he gave no indication that he was looking for a woman who, had she been anyone else, would have been stuck to his side all night to advance her position.

There was a part of him that liked her more than he should because she was nothing like the sort of socialite heiress he'd always assumed he would marry, all soft smiles to the face and a dulcet-toned knife to the back. Calista, he knew, would come at him from the front.

Something about that was deeply cheering.

He rounded a corner festooned with exultant shrubberies, then, and saw her. At last.

The soft light surrounded her, making her glow as if she was her own candle, and Orion felt…poleaxed. Frozen solid, there where he stood, though the Mediterranean night was nowhere near freezing.

As if he'd never seen a woman before.

His heart exploded inside his chest, so dramatic a sensation that he was half-afraid he'd suffered the kind of cardiac arrest that had claimed his father. But no, he realized after a breath, he was still standing.

It took him long moments—small eternities, really—to realize first, that Calista wasn't alone. She stood with her father, here in a far-off corner of the gardens. Though she was still dressed like a queen—*his* queen—she had her arms crossed and a faint frown marring her perfect brow.

Unless he was very much mistaken, her father was threatening her. He recognized that particular bulldog-like expression on Skyros's face.

"Whatever it takes, girl," Aristotle said to her, sounding angry. "You understand me?"

"Perfectly," Calista replied, her voice cool and crisp.

Orion should have stayed there, half concealed in shadow, to see what would happen next. He knew he should. But Aristotle reached out, as if to grip Calista's arm, and he couldn't stand it.

He couldn't *allow* it.

"Careful there, Skyros," he found himself belting out into the dark. "I believe we already covered this."

Father and daughter jerked, then turned to gape at him. And he couldn't say he cared that Calista looked faintly guilty, because what really mattered to him was that Aristotle dropped his hand.

"You do have a habit of popping up in the strangest places, don't you?" Aristotle growled.

Orion ignored him, inclining his head toward Calista. "The hour grows late, my lady. It's time to head back to the palace."

"Indeed," she said, shooting a look at her father that Orion wasn't sure he wanted to be able to read. "I wouldn't want to turn into a pumpkin."

Orion held out his hand. And he didn't know if she was performing for her father. He didn't know far too many things when it came to this woman he was meant to marry, it was true. But he couldn't worry about any of that as he should, because she stepped toward him and took his hand then, and for a moment, he almost thought she meant it.

For a moment, he was tempted to forget that he hadn't chosen her himself.

He nodded at her father, his tormentor, and then swept her away so that she could join him in the endless ordeal of extricating himself from the ball.

By the time they made it to the car, he'd grown so used to her hand in his that he felt a flash of something like grief, though far hotter, when she took it away.

And this time, though they both sat in the back of the car just as they had on the way to the ball, it was different. It was as if the same heartbeat pounded through both of them. Orion was aware of the blood rushing through him. He was aware of Calista, as if she was wrapped tight around him. As if she was goading him directly, when all she was doing was sitting there beside him, staring straight ahead.

He was aware of her breath, the rise and fall of her chest. And of the faint scent of the perfume she favored, light enough and seductive enough that he was never quite sure if he was imagining it.

Once in the palace they walked side by side, their footsteps echoing against the marble floors as they headed, together, for the family wing.

"I will escort you to your suite," he informed her, aware that his voice was gravelly. Low. Unduly serious.

And not quite his own.

"What's this?" Her voice was bright, if forced. Tense, the same as his. "Are we suddenly observing dating protocols? However will my tender heart cope?"

He walked next to her, that throbbing, pounding beat inside him still insistent. Dark and stirring. And it only got worse with every step.

"I will not ask you why you are forever hiding away in dark corners, whispering with your father, a man already known to the crown as a bad actor. A legitimate threat."

"I'm glad you won't ask. Because I wouldn't answer you anyway. He's my father."

"Nor will I ask you what it is he wants you to do, as I think we both know you wouldn't tell me anyway."

"That would defeat the purpose, surely, having gone to all the trouble to slip a king into a pocket in the first place."

Her voice was tart, but somehow, he thought that darkness in her gaze was the real truth. Or maybe it was only that he felt the same darkness in him.

"But it does beg the question, Calista," he said, as they drew up outside the door to her suite. "Which one of us is the greater martyr?"

She flinched at that, as if the question was another slap. And he watched, amazed—and something far darker than merely *amazed*—as her cheeks flushed red.

"I'm the very opposite of a martyr, thank you."

"Not from where I'm standing. Don't you have a sister? Where is she in all this?"

Calista surged forward, her aquamarine eyes clouded with some great emotion. And then, to his eternal astonishment, thumped him.

In the chest.

Hard.

"Don't you mention my sister. Don't you try to drag her into this. She has her own troubles, and certainly doesn't need palace drama on top of it."

"Are you sure?" Orion asked with an idleness he did not feel. "Are you protecting your sister because she needs protection? Or because you like how it feels to be the one forever in demand? The one forever spreading out the mantle of your many sacrifices far and wide, so you can complain about them?"

She thumped him again, and it was clarifying.

Because it was rage inducing. Though, if he thought about it, it wasn't rage at all that surged in him then.

It was hot, dark and deep, but it wasn't quite *rage*.

And the truth was, he felt that hair shirt disintegrating all around him. He could hardly remember the vows he'd made, or why.

Because even though she was thumping him, which would have bordered on a treasonous assault if anyone else had done it, all he could seem to focus on was that she was touching him.

Calista was *touching him*, and of her own volition.

That felt far stronger than any vow.

"You haven't the slightest idea what it's like," she threw at him.

"Says a civilian to a king."

Temper flashed over her face, and there was something almost electric about it. He could feel the same currents from earlier, but they were hotter now. Brighter.

As if the two of them, together, burned like a fever.

And she appeared to be just getting started. "You don't know the first thing about real life. You don't know about loss. You don't know what it's like to work your whole life for something only to have it snatched away from you at the last second."

"I am being blackmailed into marrying you, Calista, though I am the bloody king—and not my father. Perhaps it is you who do not understand."

"I have fought my whole life," she seethed at him. "Any sacrifices I made were not to martyr myself so I could feel better about my choices, but because they were necessary. Life and death, Orion. You weren't the only one who grew up under the whims of a terrible father. And not everyone gets to be a crown prince in that scenario. Some of us have to suffer in private. But you wouldn't know anything about that, because you live in a gilded palace, making laws and issuing commandments. You should try the real world sometime."

"Lady Calista. Please. You are the daughter of a billionaire. You live in an island kingdom the poets call enchanted. Magical. A real-life fairy tale. Perhaps you are no more acquainted with the real world than I."

She blew out a breath at that, as if she was deflating

there before his eyes. And he had the impression she wasn't entirely aware of it when instead of thumping him again, her hand flattened out, so that her palm was resting in the hollow between his pectoral muscles.

Calista might not be aware of it, but he could think of nothing else.

And for a moment, their gazes remained tangled together, and they…breathed.

As if they shared that same breath.

"I wish…" she began. "I wish that I could… You and I…"

But she didn't finish.

Orion reached up and covered her hand with his, trapping her there against his chest.

And he couldn't tell if that was her heartbeat he felt, or his own. Only that it rang in him like a warning. Like a new song.

"Then do something about it," he told her.

A command. A plea. His own *want*.

He should have known better. He should never have risked it. The control he never, ever lost felt loose around him then, precarious and dangerously close to breaking.

Orion needed to take his leave of her. He needed to pretend none of tonight had happened. He needed to march off, regain his equilibrium, and remind himself who he was, and more, who he wanted to be.

But he didn't move.

Not when she smiled, a curve of her lips that was not smirky, or edgy, or any of the weapons it usually was.

And certainly not when Calista lifted herself up onto her toes, swayed in closer, and finally kissed him.

Setting them both alight.

CHAPTER EIGHT

CALISTA FELT TWISTED. Turned inside out, and raw straight through.

But kissing Orion was a revelation.

Because it didn't make her feel less twisted, less raw or inside out. It took all of that and made it all worse, and then, by some delirious magic that only he seemed to know, heated it all up and made it better.

Until all she wanted was more.

She kissed him, her hand against his chest and his hand on hers, and he followed her lead. And it felt the way she'd always imagined fairy tales would, in those stories that belonged to others.

Soft. Sweet.

The faintest hint of heat and need—

But then Orion shifted, angled his jaw, and everything…*ignited.*

He kissed her and he kissed her.

And she forgot her goals here. She forgot all the bold words she'd thrown at him when they'd met, or the promises she'd made herself about how this would go down. She forgot everything, because he tasted too good.

Because nothing about this situation was real…but he was.

This was.

She let out a soft sound as she felt the hard wall behind her, but then the harder, far more fascinating wall of his body was pressed up against the front of her, and that was delicious. And everywhere. And she'd had no idea she could burn like this, so hot and bright.

She wound her arms around his neck and lost herself in the dance of their tongues, the taste of him, and a lifetime or two could have passed that way. Maybe they did.

But the heat was growing. The need wound around and around inside her, coiling tight, then tighter still, until she worried she might crack open. And when Orion lifted her against him so she could wrap her legs around his waist, she could do nothing but groan out her approval.

His kisses were deep, wild, perfect. But there was too much in the way. Her dress with its voluminous skirts seemed to anticipate her growing need and counter it, and all the clothes he wore seemed like an affront.

And it was as if he read her mind, because he pulled back, then. He tore his mouth from hers, but didn't put her down. For a moment all she could do was pant and wonder if her heart could really beat that hard without hurting her, and then Orion was shouldering his way into her suite, holding her against him as easily as if she weighed no more than a handful of feathers.

There was something about it. Something about being *carted about* by a man. *Effortlessly.* It made her feel feminine and sweet in all the ways she'd never been, like spun sugar. A confection.

The kind of dessert she couldn't wait for him to sample.

He carried her straight through to the bedroom without breaking his stride, then set her down at the foot of the grand bed that stood gracefully against the far wall. Across from it, the fire had been lit and danced there in its stone hearth, sending light and shadow spinning into the elegant room.

In the flickering of the flames, Orion's face seemed carved from marble, taut with need, and marked with a passion so intense it made his hazel eyes dark.

And better still, made her shudder, deep within. Where she felt exactly the way he looked.

"Orion…" she whispered, though she didn't know what she meant to say. Or how she could say it when she was so wild with wanting him, it hurt.

"I want you," he said, as if he knew. And his voice was thick with it.

With something else, too, though she couldn't place it.

It was not until his hands found her face to slide along her cheeks, then his fingers dug into her hair and pulled it loose from its pins, that she realized what it was.

Wonder.

The word seemed to shimmer inside her, heat and flame. But then he was kissing her again, and everything became a part of that. The slide of his tongue. The dizzying, glorious mastery he took of her.

And then when he pulled back and gazed at her as if he'd never beheld such beauty.

Calista felt lit up from the inside out, and trembled with it, especially when all Orion did was smile.

A very male, very dark sort of smile.

And then he undressed her.

But he didn't simply rip her clothes off, or hurry them along in any way.

He…unwrapped her, as if every bit of flesh he uncovered was a gift and he had nothing better to do than savor it. For eternity, if necessary.

Because that was what he did. He took his time, lavishing attention as much on the space between her breasts as the aching crest of each. He learned her collarbone, her shoulders, and each of her fingers. He spent a lifetime on the line of her spine, the curve of her lower back, the flare of her hips. Calista lost days, weeks, months, as he found his way down the length of each leg, then up again.

And by the time he made it between, to that place where she ached for him the most—molten and sweet and hot—she was gasping for breath.

Then her gasps turned to cries as he tasted her there, too.

Orion feasted on her with a fierce, possessive intensity that had her first falling back against the foot of the bed, and then lifting her hips up to meet the flat of his tongue, the faint scrape of his teeth, right where she needed it most.

And the first time she broke apart, arching up against him and sobbing, she understood fully why the French called it a little death.

Though there was nothing *little* about it.

Orion shifted her, moving her farther back onto the bed. Calista simply…lay there, fighting for air, as he rid himself of the suit he wore at last.

And then, despite how hard it still was to breathe, she had to prop herself up on her elbows to watch. Because the truth about the King of Idylla was that he was far more beautiful naked than he was magnificently clothed. He was a work of art. He belonged on all the statues that cluttered up this palace, and she was half-afraid that her heart would clatter its way straight out of her chest, because she was going to get to touch him. All of him.

She was going to get to lose herself in all that spectacular maleness, and even imagining that made her flush. Everywhere.

And the look on his face as he regarded her, sprawled

out naked on the bed while she waited for him, almost made her tip straight over that edge again.

It was so intense. *Too* intense, almost. He looked at her with so much focused ferocity that she felt fluttery.

And then he crawled his way up onto the bed to join her, and that only made the intensity and the fluttering worse.

Better, something in her argued.

"I want to touch you," she whispered. "I want to taste you."

"Next time," he growled.

Calista meant to protest, but he was kissing her again. Deep, drugging, intense kisses that sent her spinning.

And when Orion finally gathered her in his arms, then rolled her beneath him, she could feel how close to out of control he was. She could feel that electric tremor in him, running through him, as if he'd plugged himself into a wall socket.

His kisses grew wilder. More glorious.

And then she could feel him, the hardest part of him, flush up against the place where she wanted him the most.

It was almost too much to handle.

He blew out a breath, and she could feel his heart pounding against hers. His gaze was dark, gleaming with a kind of fierce longing, and she could hardly bear the intensity of this moment.

She could hardly bear this.

Him.

She felt as if they were both caught in a mad storm. It howled and shook the windows, but in the center of everything was Orion. In the way he notched himself into her soft heat, and then waited there, one heartbeat. Another.

And she thought there could be nothing in the world more real, more true, than this. No matter how they'd gotten here. No matter what their future held. Wanting him made her feel open wide and utterly bared, and the craziest part was that she longed for that, too.

For someone to look at her the way he did, as if he'd never wanted anything more and never, ever would.

"Please," Calista whispered. "*Please*, Orion."

And with a deep kind of growl, he thrust forward and buried himself within her.

Calista fell apart. She burst into a thousand pieces, when she would have said it was impossible for her to have hit such heights again at all tonight. Much less so soon.

She shook and she shook. And when the glorious quaking subsided, she was still clutching him to her.

But he hadn't moved.

"Orion…" she whispered.

There was a grimness about that stark expression on his face as he braced himself above her. As if he was holding himself so tightly that the slightest movement might break him.

And suddenly Calista wanted nothing more than to see him break. To see the reserved, guarded king break apart the way she had. So she shifted, rolling her hips to take him even deeper into her, and he let out a sound that could have been a laugh.

Though perhaps it sounded a bit more tortured.

But then, finally, he began to move.

And the storm they'd made moved in, wrapped itself around them, and began to howl.

Or maybe that was Calista. She couldn't tell.

Orion set a rhythm, but she didn't want that. She didn't want patience when she'd already lost hers so completely. She didn't want a single second more of his regal composure.

So she wrapped her legs around his waist and set her teeth to his neck. She met each thrust. And she knew the exact moment when King Orion Augustus Pax, King of Idylla, simply…lost it.

He dropped his head to her shoulder. His hips pistoned, tossing her straight back into that wildfire she'd thought had already burned its way out of her. Twice.

But it turned out there was so much more to burn.

He hurtled them both over that cliff, and his mouth against her shoulder while he went. And somewhere between those two things—the way he lost himself and the way he found himself with his mouth against her flesh—took her with him.

Tossing them over the edge and into oblivion.

Together.

She had no sense of falling asleep, though she knew she must have when she woke to find herself lifted up in Orion's arms. A faint alarm stirred deep inside her, but she ignored it, because perhaps not every last second of her life had to be a fight. A struggle.

It was far better to rest her head on his shoulder the way she imagined regular women might, and dream a bit as he carried her through the suite, and deposited her into the huge bathtub already full and foaming.

Calista slid into the embrace of the water, smiling, because she couldn't remember the last time someone had cared for her. That was her job. And she smiled wider when he surprised her completely and joined her.

Then liked it even more when he shifted her around so he could hold her, her back to his front.

And held like that, where no one could see her, the

hot water could sink into her bones, and Calista could simply…be.

It felt like a revolution.

She let herself relax, as if nothing outside the confines of this tub could touch her. Or could matter, one way or the other. No schemes, no goals, no worries. Just the warm water, the bubbles, and Orion.

Calista rested against him, and let the quiet soothe her. Or maybe it was him, so solid and strong behind her.

She sighed a little when he picked her hand out of the water and held it between them, once again fiddling with the ring he'd put there. The Ring of Queens. The ring, it was rumored, a besotted ruler of Idylla had created for his beloved, fashioning it from sky and sea, so she could wear it forever on her finger and think of Idylla. Of him.

And for the first time since this farce had started, Calista found herself really imagining what it would be like if this was real. If the only thing she had to do was become Orion's queen. If all the rest of it was a skin she could shed when they married, and once they did she could simply be the sort of woman who could wear a ring like this all the time, without irony. She could be the kind of woman he could hold in his arms the way he did now, the whole rest of the world at bay.

The kind of woman who could allow herself to be as real as he felt to her.

All she had to do was imagine herself anyone else alive, and this moment would have been romantic. A beautiful new beginning. The start of an unexpected chapter in the kind of arranged marriages families like hers had been mandating forever.

But wishes were never horses, and Calista didn't get to play Cinderella games. She didn't have a fairy godmother. Instead, she had a nasty, terrible father… And what was she doing?

The water was still warm, but she felt cold. How could she let herself sit here, surrendering to all these treacherous feelings for this man when nothing could ever come of them?

This could never be real. This was only a game, and if it was a game, that meant she had to win it. She couldn't let either one of them be lulled into any false senses of security when there was none.

Not when so much was at stake. Not when Melody would be the one to pay the price.

Every wish, every feeling inside her was a betrayal of her sister. Calista should have hated herself.

She squeezed her eyes shut, happy that he couldn't see her face or the torment there that shouldn't have been there, and made herself laugh. A sharp dagger of a laugh, precisely calculated to make him stiffen beneath her.

Which he did, and her heart ached. But she kept going.

Because he was her adversary, not her lover, and she really didn't know how she'd let herself forget that for a moment.

"I really am shocked, Orion," she said, making her voice arch. Insinuating. A hideous intrusion into the beauty of this moment, and she hated herself for it. But she didn't stop. "How on earth have you managed to keep your lovers from prattling on to all the tabloids about your prowess in bed? I would have thought they'd be lining up to talk about how good you are. To compare notes, even, the better to brag to each other and all the poor women out there who can only dream of touching you."

Calista wanted to cry. She couldn't let herself, however, so instead she laughed again. Another sharp knife.

And she could feel him change beneath her, going stern and harsh.

You did that, she snarled at herself. *Good job.*

It wasn't lost on her that she should have been happy that she'd done it.

"I'm not a show pony, Calista." His voice was disapproving and dark. And she could feel it inside her as if every word was carved into her ribs. Flaying her open, and deservedly. "I do not perform for the crowds—much less the filthy tabloids."

"You don't have to perform. You're you." That almost veered back into the mess of feelings that made her throat feel tight, so she kept on with that bright, brittle blade of a laugh. "And you must be some kind of magical creature to keep them all so quiet all these years. I'm not sure it's ever happened before in the history of royalty."

"I do not care to share my private life," he said, his voice a rumbling bit of thunder that she could feel against her back like a new, worse storm. "I have been at some pains to tell you this."

"Not everyone gets to choose what they keep private, Orion. Especially not when they sit on thrones and expect others to bow and scrape before them. I'm amazed you haven't learned that lesson already."

"Perhaps you will need to teach it to me," he said then, a different, silky note in his voice. It made her shudder, and she wasn't sure if that was pure sensual reaction or some kind of foreboding. "Because there is only one person who can talk to the tabloids or anyone else about my sexual prowess, Calista. I have not had to use magic spells to ensure any particular loyalty from anyone. I've maintained a dignified silence about my exploits by simply…not having any."

She didn't understand.

She blinked at the tub and the water before her. "Is that a fancy way of saying you made them all sign non-disclosure agreements?"

But he didn't reply. He simply stayed where he was, lounging there in the hot bath behind her, his back like a wall. And she turned the word she'd said over and over again in her head.

And then again, when an inkling bloomed inside her.

"Orion."

He sounded amused. "Calista."

"You don't… You can't mean…?"

"Indeed I do."

Calista pushed away from him. Something great and terrible was expanding inside her chest, fast and hot. And she really didn't know if it was a sob or if she was about to scream, or some mad combination of both—

"You can't…?"

She turned around in the water, ignoring the way it sloshed alarmingly at the sides of the tub. Then she knelt there, facing him.

Her heart kicking at her so hard she was astonished she wasn't running flat out.

His eyes glittered dark gold. But otherwise, he looked almost entirely at his ease. His mouth in its usual stern line. His head high. Not in the least bit concerned about what he'd just told her.

What he'd just admitted to her.

"You can't possibly mean…?" she whispered.

"That is exactly what I mean," he replied, quietly. Almost as if he was relishing this, she thought. "You are my only lover, Calista. And soon to be my wife and queen. Your reaction suggests you did not enjoy yourself when I feel certain you did."

"I... That's not the point! You're supposed to disclose things like that!"

He lifted a shoulder, then lowered it, looking entirely unconcerned. "I apologize if this upsets you in some way."

"Upsets me?" She felt a deep, shuddering thing, rattling through her. As if her bones were coming apart. *As if your heart is breaking,* something in her whispered. "Of course it doesn't upset me, I just don't believe it."

She didn't know what she imagined a virgin ought to look like—or someone who had so recently been a virgin—but she was sure it wasn't this. Orion, every inch of him majestic in all ways, lounging back in the bath they shared. An enigmatic look on his face and not a single shred of anything like insecurity about his performance or her reaction anywhere.

Not that he should have been insecure. But surely there should have been fumbling. Mistakes or even misfires. Not...all that fierce possession that made her clench with need all over again, just thinking of it.

"Why would a man lie about such a thing?" he asked idly. "Surely it is more likely that the lies go in the other direction. Men do like to spin tales of their prowess, do they not?"

The gleam in his dark gaze suggested that he knew full well that he did not need to brag about his prowess or anything else. That, too, made a shiver snake its way down her spine.

"But you... But that..." She ordered herself to stop stammering. To get a hold of herself. "How?"

There was the faintest curve in the corner of Orion's mouth, then. He kept his dark gold gaze on her. "It was clear to me from a very young age that one of the primary ways in which my father was weak was his complete inability to avoid the sexual invitations that came his way. He did nothing to hide them. Indeed, he flaunted his various conquests in magazines like your father's or right here in the palace. And at the age when I might have started experimenting with such things, I was too busy engaged in what was already my life's work. Cleaning up his messes." His eyes glittered. "I decided I had no need to clean up mine, as well. It started as a rash decision when I was no more than thirteen. But it became a vow, and I kept it."

"How did you possibly...?"

Calista couldn't finish the sentence. She was terribly afraid that her heart was going to claw its way out of her chest, right there in the tub. She felt weak, somehow. And more profoundly thrown than she ever had before.

Or maybe, a voice inside her that sounded suspiciously like her sister whispered, *what you actually feel is vulnerable.*

Because he had given her something he had kept to himself all this time. He had made this thing between them real, and it made her want to sob. She wanted to lean forward, take his hands in hers, or his face, and tell him to be careful. That she could not be trusted and would only betray him in the end. How could he not know that already?

"Do you imagine that men cannot control themselves?" Orion sounded amused again. "I will note that no one thinks anything of it if a woman chooses to hold on to her virtue. But there must be something wrong with a man if he does the same."

"You did this to stay virtuous?"

"My brother would tell you that I'm ill-suited to be a king, because the monastic life suits me so much better." Again, the hint of a smile played with his mouth. Not as if he couldn't understand her reaction. But as if he found it entertaining. "I have always been intensely physical. I have merely restricted myself to other expressions of it. Until now." He inclined his head. "Until you."

That same emotion walloped her again. Was she going to surrender to it and sob? Or was she going to let it wrench her apart? Was she mad to imagine she could choose when it felt as if she might burst where she sat?

"All that waiting and you just thought, *Enough's enough*, after a night at a ball."

"With the woman I am to marry," Orion said, with tremendous patience and another hint of laughter. "When if not now? It wasn't marriage I was saving myself for, Calista. I'm not a young girl with a hope chest. I simply wished to make certain that I would not repeat my father's mistakes."

"But—"

He moved then, hooking his hand around her neck and tugging her gently to him, so she fell against his chest. And the curse of it was, she liked it there. She fit him too well, and she had to close her eyes against the surge of unfortunate sensation that stirred up in her.

"This is an arranged marriage," she said crossly. "This is supposed to be distant and remote and chilly. Not… *this*."

"I think we'll muddle through, Calista. Somehow."

There was something about the way he said her name, then. It had changed. Or she had changed. There was that dark richness to it, now. There were levels of meaning in it, shades and complications.

Or maybe that was just her poor, battered, traitorous heart.

She didn't argue with him any further. She didn't tell him that *of course* she worried, and he should worry, too.

That nothing good could come of this. That whatever she might feel, she was still her father's daughter.

That her father would destroy them both, and her sister, without a second thought, and neither one of them could prevent it—or they already would have, surely.

That they were doomed.

But it was as if he heard her arguments all the same. He smoothed a hand over her hair, and that stern mouth of his even softened in the corners.

"Don't worry," Orion said, but to her, it sounded like a curse. And then he made it worse. "I trust you."

CHAPTER NINE

DECEMBER WORE ON, drawing ever closer to the twenty-third and the board meeting Calista still had every intention of disrupting.

Her father might have removed her from the office, but that didn't change all the things she'd spent years putting into motion. She told herself it was better that she was away from the company these last, critical days—because she was sure it would have been impossible to keep herself under control and seemingly subservient, the way she needed to do until it was done.

Calista spent these weeks in the palace rather than directly under her father's thumb. Not that she felt free of him, with the daily messages and calls demanding she provide him with dirt on Orion. Instead of spending her days at Skyros Media, fighting tooth and nail in meetings and building up her position behind her father's back, she found herself at the mercy of the king's private secretaries. She got a crash course in the Idyllian Crown and the duties of the king's consort, and spent hour after hour learning all the various facts they thought she needed to know—and they thought she needed to know just about everything.

In many ways, it reminded her of being back at university in Paris, sitting in endless lectures. But instead of producing essays out of café nights and too much red wine, she had to sit there and prove to them that she'd internalized their teachings on everything from international diplomacy to proper correspondence, all while fending off her father's demands.

Hour after hour after hour. Until she thought that if the whole queen thing didn't work out, she could easily become a professional historian. With a focus on Idyllian royals throughout the ages.

She should have been crawling out of her skin. She should have been beside herself, and she…wasn't. Or not in the way she'd expected she ought to have been, anyway.

Her days were spent immersed in history. But her nights… Her nights were filled with Orion, and she almost couldn't bear to let herself think about what that meant.

"I don't understand how you never…" she'd whispered one night when they both lay panting before the fire in her bedchamber. "I don't understand anything about you."

"I made a vow," he'd replied lazily, turning her over on her belly and applying himself to the line of her back, turning her to jelly.

"You broke that vow, then."

She'd felt his smile against her skin and had shuddered. "I vowed I would only indulge in the pleasures of the flesh with my queen, Calista. I have broken no vows. Nor shall I."

And even now, weeks later, she almost couldn't bear to think about such moments, because thinking about them would mean analyzing them. Making decisions. And inevitably ruining these oddly bright weeks carved out in the darkest part of the year—and her life.

These weeks that made no sense. These weeks that

made her doubt herself, her purpose, and everything she'd ever known.

All lit up and threaded through with Orion, as if the king was his own holiday light and she glowed straight through. With him.

"Maybe you just like him," her sister said drily, a week before Christmas Eve. "Maybe he's likable. Maybe someday I'll actually get to meet him and decide for myself."

"You've met him."

"I was presented to him with half the kingdom in attendance at your engagement ball. Not the same thing."

Calista wasn't deliberately keeping Melody and Orion apart. But she also wasn't going out of her way to introduce them, either. She told herself there was no point. There were only six days remaining before the board meeting and seven days before her supposed wedding. Why pretend that her sister and Orion would ever need to interact?

Then again, here she was standing in one of the many palace salons, being pinned and sewed and otherwise fitted into a sweeping white gown she had no intention of ever *really* wearing. And certainly not for the ceremony it was being made for.

The palace advisers had decided, with very little input from Calista, that what was needed here was a fairy tale. The full Cinderella treatment, they called it, complete with a dress boasting skirts so wide she could have fit half the island beneath them, a tiny waist that stole her breath, and gold embroidered everywhere.

Just in case there was any doubt that she was marrying a king.

God help her, she was marrying *the king.*

No, she reminded herself. *You're only pretending you might.*

She seemed to keep forgetting that part.

"I'll take that as a yes," Melody said then, snapping her back to the salon. The dress. The disaster that was her life. "You do like him."

"I can't think of anything that matters less than *liking* someone," she replied, perhaps a bit grumpily. "Much less a person I'm being forced to spend time with."

The fleet of brisk seamstresses had left the room en masse ten minutes before, forced to contend with some or other textile disaster. They had spared Calista the details. She was left standing on a raised dais, surrounded by a portable wall of mirrors. Melody was there in the midst of it all, looking feral and entertained in the antique chair she'd claimed, and somehow more at home in this palace than Calista was.

"I would personally consider it a good thing that I liked a man I was going to have to marry even if he was a monster I detested," Melody said mildly. "But you do you, Calista."

Calista's hands were in fists, and she was glad her sister couldn't see it. Though the expression on Melody's face made her think that she knew, anyway. The way she always did.

"I have a plan," she began, trying to keep her voice even.

"It's not the end of the world if you change your plans," Melody interrupted her, quietly. "Maybe it's even for the best. There are opportunities everywhere, if you know how to look for them."

Calista opened her mouth to snap something back at her, but then paused. She frowned. "Are you talking about you or me?"

Melody smiled with a certain edge. "Father has been talking to me about alternate living opportunities."

Such a simple sentence, yet it sent cold water straight down Calista's back.

She knew she should have found something to feed to her father. Some bit of palace dirt. Some terrible rumor. How had she imagined that she could keep fobbing him off? Ignoring his messages and acting as if she was too busy with the wedding he'd demanded to give him what he wanted?

The truth was, she'd been pretending—hoping maybe, or wishing—that if she ignored the mess she was in, it might go away.

This was their father's way of reminding Calista what he was prepared to do.

What he had every intention of doing.

How could she have been so stupid?

"I knew this would happen." And suddenly the enormous dress she wore felt like a cage. A prison, and she couldn't breathe, and Calista didn't know what would happen if she simply clawed the fabric off her body—

Breathe, she ordered herself.

But she couldn't. Not really. Not with any depth.

"I think it will be fine, actually," Melody said, sounding philosophical. "I've never been around any other blind people. I might like them. At the very least, I can learn…blind things. Whatever those are."

Calista tried to breathe. She really did try. "This is all my fault."

"I think you know it's not, Calista. I think you know that the only reason I wasn't shunted off into one of these schools at birth is because of you."

Her sister sounded calm. Resigned.

Calista was anything but. "I've been so wrapped up in what was going on here." In sex, she thought, ashamed of herself. In *glowing.* "I should have known that they would make their move. I'm surprised they haven't done it already."

Calista wanted to tear down the walls. Shatter all the mirrors—but she was still trapped in her damned fairy-tale dress.

"Melody—" she began, her voice hot with guilt and shame.

But she stopped herself, because the door swung open.

And instead of the officious seamstresses who liked to stream in and out, issuing instructions, measuring things, and clucking around as if they really were all that wild-life in a Cinderella film, a man stood there.

Calista's heart kicked at her, but it wasn't Orion.

Why did she want it to be Orion?

In her chair, Melody shifted in that way she always did, instinctively hiding the truth about herself. Not the fact that she couldn't see, but that she wasn't helpless. She was good at it. She instantly looked smaller. Fragile and pathetic, even.

"Prince Griffin," Calista said, and it cost her something to sound calm. To pretend that she wasn't about to explode into pieces, right where she stood.

"Lady Calista," Griffin replied in that smooth way of his that Calista normally objected to, on principle. It was too pat. Too practiced. But he was shifting, looking over to where Melody made a pretty little picture of a damsel in distress in the corner.

It would have been laughable, really, if any of this had been something to laugh about.

"Your Royal Highness," Calista said, because she knew her etiquette now, backward and forward, whether she wanted to or not, "may I present to you my sister, Lady Melody."

Melody did not rise from her chair and sink into the

appropriate curtsy, but she did bow her head in such a way that she gave the impression of doing it.

While Calista watched her soon-to-be brother-in-law as he did a set of rapid calculations, clearly recalling that this was the so-called "imperfect" Skyros sister.

"I am enchanted," he murmured, executing a perfect bow that Melody couldn't see. Though she likely heard it.

"Have you come to aid with the dress fitting?" Calista asked, glaring at him, because she could see him just fine. "In all the tales of your exploits, I've never heard anyone mention that you were good at dressing women. More the opposite."

"Not at all," Griffin said, and when he shifted that gaze of his back to her, Calista straightened. Because he looked lazy enough, with that half smile and the languid way he held himself. But that dark look in his eyes was anything but. "I came to warn you."

"Warn me?" Calista asked lightly.

She watched her sister in the mirrors. Melody was basically a parody of herself at this point, managing to look like the Little Match Girl. When she was perched on a brocaded chair that might as well have been a throne, here in the middle of the palace. Not out in a cold gutter.

It was quite a performance. It always was.

"The standard warning, really," Griffin said, sounding jovial. "We are all of us adults. And we understand the ways of our world, I assume. But I must tell you that if you wound my brother in any way, *he* will be the least of your concerns."

He sounded so polite. Almost apologetic. It took a moment for the words to penetrate.

"I can't wait for Melody to warn off the king in the same fashion," Calista replied.

"That's between your sister and the king." Griffin smiled

wider. "If she wishes to threaten him, that is. Most people might avoid taking that route. As it is against the law."

"No need to worry about what I might do," Melody said, in a frail, tremulous sort of voice that made that tight vise around Calista's chest lighten a bit and she fought to keep herself from laughing. "I would never dare speak in the exalted presence of His Majesty."

Calista expected Griffin to smile in that strained, pitying way people usually did. To fail to see Melody as anything more than a bit of furniture, and more drab than the average chair.

This was Idylla's Playboy Prince, who was spared the hatred aimed at his father because he was always so charming. Not because he was any different.

But instead of dismissing and demeaning the version of herself Melody was offering him, Griffin…changed. He stood a little straighter. He stopped smirking. He looked at Melody, tiny and pathetic, and the expression on his face was almost…

Surely not, Calista thought.

"He is only a man," he said. "Flesh and blood, Lady Melody. No more and no less, no matter what manner of crown adorns his head."

Melody quailed as if the idea floored her. "If you say so, Your Royal Highness."

"Call me Griffin," he said, his attention on her younger sister in a way Calista could not say she liked. At all. It made the tiny waist of her gown seem even tighter. Especially when he kept going in that silken voice of his. "After all, we are practically family, are we not?"

Calista knew her sister well enough to see that description didn't sit well with her, even as she…fluttered. But if she wanted to play this game of hers, pretending she was a helpless creature at every opportunity when she wasn't, Calista was more than happy to go along with it. Particularly if it also slapped at Prince Griffin and his *warnings*.

"Hush now," she murmured soothingly. "This is part of why I'm marrying, Melody. To give you these wonderful new brothers."

And it was worth it when Melody forgot herself for a moment, focusing her whole body in Calista's direction with what seemed like obvious fury to her.

But Griffin was none the wiser. That was what mattered.

He was far too busy looking from Melody to Calista as if the word *brother* was a vile curse.

"I cannot wait," he murmured, all silk and seduction.

But Calista thought there was something else in his gaze as he took himself out of the room.

And for a moment, the sisters stayed where they were.

"It really is like a fairy tale," Calista said merrily. "Your very own Prince Charming cannot wait to welcome you to the family, Melody, despite your simpering."

"I really ought to kill you. You know I can, right?" Melody was no longer assuming her Little Match Girl persona. She looked like herself again, capable and intent. "With my own two hands."

"Yes, yes," Calista said and sighed. "But then what would become of either one of us?"

Melody laughed, settling back against her chair. As if it was all a joke.

But Calista knew better.

Her father was calling her bluff in this game she'd never wanted to play. She had six days left before she could make her move and she had no doubt that if she didn't throw him a bone, he would cart Melody off to some horrible prison of an institution somewhere. He'd call it a wedding present.

How could she live with that? Calista knew she couldn't. She had to make a decision, soon. And it shouldn't have been a hard one.

Of course she would protect her sister. The way she always had.

And she would do it at the expense of the man she'd never wanted to marry and shouldn't have let herself care for.

Even if it killed her.

CHAPTER TEN

TWO WEEKS LATER, Orion still could not explain why it was he'd chosen to tell Calista that she was his first.

His only.

Or better yet, why she was the only thing on this planet that could make him break a vow he'd kept even when he was half-mad with adolescent hormones.

He'd rationalized it away, of course. He had always said he wouldn't touch a woman unless he married her, and he was going to marry her. He would be making new and better vows in a week's time, come Christmas Eve. But he was entirely too aware that he was excusing himself in a way he would not excuse anyone else had they been in the same position.

The trouble was, hypocrisy was entirely too delicious.

A notion that forced him to reassess the judgments he'd so happily levied on every other human alive. Like his father.

It was a particularly shattering thing indeed, to find himself feeling even vaguely compassionate about King Max. He hardly knew what to do with it.

Maybe it was easier to concentrate on his own sins, in the form of the woman he should not have touched—but he had.

Every morning for the past two weeks, he had woken

with Calista. Tangled up in her bed, eyes gritty from lack of sleep, because after holding himself back from the pleasures of the flesh for so long, he was insatiable.

And she was nothing short of a feast. An endless banquet.

He could not get enough.

And because of her, Orion understood things he hadn't before. The magic of touch. The madness of wanting anyone that much, of thinking it might cause actual, physical pain to go without. The things he longed for now could all be wrapped up with a bow and called *more*.

He wanted to be closer. He wanted to ignore every last responsibility in his life and focus only on the things they could do to each other in that bed.

Perhaps the word he was searching for when he thought about Calista was *humbled*.

She made him all too aware that the only reason he had ever been able to wrap himself in his upright, moralistic cloak of self-righteousness was because he hadn't met her yet.

"You're staring at me again," she said, archly, from beside him. They were packed into yet another royal vehicle, en route to the last Christmas ball they would attend as an engaged couple.

Because next week's ball on the night before Christmas would be their wedding reception.

He wasn't sure he could name the way that beat in him, these days. He felt…possessive. Impatient. Because it was one more way to have her, and he intended to make sure he collected them all. Every last possible way there was to make her his, he intended to do it.

There was just this last week to get through.

"Can I not behold the woman who will be my wife?" he asked idly.

He held her hand in his, as had become his habit. He could not seem to keep himself from toying with the ring he'd put there, that great and glorious symbol of the queens of his people. And Calista was the last, best queen, by his reckoning. "In a mere week, Calista. Seven short days."

She glanced at him, and as ever, he saw that tension in her. A kind of wariness in her expression, but warmth in her gaze.

He chose to concentrate on the warmth.

And if he felt a kind of drumming intensity, as if they were hurtling toward an end he couldn't foresee—well. He chose to concentrate on the fact she would be his wife. Above all else.

"I can't decide if you're counting down to the day of our wedding with joy or if it's all become a bit dire," she said then, sounding almost muted. "Remember, Orion. You are being blackmailed into doing this."

"Did you imagine I might have forgotten that?" He never forgot it. Though he was aware that somewhere in his mind, he had separated Calista from her father. Aristotle was the person blackmailing him. Maybe that made Calista innocent. Maybe he only wished it did. "I assure you, it is never far from my thoughts."

"I can't say I understand you."

Tonight she looked particularly beautiful, but then, every time he saw her it was as if she'd transformed before his very eyes. There was a point at which he wasn't certain he would be able to look at her directly. That was how much she seemed to glow, brighter than the coming Christmas.

"What is there to understand?" he asked.

"You can't possibly trust me." She sounded outraged

by the notion. "It's not possible. I'm the daughter of your enemy, and—"

"You are the daughter of my blackmailer, yes," he said. "But your father is not my enemy, Calista. How can a parasite be an enemy? It can only be what it is. A leech, nothing more."

She did not look mollified.

"The first day we met, I told you exactly who I was," she bit out, and Orion was astonished to see her eyes were stormy. "I made it clear that no matter what happened, I would never be on your side. Did you forget that?"

"It's not that I forgot it. It's that things changed."

"Things have changed for you." She sounded desperate.

And the truth was, Orion deeply enjoyed her desperation in all its forms. The fact that he could make her beg when she was naked. The sounds she made, the pleas and the sobs. He had never heard any music he liked more.

Even if this had a harder edge, it was possible he was enjoying it more than he should have.

"Is this another patronizing discussion about my virginity?" he asked, amused. "A casual observer might note that you seem…obsessed."

She pulled her hand from his, but not before he felt the tremor in it. "I'm not obsessed with it. I just think that it's entirely possible that the experience of losing it has affected you more than you imagine. Sex is just sex, Orion. It doesn't mean anything. It certainly doesn't mean that you should trust someone who's never given you any reason to do anything of the kind."

"Here's what I wonder," he said in a low voice, watching her closely. If he wasn't mistaken, her eyes were slicked with an emotion he knew she would have denied. "What would happen if you worried less about what you thought *might* happen, and more attention to what actually has?"

"That's what I'm trying to tell you. Nothing has actually happened."

"I told you," he said. "I trust you."

She winced as if he'd hit her. "Then you're a fool."

And the way she said that, as if it was torn from her, haunted him as they pulled up into the line of cars delivering Idyllian nobles and commoners alike into the rest of their evening. Tonight's ball was held in a sprawling villa on the far end of the island. Held for centuries by one of Idylla's noble families, it had at different points in history been considered something of a secondary, southern palace.

This was usually Orion's favorite ball. The villa was a work of art, marrying Idyllian architectural prowess with Italianate and Hellenic accents, as suited their position in the Aegean Sea. On a night that was cool by island standards, all the villa's many atriums were filled with glowing heaters, strong lights. The imported evergreens were trimmed and bursting with ornaments. Night-blooming jasmine wafted in the air.

He and Calista were announced to the crowd and then led on a bit of a promenade through all the villa's public rooms, as was tradition, but all Orion could concentrate on was the woman by his side. That odd gleam in her gaze. And the desperation that he knew, deep down perhaps he'd always known, had nothing to do with him.

He pulled her out onto the dance floor in the largest of the ballrooms to lead off the first song.

Was it his imagination, or did she seem more brittle than usual? More fragile?

Even…scared?

She is none of those things, something in him whispered. *You should know better.*

But this wasn't about *knowing.* This was about *feeling.* And he suspected that if he said as much, she would bite his head off, there and then.

Still, that didn't change the fact she looked haunted.

"You could always tell me what's wrong," he said quietly, holding her so she had no choice but to tip her head back and meet his gaze. "I am the king. If I cannot help you, who can?"

Calista had her usual public smile on her face, but the look in her beautiful sea-colored eyes was pure misery. "There are some things even a king can't help."

"Is it so terrible, then?"

"Orion. There's no point in this."

"There is." He held her tighter, and recognized—yet again—that when it came to her he was not as in control as he should have been. Not even close. "Because I have to think that the woman I met in my private salon all those weeks ago would not have been torn. Whatever else she had going for her, chief among them was her sense of purpose. Maybe you should ask yourself, my lovely queen-to-be, what has happened to yours."

He didn't expect her eyes to darken the way they did. With a flash of temper and vulnerability that made him want nothing more than to gather her in his arms and carry her from this place, where so many eyes were upon them, and the glare of so much public interest made it hard for him to see her at all.

"I ask myself that question every day," Calista said, her voice thick and rough.

And then the dance was done, and it was back again to the endless rounds of glad-handing and stilted conversations it was his job to make smooth.

Ever since Orion had found her out there in a distant corner of the Botanical Gardens with her father, she'd stayed close. Tonight was no exception. She stayed right there at his elbow, graceful and obliging, everything his queen should be.

He was getting used to having her there, Orion could admit. And he would never have imagined that as a possibility, so used was he to doing everything by himself. But over these past weeks, Calista had bloomed into her role—whether she liked it or not. And the more she did, like the sweet jasmine in the air all around them, the more Orion began to comprehend what it would be like if he and his queen were really, truly some kind of team.

She was nothing like his mother, who had always looked wan and pale, as if the slightest impertinence might send her into a swoon.

Calista was not delicate. She was vibrant. Just amusing enough, without being flippant. Capable of gentle flattery and asking surprisingly incisive questions with that same sweet smile.

"If you're going to betray me," Orion said as he escorted her from one set of careful, diplomatic conversations to the next, "I wish you would hurry up and do it. Then we could put it behind us and move on."

"I had no idea you were such an optimist, Your Majesty," she said, her voice a mild reproof. Though there was something bitter beneath it. "From a distance, you always appear so stern."

"There could be no point in dedicating myself to changing this kingdom for the better if I lacked optimism," he said. "How could there be? The country is bloated with enough cynicism as it is."

Again, the look she gave him was dark. It made something in him tighten, as if in foreboding.

"Optimism is a privilege," she said quietly. "A gift."

Orion did not have time to chase that up as she moved to talk with a group of foreign ambassadors. Nor would he have, in all likelihood, even if they hadn't been in public—because there was a part of him that didn't want to know what ate at her.

A part of him that was afraid he did know, more like.

Still, if they were alone, he would have kissed her. He would have reached her that way.

Sometimes he thought it was the only way he *could* reach her.

Because he was certain, deep in his bones in a way he was not sure made any sense, that if he could simply marry Calista, everything would be all right. Making her his queen would break whatever spell it was that made her eyes go dark, as if this really was a fairy tale, after all.

Complete with its own ogre, he thought darkly when he found himself face-to-face with Aristotle.

Even though he had instructed his handlers at length that was never to happen. He shot a hard look at the aide to his right, who leaned in with his usual deferential smile.

"I beg your pardon, sire," the man murmured in Orion's ear. "He claimed he would cause a scene if he did not get an audience with you."

And no doubt he would, Orion knew. No doubt he would make it into an opera, and happily. It was far better to suffer a conversation with Aristotle than to have to clean up another one of his messes.

But Orion didn't have to like it.

"Do you really think you can avoid me?" The other man snarled, his flat eyes gleaming in a way Orion really didn't like. "Surely you must know it doesn't work that way. I'm marrying my daughter to you for access."

"And here I thought I was marrying your daughter for damage control. Did we not sign documents to that effect?"

"Either way I will be your father-in-law. Your family, like it or not. And that must mean I will have the king's ear."

"No one is preventing you from speaking," Orion replied evenly. "As to whether or not I plan to take your advice, I think you already know the answer."

"You'd better watch yourself there, Your Majesty," the older man growled, in a way that moved in Orion unpleasantly. He felt his stomach clench. "You may have wrapped me up in legal nonsense concerning that portfolio. But there's more than one way to skin a cat."

Two months ago, it would not have occurred to Orion to consider how satisfying it would be to punch Aristotle in his round face. Tonight, he had to fight to keep himself from it—and succeeded only because the last thing Idylla needed was their king in a common brawl.

"I am not a cat," he said icily. "I am your king. And if I were you, Aristotle, I would endeavor to remember that before your mouth gets you into trouble."

His aide was not close enough to hear his words, but his tone must have carried, because the man winced.

Aristotle snorted. "You are king of an island," he sneered. "But I am king of a far greater kingdom. I tell people how to think. I tell them what to feel. I make up stories and convince them it's the truth. All you do is wave from the back seat of a car, or wink invitingly on a few commemorative plates."

"A person with so little respect for the monarchy should not be quite so desperate to marry into it, I would have thought," Orion replied, keeping his voice cool—but wholly unable to do much about the edge beneath it.

"I made a meal of your father and the fact he couldn't keep his pants on," Aristotle said, looking smug and entirely…satisfied. "What do you think I'll make out of a grown man as inexperienced as you are?"

For a moment, it was if everything—the villa, the world, all of creation—went blank.

Calista.

Her name was a cry inside him. A curse.

But she had already told him what she'd done, Orion realized, as if from a great distance.

She'd told him and she'd told him again, and he hadn't listened.

It shouldn't have surprised him—shocked him, even—that she had told him she would betray him, and then had.

He just hadn't expected it to take this form.

"If I have a king in my pocket," Aristotle was crowing at him, "you can bet that I have my own daughter sewed up tight. You need to adjust your attitude, sire."

And then the vile little man swaggered away from him, leaving Orion to stand there.

Stunned.

With no one to blame but himself.

CHAPTER ELEVEN

"SOMETHING MUST BE the matter," Calista said, when a solid half hour had passed in brooding silence. The drive from the far southern tip of the island to the royal city, and the palace, took almost two hours.

And she had never known Orion to be so quiet, when he was not tending to his many messages. Or more accurately, to go without speaking.

Because he might not be using words, but he was not particularly *quiet* at all. On the contrary, he seemed to be burning up as he sat there beside her seemingly staring out the window at nothing. White hot and loud.

"A great many things are the matter," he replied then, surprising her. "But none of them require conversation."

And the tone he used made her chest…hurt.

"What did my father say?" she asked, because she'd seen them, off to the side in a little alcove, where no one else could hear. And she knew full well how her father liked to take advantage of things when no one else could hear him.

She felt a clock ticking inside her, so loud that her head ached.

Time is running out, something within her whispered.

Because somehow, she'd forgotten that the point of all of this was Melody. Taking her father's power so that he couldn't hurt Melody. It was Orion's fault. He had made her feel things she would have said she didn't believe in—

But none of that mattered. It couldn't matter, not until the board meeting was done. On December 23, she would take on her father, and win. At last.

Even if, inside, it felt as if she'd already lost.

It doesn't matter how it feels, she snapped at herself. *It matters that you get it done so Melody is never at risk again.*

"What do you imagine your father had to say to me?" Orion asked, and for the first time in this interminable car ride, he actually angled his head to look at her.

The breath left her in a harsh exhalation she could do nothing to prevent.

Because for the first time, possibly ever—and certainly in as long as she'd known him—King Orion looked…

Furious.

"I've no idea," she gritted out, though that was a lie, and her heart was galloping.

"I blame myself," he said in a gritty sort of voice that didn't make anything better. "After all, you did warn me. Repeatedly. But somehow, I thought your loathing of your father would win the day."

She tried to make her heart stop racing. "Everybody loathes my father. He inspires it in everyone. I'm not sure that's newsworthy."

"Understand this," Orion told her then, his voice a hard thing and his dark gold gaze pinning her to her seat. "I am not embarrassed by my inexperience. If it were splashed across every paper in the land, I would not care at all. I kept my vows of celibacy because I wanted to keep them, and I broke them because I wanted to break them. You and your father cannot shame me with the truth."

His name was on her lips, but she bit it back. She didn't dare.

Orion held that terrible gaze on hers. "What shames me, Calista, is that I imagined you were better than him."

Calista felt sick.

She hated herself, deeply and wildly, and she hated most of all that she'd felt she had no choice but to throw her father a bone. Because she had to keep him happy and distracted or she knew she would never see her sister again. He would ship her off somewhere, never tell her where, and if Calista was lucky, she might get upsetting reports about how Melody was faring from time to time.

It was more likely that he would act as if Melody had never existed, just to torture Calista.

She could see it all unfold before her as if it had already happened.

The decision should have been an easy one. She hated that it hadn't been. That telling her father something so private had made her feel as dirty and disgusting as he was.

It had never occurred to her that he would sell her out so quickly. Not before the wedding, anyway.

"I had no choice," she said now, trying not to sound as miserable as she felt.

"No attempts to convince me it wasn't your fault, I see. No tears, no protestations."

She lifted her chin, even though there wasn't a single part of her that didn't want to curl into a ball and die. "I think you know that my father delivered me into your hands for one reason only. To funnel information back to him."

He let out a hollow laugh. "Why did I imagine otherwise?"

"I don't believe you did," she made herself say, as if

nothing had changed between them from that first meeting to now. "Not really."

Another laugh, as if he was angry at himself, not her. Or perhaps both. "It is good to know that you follow instructions to the letter, Calista. Something I will have to keep in mind in the future."

She wanted to cry. She wanted to hit things, or possibly just crawl away somewhere and sob her heart out.

Instead, she made herself glare at him. "I warned you. I told you not to trust me. There was no reason why you should have in the first place."

And her heart stuttered in her chest when he reached over and took her chin in his fingers.

"Because I wanted to trust you, Calista," he bit out. "Because I knew exactly who you were, but I hoped—I wished—that you might surprise yourself."

"Then you really are a fool," she threw back at him, though it made her shake. "What did you imagine? That you could change the world simply because you decreed it?"

She jerked her chin out of his fingers, but she was all too aware that he let her go. And more, that she wished he hadn't.

"Yes," Orion said, starkly. "I thought you would want to change."

He couldn't have hurt her more if he'd swung and hit her.

Hard.

Her breath left her as if he had.

"You will never know how much I wanted—"

But Calista cut herself off, because it was all futile. It didn't matter. This was never the part of her life that was supposed to matter. This was the distraction, and she didn't understand when or how the King of Idylla had shifted everything around inside her.

When he had got to her and got her so...*muddled.*

Some mornings, she woke up and forgot all about board meetings and Skyros Media and her lifelong dream of bringing down her father.

For hours.

And every time she remembered, it was another betrayal of her sister.

She couldn't pretend she hadn't known, when she'd chosen to give her father information about Orion—much less *that* information—that she was sacrificing those hours of freedom, no matter how much she'd loved to forget the mess of it all. The squalid dirt that had made her family's name.

She knew full well she was sacrificing the bright glow of these past weeks for the same cold future she'd always been aiming toward.

It was the right thing to do, she told herself, again and again. A king would always prosper, but the same couldn't be said of Melody, there beneath their father's thumb.

But that it was right didn't make it hurt less.

Calista was starting to think that the hurt was a part of it, and one more price she would have to pay.

Sometimes, looking at him, it almost felt worth it.

"I don't understand any of this," she said, trying to keep her eyes away from him in the shadows of the back seat, because it was too painful. But it didn't work. "You and I should never have met. You should never have told me that you were a virgin. All of this could have been avoided if you'd stood up to my father in the first place. It wasn't your sin. It was your father's."

She shook her head, terribly afraid that the sobs that

caught in the back of her throat might pour out now, whether she wanted them to or not. She felt jagged and broken and *hurt*, and she didn't have the slightest idea what to do about any of it.

"You're the bloody king, Orion. Surely you could have made this—made *him*—go away."

His mouth twisted, and there was something so savage in his eyes then it made her heart skip a beat.

"It's not my father's sins that worry me," he belted out. "It's my mother's."

She gaped at him. He muttered something that might have been a curse, then dragged his hands over his face. Then he pressed the button that allowed him to talk to his driver and ordered the man to pull over to the side of the road.

When the car stopped, Orion threw open the door and the sea rushed in.

Calista was breathing too hard. As if she'd been running all the way down the long island road from the villa instead of sitting in his car.

And she didn't want to follow him out. She didn't want to hear any more of his secrets. Because she'd told him he couldn't trust her, but worse than that, she didn't trust herself.

She was terrified, not that he would tell her more secrets that she would feel compelled to tell her father.

But that he would tell her enough of his secrets that she *wouldn't* share them with her father.

And Melody would pay the price.

What would any of this have been for?

Calista could hear the crash of the winter sea against the rocks. She told herself that was what lured her out, crawling carefully from the car and closing the door behind her. And taking a moment, then, to lean against the side of the vehicle and wait for her eyes to adjust.

When they did, the stars were so bright in the night sky above her it took her breath away.

And when she angled her gaze away from the resplendent sky, it was to see Orion standing there on a flat rock overlooking the rocky shore, like a dark dream made real.

She was as drawn to him now as ever, she understood with a little jolt inside, no matter if it was against her will. Especially now he knew exactly how perfidious she was. The lengths she was willing to go.

The betrayer she'd become to fight a man who had made her in his image after all. Because all the *whys* didn't matter. She'd sold Orion out.

Though, tonight, all the things she'd been telling herself for years to keep herself focused on felt flat inside her. Like paltry little excuses.

In order to save one person who mattered to her she'd lost another.

She didn't know how she was meant to live with that.

He didn't turn around to see what she was doing, and maybe that was why she felt so drawn to him. His certainty. How sure he was of himself, so that when he'd actually made love for the first time in his life, she would have sworn that he'd had decades of experiences.

She had let him get close to her. Close enough to shame her, and she didn't know how she was supposed to cope with that. How she was supposed to carry on doing what she'd always done when she knew that this sickening current of self-disgust could just…bloom inside her the way it did?

"I'm sorry," she whispered when she reached him.

But the December wind, cool enough to make her shiver, if not cold in any real sense, took her words away.

Orion was staring out at the dark water, as if he was fighting his own battle while standing still.

"What your father has on me is a portfolio of pictures," he told her, matter-of-factly. As if it was part of some royal decree.

"You don't have to tell me anything," Calista said, feeling wretched. "Surely by now you should know better than to want to."

"It's an old roll of film, with twenty-four exposures. The portfolio contains both prints and negatives. Your father assured me that no copies had ever been made."

"Even if there were, he likely would have found them and destroyed them," she said, clearing her throat as she thought about the squalid little bargains Aristotle called "business." "Because the value in a damaging image is lessened if there are copies. If anyone can have leverage, the leverage itself is lessened."

She felt her face go hot when Orion slanted a look her way. "Yes, these are the sorts of things I learned at my father's knee. Don't act so surprised, Orion. Surely you didn't think he sang us nursery rhymes?"

"The images are quite standard, really," Orion continued, darkly. "King Max engaged in yet another threesome. But in this case, the photos feature the king and another man focused on particular shared acts. And the woman in question..."

He didn't finish his sentence.

"No," Calista whispered.

"The woman in question is my mother," Orion gritted out, as if it hurt him. And that fury in him was a raw and pulsing thing. "She looks enthusiastic, but also as if that enthusiasm was chemically enhanced. And I can tell you that in the days leading up to her death—which, according to the date stamped on these pictures, was not long after the event—she would drink too much and say a great many things that made no sense. Then. They make more sense now."

"Orion…"

"She was concerned about gaps in her memory. She was…fragile, and she refused to eat or drink anything she did not prepare herself. I can only assume now that she was given something in her food or drink that was laced with the sort of drugs that create enthusiasm where there is none."

Calista let that sink in, though it made her stomach lurch. "And you think it was your father…?"

"Does it matter?" His voice was a vicious slap against the wind. "Whether my father slipped her a drug to make her compliant, or merely took advantage of it when he must surely have known better—does it really matter which? What *degree* of monster he was? And as I allow my outrage and sickness over this to turn around inside me, I must ask myself why it is that every other photo I've ever seen with him in various sexually explicit scenarios, I never questioned the enthusiasm of the participants. Only when it suited me."

"Because your poor mother…"

"Yes. My poor mother."

Orion shook his head, looking sick and furious and tired, suddenly. It made the rocks beneath Calista's feet seem to sway, because this was *Orion*. He *was* the rock, and it had never occurred to her that he could go weary.

It made her want to fight anything that might come at him, even if it was her.

"I'm not even certain that the kingdom would bother to react to yet another explicit photograph of my father," he said after a moment or two. "But I cannot bear to think of my mother being tarred with the same brush. Not to mention, the fact that there are pictures of one such event would lead to the inevitable speculation that it was not a one-off. And that would lead to questions about parentage. Bloodlines."

"You can't have that," she whispered, flushing with a shame so deep and hot she was surprised she could still stand.

"The truth of the matter, Calista, is that I am sick unto death of the excesses of my father's reign," Orion said, and she had never heard him sound so dark. She had never felt that darkness inside her, too. "I felt this way before it affected my direct family and I only feel it more strongly now. And yes, I am willing to marry the daughter of a man who trafficked in those photographs to prevent them ever getting out. I still am. Whatever that makes me."

Calista thought it made him a hero. Possibly even a saint.

She was afraid to put words to what it made her.

"I wish..." Her tongue felt thick in her mouth. She had no idea what to say, only that everything hurt and she hated herself. And this, because after a lifetime of being certain that she was nothing like her father, she was. She'd proved it. Maybe she had different reasons, but the end result was the same. "I thought I wasn't tainted by him. But he is like an infection in the blood. It doesn't go anywhere. It will only twist in you until it wrecks you, over time."

"That is a choice." Orion's voice was clipped and harsh, but his eyes blazed. "Do you think I don't know the temptation to become just as dark and dissipated as the man who bore me? Do you think I don't ask myself daily if it would have been easier to follow in his footsteps? It's a *choice*, Calista. You have chosen to become your father. That's on you, not him."

"You don't understand."

"Then tell me."

And the most astonishing thing by far was that he shouted that.

As if this was the same thing as what happened to him in that bed they shared.

King Orion Augustus Pax, losing control.

And this time, Calista took no satisfaction from it. This time, he made her shudder and feel like weeping, and not in any kind of delight.

"I—"

His hands were on her shoulders then. His face in hers.

"Do not tell me what you cannot do. Just do it, or do not." His grip tightened. "I have seen the tension in you from the very start. Did you think I would miss it somehow? You want so badly to be bulletproof. To care as little about the people you come into contact with as your father does. But you're not him, Calista. You don't have to do the things he does."

She felt that everywhere, half indictment, half wish.

She thought it might take her to her knees, but his hands gripped her shoulders, and she stood.

Because like it or not, she always stood. And did the horrible things no one else could—no matter what it cost her.

"I have spent my entire life working hard to get myself into a position where I can change things," she heard herself say, as if she could possibly explain herself to this man she was terribly afraid she might love.

This man she had already betrayed.

"In a week, you will become capable of simply moving your little finger and changing whatever you like, as queen. Or did you forget that when you marry me, the only person with more power than you in all the world is me?"

"That doesn't count," she threw at him, feeling desperate and despairing, all at once. "That's what he wants. Don't you understand?"

"Are you concocting some doomed attempt to make your father feel things like a normal human being?" His eyes blazed still, that terrible gold. "From sad experience, Calista, I can tell you it won't work. I tried to talk to my father once, man-to-man. It only served to entertain him."

She let out a sound that was not quite a sob. "I don't want to *talk* to my father. I want to crush him."

"And then what?" Orion demanded, his fingers pressing into her skin. "When you rise to take his place, what will become of you?"

She shook her head, but it didn't occur to her to pull away from him. Not yet. Or maybe she couldn't.

Maybe, despite everything, she didn't want to.

How had this happened? How had she lost her focus so completely?

But she knew. It was him. It was Orion.

He had gotten beneath her skin, and worse, into her bones. She couldn't take a breath without feeling him there, and she knew there'd be no changing that. That no matter what happened here, or next week in her board meeting, or on Christmas Eve, or ever after, straight on into the future, he would stay right there.

Deep in her bones, always.

For good or ill.

The inevitability was almost comforting.

"What are you going to do?" he demanded, his beautiful face close.

She thought of all the years she'd put in. Her father's

handprint on her face. Her sister, so fiercely herself despite her parents' horror that she had come out of the womb something less than perfect in their eyes.

"I will do what I have to," she said.

And understood as she did that this thing between them, these last two weeks, was only the latest thing she sacrificed on the altar of this quest of hers.

"Be certain this is what you want," Orion said, his voice like a bell deep inside her. He dropped his hands. "Because the truth, Calista, is that I am not so optimistic. No son of my father's could be. And when I stop hoping for better, that is when, I am afraid, you will find me far less accommodating and far more uncompromising than you can possibly imagine."

"Medieval," she whispered, remembering their first meeting. She cleared her throat. "You can imprison me on Castle Crag if you must, Orion. But it won't change anything. It can't."

"So be it," he whispered, and there was a finality in his voice.

And when he turned and headed back to the car, away from the sea, the ring she wore on her hand felt heavy. Like iron.

Like prison bars, close and tight around her.

You have no choice, she told herself, again and again. She had to keep Melody safe.

Maybe Orion was right, and once she became his queen—*if* she became his queen—she would find herself able to *decree* her sister safe... But what if her father acted before then?

She would risk herself. But she refused to risk her sister.

"I have no choice," she whispered, when there was only the December wind to hear.

And it seemed to her the sea itself laughed at her predicament, doused her in salt and recrimination, and then left her to the fate she'd made real with her own two hands.

CHAPTER TWELVE

On the night before his wedding, Orion stood in his office, there at the window with his back to the palace where he had always been most comfortable.

Not that anything could comfort him these days.

The royal city stretched out before him, the lights sparkling brighter than usual with holiday splendor, and more this year. Because tomorrow was the royal wedding, and the celebrating kingdom had no idea that their new king was anything but transported with joy at the prospect.

The way he might have been a week ago, it pained him to admit. And no matter the faintly sniffy headlines in some of the tabloids, which questioned the timeline the palace had given them about the king's romance.

He knew those headlines were warning shots.

But it was the word *romance* that sat in his chest like a spot of pneumonia, gnarled and heavy, and worse by the day.

He found no peace in this view tonight.

Because instead of the kingdom he planned to save, all he could see was Calista.

He had barely seen her since that fateful last ball, when he had discovered what he should already have known—that she was as devious and untrustworthy as her father.

That she could have turned her back on Aristotle and his schemes, but had chosen not to.

That she had made those choices despite what had happened between them.

That whatever it was that haunted her, she refused to share it with him.

It was that last that bothered him the most, loathe as he was to admit it.

They had run into each other once in the hallway of the family wing. She had been surrounded by a pack of seamstresses all dressed in black, a wild sort of look on her face—until she saw him.

She had gone silent. Still.

Haunted straight through, something in him had intoned, but he couldn't *help* her betray him.

A man—a king—had to draw the line somewhere, surely.

He had stared at her, not certain what he was meant to do with all the unwieldy *feelings* inside him, now. He had wanted nothing more than to be the opposite of his father. And instead, it turned out that while his temptations might not level the kingdom—they might just level him. They might just lay him out flat all the same.

Neither one of them had spoken.

He had inclined his head. She had performed the expected bob of head and knee upon one's first daily sighting of the monarch.

And he had wasted an entire day when he should have been sorting out cabinet ministers and putting out fires all over the kingdom, brooding about that interaction.

Another time, he'd heard her.

Calista and her sister, laughing together in one of the rooms where the staff was laying out her trousseau. He had stopped himself midstride, the sound of her laughter seeming to pierce straight through him.

He was an embarrassment to himself. A disappointment, certainly.

But none of that mattered as the days dragged by and he began to realize exactly what he was signing himself up for.

It had been better before. He had been fascinated, and that was far better than disappointed. He had to think that it was worse, now, to know how good it could be between them when it could never, ever be like that again.

He couldn't unknow it.

But he wasn't sure how he could live with it, either. Sometimes he would find himself in one of his meetings or ceremonies, suddenly seized with a kind of deep panic at the endless stretch of days before him. Days that would become months, then years. If he was lucky, he would keep this marriage of convenience civil, if chilly.

Year after year after year, as they both turned to stone.

Sooner or later, the vivid longing of these weeks would fade. He was sure of it. It would be like a dream he'd had once—never quite forgotten, but never repeated.

"You do not look quite the part of the happy bridegroom," came his brother's drawling voice from behind him.

Orion sighed, but turned to face him all the same. "Should I be turning cartwheels down the corridors of the palace?"

"Not looking murderous might be a start." Griffin's gaze swept over him. "Where is your lovely bride-to-be? Sequestered somewhere around here, presumably? Surrounded by the usual passel of women and dreams of her special day, one assumes?"

Even if Calista had not been her father's weapon, she

would still be Calista—but Orion did not allow himself to succumb to the urge to defend her. Not tonight.

"My bride-to-be has not shared her plans with me," Orion said instead. "Then again, I did not ask."

Griffin blinked at that, standing behind the chair he usually preferred to lounge in. Orion watched as his brother tapped his finger against the back of the chair, as if contemplating something. Deeply.

The world must have ended.

"If you've come here to give me marital advice," Orion said softly, "don't."

Griffin smiled. Faintly. "What marital advice could I possibly have to give? The closest I've been to that blessed state was witnessing our parents' union. Not exactly the sort of thing that would turn a man's thoughts to marital bliss, was it?"

Orion's smile felt thin and mean on his mouth. "You have no idea."

"If you are holding on to something that affects us both, out of some misplaced sense of duty," Griffin replied, in much the same tone Orion had used, "I will remind you that I'm not a child."

Orion knew that too well. But he also knew that he could have quite happily lived out the rest of his life without knowing what had happened between his parents. Or what had caused his mother to make the choices she had.

Why should he ruin what scant good memories Griffin had, too? He didn't see the point.

"I will always do my duty," he said instead, and felt far more tired than he had when he'd used to make such statements. When they had been hopes and dreams instead of simple facts. "I made that promise to you years ago. And to the rest of the kingdom."

"Yes, yes," Griffin murmured. "No one doubts your

commitment, brother. What I do wonder, though, here on the eve of your wedding to a woman so unworthy of you that it is almost laughable—"

"You are speaking of my queen," Orion growled, all steel and menace, and only then recalled that he did not plan to defend her. Not tonight. But he had already started, so he kept on. "I will not have it. Not even from you, Griffin."

His brother looked as if he wanted to laugh, but wisely did not.

Instead, he nodded. "Understood. But while you are busy being on her side, whether she deserves it or not, know that I'm on yours. And not because I want your job, because I don't. I never have and I never will."

"I am aware." Orion thought his voice was too harsh, then. Too rough, but he had lost the ability to moderate it. "It's maddening, if you must know the truth. Younger royal siblings are supposed to want nothing more than to usurp the heir's position, with all the usual sniping and backbiting."

"I would rather dic."

Orion smiled despite himself. "This I know."

And the two of them looked at each other, then away. It might have been an embrace, had they been different men.

"Tomorrow I will stand at your side and welcome your new queen to our family and this kingdom," Griffin told him, his voice as solemn as his gaze was uncharacteristically serious. "I represent the entirety of the royal family besides you, and so I can say with certainty that she will be supported. As long as you wish it."

Orion thought of Calista. Beautiful, faithless Calista.

He thought of the betrayal she had already enacted, and the others that were sure to follow. And he had lied to Griffin. He knew that Calista was not in the palace tonight. He had been informed when she left and with a single phone call, he could determine where she was now—but did he really want to know?

Orion would have asked himself why he was bothering to protect her, but, of course, he knew.

Because he loved nothing more than exercises in futility, particularly if it came with a side dose of martyrdom. Except possibly the one woman who had ever gotten beneath his skin.

But he said nothing of these things to his brother.

"I wish it," he said. "I want her supported, no matter what."

Griffin nodded. And turned to go, but Orion stopped him.

"But while we are discussing duties in support," he said.

"I promised you that I would do my bit to stabilize the kingdom," Griffin replied, a bit tightly. "I haven't forgotten."

"I'm glad to hear it. Part of why I'm getting married is so that there can be no more gossip. No more innuendo. No more dating, Griffin. No more scandalous exploits. The next woman you are connected with I will expect you to marry, do you understand me?"

He thought there was something in his brother's gaze then. Griffin looked…arrested, perhaps.

But he only swallowed, hard. Then nodded.

"As you wish, brother," he said gruffly.

Orion turned again once Griffin left and found himself scowling out into the dark, past the lights of the city, down to where the nearly full moon danced along the waves of the Aegean.

The moonlight made a silvery path across the water,

and he wished he could figure out a path through the mess this had all become as easily.

He had no idea how long he stood there, but when he heard the door to his office open again, he sighed.

"I have already told you," he began, turning with every expectation of finding his brother there again.

But it was not Griffin who stood there.

It was Calista.

For a moment his mind blanked out. At first glance, she looked cool, impenetrable. She wore a sleek corporate outfit that made his mouth water. A pencil skirt that hugged her figure and a silk blouse that showed absolutely nothing of her beautiful breasts, yet made him so hungry for a taste of them that he thought he might shake with need. Another pair of those gloriously high, impractically dangerous shoes that did things to her calves a man could have written whole sonnets about.

Even her blond hair was ruthlessly controlled, wrenched back into something conservative and appropriate.

She looked absolutely ruthless from head to toe—except for her eyes.

They were as aquamarine as ever, blue and green and wild tonight.

Hectic, even.

"What are you doing here?" Orion asked coolly. "I assumed you had already made your choice. A week ago."

She moved farther into the office, her hands clutching the strap of the bag over her shoulder, another sign that she was not as controlled as she wished to appear.

Though he dared not hope.

Hope had already gotten him in enough trouble.

"I did."

Calista stopped, there on the other side of his desk, and

he watched as she swallowed. Hard. And hated the part of him—that terrible weakness in him—that wanted to vault over the desk and hold her to him, as if he could somehow protect her from danger when the danger was her.

"Then I assumed we would march into our royal marriage the way most do," he said, when it appeared she planned to say no more. "With cold reserve. A pretense of civility, when necessary. And after you provide me with an heir, we can repair to completely separate lives."

Orion told himself he was imagining the look of misery on her face then, the one that matched the misery in him at the very notion—because of course he was imagining it. Because any possibility of something different between them was gone. She had said so herself.

It was his burden to bear that he had broken his vow and lost himself in the process. He had the rest of his life to mourn his one and only loss of control.

Or to dream about it in Technicolor detail, more like, a voice in him whispered.

"Tonight I went to the Skyros Media offices for the annual board meeting," she told him, and he had the sense she was picking her words. That she was walking on eggshells he couldn't see.

He frowned. "I thought you were fired."

"From my position as vice president, yes." She nodded. "But years ago, in an effort to cheat more effectively on his taxes, my father transferred shares of the company to members of the family. My sister sold me hers long ago, for a single shiny penny. My mother gave me hers in a lovely show of entirely feigned maternal support when I was promoted to vice president, something she has long regretted. That gave me, in total, forty-five percent of the company. My father has never concerned himself about that, because I'm so obedient. A tool for him to use, as I believe you put it so succinctly."

She loosened her grip on the strap of her bag, and shifted it off her shoulder, then set it down on the desk that stood between them.

There were so many things Orion wanted to say to her, but something about the too-still way she stood, and that look on her face, kept him from it.

"I have worked for years to get to this meeting," she told him, her voice quiet, but racked with some emotion he couldn't name. "And finally, after years and years of near misses, setbacks, and disappointments, it was all finally going to happen. I managed to convince just enough members of the board to throw their lot in with mine. That would put me at fifty-one percent. Meaning, a controlling interest in Skyros Media. My first act would be a vote of no confidence in my father, which he would not survive. I intended to reject him from his own company by the end of the year."

"Why?" Orion asked, his throat so tight he wasn't sure the word would come out right.

"Because I want my sister safe," Calista said fiercely. "That has always been my first and foremost priority. He has threatened me with her all my life. If I misbehaved, he would have her minders lock her in her room, without food. If he was truly angry at me, he might slap me—but he'd leave her black-and-blue. And if I didn't tell him what he wanted to know about you, Orion…" Her voice wavered then, but she lifted her chin. "He told me he would send her to an institution. For life. Kicking him out would mean substantially reducing the amount of time, money, and energy he can dedicate to bullying me and her."

"You are discussing the sister-in-law of the King of

Idylla," Orion reminded her, raising his brows, even as a rush of sympathy moved in him for her predicament—when he would have said he could never forgive her for betraying him in the way she did. "I will make it a law, if you wish, that your sister must remain free." He shook his head. "Why did it not occur to you that all you needed to do was ask?"

"Because I was so close," she threw at him, and she sounded much less composed, then. "My whole life was leading to tonight, and I thought it was nothing more than a strange tangent that I was suddenly thrown in your path. What did I care if my father wanted to marry me off? Soon enough what he wanted wouldn't matter. I could break off our engagement. I could divorce you. I didn't really care what I did, when you were just a figurehead to me. Just a king. Not a person, Orion. And not when Melody was the one who would suffer if I lost focus."

He stayed where he was, every muscle in his body tense, focused on her so intently he should have been worried it would rip him asunder.

But all he could manage to think about was her.

"I never expected…you," Calista whispered. She looked away then, blinking rapidly. And he wondered if that sheen in her gaze was what he thought it was when she looked back at him again. When he was sure she would have sworn she never cried. "But then, last week, it seemed that everything was…"

"In ruins all around us?" he asked starkly.

"Clarified," she said instead. "However harshly. So tonight, I went to the board meeting. It was exactly as I imagined it. I arrived late, to make an entrance. There were the expected whispers and mutterings when I walked into the meeting and took my place. My father looked apoplectic, because he expected me to be sequestered off in the palace, allowing him to cast my vote by proxy, as he preferred."

She sniffed. "Only once every few years has he allowed me to attend the meetings, so I could have the pleasure of voting the way he told me to, but in person. In some ways that is a gift, as this is the sort of meeting that goes on for hours and takes a long while to get to the voting. At the first break, I knew that if I stayed, my father would become abusive. As usual."

Orion heard himself growl. "The next time he puts his hands on you, Calista, there will be consequences."

Her lips twitched and something in him warmed at the site. That optimism that he claimed came and went—but, in truth, only hunkered down within him, waiting for its moment—burst to life all over again.

Like fireworks.

But he tried to tamp it all down and assume his usual stern expression.

"I didn't intend to give him the opportunity to put his hands on me," she assured him. "I ducked out the door and slipped away because I knew that he would get caught up in conversation, and I needed to ready myself for the final act of this thing. At last."

"Have you come here to tell me that you are breaking off our engagement?" Orion asked then, the fireworks starting to feel a bit more like gunfire. "I suppose I should thank you for doing it in person."

His mind spun out, then. He thought of the scandal it would cause. The crowing in the papers that as they'd suspected, the king had been played for a fool by a member of the toxic Skyros family. And, really, how could anyone esteem a king who was a fool? Better, really, to be a villain. At least there was power in it instead of pity.

But Calista was talking again. "I went and hid in my

office. It's right next my father's, so I knew there'd be no particular rush for someone else to take it over. I left all the lights out and stood there, staring out at that very same moon."

"It is not quite full," he heard himself say. "It will be full tomorrow."

Again, that sheen in her gaze made his chest feel tight.

"There was something about the moon, full or not." She looked down at the ring on her hand. That ring he'd put there, and now could not imagine gracing any other hand, ever. Everything in him rejected the very idea. "It was as if the moon and the sea caught the stones. And they all twisted around and around inside me. And all I could think about was last week. When we stood in the dark, with only the sea and the rocks as witness, and you asked me to make a choice I was certain was already made."

"Was it not?" he hardly dared ask.

"I could hear it when they started calling the meeting back to order," she said, her voice barely above a whisper. A rough, harsh whisper, her eyes fixed on his. "And everything I had always wanted was in that boardroom. Mine for the taking. I could hear my father's voice, booming down the hall as he told one of his vile, off-color jokes. All I had to do was move. Turn on my heel, walk down the hall, and crush him beneath my foot the way I've always dreamed."

"Calista."

And then again, just her name, like a prayer.

"Instead, I went into his office." She sounded as if she was running, but she stood still, there on the other side of the old desk that had once been his grandfather's. "I went to his safe. It only took me three or four tries to guess his combination, because it never occurs to my father that anyone might be observing him. He thinks he's too busy studying everyone else, looking for weaknesses, for anyone to return the favor."

She looked down, then, and it felt like a slap. Orion blinked. But she was reaching into the bag she'd tossed on his desk. And she pulled out a very familiar portfolio.

Then she set it on the expanse of the desk between them tenderly, as if it was a bomb.

"Is that…?" But his pulse was going crazy in his veins. And he was staring at her as if she was a ghost, or the sun, or some beautiful, complicated combination of both. "Calista. You didn't."

"I made my choice," she whispered, her voice thick. "The board voted to remove him, but in the end, I knew my place wasn't there. It's here. With you."

And then, her eyes really did fill with tears.

More astonishing, she did nothing to hide them.

Orion had no memory of moving. But he was around his desk, with his hands on her, before his next breath was through.

"I want to be the woman you thought I was when you told me you could trust me," she cried, her head back and her face…open. Tears in her eyes and nothing but stark honesty stamped across her features.

And in all his life, Orion had never been so humbled.

"I want the future," she told him, her voice broken. "I want a future with you. I've spent my whole life battling the past, and it's done nothing but make me sick and slimy, just like him."

"Never," he growled.

"I want those weeks we shared to become our life," she continued, as if it scared her. But she kept going. "And I want you to know, Orion, that betraying you almost killed me. Because none of what happened between us was anything to me but sacred. And the thought that I destroyed it, forever, breaks my heart."

She pulled in a ragged breath that sounded like a sob. "So I've proved it to you the only way I could. By setting you free."

"Calista." He pulled her closer to him, holding her tightly, the way he wanted. The way he always wanted—he, who had taught himself not to want at all, until her. "I've already told you. You cannot shame me with the truth."

"I'm not ashamed of your truths," she sobbed. "I'm ashamed of *me*. I'm ashamed that it took me right up to the eleventh hour to understand what I was becoming."

"You were fighting fire with fire," he said, surging to her defense without stopping to think about it. The way he always would. "There's nothing wrong with that."

"You found another way." Her hands were braced against his chest and the way she looked at him made him feel like a god, not a king. "You always find another way. You never sink to anyone's level, you make your own."

"Of course I do," he said, and allowed himself a small hint of a smile. "I am the king."

"I only hope that you will help my sister in the way I tried to do, but couldn't," she whispered.

He pulled out his mobile and shot off a text to the head of his security. "She will be removed from your family's home within the hour and installed in the palace. Will that do?"

"Orion." And the way she said his name was like an ache. "I didn't come here to tell you that I was calling off our wedding. I came to give you those pictures, so that part would be ended. And with the full understanding that once my father's leverage over you was gone, you might be perfectly happy to see the back of me. I accept that."

Though he noted, with some satisfaction, that she sounded wretched. Not accepting.

"If you wish to leave me at the altar, Calista, you will have to do it yourself," he growled at her. "I will be there tomorrow in the Grand Cathedral, ready and waiting to make you my queen. All you need to do is show up. Or not."

She pushed against him, shaking her head. "You can do so much better than me. You could have anyone. Why would you want the daughter—"

"I don't care who your father is," he told her, his face low, and his mouth against hers, like a vow. "I don't care who my father is, either. It's time for us to bury them, Calista. You and me, together. We will put them in the ground, one way or another, and we will find our way into our own future. A future that has nothing to do with either one of them."

She gazed up at him, looking caught somewhere between despair and hope, and so he kissed her.

Because words were only words, but this—

This was real.

This was them.

It had already changed both of them. So deeply that Orion doubted either one of them could ever go back to who they'd been before.

Good, a voice in him said. Smugly.

"I love you," Calista whispered, there against his mouth. And the words made his heart thud. "I tried so hard not to love you. I told myself I couldn't love anyone. But in the end, I thought of you and I emptied out my father's safe, and I ran straight here."

"Calista," he said, like her name was a song. He rested

his forehead against hers. "Tomorrow you will be my queen. But I believe I have loved you from the first moment I saw you, standing out on the balcony with your eyes on the sea. I loved you then. And if you will let me, I will dedicate my life to loving you forever."

"I don't know if I believe in forever," she replied, tears pouring down her face. "But if you do, then I'll try. I'll dedicate my life to trying, and giving you every reason in the world to trust me. I promise."

"And I promise you, I will give you the same." His lips crooked into a smile. "And you know I am excellent at keeping promises."

"Just as you know I'm terrific at keeping my focus," she replied, the sparkle he loved so much returning to her gaze.

It felt like another song.

And then his mouth was on hers, she was wrapped around him, and he bore her down to the floor before the fire.

He kissed her and he kissed her, over and over, hardly able to believe that this was real.

"Orion..." she whispered.

He took his time, peeling her out of the sharp, sleek clothes that made her look so dangerous. Then he feasted upon her.

He took her breasts in his hands, tasting one hard nipple, then the other. She moaned, arching against him, and he wanted too much. He wanted everything.

Orion shrugged out of his own clothes, sighing with a kind of relief when her hands found the hard ridges of his abdomen, then moved lower to worship the hardest part of him.

Her eyes were wide with a kind of mute pleading as she shifted, moving lower so she could take him in her mouth.

A sweet promise. A wicked temptation.

A kind of vow, he thought, as she licked her way along the length of him as if tasting his heat was a sacred act all its own.

And when he could take no more, he pulled her up and astride him, settling her so he could feel the molten heat of her all over him, where her mouth had just been.

"You are mine," he told her, like a vow. "Always."

"Forever," she agreed, and then she impaled herself upon him.

And they both groaned with the pleasure of it. The slick, hot glory that was only theirs.

She moved her hips, an endless seduction. And together, they made vows to each other that would last a lifetime. With their bodies and their words. With the deep thrust and breathless retreat.

With the spiraling heights he took her to, his hands gripping her hips as he took control, lifting and lowering her. He watched her shake apart, flying over that cliff into a thousand bright pieces. He kept going, flipping her over and driving himself in deeper.

His first. His last. His only.

He waited until the fire in her burned anew, and only when she cried out his name again did he let himself go, following her over the edge of the world.

Later tonight they would burn to ash the bitter legacy her father had collected. They would render him even more toothless and dismissible than he already was this night.

Here before the fire, they were new.

Come the dawn, it would be Christmas Eve. He would make her his queen.

And he was His Majesty Orion Augustus Pax, King of Idylla, so he did exactly that—and then he set about loving her for the rest of his life, because she deserved no less.

And because she loved him right back.

Hard and true, fierce and faithful, until they were both so happy it was hard to remember that they had ever been anything else.

CHAPTER THIRTEEN

CALISTA MARRIED KING ORION OF IDYLLA in the Grand Cathedral with the whole of the kingdom watching.

The people poured into the cathedral itself. They lined the streets, though it was a blustery day, which everyone said felt appropriately Christmassy, with the holiday decorations lighting up the trees and every house in the land bright with celebratory candles.

Inside, she took Orion's hands. She gazed into his eyes and she said her vows.

Then she kissed him in front of the world and made it real.

And when he led her out of the cathedral again, she was a queen.

His queen.

Together, they sat in a carriage open to the elements, and though it was not warm, neither one of them felt the chill. The carriage led them up a winding road toward the palace, lined all the way with Christmas lights and cheering subjects.

And at the final ball of the Idyllian holiday season, always traditionally held in the palace, they celebrated their wedding—and more than that, their miraculous love for each other, where everyone could see it.

Feel it. Wonder at it, if they liked—or wonder why her parents weren't at the ceremony, which would no doubt be in all the papers the next day.

Calista found she couldn't care less. Melody was safe.

Her parents were the past.

Orion was the future.

This time, when Orion led her out onto the dance floor, he didn't pretend to be stern and austere. He smiled down at her in her Cinderella dress, until she thought that surely every person in the whole of the kingdom of Idylla could see that he was besotted.

But then, so was she, and she didn't care who saw it.

"My queen," he said formally, as he swept her into his arms. "Your Royal Highness."

"My love," she said in reply.

And they danced.

They danced and they danced, and they celebrated the love they'd almost lost, before finding it at the very last moment.

They danced. They celebrated. The king made a speech, and outside the crowds cheered them by name.

Most of what Calista would remember of this night was him. Her beautiful Orion, his eyes gleaming gold, as they claimed each other at last.

And when the clock struck midnight, it really was Christmas, at last.

Her king and her love—her husband—dispensed with tradition and tedious royal decorum. He swept her up into his arms to the delight of the crowd, and then he carried her up the grand staircase, heading for the family wing of the palace.

He didn't put her down when he'd climbed the stairs. Nor did turn toward her suite.

Instead, he carried her into the sprawling King's Suite.

"I have already moved your things," he told her sternly. "And I will tell you now, Calista, that I have no intention of maintaining separate lives. Or rooms. Or anything of the sort."

"Perish the thought, my liege," she said, smiling, with her head on his shoulder.

"It is clear to me that I am going to require access to my queen," he said, as he strode into a chamber with a bed raised high on a dais, with four posters soaring high, as befitted a king.

"You have all the access you like," she assured him. "As long as I can access the king in turn."

He laid her down on the bed, came down with her, and for a moment, they both smiled so wide, so bright, it was as if they created their own full moon there between them. To watch the one outside that hung there, for them, lighting up the sea.

"Merry Christmas, my love," Orion said.

"Merry Christmas," Calista replied.

And then, together, they set about unwrapping their gifts.

That night, each other.

And nine months later a red-faced, squalling crown prince.

Followed not long after by a fierce little princess.

And one more of each.

"For good luck," Orion liked to say, gathering their children in his arms and looking at her over their heads with those beautiful hazel eyes gone gold.

Calista knew they had no need of luck.

Because they had each other and that was better and sweeter than luck could ever be.

But to make sure, she loved him with all her heart, and let him love her the same way in return.

Forever and ever, and that was just the start.

* * * * *

THEIR IMPOSSIBLE DESERT MATCH

CLARE CONNELLY

PROLOGUE

Nineteen years ago. The Royal Palace of Ishkana, on the edge of the Al'amanï ranges.

'Tell me immediately.' It didn't matter to His Royal Highness Prince Amir Haddad that he was just twelve and the advisors in his bedroom were all at least three times that in age. From birth he had been raised to know his place in the kingdom, the duty that would one day be his.

Having six men sweep into his private quarters at four in the morning might have caused a ripple of anxiety deep in his gut, but he revealed nothing. His dark eyes fixed on advisor Ahmed, one of his father's most trusted servants, and he waited quietly, with an unintended look of steel in his eyes.

Ahmed took a step forward, deeper into Amir's bedroom. Ancient tapestries adorned the walls and a blade of moonlight caught one, drawing Amir's attention for a moment to the silver and blue threads that formed an image of the country's ancient western aqueducts. He felt that he should stand up, face whatever was coming with his eyes open, and so he did, pushing back sheets made of the finest linen, pressing his feet to the mosaics—gold and blue and green, they swirled like water and flame beneath him. At twelve, he was almost as tall as any of the men present.

'Tell me,' he repeated, the quality of steel shifting from his eyes to his voice.

Ahmed nodded slowly, swallowing so his Adam's apple shifted visibly. 'There was an attack, Your Highness.'

Amir waited.

'Your parents' convoy was targeted.'

Amir's only response was to straighten his spine; he continued to stare at Ahmed, his young face symmetrical and intent. Inside, his stomach was in knots and ice was flooding his veins.

'They were hurt?'

He heard one of the other servants groan, but he didn't take his eyes off Ahmed. With Ahmed he felt a degree of comfort; he trusted him.

'Yes. They were badly hurt.' Ahmed cleared his throat, his gentle features showing anguish. He put a hand on Amir's shoulder—a contact that was unprecedented. 'Amir, they were killed.'

The words were delivered with compassion and a pain all of his own—Ahmed had served Amir's father for a very long time, since he himself was a boy. The pain he felt must have run deep.

Amir nodded, understanding, knowing he would need to deal with his grief later, when he was alone. Only then he would allow his pain to run through his body, felling him to his knees for what he had lost. He wouldn't mourn publicly; that was not his way, and it was not what his country required of him. How long had that message been instilled in his heart? He was now his country's King, his people's servant.

'By whom?'

One of the other servants stood forward. Amir recognised the military medals he wore across the breast of his white uniform. He had a thick moustache, black and long. 'A band of renegades from Taquul.'

Amir's eyes closed for a moment. The country directly to the east, with whom Ishkana had been embroiled in bitter unrest for over a century. How many lives had been lost because of it? And now his parents were gone.

He, Amir, was Sheikh of Ishkana.

'A band of renegades,' Ahmed continued gently, 'led by His Highness Johar Qadir.'

Amir dug his hands into his hips, rocked on his heels, and nodded slowly. The King of Taquul's brother was a well-documented troublemaker. It was known that he sympathised with the people who inhabited the borders of their two lands, a people who had benefited for years from the ongoing conflict and wanted it to continue, at all costs. But this?

This was a step further. This was a new twist in the century-old war, one that was unforgivable. And for as long as he lived, Amir would make the Qadirs pay. He hated them with a vengeance that nothing—and no one—could ever quell.

CHAPTER ONE

PRINCESS JOHARA QADIR cut through the room with an innate elegance, pleased the evening was a masquerade for the anonymity it afforded her. The delicately constructed mask she'd been given to wear was made of onyx and pearl, with diamonds around the eyes and ostrich feathers on one side, which rose at least two feet above her head. The mask concealed everything but her eyes and lips, meaning she could pass unrecognised on this evening to all but those who knew her very, very well and could recognise the sparkle that lit the depths of her golden brown eyes.

'You have no choice, Johara. The whole family must appear to be united behind this decision. For our people...'

Yes, for their people. The prospect of peace with neighbouring Ishkana meant too much, would save lives, improve safety and lifestyle—of course she must support her brother's decision to enter a treaty with the neighbouring Sheikh.

It wasn't that that bothered her.

It was being summoned to return to the kingdom—for good. To leave behind her life in New York, the important work she was doing to support childhood literacy; it was leaving behind the identity she'd carved out for herself there. And for what? To come home to Taquul where her future was all mapped out for her? A ceremonial title and marriage to the man her brother deemed most suitable,

Paris Alkad'r? A role in this kingdom as ornamental but useless and ineffective?

It felt like a form of suffocation to even contemplate that kind of life and yet she understood her over-protective brother's thinking. He'd seen the way she'd been after Matthew—the American she'd fallen in love with and who had broken her heart. The newspaper articles had been relentless, the tabloids delighting in her pain. Malik wanted to spare her that—but an arranged marriage was about ten steps too far. Besides, the kind of marriage he and Paris envisaged—a political alliance—was the last thing she wanted!

A spirit of rebellion fired inside her.

Her brother was the Sheikh. He was older, true, but, more importantly, he had been raised to rule a country. Johara's importance—compared to his—had never been considered as particularly great—at least, not by their parents. Even Malik seemed, at times, to forget that she was a person with her own free will, simply snapping his fingers and expecting her to jump. Her closest friend in New York had commiserated and said that it was the same with her and her older sister—'older siblings are always bossy as hell'—but Johara doubted anyone could match the arrogance of Malik. She adored him, but that didn't mean she wasn't capable of feeling enraged by his choices, at times.

She expelled a sigh, took a glass of champagne from a passing waitress and had a small sip, then replaced it on another waitress's tray. Every detail of the party was exquisite. The National Ballet were serving as wait staff, each ballerina dressed in a pale pink and silver tutu, dancing as they moved through the crowd, mesmerising, beautiful, enchanting. The enormous marble hall had been opened for the occasion—showcasing the wealth and ancient prestige of the country, the windows displaying views of the desert in one direction and the Al'amanï ranges in the other. Large white marble steps led to an enormous lagoon; man-made, centuries ago, it had a free-form shape and was lit with small fires all around it. Glass had been carefully laid over the edges, allowing guests to hover over the water. Gymnasts danced in the water, their synchronised routines drawing gasps from those who stood outside. Fairy lights were strung overhead, casting a beautiful, 'midsummer night's dream' feeling.

Nothing had been missed.

Another sigh escaped Johara's lips. In New York, she had still been a princess, and the trappings of home had, of course, followed her. She'd had bodyguards who accompanied her discreetly wherever she went, she'd stayed at a royal apartment, and from time to time had taken part in official functions. However, she had been, by and large, free to live her own life.

Could she really give that up to come home and be, simply, ornamental? What about her burning desire to be of use?

Her eyes flicked across the room. Dignitaries from all corners of the globe had travelled to Taquul for this momentous occasion—an occasion most said would never happen. Peace between Ishkana and Taquul was almost an oxymoron, despite the fact the war had raged for so long that it had become a habit rather than anything else. A foreign diplomat was strutting proudly, evidently congratulating himself on bringing about this tentative peace accord. Johara's lips twisted into an enigmatic smile. Little did the diplomat know, no one could force her brother into anything that was not his desire.

He wanted this peace. He knew it was time. The ancient enmity had been a part of their life for generations, but it didn't serve the people. The hatred was dangerous and it was purposeless. How many more people had to die?

Perhaps in the beginning it served its purpose. The landscapes of Ishkana and Taquul were inhospitable. True, there was beauty and there was plenty in parts, but not enough, and the regions that had been in dispute a hundred years ago were those most plentiful with water, most arable and productive. Though a property accord had been reached, the war had continued and the accord had always seemed dangerously close to falling through. Add to that a group of tribes in the mountains who wanted independence from both countries, who worked to ensure the mistrust and violence continued, and Johara could only feel surprise that this peace had finally been wrought. Detailed negotiations between both countries and an agreement to impose strict laws on both sides of the mountains had led to this historic, hopeful event.

She hoped, more than anything, the peace would last.

'You are bored.' A voice cut through her thoughts, drawing her gaze sideways. A man had moved to stand at her side. He wore a mask over the top half of his face—soft velvet, it hugged the contours of his features, so she could still discern the strength and symmetry that lay beneath. A jaw that was squared, a nose that was strong and angular, and lips that were masculine yet full. His hair was dark as the depths of the ocean might be, and just as mesmerising—thick with a natural wave, it was cut to the collar of his robe and, though it was neat, she had the strangest feeling it was suppressed wildness, that it wanted to be long and loose, free of restraint. His eyes were dark like flint, and his body was broad, muscular, tall, as though cast in the image of an ancient idol. The thought came to her out of nowhere and sent a shiver pulsing down her spine. He wore an immaculate robe, black with gold at the cuffs and collar, complementing the mask on his face. He looked…mysterious and fascinating.

Dangerous.

He looked temptingly like the rebellion she wanted to stage, so she forced herself to look away while she still could.

'Not at all.' She was unrecognisable as the Princess of Taquul, but that didn't mean she could speak as freely as she wanted. And not to a stranger.

But she felt his eyes on her, watching her, and an inexplicable heat began to simmer inside her veins. She kept looking forward. 'There is somewhere else you'd rather be though?' he prompted, apparently not letting his curiosity subside.

She felt a burst of something shake her, willing her to speak to him, to be honest.

'I—' She swallowed, tilting her gaze towards him. The mask emboldened her. She was hidden, secret. He didn't know who she was, and she had no idea who he was. They were simply two strangers at a state function. No rank, no names. A smile curved slowly over her lips. 'Up until twenty hours ago, I was in Manhattan.' She lifted her shoulders, conscious of the way the delicate gown moved with her.

'And you would prefer to be there.'

'It is a momentous occasion.' She gestured around the room, then turned back to face him fully. 'Everyone in Taquul will be rejoicing at the prospect of peace with Ishkana after so long.'

His eyes gave little away; they were stony and cool. 'Not everyone.'

'No?'

'There are many who will harbour hatred and resentment for their lifetimes. Peace does not come about because two men snap their fingers and decide it should.'

Fascination fluttered inside her. 'You don't think people see the sense in peace?'

His lips curved in an approximation of a smile. There was something about its innate cynicism that sparked a fire in her blood. 'Ah, then we are talking about sense and not feeling. What one feels often has very little to do with what one thinks.'

Surprise hitched in her throat. It was an interesting and perceptive observation; she found herself more interested in him than she'd expected to be by anyone at this event. She took a small step without realising it, then another, leading them around the edges of the space.

'Nonetheless, I believe the people of Taquul will feel enormous relief, particularly those in the border regions. What's needed is a unified front to quell the unease in the mountain ranges.'

His eyes burned her with their intensity—strange when a moment ago she'd been thinking how like cool stone they were.

'Perhaps.'

'You don't agree?'

His lips curved in another mocking smile. 'I do not think peace can be so easily achieved.'

'I hope you're wrong.'

'I doubt it.'

She laughed; she couldn't help it. His cynicism was so completely natural, as though he barely realised he was doing it.

'I believe people can obey a peace treaty,' he said quietly, his voice dark. 'But that hatred dies a long, slow death. Many lives have been lost on both sides. How many deaths have there been in this war? Would you not wish to retaliate against a man who murdered someone you loved?'

Sadness brushed through her at his words and she

couldn't help wondering if he'd lost someone to the awful unrest of their people. 'I think vigilantism is bad for that very reason. It's why victims should never get to enact retribution—how easy it would be to answer death with death, pain with pain, instead of finding the restorative properties of forgiveness.'

He was silent; she couldn't tell if he agreed or not, only that he was thinking. They reached the edge of the enormous marble room and by unspoken agreement proceeded down the stairs. They were not steep, but his hand reached out, pressing into the small of her back in a small gesture of support.

It was meaningless. Absolutely nothing—yet it was the sort of thing that would never have been allowed to happen if he knew who she was. The Royal Princess of Taquul could never be simply touched by a commoner! But no one knew her identity except the few servants who'd helped her get ready. She moved down the steps and unconsciously her body shifted with each step so that they were pressed together at the side, touching in a way that sent arrows of heat darting through her body.

At the bottom of the stairs, he gestured to the edge of the pool. 'Stand with me a while.' He said it like a command and she suppressed a smile. People didn't dare speak to her like that in Taquul—or anywhere.

She nodded her agreement. Not because he'd commanded her to do so but because there was nowhere else she wanted to be. His hand stayed pressed to her back, guiding her to the edge of the pool. There was a tall table they could have stood at, with ballerina waitresses circulating deftly through the crowds. It was everything they needed, so Johara wasn't sure why she found herself saying, 'Would you like to see something special?'

He turned to face her, his eyes narrowing in assessment before he moved his head in one short nod of agreement.

Relief burst through her. It should have signalled danger, but she was incapable of feeling anything except adrenalin. No, that wasn't true. She felt excitement too, and in the pit of her stomach, spinning non-stop, she also felt a burst of desire.

The man strode beside her, completely relaxed, his natural authority impossible to miss. She wondered if he was a delegate from a foreign country, or perhaps one of the powerful industry leaders often included in palace occasions. A wealthy investor in the country's infrastructure? He certainly moved with that indefinable air of wealth and power.

Steps led away from the pool—these older and less finessed than the marble—giving way to a sweeping path. She walked down it, and his hand stayed at the small of her back the whole way, spreading warmth through her body, turning her breath to fire inside her and deep in the pit of her stomach she had the strangest sense of destiny, as though something about him, this night, her choice to walk with him had been written in the stars a long, long time ago.

He couldn't have said why he was walking with her. From the moment he'd seen her across the crowded ballroom he'd felt a lash of something like urgency; a *need* to speak to her. The room had been filled with beautiful women in stunning couture, dripping in gemstones with ornate face masks. While her black gown clung to her body like a second skin, showcasing her generous curves to perfection, it had been a long time since Amir had allowed physical attraction to control his responses.

Desire wasn't enough.

So why was he allowing her to lead him away from the party—knowing he had to stand beside Sheikh Malik

Qadir within the hour and showcase their newly formed 'friendship'? At least, for the sake of those in attendance, they had to pretend.

Nothing had changed for Amir though. He still hated the Qadirs with a passion. Nineteen years ago, with the death of his parents, he had sworn he would always hate them, and he intended to keep that promise.

'Where are you taking me?'

'Patience. We're almost there.' She spoke with a slight American accent and her voice was smooth and melodious, almost musical.

'Are you in the habit of taking men you don't know into the wilderness?'

She laughed, the sound as delicate as a bell. 'First of all, this is hardly a wilderness. The gardens are immaculately tended here, don't you think?'

He dipped his head in silent concession.

'And as for dragging men I don't know anywhere...' She paused mid-sentence, and stopped walking as well, her eyes latching to his in a way that communicated so much more than words ever could. He felt the pulse of response from her to him, the rushing of need. Her breathing was laboured, each exhalation audible in the quiet night air. Overhead, the stars shone against the desert sky, silver against velvet black, but there was no one and nothing more brilliant than the woman before him. His hands lifted to her mask; he needed to see her face. He wanted to see all of her. But her hands caught his, stilling them, and she shook her head a little.

'No. I like it like this.'

It was a strange thing to say—as though she liked the anonymity the mask provided. He dropped his hands lower, but instead of bringing them to his side he placed them at hers. His touch was light at first, as though asking a question. In response, she swayed forward a little, so her body brushed his and he was no longer able to deny the onslaught of needs that were assaulting him. He felt like a teenager again, driven by hormones and lust. How long had it been since he'd allowed himself to act on something so base?

'Come with me,' she murmured, hunger in the words, desperation in the speed with which she spoke. She reached down and grabbed his hand, linking her fingers through his, pulling him beside her. The night was dark and here they were far from the revellers, but as an enormous shrub came out of nowhere he was grateful for the privacy it created. She reached for the loose branches and brushed them aside, offering him a mysterious look over her shoulder before disappearing through a wall made of trees. Her hand continued to hold his, but he stood on the other side a moment, looking in one direction and then another before stepping forward. Large, fragrant trees surrounded them, the foliage thick to the ground.

The sky overhead was the only recognisable feature, but even that was unable to cast sufficient light over the structure. It was black inside, almost completely, a sliver of moonlight offering the faintest silver glow.

'This way.' She pulled him a little deeper, her other hand on the leaves as if by memory, turning a corner and then another, and as they turned once more he could hear water, faint at first but becoming louder with each step. She didn't stop until they reached a fountain in the centre of this garden, this maze.

'It's beautiful, isn't it?' she asked, turning to face him. He didn't spare a glance for the space in which they stood. He was certain she was right, but he couldn't look away from her. He ached to remove her mask; even if he did so, he would barely be able to see her face, given how dark it was this deep in the maze.

'Yes.' The word was guttural and deep.

He lifted a hand to her chin, taking it between his thumb and forefinger and holding her steady, scrutinising her as though if he looked hard enough and long enough he could make sense of this incredible attraction.

'It's famous, you know. The Palace Maze.'

He nodded. 'I've heard of it.'

'Of course. Everyone in Taquul has.' She smiled, a flash of dark red lips. He didn't correct her; she didn't need to know he was from Ishkana—nor that he was the Sheikh of that country.

He continued to stare at her and her lips parted, her eyes sweeping shut so beyond the veil of her mask he could see two crescent-shaped sets of lashes, long and thick.

He should leave. This wasn't appropriate. But leaving was anathema to him; it was as though he were standing in quicksand, completely in her thrall.

'How long are you in Taquul for?'

Something shifted in her expression, in the little he could see of it, anyway. 'I don't know.'

'You don't like it here?'

She expelled a soft sigh. 'I have mixed feelings.'

It made more sense than such a vague statement should have. 'What do you do in New York?'

Her smile now was natural. 'I started the Early Intervention Literacy Association. I work on childhood literacy initiatives, particularly for children aged four to seven.'

It surprised him; he hadn't been expecting her to say anything like that. She looked every inch the socialite, the heiress, rather than someone who rolled up her sleeves and worked on something so important.

'What drew you to that?'

Her eyes shuttered him out even as she continued to look at him, as though there was something she wanted to keep secret, to keep from him. He instantly hated that. 'It's a worthwhile cause.'

He wanted to challenge her, to dig deeper, but he felt he was already balancing on a precipice, and that the more he knew was somehow dangerous.

'Yes.' Silence wrapped around them, but it was a silence that spoke volumes. His dark eyes bore into hers—a lighter shade of brown, like oak, sunshine and sand. He stared at her for as long as he could before dropping his eyes to her lips, then lower still to the curve of her breasts. The dress was black but so glossy it shimmered in the gentle moonlight.

'This is incredible,' he muttered, shaking his head as he ran his hand along her side, his fingertips brushing the flesh at her hips, then higher, tantalising the sweet spot beneath her arms, so close to her breasts he could see her awareness and desire, the plea in her eyes begging him to touch her there. His arousal hardened; he wanted to make love to her right here, beneath the stars, with the trees as their witness to whatever this madness was.

'How long are you in Taquul for?'

Only as long as he absolutely needed to be.

Every moment in this kingdom felt like a betrayal to his parents and their memory. 'Just this event. I leave immediately afterwards.'

Her eyes glittered with something like determination and she nodded. 'Good.' It was a purr. A noise that was half invitation, half dare. The latter made no sense but the former was an utter relief.

'In answer to your earlier question, I don't ever do this.'

He was quiet, waiting for her to say something else, to explain.

'I don't ever drag men I don't know into the maze, or anywhere.'

Her breath snagged in her throat, her lips parted and her head tilted back, her eyes holding his even as she swayed forward, totally surrendering to the madness of this moment.

'But you're different.'

His smile was barely a shift of his lips.

'Am I?'

'For starters, you're the only man here wearing black robes.'

He nodded slowly. There was a reason for that. Robes just like these had been worn at an ancient meeting between these two people, an event to mark their peace and friendship. His choice of attire was ceremonial but yes, she was right. All the other men wore either western-style suits or traditional white robes.

'Except, it's not what you're wearing.'

She lifted a hand, pressing her fingers to his chest. The touch surprised them both, but she didn't pull away.

'Have you ever met someone and felt…?' She frowned, searching for the right word.

But it was unnecessary. She didn't need to explain further. He shook his head. 'No. I've never felt this in my life.'

And before either of them could say another word, he dropped his mouth to hers and claimed her lips with all the desire that was humming inside his body.

CHAPTER TWO

THE DRESS WAS impossibly soft and, at its back, small pearls ran the length of her spine, so he had to undo each one in order to free her from the stunning creation. He was impatient and wanted to rip the dress—but the material was seemingly unbreakable. Besides, he had just enough sense left to realise he'd be doing this woman a great wrong if he left her to emerge from the maze with a snagged dress.

What they were doing was mad on every level. He knew nothing about her—he could only be grateful she knew nothing about him either. The last thing he needed was a complication that would detract from the peace accord.

She'd been right about the masks. Anonymity was perfect. He removed the dress as quickly as he could, stripping it from her body with reverence, a husky groan impossible to contain when he saw the underwear she wore. Flimsy white lace, it barely covered her generous breasts and bottom. The effect of the silk and her face mask had his cock growing so hard it was painful.

He swore under his breath, dispensing with his own robes with far less reverence, stripping out of them as he'd done hundreds of time before, unable to take his eyes off her as he moved. He was half afraid she'd change her mind, that she'd tell him they had to stop this. And she'd be right to do so! This was utter madness, a whim of desire and pleasure and hedonism, a whim he should deny himself, just as he'd denied himself so many things in his time for the sake of his country.

He knew that his kingdom required him to marry—he was the sole heir to the throne and without a wife the necessary children were impossible to beget. Yet he had only ever engaged in careful, meaningless affairs, and only when he'd felt the conditions were right—the right woman, who would understand he could give her nothing in the way of commitment, because he had an obligation to marry for the good of his kingdom. Did this woman understand that?

She reached around behind her back, as if to unclasp her bra, drawing his mind away from his thoughts and back to the present. He watched as she unhooked the lace, her breath hissing between her teeth, her eyes on his as the garment dropped to the ground beside her, revealing two perfect, pale orbs with dark, engorged nipples.

He swore again, and when her eyes dropped to his very visible arousal, he felt a little of his seed spill from his crown. Her eyes looked as though they wanted to devour him.

Aljahim, he wanted this. He wanted to feel her, to taste her, to touch her all over, but time was against them. This would be so much faster than he wanted.

'I cannot stay long,' he said quietly; it was only fair to forewarn her of that before they began.

'Nor can I.' She reached for the elastic of her tiny scrap of underwear but he shook his head.

'Allow me.'

Her eyes widened and she dropped her hands to the side, nodding once.

He closed the distance between them, pausing right in front of her, his pulse slamming through his body.

'This is what you want?'

She nodded.

'You're on the pill?'

Another nod, wide-eyed, as though the reality was just dawning on her.

'I don't have any protection—'

'I'm safe.'

He nodded. 'As am I.'

She bit down on her lip, a perfect cherry red against the dark hue of her skin. He ached to remove the mask and see her face, and yet it also served to draw attention to her lips and eyes, both of which were so incredibly distracting.

'Please.'

The single word was his undoing. He groaned, kissing her once more, dragging her lower lip into his mouth and moving his tongue so that it duelled with hers, teasing her at first before dominating her completely, so her head dropped backwards in surrender and he pillaged her mouth, each movement designed to demand compliance—yet it was he that was complying too, with the current of need firing between them a most superior force.

His hands cupped her naked breasts, feeling their weight, their roundedness, pushing his arousal forward against the silk of her underpants so she whimpered with need—a need he understood.

Her fingers dug into his shoulders, her body weak against his. He understood. It was overwhelming. He broke the kiss simply so he could drag his mouth lower, over her décolletage, conscious of the way his facial hair left marks as he went, his teeth adding nips, something primal and ancient firing inside him at the sight of his proof of possession. If he were less fired by desire he might have felt ashamed by such an ancient thrill, but he didn't.

He took one of her ample breasts into his mouth, seeking her nipple with his tongue, rolling the sweet flesh until she was whimpering loudly into the night sky. Only then did he transfer his attention to the other breast, lifting his thumb and forefinger to continue the pleasurable torment on the other. She bucked her hips forward; he knew how she was feeling, for his own body was racked with the same sense of desperation.

He wanted her but he didn't want to stop this yet. He could feel her pleasure tightening, her body responding to his instantly, and he wanted to indulge that responsiveness, to show her how perfectly they were suited. With his teeth clamping down against her nipple and his fingers teasing the other, he wedged her legs apart with his knee then brought his spare hand to rest there, parting the elastic from her with ease to allow a finger to slide into her warm, feminine core.

She groaned, a sound of complete pleasure and surrender and delight. He didn't stop. He pushed another finger into her depths and then used his thumb to stroke her, pleasuring her breasts as he paid homage to her.

She crumpled against him; his arms, his mouth, were holding her body in place. He felt her stiffen then, and begin to shake; she was exploding, gripping him hard as her body was racked with an intense, blinding release. He didn't relinquish his touch; he held her close, the squeezing of her muscles against his fingers eliciting an answering response from him.

He needed her; there was nothing else for it. Before her breath could calm he let her go, moving his hands to her hips instead, holding her steady as he knelt in front of her. His teeth caught the elastic of her underpants, pulling them loose and lower, low enough for her to step out of, and then he kissed her feminine core, his tongue flicking her until she was crying again, moaning, and, for lack of a name, she could only say 'please', again, and again, and again.

He smiled against her. Yes, he'd give her what she wanted—and what he wanted—and he'd do it soon. He stood, scooping her up and kissing her lips, unspeakably aroused by the idea that she might taste herself in his kiss, carrying her to a soft patch of grass to the right of the fountain. He laid her down, then took a moment to simply marvel at the view she made. Her body was curvy and slim all at once, her hair dark and tumbled around her shoulders, her mask adding an element of mystery and allure—not that she needed it.

This woman was the definition of alluring—distracting and perfect. What other explanation could there be for the instant attraction he'd felt for her? It was as though the very heavens had demanded this of him—of them. This was so out of character and yet it didn't feel wrong.

He brought his body over hers, feeling her softness beneath the hard planes of his frame, his mouth seeking to reassure her with kisses as his knee parted her legs, making way for him. He hovered at her entrance, the moment one he wanted to frame in time, caught like one of the butterflies he'd chased as a child and occasionally held in the palms of his hand for a precious instant before releasing it back into the forest. He caught her wrists in his, pinning them above her head, holding her still, and as he pushed up to watch her face as he entered her, he committed every instant of their coming together to his memory. Her eyes widened before sweeping shut as her lips parted on a husky moan, her hips lifting instinctively to welcome him to her body.

She was so tight, her muscles squeezing him almost painfully, so he moved more slowly than his instincts wanted, taking her bit by bit until he was buried inside then pausing, allowing her to grow used to this feeling before he moved, pulling back a little then driving forward, his hips moving slowly and then, as her cries grew more fervent, taking her harder, faster. His grip on her wrists loosened, his fingers moving instead to entwine with hers, squeezing her hands before releasing her so she wrapped her arms around his back, her nails scoring his flesh with each thrust. Her cries grew louder and her muscles tightened then fell into spasm and he felt the moment she lost her grip on reality and tumbled off the side of the world in an intense orgasm. She writhed beneath him and a moment later he joined her in that ecstasy, allowing his body the total surrender to hers and this moment, releasing himself to her with a hoarse cry that filled the heart of this maze with their pleasure.

She should have felt regret but she couldn't. She watched as he dressed, covering his body with the black robes—a body that she had somehow committed to memory. It was a honed frame, all muscle and strength, and on his left pectoral muscle, he had words tattooed in Latin in a cursive font: *amor fati.* His back bore signs of her passion all over it. Her fingernails had marked his smooth, bronzed skin, leaving a maze of their own in bright red lines, frantic and energised. A smile played about her lips, her body still naked beneath the glorious night sky, the sound of the water fountain adding an air of magic to what they'd just done. Or perhaps it wasn't the fountain, it was just the act.

Pleasure exploded through her. Relief. As though what she'd done was a connection to her true self, a timely reminder that she was an autonomous being, not controlled by this kingdom and her brother, by the expectations upon her. And it was more than that—it was as though the heavens themselves had conspired to bring them together. It had all happened so quickly, so completely, his possession of her so absolute. She'd only been with one other man before,

Matthew, and she'd thought herself to be in love with him. She'd presumed that was a prerequisite to enjoying sex.

Enjoying sex!

What a bland way to express what she'd just felt! Her soul had changed orientation. North was now south, the world had altered shape, everything was different. She hadn't known what her body was capable of until a master such as this man had taught her how to truly feel. Wonderment filled her.

She knew only one regret then—that this wasn't the beginning of something more. It was impossible to hope for that. She wasn't utterly deluded as to her position in the royal family to think she could shun her obligations so completely and pursue a sexual fling with some random man—even onc of obvious wealth and importance.

A sigh left her lips; she reached for a blade of grass, the dew on its tip delicate and glistening in the moonlight. The man turned to face her, and she smiled at him as though it were the most natural thing in the world. He smiled back; there were no barriers between them.

'Let me help you.' His voice was deep and husky, tinged with a slight accent. She couldn't quite pick it. She'd presumed he was from Taquul but perhaps he was from a neighbouring state, here to mark the new peace in the region.

Her brain was beginning to work again, after the fog of desire had made thinking impossible. He reached for her underwear, holding it out to her, the smile still on his face so something shifted in the pit of her stomach. He was so handsome, but it was more than that. She'd met plenty of handsome men before, and never felt like this. Powerful men, too. Handsome, strong, wealthy, sophisticated. After Matthew, she'd been difficult to impress. *Once bitten, twice shy* had become somewhat of a mantra for Johara without her realising it.

Perhaps it came down to the fact she knew nothing about him—he hadn't lied to her, he couldn't have, because they hadn't spoken. They'd let their bodies and mutual desire do all the communicating. Pleasure had been paramount.

Her nipples tingled as she slipped the bra into place, and he expelled a harsh breath as her underpants covered her femininity, so she knew he too regretted the necessity of ending this. Beyond the walls of this maze a party raged, a party at which she was expected to stand at her brother's side. Soon, the masks would come off, for the members of royal family at least, so that they could stand before the Sheikh of Ishkana as their true selves, and see his true self, pledging a better future for their two countries. And just for a moment, a blade of something like worry punctured the perfection of this moment. She pushed it away; she couldn't let it ruin this wonderful thing she'd just done.

Yet she had always hated everything the Haddad family was—that hate had been taught to her from a young age and even now, as a twenty-five-year-old woman, when she could acknowledge it was an ancient prejudice she'd been brought up to bear, she couldn't free herself from those feelings.

The idea of standing beside Malik and pretending she welcomed the Sheikh of Ishkana filled her with abhorrence. But she must do it. This encounter had been her act of rebellion, a last, secret giving-in to her own needs. Now she must be what her country needed.

'This dress is unlike anything I've ever seen.' He ran his fingers over it then held it open for her to step into. She moved closer, lifting one foot and placing it in the middle of the dress, putting a hand on his shoulder to steady herself. She'd marked him there too; little fingernail crescents were woven over his skin like a pattern that told of her impatience and need. She stroked the marks absent-mindedly as she moved her other foot into the dress.

'It's made of spider silk.'

The jerk of his head towards hers showed surprise.

'It was my mother's,' she added. 'Made a long time ago, and over the course of many years. A tribe to the west spent a long time harvesting the silk of spiders and spinning it using a special loom.' She ran her hands over it then turned, so he could fasten the buttons at the back. 'It's virtually unbreakable. It's supposed to signify strength and courage.'

His hands stilled a little at the small of her back before continuing with her buttons. 'Do you need these things?'

She thought of what was ahead and nodded. 'We all do, don't we?'

He reached the top button and pressed it into place, then let his hands move over her shoulders without answering. She turned to face him, looked up into his face and smiled.

'Thank you.' It was a strange thing to say but she felt gratitude. They'd never see each other again but what they'd just done had been incredibly important to her.

He dipped his head in silent concession. 'I have to go back.'

Her brow furrowed behind her mask as she looked to the entrance of the heart of the maze. 'Me too.'

He took her hand in his. 'Lead the way, *inti qamar*.'

My moon. She smiled at the casual term of endearment, pushing through the maze effortlessly.

'You know the way well.'

'Yes.' She could have elaborated on that. She could have said that she used to come here to hide as a child, that the maze was hers alone. The gardeners who tended it had brought her treats for the days when she would come with a book and lie on the grass for hours on end. Not the kind of food that was served in the palace, all perfect and delicate and with the expectation that she sit with her back ramrod straight and make polite conversation with the children her parents had deemed suitable companions. No, here in the maze she'd feasted on food from beyond the palace walls, street food and market delicacies that the gardeners had brought in for her. Sticky pastries, figs that were sun-dried and exploding with flavour, spiced meatballs, marinated cheese, rice stuffed into vegetables and packed with spices. It was messy and organic, each mouthful a tribute to life and goodness. She could have told him that in this maze she'd spent some of her happiest times—and that tonight had simply added to that.

But instead, she simply nodded, already feeling as though the woman who'd just done such a daring and spontaneous thing was disappearing, being pushed deep inside Johara. The closer they moved to the start of the maze, the more she was reminded of the life that was ahead of her.

Rebellion aside, she couldn't keep hiding in mazes for ever. She was a princess of Taquul and that brought with it obligations and expectations. She would do as her brother said. She would stand at his side tonight and welcome the peace accord and then, if he insisted on it, she would consider the marriage to Paris, even though the idea turned her blood to ice.

At the entrance to the maze, she paused, pulling her hand from his and rubbing her fingers together.

'You go ahead of me,' she said, simply. 'It's not worth the trouble of being seen coming out of the maze together.'

He seemed to consider that a moment and then nodded. She had no idea what else she could say.

'If things were different,' he murmured, lifting a hand to her chin, holding her steady beneath him, 'I would have liked to see you again.'

Her answering smile was lopsided with wistfulness.

'If things were different,' she agreed, 'I would have liked that too.'

Neither said what their commitments were and why it wasn't possible. They didn't need to.

'Goodnight.' He bowed his head low in a mark of deference and respect, something she was used to, so for a moment she wondered if perhaps he'd guessed at her identity. But, no. He was simply showing her what their assignation had meant to him; how he viewed her. Her heart felt as though it had exploded to three times its size. She kept a polite smile in place, used to maintaining an expression of polite calm when she felt anything but.

'Goodnight…sir.'

CHAPTER THREE

'GOODNIGHT, SIR.'

Her words hummed through his brain, flooding him with memories. His body felt as though it was infused with a special kind of energy. He emerged from the maze, stalking past the pool, deliberately evading anyone who might try to catch his eye. At the entrance to the ballroom though, he could no longer ignore his reason for coming to this place he'd always despised.

Ahmed, his long-time servant, stepped from the shadows. 'Your Highness.' He bowed low, and Amir stilled, pushing aside thoughts of the beautiful woman and what they'd just shared. The entire encounter had been like a dream and already the threads of it were drifting away, impossible to catch.

'It's time.'

Amir nodded once, scanning the ballroom. 'Where is he?'

'In the stateroom.'

Amir's eyes narrowed with determination. 'Take me there.'

'Yes, sir.'

Amir paused as her words filled his brain once more. He walked beside his servant, using every ounce of willpower not to look over his shoulder to see the woman return to the ballroom. He wouldn't look for her again; he couldn't.

At the doors to the stateroom, Ahmed said something low and quiet to one of the guards. Both bowed low then opened the doors inwards.

There were only three men in the room, though the space was opulent and large enough to house two hundred easily. Marble, like the ballroom, with pillars to the vaulted ceilings, and tapestries on the walls—burgundy and gold with threads of navy blue to add detail.

Amir strode through the room as though he belonged. These men had removed their masks; he identified Malik Qadir easily enough.

'Your Majesty.' Malik silenced the other two with the address, extending a hand to Amir's. Amir hesitated a moment, his veins pounding with hatred and enmity. Only a love for his kingdom had him lifting up to remove his own mask before taking the outstretched hand and meeting Malik's eyes.

'Your Majesty,' he returned. But it felt like a betrayal of everything he knew in the world; he felt as though he was defacing the memory of his parents by treating this man—the nephew of his parents' murderer!—with such civility. He had always sworn to hate this family, and that included the Sheikh and Princess of Taquul.

'My chief aide, Tariq.' Malik indicated the man to his left. Amir nodded and introduced Ahmed with the same title.

'And Paris—my friend, and the man my sister is to marry.'

Amir nodded. He didn't say that it was a pleasure. He was honest to a fault and always had been. But he forced his lips into something approximating a smile. 'Let's get this over with, then.'

Malik's eyes glittered, showing a matching sense of antipathy. They were both putting aside their personal hatred for the sake of their kingdoms. For peace and prosperity and in the hope that more senseless deaths could be avoided.

'One moment,' Malik murmured, turning to Tariq and speaking low and soft. They shared the same language but he swapped to an ancient dialect that Amir only passingly understood.

A moment later, Malik looked at Amir. 'My sister is expected.'

Paris's smile was indulgent. 'She is often late.'

It was clear from Malik's expression that he disapproved of that quality. It was a sentiment Amir shared. Punctuality was not difficult to master and was, at its base, a sign of respect.

'Would you care for some wine?' Malik gestured to the wall, where a tray had been placed with several drinks.

Amir shook his head.

'Then we shall simply wait.'

The silence was tense. It was not natural. To be in the depths of this palace, surrounded by men who a year ago might have wished him dead? Hell, who probably still did. The peace talks had been ongoing, difficult and driven by emotion on both sides. It had taken Amir and Malik's intervention with their aides to achieve what they had.

And now, there was simply this. To stand in front of the assembled guests and speak to the importance of what they hoped to achieve, the ancient bonds that had, at one time, held these countries together. The mountain ranges separated them but that had, generations ago, been a passage alive with trade. The cooler climates there had created villages full of people from both countries. Only in recent times had the mountain range come to serve as a barrier.

He must focus on their past, on the closeness that had once been natural to their peoples, and on the future they intended to forge.

* * *

'I know, I know.' Johara ran a hand over her hair, meeting her servant's eyes in the gold-framed mirror. 'I'm late.'

'Very,' Athena agreed, pursing her lips into a small smile. 'Your brother was expecting you in the staterooms fifteen minutes ago.'

Another flicker of rebellion dashed through her soul. So she was keeping her brother waiting. It was juvenile and silly, particularly given the importance of the evening, and yet there was pleasure in the perversity of running behind schedule.

'Send word that I'm on my way,' she murmured to another servant, reaching up to remove the thick black ribbons that held the mask in place. Her hair was loose; it tumbled over her shoulders, but for this meeting, she wanted it styled more severely, more formally. That felt like an armour she would need.

Her hands worked deftly, catching the lustrous brown waves low at her nape and swirling them into a bun. 'Pins?'

Athena reached into her pockets—from which she seemed capable of removing all sorts of implements at will—and handed several to Johara. 'I can call a stylist?'

'Is it necessary?' Johara returned archly, pressing several pins into place to secure an elegant chignon.

'No. It's perfect. Neat and ordered.'

The opposite of how she presently felt. When she lifted her hands to her cheeks to pinch them for a hint of colour, her nipples strained against the lace of her bra and she felt a hum of memory, a reminder of what she'd shared with the stranger. A *frisson* ran the length of her spine—had it really happened? It was the most uncharacteristic thing she'd ever done in her life and yet she didn't regret it. Not even a little.

'Lipstick.' Athena passed a black tube over and Johara coloured her full lips and then nodded.

'Fine. Let's go.'

She didn't portray a hint of the turmoil she was feeling. Her country stood on a precipice. Everything was new. The old ways must be forgotten. He had been wrong to say hatred would persist. The possibility of peace and safety was too alluring. Surely their people would force themselves to forget the anger and bigotry and come to see the people of Ishkana as their brothers and sisters?

She was barely conscious of the way servants bowed to her as she walked. It hadn't been like this in New York but, despite the fact she'd lived there for several years, she had grown up here in Taquul, for the most part, and this sort of respect came part and parcel with her position.

At the doors of the stateroom, she paused, turning to Athena. 'You'll come with me.'

'Of course.' Athena's eyes dropped to the marble floor a moment, as though she too was fortifying herself for the night ahead. And that was natural—Athena had served the Taquul royal family since she was a teenager, her sentiments matched theirs.

Beyond that, she was a friend to Johara. Johara reached out and squeezed Athena's hand for comfort. 'Let's just get it over with.' She unknowingly echoed Amir's earlier sentiments. The doors swept open, the noise of their intrusion drawing the attention of all in the room.

Her eyes naturally gravitated towards her brother's. His gaze held a warning, as though he expected her to make trouble in some way. From him, she turned to Paris. His smile was kind; she returned it. She might not find him at all attractive but he was sweet and they'd been friends for a long time.

Someone moved at the side of the room, catching her attention. She turned that way naturally, and missed her step, stumbling a little awkwardly as her eyes tried to make sense of it.

The man across the room was…unmistakably…the same man she'd made love to in the heart of the maze. His dark robes were instantly recognisable, but it was more than that. Though he'd worn a mask his face was…she'd seen it as they'd kissed. She'd *known* what he looked like.

Had he known who she was? Had it been some kind of vile revenge?

No. Shock registered on his features too, though he covered that response much more swiftly than she was able, assuming a mask of cool civility while her blood was threatening to burn her body to pieces.

'Jo.' Malik crossed to her but she couldn't look away from Amir. She saw the way he flinched at her name and wondered why. The world was spinning, and not in a good way. Malik put his hand under her elbow, guiding her deeper into the room, and she was glad for his support. She could hardly breathe. What were the chances?

He *had* to have known. He had come to speak to her out of nowhere—why else had he approached her like that? It couldn't have been random happenstance.

Except he hadn't known; she was sure of it. They'd both sought anonymity. It had been a transaction between two people: faceless, nationless, without identity. It had been about him and her, their bodies and souls, and nothing more.

She dropped her head, almost unable to walk for a moment as the reality of what had happened unravelled inside her.

He'd use this to destroy her. To destroy her brother. If Malik knew what she'd done… Oh, heck.

Panic seized her.

'Calm down,' Malik muttered from the side of his lips.

'This is to commemorate a peace treaty, remember? He is no longer the enemy yet you look as though you would like to kill him.'

Startled, she jerked her eyes away from Sheikh Amir of Ishkana and looked at her brother instead. 'I would.'

Malik's expression showed amusement and then he shook his head, leaned closer and whispered, 'Me too, but my advisors tell me it would be a bad idea.'

She forced a smile she didn't feel. Paris moved to them, putting a familiar hand on hers and pressing a kiss to her cheek. It was a simple greeting, one that was appropriate for old friends, but in front of Amir, after what they'd just shared, she felt as though she should distance herself. She needed space. From him, from everyone. But it wasn't possible. There were far greater concerns than her personal life.

'Amir.' Malik addressed him by his first name, and it didn't occur to Amir to mind. In that moment, all of his brain power was absorbed in making sense of what the hell had just happened.

She was… Johara? The Princess of Taquul? The woman he'd made love to, been so blindsided by that he'd given into physical temptation against all common sense was…a Qadir?

He wanted to shout: *It can't be!* Surely it wasn't possible. And yet…there was no refuting it. Her dress…she moved and he remembered how she'd felt in his hands, how her body had writhed beneath his. He could close his eyes and picture her naked, her voluptuous curves calling to him, even as she now walked elegantly towards him, her hair neat, her make-up flawless, and he saw only a Qadir princess. Her parents had hated his. Her uncle Johar had killed his parents. Johar… Johara. She'd been named for that murderous son of a bitch.

Something like nausea burst through him. Hatred bubbled beneath his skin. As she came close, he inhaled and caught a hint of her fragrance, so familiar to him that his body couldn't help but respond, despite the fact he now knew who she was.

'This is my younger sister, Princess Johara of Taquul.'

Their eyes met and locked. It was impossible to look away. He saw fear there. Panic. But why? Because of what they'd done? Or because of what she thought he might do next? Did she believe he was going to announce their prior relationship? That he'd do something so foolish as confess what they'd shared? To what end?

His eyes narrowed imperceptibly and he extended a hand. 'A pleasure to meet you.'

He saw the moment relief lit her eyes. Her smile was barely there—a terrible facsimile of the vibrant smiles she'd offered in the maze. She hadn't known who he was. Neither of them had understood.

How had he failed to notice the signs though? Her familiarity with the maze. A dress made of spiders' silk. Both such obvious signs of her place within this family. Yet he'd been blinded by her, and by the attraction he felt. It was the only answer.

'Likewise.' Her accent. It was so American—naturally he'd assumed she was a foreigner, here in Taquul just for the ball. But now he recalled the biographical details he'd been furnished with prior to this treaty: that her mother had been American, that she'd gone to school in America for some time, and had lived there for several years.

'You look flushed. Do you feel well?' It was Paris, to her left. Something else flared in Amir's mind.

The man my sister is to marry.

'I'm fine.' At least she had the grace to look ashamed.

'Your Highness? They're ready.'

* * *

It was a blur. Johara stood between her brother and Paris as the peace accord was announced. Fireworks burst overhead to celebrate the occasion, and answering displays were seen across the countries. Peace had come—she could only hope that it would hold.

And all the while, those in attendance smiled and nodded with rapt faces, and finally cheered, so Johara smiled along with them and nodded as her brother spoke. But it was when Amir began to address the crowd that everything inside her dissolved into a kind of never-ending tumult.

'For too long we have seen our people die. We have fought over nothing more significant than on which side of the mountains we were born; this war has been a plague on both our countries. Our people were once unified and great, strong in this region, capable of anything. Our prosperity was shared, our might universally known. It is time to set aside the last one hundred years. It is time to forge a peace between our people, a lasting peace—not into the next century, but the next millenium.' She was captivated, staring at his deep, dark eyes as he scanned the crowd.

'It will take work. It will require us to actively forget how we have been taught to feel. We will need to look behind the masks of what we believe our peoples stand for, to see the truth of what is there. A baker in Ishkana is no different from a baker in Taquul. We see the same stars, worship the same god, dance to the same songs, have learned all the same tales. We can be unified once more.' He turned to look at Malik, but his eyes glanced over Johara, so she was sure he must have seen the effect his rousing speech had on her.

She couldn't hide her admiration, she was sure of it.

'Tonight begins a new way of life for us, a life of peace.'

Silence lasted for several seconds and then applause broke out, loud and joyous. If Johara had been in any doubt as to how desperately the people wished for peace, the proof was right before her now. And for Amir to take what was largely a crowd of Taquul dignitaries and have them eating out of his hand—it showed the magnetism he had.

Not that she needed any further indication of that.

The official requirements of the evening were at an end. She left the makeshift stage gratefully, giving a brief farewell to Paris before slipping through thick gold curtains that hung along the edge of the ballroom. She moved quickly, desperately needing air, space, a way to breathe. She found her way to a long marble corridor and moved through it until she reached glass doors at the end.

The cool desert air glanced across her skin as she pushed them open, onto a small Juliet balcony that overlooked the Sheikh's aviary, where his prized falcons were kept. In the evening, the stark outline of trees was striking. Beyond it, the desert lay, and the light breeze stirred the sand, so when she breathed in she could smell that acrid clay that was so reminiscent of her childhood. How she'd loved to carry bottles of water into the desert and pour it over the sand to make little streams, turning the sand into a malleable substance from which she could build great structures.

For a child who could barely read, making things with her hands had been her own source of satisfaction.

'Your Highness.'

She stiffened, curving her hands over the railing of the balcony as his voice reached her ears. Had she known he would follow? No. And yet, she was hardly surprised.

She turned slowly, bracing for this—or at least attempting to. Nothing could prepare her for what was to come. Without his mask, alone on the balcony, so close she could touch him. And more than that, the coldness in his face. The anger. Oh, he was trying to control it but she felt it emanating from him in waves so she rushed to say, 'I didn't know who you were. I had no idea.'

She knew, even as she spoke the words, that it wasn't completely true. Their connection had defied logic and sense. Perhaps she might have been able to resist him, but not if he'd set his mind on seducing her.

'So you simply took the chance to sleep with another man behind your fiancé's back?'

'I…' She frowned. 'I don't have a fiancé.'

That surprised him.

'There is a man my brother wishes me to marry,' she stressed, 'but that's not quite the same thing. Last time I checked, I still have some say in the matter, so no, I didn't "cheat" on anyone.'

He dipped his head forward. 'I apologise. I was misinformed.'

She was surprised by the instant apology, and more so how he could deliver it in a way that was both genuine and infused with icy coldness. If she turned to the right, she'd see the edge of the maze. She couldn't look that way. She'd likely never look at it again, certainly never walk within its verdant walls.

'You're named for him.'

She frowned, but only for a second. She should have remembered sooner, the awful, bloody death in her family's—and his family's—history. 'My uncle Johar? Yes.'

'You're named as a tribute.'

'I was born before he…'

Amir's shoulders squared. 'Murdered my parents?'

Her eyes swept shut in anguish. 'Yes.'

'And yet he had knowingly hated them for a long time.'

'You said yourself, hate has been felt by all our people for a very long time.'

'True.' He crossed his arms over his broad chest. She

wished he hadn't done that. It drew her focus in a way that was dangerous, flooding her body and brain with too many feelings.

'A moment ago, I listened to you implore us to move on from those feelings. To remember that we were once allies.' She swallowed, not realising until that instant how badly she wanted that to be the case. 'Let's not speak of Johar. Not when a new period of peace is upon us.'

His lips curled into what she could only describe as a grimace of derision. 'Publicly I must advocate and encourage peace. Privately I am allowed to feel whatever the damned hell I please.'

His anger and vehemence were palpable forces, rushing towards her. 'And what do you feel?'

He stared at her for several seconds and then looked beyond her, beyond the aviary, to the desert planes in the distance, made silver by the moonlight. 'It's better not to discuss it with you.'

'If you'd known who I was…' She let the question hang between them unfinished.

'Would I have allowed it to happen?' He compressed his lips. 'No.'

'You think you could have stopped it?'

His eyes shifted back to hers and she saw it—what she'd been conscious of and yet not fully understood before. He was a king. Born all-powerful to a mighty people. Born to rule and fully cognisant of what the world required of him. His natural authority was exactly that. She'd perceived it from the outset and she felt it now. She shivered involuntarily, a whisper of cold seizing her core.

'Absolutely.'

Courage was failing her, but she wouldn't allow what they'd shared to be lost completely. 'You're wrong.' She moved forward, putting a hand on his chest, but he flinched away from her, his eyes holding a warning. Pain lashed her. She had to be brave; he couldn't deny that what had happened between them was real. That it held meaning. 'There was something about you, and me, that needed us to do that.'

He made a noise of disagreement. 'It was a mistake.'

Hurt pounded her insides. She shook her head in disagreement.

'Let me be clear.' His voice was deep and authoritative. She stayed where she was, but her body was reverberating with a need to reach for him, to touch him. 'If I had known you were a Qadir I would not have touched you. I would not have spoken to you. I will always regret what happened between us, Johara.' And her spat her name as though it were the worst insult he could conjure. 'Tonight, I betrayed myself, my parents, and everything I have always believed.'

Pain exploded in her chest. She blinked at him, uncertain of how to respond, surprised by how badly his words had cut her. 'I'm not my uncle. I'm not my parents and I'm not my brother.' She spoke with a quiet dignity, her voice only shaking a little. 'You cannot seriously mean to hate me just because of the family I was born into?'

His eyes pierced her. 'I'm afraid that's exactly what I mean, Your Highness.'

CHAPTER FOUR

'IT'S IMPORTANT.'

'It's dangerous.' Paris spoke over Malik in a rare sign of anger. Johara watched the two of them discussing her fate with an overarching sense of frustration. As though where she went and why came down to what they said.

'The peace is already fraying, and only eight weeks after the accord was signed. We need to do something more to underscore our intent that this be meaningful.' He turned to Johara, frowning. 'I hate to ask it of you, Johara, but you know that it's time.'

She said nothing, simply lifting a brow in a silent invitation for him to continue. 'You've avoided your obligations for years, and I've allowed it.' Inwardly she bristled. Malik crouched before her. 'Because you're my sister and I love you; I want you to be happy. But I *need* you now. Someone has to go and do the sorts of visible politicking I don't have time for.'

She ignored the way her brother so easily relegated the responsibilities he was trying to foist on her as though it were just glad-handing and smiling for cameras, rather than wading into enemy territory and attempting to win the hearts of the Ishkana people.

'You should go.' Paris spoke quietly, addressing Malik, his eyes intense. 'For a short visit.'

'It's not possible.' Malik sighed. 'You know there are matters here that require my urgent attention.'

Paris expelled a breath. 'Then send someone. A diplomat. A cousin.'

'No. It can't be a snub, nor a regular visit. This has to have meaning to his people, the way his visit did for ours.'

'It can't have meant that much,' Paris pointed out, 'for the skirmishes to be continuing.'

'Sheikh Amir is right. We have to be unified in this.' Johara spoke above both of them, standing with innate elegance and striding towards one of the windows that framed a view of the citrus gardens. Their formal layout was designed as a tribute to a French palace, each tree surrounded by bursts of lavender, white gravel demarcating the various plantings.

Paris and Malik were silent; waiting.

'I hate the idea of going to Ishkana.' She did, but not for reasons she could ever share with either man. She had tried to forget everything about Sheikh Amir and his hateful kingdom since they'd spoken on the balcony; to be sent there now as a guest of the palace? She trembled at the idea, and with outrage, nothing more!

'So don't go,' Paris murmured.

'I have to.' She turned to face him, her smile dismissive. He was a good friend but the more time she'd spent back in Taquul, the more certain she'd become that she could never marry him. There was no doubt in her mind that he had her brother's best interests at heart, and yet that wasn't enough. She would speak to him about it, put the idea from his mind once and for all. His concern was worrying because it suggested he cared for her in a way that went beyond duty to the Sheikh, and the last thing she wanted to do was hurt Paris.

'Malik is right. We have to show the people of Ishkana

that we value this peace accord,' she said with quiet resolve. 'For our people, we must appear to be moving forward. We have to lead the way. How can we expect them to find peace in their hearts if we don't demonstrate it? I will go to Ishkana as a guest of the palace. I will attend state dinners and speak to the parliament. I will tour their ancient ruins and libraries and smile for the cameras. Is that what you want, Mal?'

He made a small noise of agreement. 'You know how I hate to ask it of you.'

She waved a hand through the air. 'If you hadn't asked, I would have suggested it. It's the best thing for everyone.'

'No, Johara. You will be exposed—'

'I'll be a guest of their King, will I not?'

Malik dipped his head forward in silent agreement.

'And staying in the palace?'

Another nod.

'So I presume His Majesty will vouch for my safety?'

'For what it's worth,' Paris responded dubiously.

At that, Malik held up a hand. 'I believe Amir is a man of honour.' The words were dark, troubled. 'He is a Haddad, so naturally I mistrust him, but I believe that, having invited you to the palace, he will go out of his way to ensure your safety.'

Johara's heart skipped a beat. 'Sheikh Amir invited me?'

Malik's smile was dismissive. 'A figure of speech. The suggestion came through diplomatic channels and no specific guest was mentioned. It was my idea that you should attend.'

'Of course.' She turned away again quickly, hoping she'd hid the look of disappointment she knew must be on her face. What had she expected? That he'd roll out the red carpet for her eight weeks after they'd last seen each other? He'd made his feelings perfectly clear that night.

It was a mistake. Her heart skipped another beat. It wasn't a mistake. It was the single greatest moment of her life and she wouldn't let him take that away from her. Oh, she desperately wished that they weren't who they were—the Haddads and Qadirs had hated each other for too long to allow it to be forgotten. But in that moment, it had been too perfect so even now she struggled to care.

'So you'll go?'

What would it be like to enter his kingdom? His palace? She'd never been to Ishkana. It wouldn't have been safe until recently. She'd seen photographs and knew much of its history, but to see it for herself? Curiosity sparked inside her, and she told herself the rushing of her pulse was owing to that alone.

'Yes, Mal. I'll go to Ishkana.'

In many ways, it was just like Taquul. The sand was the same colour, the heat was the same, the trees innately familiar. But as the limousine approached the palace she felt a flash of anticipation warm her skin. The approach to the palace was lined with palm trees, and on one side, a colourful market had been set up. The limousine was obliged to slow down as pedestrians meandered across the road, in no hurry to clear the way for the car. It gave her time to observe. An old woman sat in the shade cast from her brightly coloured market tent, an ancient spinning wheel before her. She moved effortlessly, each shift of the wheel an act she'd obviously repeated millions of times in her long lifetime. A vibrant red wool was being formed at one side. Another woman sat beside her, talking and cackling with laughter. The next stall showed spices, piled high in pyramids, just as vendors did at home, the next sold sweets—she recognised many of the same illicit delicacies she'd been introduced to by the gardening staff who'd tended the maze.

As the car neared the palace gates, she saw something that broke her heart. Several people stood in a cluster, shaded by a large, old umbrella. Their clothes were poor, their faces grubby and bodies frail. She turned to the driver, leaning forward. 'Stop the car.'

He pressed the brakes, looking over his shoulder. 'Madam?'

'A moment.' She spoke with all the authority she could conjure, unlocking her door and stepping out. The sun beat down on her relentlessly, causing a bead of perspiration to break out on her brow. She wiped at it but continued to walk to the group. There were perhaps eighteen people. She was conscious of one of the palace guards stepping out of the car and following behind her—she resented his intrusion, and the suggestion that these people must be dangerous because they happened to be poor.

Fixing him with a cool stare, she turned back to the people at the gate and smiled. 'It's warm,' she said to a woman in perhaps her early thirties, nursing an infant on her hip. The child looked at Johara with enormous brown eyes.

'Very hot, yes.'

'You need some lemonade from the markets,' Johara said with a smile. The mother's eyes widened but she shook her head almost instantly.

'It's not possible.'

'Here.' Johara reached into the folds of her linen dress, removing enough bank notes to pay rent for a month. She handed them to the mother, who shook her head.

'Please, take it. Buy some food and drink.' She gestured to the group behind her. 'For all of you.'

'But…it's very generous…'

Johara's heart turned over, and simultaneously she felt a blade of anger pierce her. How could Amir sit in his palace and allow this kind of poverty to exist on his doorstep? True, Taquul wasn't perfect but this was so blatant! So heart-wrenching.

'I insist.' She leaned out and tousled the little boy's hair. He didn't react at first but then he giggled, so Johara did it again.

'He likes you,' the woman said wistfully. 'It's the first time he's smiled in days.'

'I'm sorry to hear it,' Johara murmured truthfully. 'He has a beautiful smile.'

She turned to leave but before she'd gone three steps, the woman arrested her. 'What is your name, miss?'

Johara paused, aware that it was a turning point. She'd come to this country to spread word of the alliance and reverse people's opinions; now was as good a time to start as any.

'Johara Qadir,' she said without inflection—not anger, not cynicism, not apology.

A rippled murmur travelled the group but the woman spoke over it. 'Thank you, Your Highness.' And she bowed low, but with a smile on her face, so Johara was glad the people knew who she was.

The security guard followed her back to the car, and as he opened the door he said firmly, 'You should not have done that, madam.'

Johara's surprise was obvious. In Taquul, a servant would never speak to a guest in such a manner! 'I beg your pardon, why exactly not?'

'Because it is dangerous and the Sheikh gave your brother his word you would be safe here. That means he will want to control every aspect of your safety. If you display a tendency to make such poor decisions he'll likely confine you to the palace.'

She stared at him in disbelief. 'Confine me…*me*…to the palace?'

The guard lifted his shoulders. 'We should go. He will be waiting.'

Emotions flooded Johara's body. *He will be waiting.* The idea of Amir waiting for her did unreasonable things to her pulse.

She slid into the car, waving at her newfound friend as the car drove through the palace gates, trying to work out why her nerves wouldn't settle.

This wasn't about him. He'd made it very clear that he regretted what had happened between them and she had no choice but to accept that, to feel as he did.

Johara held her breath, marvelling at all the many ways in which the palace differed from the photographs she'd seen. Oh, it was enormous and impossibly grand, she knew parts of it had been constructed in the fifth century—the old stone foundations and underground tunnels and caverns rumoured to run all the way to the mountains—but the rest had been completed in the sixteen hundreds; enormous white stone walls with gold details formed an impressive façade. The windows were arched, the roofs shaped to match with colours of gold, turquoise and copper. Around the entire palace there was a moat of the most iridescent water, such a glorious pale blue it reminded her of the clearest seas of the Mediterranean.

She peered at it as they drove over the moat, then fixed her attention on the palace. The car stopped at a large golden door. Servants and guards stood to the ready and at the top of the stairs, him.

Amir.

His Majesty, Sheikh of Ishkana. Nerves fired through her but she refused to let them show, especially to the bossy security agent who'd told her she shouldn't have stopped to speak to the poor people at the gate. Since when was compassion forbidden?

The security agent opened the door without meeting her eyes and she stepped from the car, conscious of everything in that moment. Her dress, her hair, the fact *he* was staring at her and that everyone was watching them. Conscious of the photographer who stood poised to take an official photograph that would be printed in all the newspapers in both countries and around the world the following morning.

Most conscious of all though of Amir as he moved down the stairs towards her, his eyes not leaving her face, his face so familiar, so achingly familiar, that she could barely remember to act impassive.

It took all her self-control to stay where she was, a look of polite calm on her face. He extended a hand in greeting; she placed hers in it. The world stopped spinning all over again. Arrows drove through her skin. Her mouth was dry, breathing painful. She stared at him in bewilderment—she hadn't thought he'd still be able to affect her like that. She'd thought knowing who he was and how he felt about her might have changed…something.

She pulled her hand away as though he'd burned her, with no idea if the photographer had succeeded in capturing a suitably friendly photograph—and not particularly caring.

'Welcome, Princess,' he murmured, and, though it was a perfectly acceptable thing to say, she felt her skin crawl, as though he were condemning her title just as he had her name on that last night. 'Johara.' He'd spat it at her and she felt that again now.

'Thank you.' She didn't flinch.

'Smile for the camera,' he said quietly, leaning down so only she caught the words. She looked in the direction he'd nodded, eyeing off the photographer and lifting her lips in a practised smile. They stood there for a moment before the Sheikh put his hand to the small of her back, to guide her to the palace. It was too much. She wanted to jerk herself away from the simple contact, or she wanted to throw herself at his feet and beg him to do so much more.

She did neither.

Her upbringing and training kicked in; she put one foot in front of the other until she reached the top of the steps and then beyond them, into the cool corridor of the palace. Then, and only then, when out of sight of photographers, did she casually step beyond his reach.

If he noticed, or cared, he didn't show it. 'How was your flight?'

Like you care. The acerbic rejoinder died on the tip of her tongue. This would never work if she went out of her way to spar with him. 'Fine. Easy.'

'Easier still when we can repair and reopen the mountain roads; the drive will take a matter of hours.'

Johara looked towards him. 'That's what you intend?'

He began to move deeper into the palace and she followed after him. 'Why not? There were always easy links between our people. It's only as a result of the conflict that these have been shut down.'

'And trade?' she prompted.

'Naturally.'

She nodded, considering this. 'Even as the peace seems so tenuous?'

'I expected it would.' He shrugged. 'Surely you didn't truly believe it would be smooth sailing simply because Malik and I signed an accord?'

Her brow furrowed as she considered that. 'I…had hoped.'

'Yes.' The word was delivered enigmatically. 'You had hoped.'

'You're still cynical about this?'

They reached a pair of thick, dark wood doors, at which four guards stood sentinel. He gestured for her to precede him. She did so, without looking where she was going, so when she stepped into the space she was completely unprepared for what awaited her. She drew in a sharp breath, wonderment filling her gaze. She hadn't been paying attention; it had felt as though they were moving deeper into the palace, yet this room was a sanctuary of green. A stream ran in front of them, covered by dark timber bridges. The walls were dark wood, but filled with greenery. Vines had tentacles that reached across everything. Johara reached out and ran her fingers over the velvety surface of one of the plants.

Amir watched Johara.

'What is this?' She turned to face him, a smile unknowingly lifting her lips. It was impossible to feel anything but uplifted in this room.

'A private hall, now just for my use. It's one of the oldest spaces in the palace.'

She nodded, looking upwards, where several openings showed views of the sky. She could only imagine how stunning it would be in the evening.

'I'd never heard of it. It's not in any of the information we have.' Her cheeks grew hot. 'The texts, I mean.'

He lifted a brow. 'You've been studying my country?'

'As children, my brother and I were taught much about Ishkana.'

'And how to hate us?'

Her eyes flashed. 'As you were taught to hate us.'

'A lesson that I never really understood until I was twelve years old.'

She stared at him blankly.

Amir moved deeper into the room. 'The age I was when my parents were assassinated.'

Her heart squeezed for the boy he'd been. She wanted to offer condolences, to tell him how sorry she was, but both sentiments seemed disingenuous, given the strained nature of their relationship. So instead, she said, 'That must have been very difficult.'

He didn't respond. His profile was autocratic, his features tight. Where was the man she'd made love to in the maze? It felt like such a long time ago. Then, she'd had no inhibitions, no barriers. To him she would have known exactly what to say, without second-guessing herself.

'This room is completely private—for my use only, and for those guests I choose to invite here with me.' He tilted a gaze at her. 'I'm sure you are aware of how difficult it is to have true privacy in a palace.'

'Yes,' she agreed, looking around. The more she looked, the more she saw and loved. In the far corner, an old rug had been spread, gold and burgundy in colour, and against it, sumptuous pillows were spread. 'Thank you for showing it to me.'

He turned to face her, his eyes glittering like onyx in his handsome face.

'I wanted to speak to you. Alone.'

Her body went into overdrive. Blood hummed just beneath her skin, her heart slammed into her ribs and her knees began to feel as though they were two distinct magnetic poles. She walked slowly and deliberately towards the centre of the room, where an enormous fiddle leaf fig was the centrepiece. 'Did you, Amir?'

Using his name felt like both a rebellion and a comfort. She didn't look at him to see his reaction.

'It's been two and a half months since the masquerade.'

She studied the detailed, intricate veins in the leaves of the fig tree, her eyes tracing their patterns, every fibre of her being focussing on not reacting visibly to his statement.

'So you would know by now.'

'Know?'

'If there were any consequences to that night.'

Consequences? Her brain was sluggish. The heat, and having seen him again, made her feel a thousand things and none of them was mentally acute, so it took a few seconds for his meaning to make sense. Her breath snagged in her throat as she contemplated what he meant—something which hadn't, until that moment, even occurred to her. 'You mean to ask if I'm pregnant?'

The room seemed to hush. The gentle vines no longer whispered, the water beneath them ceased to flow, even the sun overhead felt as though it grew dim.

'Are you?'

Something painful shifted in her belly. She swallowed past a lump in her throat, turning to face him slowly. 'And if I were, Amir?' This time, when she said his name, she was conscious of the way he reacted, heat simmering in his eyes.

'I will not speak in hypotheticals.'

It was so like him. She felt a ridiculous burst of anger at his refusal to enter into a 'what if?'. 'No, that's not fair. You asked the question, I'm entitled to ask mine back. What would you do if I were pregnant?'

His face became shuttered, impossible to read, unfamiliar and intimidating. 'What would you have me do?'

She should have expected that. 'No, I'm asking what you would *want* to do.'

'Are you hoping I'll say something romantic, Johara? Do you wish me to tell you that I would put aside our ancient feud and marry you, for the sake of our child's future?'

Her lips parted. The image he painted was painful and somehow impossible to ignore. She shook her head even when she wasn't sure what she felt or wanted.

'Even for the sake of our child, I would not marry you. I couldn't. As much as I hate your family, you deserve better than that.'

Curiosity barbed inside her. 'You think marriage to you would be a punishment?'

'Yes. For both of us.'

'Why, Amir?'

He moved closer, and she held her breath, waiting, wanting, needing. 'Because I would never forgive you, Johara.' It was just like the first time he'd said her name. An invocation, a curse, a whip lashing the air in the room and crashing finally against the base of her spine.

'For what? What exactly have I done that requires forgiveness?'

'It is not what you've done.'

'But who I am? Born to the Qadir royal family?'

The compression of his lips was all the confirmation she needed.

'And what we shared changes nothing?'

'What we shared was wrong. It should never have happened.'

'How can you say that when it felt so right?'

His eyes closed for a moment then lanced her with their intensity. 'It was just sex.'

She stared at him in surprise. It was such a crude thing to say, and so wrong. She hadn't expected it of him.

'You weren't a virgin. You knew what sex was about.'

Her eyes hurt. It took her a second to comprehend that it was the sting of tears. She blinked furiously, refusing to give in to such a childish response.

'So that night meant nothing to you?'

He stared at her without responding. Every second that stretched between them was like a fresh pain in her heart.

'I'm not here to discuss anything besides the possibility that you conceived our child.'

Her heart lurched. She couldn't help it—out of nowhere an image of what their baby might look like filled her eyes, all chubby with dark hair and fierce dark eyes. She turned away from him, everything wonky and unsteady.

'I'm not pregnant, Amir. You're off the hook completely.'

She heard his hiss of relief, a sharp exhalation, as though he hadn't been breathing properly until then. She wanted to hurt him back, to make him feel as she did, but she feared she wasn't properly armed. How could one hurt a stone wall? And whatever she'd perceived in him on the night of the masquerade, she could see now that he was impenetrable. All unfeeling and strong, unyielding and determined to stay that way.

'If that's all, I'd like to be shown to my suite now.'

CHAPTER FIVE

'It is called *albaqan raghif*,' he said quietly, his eyes on her as she fingered the delicate piece of bread, his words murmured so they breathed across her cheek. She resisted the impulse to lean closer. This was the first she'd seen of him since their discussion earlier that day. For most of the day, she'd been given a tour of the palace by a senior advisor, shown the ancient rooms—the library, the art galleries, the corridors lined with tapestries so like those that hung in the palaces of Taquul. Looking at them had filled her with both melancholy and hope. A sadness that two people so alike and with such a richly shared history could have been so combative for so long, and hope that their shared history would lay the foundations for a meaningful future peace.

Now, sitting at the head of the room with him, various government ministers in attendance, she concentrated on what she'd come here for—this was a state visit and she the representative of Taquul—how she felt about the man to her right was not important. 'We have something similar in Taquul.' She reached for a piece of the pecan bread and bit into it. She concentrated on the flavours and after she'd finished her mouthful said, 'Except ours generally has different spices. Nutmeg and cardamom.'

'My mother made it like that,' Amir said with obvious surprise.

She took another bite and smiled at him politely. 'This is very good too.'

His eyes narrowed. 'But you prefer it the way you're used to.'

'I didn't say that.'

Silence stretched between them, all the more noticeable for how much conversation was swirling around the room. The mood was, for the most part, festive. Some ministers had treated her with suspicion, a few even with open dislike, but generally, people had been welcoming. It saddened her to realise how right Amir had been—the peace would not come easily. Prejudices died hard.

'I'm sorry your brother sent you.'

She was surprised by the words. She squared her shoulders, careful not to react visibly. 'You'd prefer I hadn't come?'

He angled his face to hers. 'As I'm sure you would have wished to avoid it.'

'On the contrary—' she reached for her wine glass '—I relished the opportunity.'

His eyes held hers curiously.

'I've heard a lot about Ishkana. All my life, stories have been told of your people, your ways, your ancient cities. To be here now is an exercise in satisfying my curiosity.'

He lifted his brows. 'What are you curious about?'

'Oh, everything.' She sipped her wine. 'The ruins of *wasat*, the wall that spans the *sarieun sea*, the theatres in the capital.' She shook her head, a smile playing about her full red lips. 'I know there won't be a chance on this visit, but in time, with continued peace between our people, these landmarks could open up.'

He appeared to consider that for a moment. 'Yes. In time.'

'And our historical sites will be open to your people as well.'

He regarded her for several long moments, then sighed. 'You are an optimist.'

She laughed softly, spontaneously. 'Am I?'

Photographers were not permitted at royal banquets. It was a long-established protocol and even in this day of cell phones no cameras were used during meals. If anyone had taken a photo in that second though it would have captured two royals with their faces close together, their eyes latched, a look of something very like intimacy in their position. To a few of those present, the idea of the powerful, feared and adored Sheikh Amir Haddad sharing a meal with the Princess of Taquul was likely a bitter pill to swallow.

'If I am,' she murmured, after several seconds, 'then you must be too.'

His cxprcssion was unchangcd. 'I don't think I'vc cvcr been accused of that.'

'It's not an accusation so much as an observation,' she corrected.

'Fine. That has never been…observed…of me before.'

'Doesn't it take a degree of optimism to proceed with a peace treaty? You must believe it will succeed or why bother with all this?' She gestured around the room, as if rousing them both, reminding them of where they were and how many people were watching.

Both separated a little, straightening in their seats. 'Acknowledging the necessity of something has no bearing on its likely success.'

'I take it back. I think I was right the first time we met. You're a cynic.'

'*That* I have been called frequently.'

The air between them seemed to spark. Awareness flooded Johara's body. Sitting close to him, speaking like this, she found the tension almost unbearable. She felt as though her skin was alive with an itch that she wanted to scratch and scratch and scratch.

The evening was long. After the dinner—which spanned six courses—there were speeches. The trade minister, the foreign minister, the culture minister. Johara sat beside Amir and listened, a polite smile on her face even when many small, barbed insults were laid at her country's feet. She wanted to respond to each that it took two to tango—a war couldn't be continued at only one country's insistence. Wrongs had been perpetrated on both sides. But all the while, the knowledge of what the man beside her had lost at her uncle's hand kept her silent.

She nodded politely, reminding herself again and again that her place in all this was not to inflame tensions so much as to soothe them. A necessary part of the peace process would involve humility—from both sides. The thought made her smile. Imagining Sheikh Amir Haddad humbling himself was not the easiest thing to do.

Finally, when all the speeches had been made, Johara stood. She ignored the small insults she'd heard and focussed on the bigger picture, and the fact Amir had invited her here.

'I'm gratified to sit here with you as a representative of my brother, Sheikh Malik Qadir, and the people of Taquul. I hope this is the first of many such events enjoyed by our people in this new age of peace and understanding.' She paused and smiled, her eyes skimming the room before coming to rest on Amir. He didn't return her smile and the expression on his chiselled face made her pulse rush through her body. 'I'm grateful for the hospitality of your kingdom, your people, and your Sheikh.' She wrenched her eyes away from him with difficulty. 'I look forward to getting to know the ways of your people better.'

When she sat down, it was to the sound of muted applause. Even that earned a wry smile from her, though she dipped her head forward to hide it. Only Amir caught the look, his eyes still trained on her face.

As was the custom, he led her from the room, the official engagement at an end. It would be ordinary for him to hand her off as soon as they'd left the palace hall, and yet he didn't. He continued to walk with her. On either side, they were flanked by enormous flower arrangements—filled with natives of the region, blooms, foliage, pomegranate, citrus, all in their infancy so the fruit was miniature and fragrant. There were security personnel too, carefully watchful, discreet and respectful, but Amir felt their presence with a growing sense of frustration.

At the bottom of the stairs that led to the wing of the palace reserved for visiting dignitaries, he paused, wondering at the sense of hesitation that gripped him.

'You must be tired.' His voice was gruff. He made an effort to soften it.

'Must I be?' She lifted both brows, her lips pursed.

'You arrived early this morning. It's been a big day.'

'Yes,' she agreed, looking sideways with a small sigh. 'But I'm not tired.'

Neither said anything. He could only look at her, the face held in profile, so beautiful, so achingly beautiful, but so full of the Qadir features that even as he yearned to reach for her he stayed where he was, his body taut, old hatreds deep inside his soul refusing to be quelled.

'In truth, I'm restless,' she said after a moment. 'I feel as though I've spent all day saying and doing what's expected of me and what I'd really like is just a few minutes of being my actual self.'

The confession surprised him.

'I don't suppose you have a maze I could go and get lost in for a bit?'

It was said light-heartedly, as a joke, but he couldn't fail to feel jolted by the reminder of that damned maze.

'No.' Too gruff again. He shook his head. This was no good. How could she be so effortlessly charming despite their long, bitter past? 'We have something even better.'

She put a hand on her hip, drawing his attention downwards, to her waist and the curves that had driven him crazy long before he'd known who she was. 'I doubt that.'

His laugh was deep and throaty. 'Want to bet?'

'Sure. Show me.'

What was he doing? He should tell her to go to bed; in the morning, she'd have another busy day. But a thousand fireworks seemed to be bursting beneath his skin. He wanted to be alone with her, even when he knew every reason he should fight that desire.

'May I go and change first?'

His lips tugged downwards. 'Your Highness, you're here as my guest. You do not need to ask my permission for anything.'

He'd surprised her. She bit down on her lip and he had to look away, before impulses overtook him and he dropped his head to kiss her. It would have felt so natural and easy.

'I'll wait here.'

She nodded once then turned, walking up the wide, sweeping staircase. He couldn't help but watch her departure.

Fifteen minutes later, Johara was ready. Having played the part of dutiful princess all day, she had found it a sheer, blissful relief to slip out of the couture dress she'd worn to the state dinner and pull on a pair of simple black trousers and an emerald-green blouse, teamed with simple black leather ballet flats. It was the kind of outfit she would wear in New York—dressy enough to escape criticism but comfortable and relatable. Her hair had been styled into an elegant braid that wrapped around her head like a crown to secure the actual crown she'd worn—enormous diamonds forming a crescent above her head. She deftly removed the two dozen pins that had been used to secure it, laying the tiara on the dressing table, then letting her hair fall around her shoulders in loose voluminous waves.

With more time, she might have washed her face clean of the make-up she wore, but impatience was guiding her, making her work fast. As she walked back down the staircase, she only had eyes for Amir. He was standing exactly where she'd left him, dressed in the formal robes he'd worn to dinner, his swarthy complexion and the jet black of his hair forming a striking contrast to the snowy white robes.

All night he'd been businesslike, treating her as though they had no history beyond that of their countries, but now, there was more. He was incapable of shielding his response to her—the way his eyes travelled her body with a slow, possessive heat, starting with her face, which he studied with an intensity that took her breath away, then shifting lower, moving over the curves of her breasts, the indent of her waist, the generous swell of her hips, all the way down to her feet as she walked, one step at a time, holding the handrail for fear she might stumble. And as his eyes moved, heat travelled the same path, setting fire to her bloodstream so by the time she reached him she felt as though she were smouldering.

'Well?' Her voice shook a little; she didn't care. 'What do you have to rival the maze?'

His eyes lifted to her lips and she didn't breathe—she couldn't—for several long seconds. Her lungs burned.

He was going to kiss her. His eyes were so intent on her lips, his body so close—when had that even happened?—

his expression so loaded with sensuality that memories weaved through her, reminding her of what they'd shared.

She waited, her face upturned, her lips parted, her blood firing so hard and fast that she could barely think, let alone hear. She knew she should step backwards, move away from him—this was all too complicated—but she couldn't. She wouldn't. Just as the hand of fate seemed to guide them in the maze, a far greater force was at work now.

She expelled a shuddering breath simply because her lungs needed to work, and with the exhalation her body swayed forward a little, not intentionally and not by much, but it brought her to him, her breasts brushing to his chest lightly, so that her nipples hummed at the all too brief contact.

'Johara.' He said her name with intent, with surrender, and with pain. It was all too hard. Where she could push the difficulties aside, at least temporarily, he appeared unable to. He swallowed so his Adam's apple moved visibly, then stepped backwards, his face a mask of discipline, his smile a gash in his handsome face.

Disappointment made her want to howl *No!* into the corridor. She did nothing.

'Your Highness.' He addressed her formally, gesturing with the upturned palm of his hand that she should precede him down the corridor. Her legs felt wobbly and moist heat pooled between her thighs, leaving her in little doubt of just how desperately she wanted him.

She moved in the direction he'd indicated, and when he fell into step beside her he walked closely, close enough that their arms brushed with each stride, so heat and tension began to arrow through her, spreading butterflies of desire and hope in her gut. But why hope? What did she want? He was—or had been until recently—the enemy.

Not my enemy.

No, not her enemy. Though she'd accepted the war between their countries and the family feud that had defined the Qadirs and Haddads for generations, she had felt no personal hatred for him, nor his parents. The fact their countries had been at war until recently wasn't enough of a reason to ignore her instincts and her desires.

But for Amir, their history was so much worse. Where she had no personal wrong to resent him for, he'd lost his parents because of her uncle's malicious cruelty. His hatred for her family was understandable. But did he have to include her in that?

What did she want? The question kept circling around and around and around her mind, with no answer in sight. After several minutes, they reached a wide-set doorway, thrown open to the desert evening. He stood, waiting for her to move through it first, his manners innate and old-fashioned.

She stepped into the cool night air as Amir spoke to the servants. 'We are not to be followed.'

There was a pause and then a deferential nod of agreement. Johara turned away, amused to imagine what they must think—their Sheikh going out of the palace with a Qadir? Did they suspect Johara, all five and a half feet of her, posed a threat to the man?

Her lips curved in a smile at the notion, a smile that still hovered on her lips when he joined her. 'Care to share the joke?'

'I was just thinking how suspicious your guards looked,' she murmured, nudging him with her elbow, so his eyes fell to hers. Heat passed between them.

'You are from Taquul,' he said simply.

She ignored the implication. 'As though I might have a three-foot scabbard buried in here somewhere.' She ran her hands over her hips, shaking her head at the preposterous idea.

'I take it you don't?'

Her laugh was soft. 'You're welcome to check, Amir.'

As soon as she said the words she wished she could unsay them. She lifted a hand to her lips and stopped walking, staring at him with eyes that offered a silent apology. 'I didn't mean for you to...'

But he stared at her with a look that was impossible to read, his breath audible in the stillness of the night.

'It wasn't an invitation?'

Her heart was beating way too fast. How could it continue at that pace?

'We agreed that night was a mistake,' she reminded him.

'No, *I* said it was a mistake. *You* said it felt right.'

Her lips parted at the reminder. 'Yes, I did say that.'

He turned to look back to the palace. They'd moved down the steps and into a garden fragrant with night-flowering jasmine and citrus blossoms, out of sight of the guards. But he turned, moving them further, into an area overgrown with trees. It was unlike the maze in Taquul. Where that was all manicured and enchanting for its formal shape—like a perfect outdoor room—this was more akin to something from a fairy tale. Ancient trees with trunks as wide as six of Amir's chests grew gnarled and knotted towards a sky she knew to be there only because it *must* be there, not because she could see it. The foliage of each tree formed a thick canopy, creating an atmosphere of darkness. Were it not for Amir's hand, which he extended to take hers, she might have lost her footing and fallen. But he guided her expertly, leading her along a narrow path as if by memory. Deeper in the forest, the beautiful fragrance grew thicker and here there was a mesmerising birdcall, like a bell and a whip, falling at once. She paused to listen to it.

'The *juniya.*' He said the word as most people said her name, with a soft inflection on the 'j', so it was more like 'sh'.

'Juniya,' she repeated, listening as at least two of them began to sing back and forth.

'They're native to this forest. In our most ancient texts they are spoken of, depicted in some of the first scrolls of the land. But they exist only here, in the trees that surround the palace.'

'I can't believe how verdant the land is here.' She shook her head. 'It's like the foot of the mountains.'

'That's where the water comes from.'

'The moat around the palace?'

'And in my private hall,' he agreed, reminding her of the little stream that flowed through that magical place he'd taken her to when first she'd arrived at the palace—had that only been earlier on this same day? 'There's an underground cavern that reaches the whole way; the river travels through it. In ancient times, it was used to send spies into Taquul,' he said with a tight smile she could just make out. They continued to walk once more, and eventually the canopy grew less apparent, light from the stars and moon reaching them, so she could see his face more clearly.

'But not any more?'

'It's more closely guarded on the other side.' He laughed. 'And our own guards do the same,' he added, perhaps wondering if she might take the information back to her brother, to use it as a tactical strength against him. The thought brought a soft sigh to her lips.

'Even now in peace?' she prompted him.

'Always.' The words vibrated with the depth of his seriousness. 'The water runs underground to the palace, the heart of our government. We will protect it with our lives.'

A shiver ran down her spine, his passion igniting something inside her.

'The war went on for a long time. It's only natural to think like that.'

'You consider yourself immune from the effects of it?'

She lifted her slender shoulders. 'I've spent a lot of time in New York. In truth, I've always felt I straddled two worlds, with one foot in my Taquul heritage and another in my mother's America. That isn't to say I feel the connection to my people any less, nor that I don't see the seriousness of the war, but I see it—at times—with something akin to an outsider's perspective.'

He reached out and grabbed an overhanging leaf, running his fingertips over it before handing it to Johara. She took it, lifting it her nose and inhaling gratefully. The smell was sweet and intoxicating. 'With an outsider's clarity, perhaps,' he said darkly.

It jolted her gaze to his face. 'You think I have greater clarity than you in this matter?'

He stopped walking, his expression tight. 'I think war has become a way of life,' he said with a nod. 'Like you said. Those habits will die hard.'

'It's ironic,' she murmured softly, 'that you remind me of him, in many ways.'

He braced. 'Who?'

'My brother.'

His expression was forbidding. 'I'm not sure I appreciate that.'

'I didn't expect you would, but it's true. I think it's probably an important thing to remember in war. You were the one who said that—we're more alike than we are different.'

'I was speaking generally.'

She shrugged once more. 'And I'm speaking specifically.'

'Don't.' He shook his head, his eyes locked to hers. 'Don't compare me to him.'

'He's my brother,' she reminded him. 'You can stand here with me, showing me this incredible place—' she gestured beyond her '—but you can't even speak his name?'

Amir stiffened. 'Believe me, Johara, I am conscious, every minute we're together, of who you are and what my being here with you means. You think I don't feel that I am, right this second, betraying my parents' memory?'

She sucked in a jagged breath, pain lancing her at the fact he could perceive anything to do with her as a betrayal of his parents. She spun away from him, looking back towards the palace. It was too far to see. She knew it would be there, beyond the enormous trees, glowing like a golden beacon. But it was no beacon, really. Not for her. The pain would be impossible to escape so long as she was here in Ishkana.

Her voice wobbled. 'I think you're honouring their memory by striving for peace. I think they'd be proud of you.'

His breath was ragged, filling the air behind her. His hand curved around her wrist, spinning her gently back to face him. 'Perhaps,' he agreed. 'But that doesn't make this any easier.'

His face showed the burden of his thoughts, the weight of his grief. She looked at him for several seconds and then went to pull her wrist away. He didn't release her.

'You are a Qadir,' he said darkly, as if reminding himself.

She lifted her chin, fixing him with a determined glance. 'And you are a Haddad. What's your point?'

'When my parents died, I could not show how I felt. I was twelve years old—still a child—but, here in Ishkana, old enough to become Sheikh. My life changed in a thousand ways. There was no time to grieve, to mourn, to process the loss of my parents. We were at war.' His thumb began to pad the flesh of her inner wrist, rhythmically, softly, but almost as though he didn't realise he was doing it.

'I used to fall asleep at night with only one thought to comfort me.'

A lump had formed in her throat, making it difficult to swallow. 'What was that?'

'That I would hate the Qadirs and what they had done for the rest of my life.' His eyes seemed to probe hers, his expression tense—his whole body, in fact, radiated with tension.

'You were twelve.' The words came out as a whisper. She cleared her throat and tried again. 'Of course you were angry.'

'Not angry,' he corrected. 'I was calm. Resolute. Determined.' When he breathed, his chest moved, brushing her.

'And yet you've signed a peace treaty.'

'For as much as I hate your family, I love my country and its people. For them I will always do what is best.'

Her heart felt as though it were bursting into a thousand pieces. Her stomach hurt. 'I don't know what to say.' She dropped her gaze to his chest, unable to bear his scrutiny for a moment longer. 'My uncle was imprisoned by my family after his despicable action—where he still languishes, at my brother's behest. He had no support from my parents, my brother, and certainly not from me. Our war was an economic one, a war of sanctions rather than violence.' She tilted her head, willing his defiance. 'Oh, there are the renegades on the borders and of course the military posturing that seems to go hand in hand with war, but to stoop to something so violent and...and...wrong as assassinating your parents? That was my uncle's madness, Amir. If you are to hate anyone—and I cannot stress enough how futile and damaging that kind of hatred is—but if you insist on hating anyone, have it be Johar. Not every single person who shares his surname. Not me.'

He groaned, low and deep in his throat. 'What you say makes perfect sense.'

'And yet you don't agree?' Her words sounded bleak.

'I don't *want* to agree.'

She lifted her eyes back to his. 'Why not?'

'Because this ancient hatred I feel is the only thing that's been stopping me from doing what I wanted to do the second you arrived at the palace this morning.'

Her heart stopped racing. It thudded to a slow stop. 'Which is?'

His eyes dropped to her lips. 'I want to kiss you, Johara.'

Her heart stammered.

'I want to claim your mouth with mine. I want to lace my fingers through your hair and hold your head still so I can taste every piece of you, bit by bit, until you are moaning and begging me, surrendering to me completely as you did in the maze.'

Her knees were knocking together wildly, her stomach filled with a kaleidoscope of butterflies.

'I want to strip these clothes from your body and make love to you right here, with only this ancient forest to bear witness to whatever madness this is.'

She could barely breathe, let alone form words. 'Would that be so bad?'

His eyes closed, as if it were the worst thing she could have said. 'The first time was a mistake, but I didn't know who you were then.'

'Now you do, and you still want me,' she challenged softly, aware she was walking on the edge of a precipice, so close to tumbling over.

He swore softly in one of the dialects of his people. 'You deserve better than this. Better than for a man who can offer you nothing, wanting you for your body.'

She didn't—couldn't—respond to that.

'I can offer you nothing,' he reiterated. 'No future, no friendship beyond what is expected of us in our position. I cannot—will not—form any relationship that might jeopardise what I owe my people.'

'Damn it, Amir, I have no intention of doing anything to hurt your people…'

'Caring for you would compromise my ability to rule. There are lines here we cannot cross.'

She swallowed, the words he spoke so difficult to comprehend and yet, at the same time, on an instinctive level, they made an awful kind of sense. Amir had been running this country since he was twelve years old. His life was impossible for Johara to understand. But she knew about duty and sacrifice; she had seen both these traits ingrained into her brother, she understood how his country would always come first.

And it wasn't that he perceived *her* as a threat to the country. Not Johara, as a woman. Johara as a Qadir, as a member of the Taquul royal family. It was symbolic. The peace was new. His people would take time to accept it, to trust it, and if news of an affair between Amir and Johara were to break, it could threaten everything by stirring up strong negative feelings in response. Retaliation could occur.

The war had been too costly, especially on the border.

She closed her eyes and nodded, a sad shift of her head, because the futility of it all felt onerous and cumbersome.

'I don't hate you, Amir.' She pulled her hand out of his and this time he let her. Her flesh screamed in agony, begging to be back in his grip. Her stomach looped again and again. 'But you're right. I deserve better than to be the scapegoat for all the pain you've suffered in your life.' She straightened her spine and looked beyond him. 'Shall we go back to the palace now? I think I've seen enough for tonight.'

CHAPTER SIX

THE SUN WAS UNRELENTING, the sands from the deserts stirred into a frenzy and reaching them even here, on the outskirts of the city where one of the oldest libraries stood in existence. He'd had this added to the itinerary days before she arrived. Memories of the maze had been running thick and fast through his mind. The pride with which she'd spoken of her work with childhood literacy had been impossible to forget—her eyes had sparkled like diamonds when she'd discussed the initiative she'd put together.

He knew she'd find the library itself beautiful—the building was very old, the books, parchments, scrolls, tapestries and stone walls contained within dated back thousands of years, but more than that, there were the spaces that had been built in the last fifteen years, during his reign, specifically to make books and reading more accessible to the youth of Ishkana.

This was the last stop on what had been a day filled with formal events. So much polite meeting and greeting, smiling, posing for photographs, and all the while Johara's features had never shown a hint of strain or discomfort. Not at the proximity to a man who had been, as she claimed, using her as a 'scapegoat'. Nor in exhaustion from the heat, nor after hours on her feet in dainty high heels that must surely pinch.

Even now, she listened with a rapt expression on her face as his Minister for the Arts explained how the library spaces worked.

Impatience coursed through Amir's veins. He no longer wanted to stand to the side as she was shown through the library. He wished everyone to leave, so that it was just Johara and him, so that Amir could tell her what he'd hoped when he'd had the rooms built, so that he could tell her his favourite memories of being here in this building. Even when he was a boy, it had been one of his most delighted-in haunts.

'What an incredible programme,' she said, almost wistfully, running a finger over the bottom of a windowsill. Beyond them, the classroom was full of children—some of the poorest of Ishkana. Buses were sent each morning to various districts, a bell loudly proclaiming its arrival, giving all children who wished it a chance to get on board.

'We are working towards universal education,' Amir found himself saying, moving closer, half closing the Minister for the Arts from the conversation and drawing Johara's eyes to his. It was only then that a sense of reserve entered her expression—just a hint of caution in the depths of her eyes but enough for him to see it and recognise it. 'It was a passion of my father's.' He took a step down the marble corridor, urging her to follow him. It was impossible not to remember the group that followed them—staff, servants, media—and yet he found himself tuning them out, thinking only of Johara as they walked.

'Education?' she prompted, falling into step beside him.

'Yes. The benefits to the whole country can't be underestimated.'

'I agree,' she said, almost wistfully.

'This is the state library,' he continued. 'So we were limited in the scope of what we could achieve. Naturally there is much here that is protected from too much public access—the oldest texts are stored on the second and third floors and kept out of the way of children.' His smile was genuine.

She nodded. 'Naturally.'

'This is just an example of what we're prioritising, and serves only the inner-city children. Beyond this, we've built twenty-seven libraries in the last decade, starting in the poorest regional communities and working our way up. The libraries aren't just for books, though. There are computers and tablets, lessons in how to use both, and for the children, six days per week, classes are offered. Book hiring is incentivised, with small tax breaks offered to regular borrowers.'

She gasped. 'Really?'

'Oh, yes. Really.'

'What an incredible initiative.'

He lifted his shoulders. 'Reading is a habit that brings with it many benefits.'

She seemed to miss her step a little. He reached out and put a hand under her elbow, purely to steady her, but the sparks that shot through him warned him from making such a stupid mistake—particularly in public.

'You must feel likewise to have established your childhood literacy initiative?'

'Yes.' Her smile was more natural. She casually pulled her arm away, putting a little more distance between them.

'You enjoy reading?'

She kept her eyes straight ahead, and didn't answer. Instead, after a moment, they came to the opening of a large room, this one filled with straight desks at which students could study during term time, and dark wooden walls filled with reference texts.

'What a lovely room.'

He wondered if she was changing the subject intentionally, but let it go. There would be time later to ask her again—he wasn't sure why it mattered, only it felt as if she was hiding something from him and he didn't want that. He wanted to know…everything.

The thought almost made *him* miss a step, for how unwelcome it was.

Why? What was the point? He didn't want to analyse it, he knew only that his instincts were pushing him towards her, not away, and he could no longer tell what was right or wrong.

The rest of the library tour took forty-five minutes. At the end of it, he paused, with one look keeping the rest of their contingent at a distance, leading her away separately. 'Would you like to see what's upstairs?'

'The ancient texts?'

He dipped his head.

'I…would have thought they were too precious to share with someone like me.'

His stomach tightened. Because she was a Qadir? Why wouldn't she feel like that, particularly after the things he'd said the night before? 'They are not something we routinely display to foreign guests.' He deliberately appeared to misunderstand her. 'But would you like to see them?'

Her breath grew louder, her eyes uncertain. He could feel a battle raging within her, the same kind of battle that was being fought inside him. 'I would,' she said, finally, not meeting his eyes.

Without a response to her, he spun on his heel and stalked to the group. He addressed only Ahmed, giving brief instructions that the motorcade should wait twenty minutes—that he and the Princess were not to be disturbed.

It was a break from protocol, but nothing he couldn't explain later.

Before he could see the look of disapproval on Ahmed's face, Amir walked Johara towards a bank of elevators, pressing a button that immediately summoned a carriage. The doors swished open and he waited for her to step inside before joining her and pressing a gold button. Even the elevators were very old, built at the turn of the nineteenth and twentieth centuries. It chugged slowly, and he tried not to pay attention to how close they stood in the confines of the infrastructure.

The doors opened and he felt relief—relief to be able to step further away from her, to stop breathing in her scent, to be able to resist the impulse to touch her, just because she happened to be standing right in front of him.

'Many of these are relevant to your country,' he said, indicating one tapestry that hung opposite the elevator, dimly lit with overhead lights to preserve its beautiful threads.

She studied the pictures, a look of fascination on her features. He led her through the area, showing some of his favourite pieces.

'You sound as though you know this place like the back of your hand,' she said after ten minutes.

He smiled. 'I do. I came here often as a child. I loved to sit up here and read while my parents attended to business at parliament. I was fortunate that they indulged my every whim.' He laughed.

Her tone was teasing. 'Are you saying you were spoiled?'

'Actually, I wasn't.' He grinned. 'Only in this aspect—my mother found my love of books amusing.'

'Why?'

'Because for the most part, I preferred to be out of doors. I hated restriction. I liked to run and ride and swim and climb. In that way, I was cast in my father's image. But then, here at the library, I saw the opening to all these other worlds and found a different way to run and be free.'

She was transfixed by his words, her expression completely engaged by what he was saying. 'It was a catalyst for them. Seeing how I loved these texts, how they opened my eyes and mind—I still remember the conversation between them, travelling back to the palace one night, when my father remarked that every child should be able to lose themselves in a library as I seemed to want to.'

Johara paused, looking at a small book with a golden spine and beautiful cursive script.

'They were right.' Her voice was small.

'Was this similar to your own childhood?'

A beat passed, a pause which seemed somehow unnatural. 'I…spent my childhood undertaking ceremonial duties on behalf of the palace,' she said calmly. But too calm, as though her voice was carefully neutralised to hide any real feeling. He didn't speak, sensing that she would continue only if he stayed silent.

He was right. 'My mother died when I was six. I have vague memories of attending events with her. But after she passed, I was expected to take on her role.' Her smile was laced with mockery. 'Something you know about.'

'At such a young age?'

'I didn't question it at the time. My *amalä* had focussed a lot of my education on etiquette, socialising, on how to speak and be spoken to.' She shrugged as though it didn't matter. 'It was second nature to me.'

'But you were still a baby.'

She laughed. 'I was old enough.' Her brow furrowed. 'There wasn't much time for libraries and reading, nor even for studying. None of which was deemed particularly important for me anyway.'

Amir stopped walking, something like anger firing through him. 'So your education was sacrificed in order for you to cut ribbons and make speeches?'

'I sit on the board of many important charities and foundations,' she contradicted defensively, then dropped her head in a silent sign of concession. 'But yes. Essentially, you're correct.'

'And your brother?' He couldn't conceal his anger then. It whipped them both, drawing them closer without their knowledge.

'Mal had an education similar to yours, I imagine. Well rounded, with the best tutors in various subjects being flown in to instruct him. He was taught to be a statesman, a philosopher, to govern and preside over the country from when he was a very young boy.'

Amir wanted to punch something! 'That's grossly unfair.'

Johara's eyes flashed to his; he felt her agreement and surprise. 'It's the way of my people.'

'It's as though nothing has changed for *your people* in the last one hundred years.'

She lifted her shoulders. 'And Ishkana is so different?'

He stared at her as though she had lost her mind. 'Yes, Ishkana is different. You've seen the facilities we've created. You've heard me talk about the importance of books and education for children. Have you heard me say, at any point, "for boys", as opposed to "children"?'

She didn't speak. Her eyes held his, and something sparked between them.

'My grandfather made inroads to gender equality, but he was hampered—if you can believe it—by public opinions. By the time my father was Sheikh, the Internet had been born, and a homogenisation of attitudes was—I would have thought—inevitable. My mother was progressive, and fiercely intelligent. The idea of her skill set languishing simply because women weren't seen as having the same rights to education as men…'

'I am not languishing,' she interrupted. 'I get to represent causes that matter a great deal to me.'

He stared at her, not wanting to say what he was thinking, knowing his assessment would hurt her.

'What?' she demanded. 'Say what you're thinking.'

Surprise made him cough. How could she read him so well? What was this magic that burst around them, making him feel as though they were connected in a way that transcended everything he knew he *should* feel about her?

'Only that it sounds to me as though your representation is more about your position and recognisability than anything else.'

She jerked her head back as though he'd slapped her and he instantly wish he hadn't said such a cruel thing. He shook his head, moving a step closer, his lips pressed together.

'I'm sorry.'

'Don't.' She lifted a hand to his chest, her own breathing ragged. 'Don't apologise.'

They stood like that, so close, bodies melded, breath mingling, eyes latched, until Johara made a sort of strangled noise and stepped backwards, her spine connected with the firmness of a white marble wall.

'Don't apologise,' she said again, this time quieter, more pained. He echoed her movement, stepping towards her, his body trapping hers where it was, his own responding with a jerk of awareness he wished he could quell.

'You're right.' She bit down on her full lower lip, reminding her of the way she'd done that in the maze, and the way he'd sought it with his own teeth. 'I'm ornamental. Unlike your mother, I'm not fiercely intelligent. I can't even read properly, Amir. Educating me in a traditional way would have been a waste of effort. So my parents focussed on what I was good at, at my strengths—which is people. I serve my country in this way.'

He could hardly breathe, let alone speak. 'You were not even taught to read?'

'I was taught,' she corrected. 'But not well, and it didn't seem to matter until I was much older. At twelve, I sat some tests—and was diagnosed with severe dyslexia.' A crease formed between her brows. 'It wouldn't have made any difference if they'd discovered it earlier. It's not curable. My brain is wired differently from yours. I can read—passably—but it takes me longer than you can imagine and it will never be what I do for pleasure.' Her eyes tangled with his and she shook her head. 'Don't look at me like that.'

'How am I looking at you?' he interrogated gently.

'As though you pity me.' She pressed her teeth into her lip once more. 'I still love books—I listen to recordings whenever I can—and let me assure you, I derive the same pleasure from their pages as you do.'

He listened, but something was flaring inside him, something he hadn't felt in such a raw and violent form for a very long time. Admiration. Respect.

'This is why you founded the literacy initiative in New York?'

'Yes.' Her smile, as he focussed conversation on something that brought her joy, almost stole his breath. 'To help children. Even children like I was—if a diagnosis can be made early enough—will be spared years of feeling that they're not good enough, or smart enough.'

'And you felt these things.'

Her smile dropped. His anger was back—anger at her parents, and, because they were dead and no longer able to account for their terrible, neglectful parenting, anger at the brother who hadn't troubled himself to notice Johara's struggles.

'Yes.' Her eyes held defiance. 'I *used* to feel that way. But then I moved to America and I came to understand that the skills I have cannot be taught. I'm great with people. I'm great at fundraising. I can work a room and secure millions of dollars in donations in the space of a couple of hours. I can make a real difference in the world, Amir, so please, for the love of everything you hold dear, stop looking at me as though I'm an object of pity or—'

Something in the region of his chest tightened. 'Or?'

'Or I'll… I don't know. Stamp my foot. Or scream.' She shook her head. 'Just don't you dare pity me.'

He gently took her chin between his finger and thumb. 'I don't pity you, Johara.' His eyes roamed her face and, in the distance, he could hear the beating of a drum, low and solid, the tempo rhythmic and urgent all at once. It took him moments to realise there was no drum, just the beating of his heart, the torrent of his pulse slamming through his body.

'You don't?'

'I admire you,' he admitted gruffly. 'I admire the hell out of you and damn it if I don't want to kiss you more than ever right now.'

Her knees could barely hold her. If he weren't standing so close, pinning her to the wall, she wasn't sure she would have trusted her legs to keep her upright. His face was so close, his lips just an inch from hers. She tilted her face, her own lips parting in an unspoken invitation, and she stared at him, hoping, wanting, every fibre of her being reverberating with need.

'How do you make me forget so easily?'

'Forget what?' Closer. Did she lift onto the tips of her toes or did he lower his face? Either way, her mouth could almost brush his now. Adrenalin surged through her veins, fierce and loud.

'Who you are.' He threw the words aside as though they were inconsequential, and then finally he kissed her, a kiss that was for him exultant and for her drugging. Her need for him obliterated every shred of rational thought, every ability to process what was happening. But even as his tongue slid between her lips, tangling with hers, and his knee nudged her legs apart, propping her up, her sluggish brain threaded his simple statement together. *Who you are.*

Who she was. It was so fundamental—her parentage, her lineage, her place in the Taquul royal family.

His hands gripped her hips, holding her possessively and almost fearfully, as though she might move away from him; he held her as though his life depended on her nearness. His kiss stole her breath and gave her life. She lifted her hands, tangling them behind his neck, her fingers running into the nape of his hair, pressing her breasts against his chest, her nipples tingling with remembered sensations.

How do you make me forget so easily?

But they couldn't forget. It wasn't that easy. He was a Haddad and she a Qadir and somewhere over the last one hundred years it had been written in stone that they should hate each other. Yet she didn't. She couldn't hate him. He'd done her no wrong and, more than that, she'd seen qualities that made her feel the opposite of hate. She *liked* him. She enjoyed spending time with him. She found talking to him hypnotic and addictive. And kissing him like this lit a thousand fires in the fabric of her soul.

But Amir would never accept her. He would always resent her, and possibly hate her. And that hatred would destroy her if she wasn't very, very careful. And what of her brother if he learned of this? Even her defiant streak didn't run that deep.

With every single scrap of willpower she possessed, Johara drew her hands between them and pushed at his chest, just enough to separate them, to give her breathing space.

'Your Majesty.' She intentionally used his title, needing

to remind him of what he claimed she made him forget. 'Nothing has changed since last night.' She waited, her eyes trying to read his face, to understand him better. 'Has it?'

His eyes widened, as though her reminder had caught him completely unawares. She could feel the power of his arousal between her legs, and knew how badly he wanted her. Yet he stepped backwards immediately, rubbing his palm over his chin.

'You're right, Princess.' His smile was self-mocking. 'That won't happen again.'

CHAPTER SEVEN

'IT'S ONLY THREE more days.' Malik's voice came down the phone line, in an attempt to offer comfort. He could have no way of knowing that, far from placating her, the reminder that the week she'd been invited to Ishkana for was half-way over would spark something a little like depression inside her belly.

She looked out of her magnificent bedroom window over an aviary very like the one in Taquul, and again felt how alike these two countries were—just as Amir had said.

'I know.' It was the end of a busy day, filled with commitments and engagements. She'd seen so much of the city, met so many politicians and leaders, and the more she saw of this country, the less contented she felt.

The war had been so futile.

This was a beautiful country, a beautiful people. They'd been hurt by the past, just as the people in Taquul had been. Not for the first time, frustration with her parents and grandparents gnawed at her. Why hadn't they been able to find a peaceful resolution sooner? Why had it rested on two men, one hundred years after the first shot was fired?

'What's it like?'

'It's…' A movement below caught her attention. She swept her gaze downwards, trying to catch it again. Something white in amongst the olive and pomegranate trees below. Another movement. Her heart recognised before her mind did.

Amir.

He moved purposefully towards one of the aviaries, his frame powerful, his movements everything that was masculine and primal. He opened the door, and made a gesture with his hand. A large bird, with a wingspan half the height of Amir, flew from the cage and did a circle above his head, above Johara, its eyes surveying what they could, before neatly returning and hooking its claws around Amir's outstretched arm. Its feathers were a pale, pearlescent cream with small flecks of light brown, its beak tipped in grey.

'What?' Malik was impatient. 'Terrible? Awful? Are you hating it?'

'No!' She had forgotten all about her brother, on the other end of the phone. She shook her head despite the fact he wasn't there to see her. 'It's…wonderful.'

Amir's lips moved; he was speaking to the bird. She wished, more than anything, that she could hear what he was saying.

'Wonderful?' Malik's surprise was obvious. She ignored it.

'Yes. I have to go now.'

'But—'

'I'll call you another time, okay?' She pressed the red button on her screen, her eyes fixed on Amir. She could not look away. The dusk sky created a dramatic backdrop to an already overpoweringly dramatic scene. With the falcon perched on his forearm, he looked every bit the powerful Emir. She held her breath as he began to move towards the palace, her eyes following every athletic step he took, her mind silently willing him to look towards her, to see her. And do what? She stared at him as though with her eyes alone she could summon him.

When he was almost beneath her, he looked up, his eyes sweeping the windows of her suite before locking to her. He stopped walking, and he stared at her as she had been staring at him.

Hungrily.

Urgently.

As though seeing one another were their sole means of survival.

He dipped his head a moment later, a bow of respect, and her heart stammered; he was going to go away again. She wanted to scream. Impatience and frustration were driving her mad. Since their kiss in the library, she'd barely seen him. Brief photo opportunities and nothing more. And at these interludes he was polite but went out of his way to keep a distance, not touching her, his smile barely reaching his eyes before he replaced it with a businesslike look.

But here, now, the same fire that had burned between them in the library arced through the sky, threatening to singe her nerve endings.

'I…' She said it so quietly she wasn't sure he'd hear. And she had no idea what she even wanted to say. Only that she didn't want him to walk away from her.

His eyes lifted, held hers a moment, and then he grimaced, as though he was fighting a war within himself. A moment later, he began to walk, disappearing from her view completely. She stamped her foot on the balcony and squeezed her eyes shut, gripping the railing tightly. Her heart was frantic and, ridiculously, stupid tears filled her throat with salt, threatening to douse her eyes. She blinked rapidly to ward them off, hating how he could affect her, hating how futile their situation was. Of all the men she had to meet, of all the men who had the ability to make her crazy with desire, why did it have to be a king who saw himself as her sworn enemy? A man who had every reason in the world to hate her family?

With a growling sound of impatience she stalked back into the beautiful suite of rooms she'd been appointed, deciding she'd take a cool shower. Three more days. She could get through this. And then what? Forget about Amir?

Her skin lifted with goosebumps. Unbidden, memories of the maze flooded her mind, filling her eyes with visions of him over her, his handsome, symmetrical face, she felt the movements of his body in hers, and she groaned, the shower forgotten. She closed her eyes, allowing the memories to overtake her, reliving that experience breath by breath until her skin was flushed and her blood boiling in her veins.

She would never forget about him. She would return to Taquul and he would return with her—a part of him would anyway. What they'd shared had been so brief yet in some vital way he'd become a part of her soul.

A knock drew her from her reverie. She turned her attention to the door, wondering what she must look like—a quick glance in the mirror confirmed her cheeks were flushed and her eyes sparkling. She pressed the backs of her hands to her cheeks, sucked in a breath and then opened the door.

If she'd been hoping for Amir—and of course, on some level, she had been—she was to be disappointed. A guard stood there, his impressive military medals on one shoulder catching her eye. Medals that had been won in the service of his army—against her country. Another blip of frustration. The war was over now, but the hurts went deep on both sides. Did this soldier hate her because of who she was and where she came from? It was impossible to tell. His face was impassive as he held a piece of cream paper towards her, folded into quarters.

'Thank you,' she murmured, offering him a smile—perhaps enough smiles given genuinely and freely could turn hatred to acceptance, and eventually fondness.

She waited until the door was clicked shut again, then unfolded the note.

Come to the West Gate. A

Owing to her dyslexia and his hastily scrawled handwriting, it took her several moments to read it and when she finished, her fingertips were unsteady, her breathing even more so. She flicked another glance to the mirror, running her hands across the simple outfit she wore—loose pants and a tunic—then over her hair, which was loose around her shoulders. She reached for some pins and secured it in a low bun, added a hint of lipstick and then moved to the door.

Athena was coming in as Johara opened the door.

'Your Highness? You're going somewhere?'

'I— For a walk,' she said with a small nod.

'Shall I accompany you?'

'No.' Johara's smile was reassuring, when inside she was panicking. The company of her servant—even one she considered a friend, like Athena—was the last thing Johara wanted! 'I'd like to be alone,' she softened the rebuke, reaching out and touching Athena's forearm. 'Goodnight.'

The West Gate was not difficult to find. She had a vague recollection of it having been pointed out to her on her first day, when she'd been given a thorough tour of the palace. She retraced the steps she remembered, until she reached a wall of white marble that stretched almost impenetrably towards the sky, creating a strong barrier to the outside world. Halfway along the wall there was a gate made of gold and bronze, solid and beautiful, with ancient calligraphy inscribed in its centre.

As she approached it she slowed, scanning for Amir. She couldn't see him. But to the right of the enormous gates there was a doorway, made to blend in completely with the wall. It was ajar. She moved towards it, then pushed at it. Amir stood waiting for her.

Her breath hitched in her throat. She'd come so quickly she hadn't paused to consider what she might say to him when she arrived.

Neither smiled.

'Thank you for coming.'

A frown quirked her brows. Had he thought she might not?

'You mentioned that you wanted to see the ruins of *wasat*. They're at their best at sunset.'

It was then that she became aware of a magnificent stallion behind him. Beneath the saddle there was a blanket over its back, gold and black, and a roll of fabric hung to one side. She could only imagine it contained the sorts of necessities one might need when riding horses in this harsh climate—water, a satellite phone.

'Are they—far from here?'

'No.' He gestured to the horse. 'Ride with me.'

It was a command. A shiver ran down her spine, and a whisper of anticipation. She eyed the horse, trying to remember the last time she'd been on the back of one—years. Many, many years. Her gaze flicked uncertainly to his.

'It's like riding a bike,' he said, a smile lifting his lips now, a smile that sent little bubbles popping inside her belly.

She walked towards the horse. It was magnificent. A shimmering black, it reminded her of a George Stubbs painting—all rippling muscles and intelligent eyes. She lifted a hand and ran it over his nose. The horse made a breathy noise of approval then dipped his head.

Amir watched, transfixed.

'He's beautiful.'

'He likes you,' Amir murmured, moving closer, pressing his own hand to the horse's mane, running his fingers over the coarse hair. 'Let me help you up.'

She was tempted to demur, but, looking at the sheer size of the horse, she knew it wouldn't be wise. Or possible.

'Thank you.'

He came to her side, his eyes probing hers. 'Ready?'

She nodded wordlessly.

He caught her around the waist easily, lifting her towards the horse so she could push one leg over and straddle it. Amir's hands lingered on her hips a moment longer than was necessary and still she resented the necessity of their removal.

A moment later, he'd pressed his foot into a stirrup and swung his leg over, nestling in behind her, reaching around and taking the reins, his body framing hers completely. She closed her eyes, praying for strength, because sitting this close to him was its own form of torment. She could smell him, feel him, his touch confident and reassuring as he moved his leg to start the horse in motion.

'We'll go fast,' he said into her ear, the words warm against her flesh. Her heart turned over. She nodded, incapable of speaking.

They sped. The horse galloped north, towards the Al'amanï ranges before tacking east. The sun was low in the sky, the colours spectacular as day blurred towards night. They rode for twenty minutes, each step of the horse jolting Johara against Amir, so after a while she surrendered to the sheer physicality of this, and allowed herself to enjoy it. The feeling of his chest against her back. His thighs against hers. His arms around her, flexing the reins. Every jolt bumped her against him and by the time he brought the horse to a stop, she was so overcome by the sensations that were flooding her body she barely realised they were at an ancient site.

'These are the ruins,' he said, his face forward, beside hers, so if she turned her head just a little her lips would press against his. She could hardly breathe. Her eyes traced the outlines of the ancient building, barely registering the details. She saw the pillars and columns, one of the ornate rooftops remained, the windows carved into arches. Yes, she could imagine this would have been a resting point in the desert, thousands of years earlier. A lodging as a midway point across the landscape. It was beautiful but she was so overwhelmed, it was impossible to react. A noise overhead caught her attention. She glanced up to see the enormous wingspan of a bird—his falcon. As she watched, it came down to land atop the ruins, its eyes surveying the desert.

'They're…' She searched for the word and instinctively looked towards Amir. It was a mistake. Just as she'd imagined, he was so close, and in turning her head towards him she almost brushed his cheek with her lips. He shifted a little, so that he was facing her, their eyes only an inch apart. The air around them crackled with a heat that had nothing to do with the desert.

'The ruins are…'

She still couldn't find the words. Every cell of her DNA was absorbed by this man. He was too close. Too much. He was…perfect. Superlatives were something she had in abundance, when it came to Amir. The ruins just couldn't compete with him.

'Would you like to see inside?'

No. She wanted to stay right where she was. She bit

down on her lip, sure what she was feeling must be obvious in her expression.

'I—' She frowned, her brows drawing together.

'The view from the top is worth seeing.'

Was he oblivious to the tension that was wrapping around her? Did he not feel it?

She nodded slowly, awkwardly, but when he climbed down from the horse she had to tilt her face away from him because of the disappointment she was sure must show in her features. He held his hands out. 'May I?'

He was asking to touch her, again. The small sign of respect came naturally to him.

'Please.' She nodded.

He reached out and took hold of her curved hips, guiding her off the horse. The act brought her body to his, sliding down his length, so a heat that was impossible to ignore began to burn between her legs. She stood there, staring up at him, the sky bathing them in shades of violet and orange, the first stars beginning to twinkle overhead.

'Why did you bring me here?'

A muscle jerked low in his jaw. She dropped her eyes to it, fascinated. Her fingertips itched to reach up and touch, to explore the planes of his face, to feel him with her eyes closed and see him as he'd been in the maze.

'You wanted to see it.'

Her lips twisted in a half-smile. 'There are many things I want to see.'

'This was easy to arrange.'

The answer disappointed her. He was right. This had been easy—a short ride across the desert. He'd undoubtedly wanted to give the bird an outing—bringing Johara was just an afterthought.

It meant nothing to him. She was embarrassing herself by making it into more.

His voice rumbled through her doubts. 'And I wanted to see it with you. Through your eyes.' And then, with a frown, he lifted his hand to lightly caress her cheek. 'I wanted to see your wonderment as you looked upon the ruins. I wanted to be here with you.'

Disappointment evaporated; pleasure soared in its place.

He dropped his hand and took a step backwards. She wanted to scream. He stalked away from her, pulling the blanket from the side of the horse and removing a silver bottle. 'Would you like some water?'

She took it gratefully, taking a drink before handing it back to him. A drop of water escaped from the corner of her lips and before she could catch it, he'd reached out, his fingertip chasing it away then lingering beside her mouth.

She was in a world of trouble.

He took the bottle, had a drink then replaced it. 'Come on.' The words were gruff but she knew why. He wasn't impatient or annoyed. He was fighting himself, trying to get control of how he felt about her and what he wanted. He was fighting the same war he'd been fighting since the night of the masquerade, when they'd learned who they truly were.

It was a war, she realised in a blinding moment of clarity, that they were both destined to lose. Just as passion had overpowered them on that first night, without reason or sense, it would triumph again.

'Do you—?'

Another sentence she didn't—couldn't—finish.

'Do I?'

'Need to tie him up?' She jerked her thumb towards the horse without looking away from Amir. His eyes briefly flicked to the animal, his lips curling when he returned the full force of his attention to Johara.

'No. He will stay nearby.'

A *frisson* of awareness shifted across her spine. 'Because you're the Sheikh and everyone and everything in this kingdom must obey you?'

His brows lifted, amusement and something far more dangerous flickering in the depths of his eyes. 'Because he is well trained.' He shifted his body weight from one foot to the other, the act bringing him infinitesimally closer. 'And yes, because he obeys me.'

Every feminist bone in her body despaired at the pleasure she took in that—the idea of submitting to this man was sensual and pleasing and answered some archaic desire deep within her. She revolted against it, blinking to clear those desperately unworthy thoughts and forcing herself to step away from him, pretending fascination with the ruins. It was a fascination she shouldn't have needed to pretend. The ruins were beautiful, ancient, endlessly steeped in history and folklore; Johara had longed to see them since she'd first heard about them as a teenager.

Amir clearly knew them well. He guided her through the buildings, or what was left of them, describing what each would have housed. The accommodations, the stables, the hall for dining and the communal courtyard from which announcements were made.

With his words and his knowledge, he brought the ruins to life for Johara. As he spoke, she could see the colours, the people, she could imagine the noise—horses snorting and stomping, people talking, laughing. It was all so vivid.

'I never thought they would be this beautiful,' she said, shaking her head as he led her across the courtyard and through a narrow opening. A tower stood sentinel over the ruins.

'For security,' he murmured. 'This gave a vantage point in all directions.' The stairs were time-worn, carved into low depressions at the centre of each courtesy of footsteps and sandstorms.

'It's perfectly safe,' he assured her as they reached the top and he pushed open another door to reveal a small opening. The balcony was not large—with the two of them standing there, it left about a metre's space, and there were no guard rails, which meant Johara instinctively stayed close to Amir.

'Do you come out here often?'

'I used to.' The sun was so close to the bottom of the horizon, and the sky was now at its finest. Vibrant pink streaks flew towards them, spectacular against a mauve sky with diamond-like stars beginning to shine.

'Not any more?' She looked towards him.

'I have less time now.'

'Right. The whole sheikh thing.' She banged her palm to her forehead, feigning forgetfulness. 'If I were you, I think I'd come here every day, regardless.'

Her sigh made him smile. 'What do you like about it so much?'

'The history.' She answered automatically. 'The tangible connection to the past. When you described the purpose of each of the buildings I felt generations of people come back to life.'

'And you like history?'

'I like the lessons it can teach us,' she said without missing a beat. 'Nothing we do is new. It's important to remember the way things have played out in the past, otherwise humanity will keep making the same mistakes over and over again.'

He studied her face thoughtfully. 'Such as war?' he prompted.

'Well, yes. Such as war.'

'And yet, regardless of the fact we know what war entails and how badly it always ends, we keep finding ourselves in that state. Perhaps it's simply inherent to human nature to want to fight?'

'And assert our dominance?' She pulled a face. 'I'd like to think we can evolve beyond that.'

'There is a lot of evidence to the contrary.'

'We're in a state of evolution,' she retorted, a smile on her lips.

'And you are a hopeless optimist,' he remembered, and just like that, the first night they'd met was a binding, wrapping around them, making it impossible to forget a similar exchange they'd once shared.

'I'm not really. I think I'm a realist who looks on the bright side wherever possible.'

'Ah.' He made a sound of having been corrected. 'And I'm a realist who doesn't look on the bright side?'

'You're just a hyper-realist.' She smiled at him, an easy smile that morphed into something like a grin and then slowly began to fade from her face as the sun began to drop towards the horizon, so close to disappearing. She angled her face towards it, wondering why she felt as though she'd run a marathon, why her breath felt so tight in her lungs.

'From here, you can see all the way to the mountains in this direction.' He lifted his arm towards the north. She followed and nodded, her throat thick with feeling. 'And in this direction, the palace—though it wasn't there when this was built.'

'No,' she agreed, the words just a croak. The sun was a fireball in the sky, burning close to the horizon. The colours emanating from it were magnificent. Amir's falcon circled overhead and Johara's eyes followed its stately progress, each span of its wings spreading something before her. Magic. Destiny. A sense of fate.

She wrenched her gaze back to Amir's. 'Thank you for bringing me here.'

That same muscle throbbed low in his jaw. 'Don't thank me. My reasons were purely selfish.'

'Oh?' It was just a breathy sound. 'You're not planning on throwing me off the tower, are you?' She strove for lightness, something to alleviate the suffocating tension that was tightening around her.

He shook his head slowly. His hand lifted to her hair, touching it so gently, so reverently, that she pressed her head towards him, craving a deeper touch.

'I wanted to be alone with you, as we were in the maze.'

Her stomach swooped and dropped.

'You were right the other night.'

She didn't say anything.

'I intended to use you as—how did you put it?'

'A scapegoat,' she murmured quickly.

'Yes, a scapegoat.' His smile was laced with self-mockery. 'You were right.'

'I know.' She looked away from him but he lifted his fingers to her chin, gently tilting her face back to his. His fingers moved lower, tracing the pulse point at the base of her neck. He must have been able to feel the frantic racing of it.

'I do want you.'

She didn't say anything.

'But the boundaries of what this is—of what it can be—are something I have no power to affect.'

Her head felt dizzy. She swayed a little. He put a hand out, wrapping it around her waist, holding her against him. They were bound like that, drawn together, unable to be apart. At least for now.

'The peace is tenuous. And making it last is the most important thing I will ever do in my life. I must make this work—my people deserve my absolute dedication to this cause. If news were to break that something personal was happening between us, you a Qadir and me a Haddad…'

She swallowed. 'We slept together once. No one needs to know.'

His brow creased, his eyes grew serious. 'I'm not talking about then. Right now, this day, standing here with you, I want you, Johara. I want more of you. All of you. While you're here in this country, I want you in my life, my bed, I want you to myself whenever we can manage it. I can offer you nothing beyond this—the decision is yours. Is this enough?'

CHAPTER EIGHT

'IS THIS ENOUGH?'

The sun slipped beyond the horizon, bathing the sky in the most magical, iridescent colours. The beating of the falcon's wings was slow and rhythmic, lulling her even as she felt the urgency of what he was asking. She tried to swallow; her mouth was drier than the desert sands.

There was a small part of her capable of rational thought and it was telling her that no, what he was offering wasn't enough. But it had to be. A little time with Amir was better than nothing; she knew it was temporary but she couldn't muster the strength to object to that—not if the alternative was that they close the door on whatever this was once and for all.

She blinked up at him, the inevitability of this completely breathtaking, and swayed closer. He inhaled deeply, as though breathing her in, and she smiled.

'Yes.' Relief flooded her. It was the right decision.

He made a groaning sound as he dropped his mouth to hers, kissing her even as his hands reached for the bottom of her tunic and pushed at it, lifting it just high enough to expose an inch of midriff. It was like breaking a seal; the moment his fingertips connected with her naked flesh she ached for him in a way that wouldn't be repressed. Her hands pushed at his robes, impatient and hungry, stripping them from his body as he did the same to her, revealing their nakedness simultaneously.

The sun dropped down completely; darkness began to curl through the sky. He drew her to her knees, kneeling opposite, kissing her, his hands wrapping around her as he eased her backwards: carefully, gently. The rooftop wasn't large, there was just space for them to lie together, and little more. He brought his body over hers, his eyes scanning her features, searching for something she couldn't fathom. Or perhaps she could, because she smiled and nodded, in response to his unanswered question, and then pushed up and kissed him, her mouth teasing him, her fingertips playing with the hair at his nape.

He drew his mouth from her lips to her collarbone, lighting little fires beneath her skin everywhere he kissed, his tongue lashing her to the edge of her sanity. She was tipped over the brink when he flicked one of her nipples; she arched her spine in a silent invitation, her fingernails dragging down his back. It reminded her of the way she'd marked him in the maze, making her smile—she lifted up and bit his shoulder, sinking her teeth into the flesh there and laughing as he straightened to fix her with a look that was equal parts smouldering and surprised.

His hands trapped hers, holding them over her head; she was no longer laughing. She couldn't. The power of what they both wanted was almost terrifying. He pushed her legs apart with his knee then kissed her, hard, her body completely trapped by his, her needs driven by him.

'No turning back,' he said into her mouth, pushing the words deep into her soul, where they took hold and filled her with relief. She didn't want to turn back. From the moment she'd discovered who he was, she'd wanted this—come hell or high water.

'No turning back,' she agreed, breaking the kiss just so

she could meet his eyes, in the hope he would see the seriousness of her response.

He claimed her mouth as he drove his arousal between her legs and into her feminine core. The relief of welcoming him back brought tears to her eyes. She kissed him with all the fierceness of her desire, lifting her legs and wrapping them around his back, holding him deep inside, allowing her body to glory in his possession. He began to move, hard and fast, as though driven by an ancient tempo that only they could hear.

His body was her master, and hers was his. Beneath the darkening sky, Amir made her his, watching as pleasure exploded through her again and again before giving into his own heady release, filling her with all that he was, holding her to him, their breath racked, their pleasure beyond compare.

Amir lay atop Johara for several minutes after, but it could have been days or months; there on the roof of a tower in the middle of the desert, time had no meaning. They were particles of life in amongst the sand and the history, as utterly a part of the earth as the elements that made this striking, barren landscape what it was.

Johara felt every bit a desert princess, overcome with a sense of her own power. Seeing the effect she had on him—that they had on each other—made her wonder at how they'd been able to resist doing this for as many days as they had!

Her eyes found the stars overhead—the sky had darkened to an inky black now—and she smiled at the thought that the celestial bodies alone had witnessed this coming together. It made it feel all the more powerful and important; all the more predestined.

Eventually, he pushed up onto one elbow, his gaze roaming her face possessively, as if looking for a sign of how she felt. So she smiled, and lifted a hand to cup his cheek, drawing his attention to her eyes. 'That was perfect.'

His features bore a mask of tightness but then he relaxed, smiling, rolling off Johara but simultaneously catching her and bringing her to lie with her head on his chest, his arm wrapped around her. She curled her body to his side, and his hand stroked her hip, his fingers moving with a slowness that could have induced drowsiness. Except Johara wasn't tired; far from it. She felt alive in a thousand and one ways. Her body had caught fire and she wasn't sure those fires would ever be extinguished.

'This is…complicated,' he said with a shake of his head, and then laughed, turning to face her. She saw the same thing in his expression that she felt in her heart. Surrender. This was bigger than them, bigger than the war. It was something neither could fight.

'No.' She shook her head and smiled, pushing up to press her chin to his chest. 'It's the opposite of that—it's so simple.'

He reached out, lacing his fingers through hers, stroking the back of her hand with his thumb. 'Yes.' He sighed. 'It is also simple.'

She put her head back down, listening to the strong, steady hammering of his heart. All her life she'd been told that the Haddads were the worst of the worst—not to be trusted, not to be seen as anything but the enemy. Yet here she lay listening to Amir Haddad's heart and she knew the truth—it was a good heart. A kind heart. A heart that lived to serve his people.

A heart that would never belong to anyone but his people.

Especially not her—a Qadir.

She pushed those thoughts away. They both knew what

they were doing, and what the limitations of this were. That didn't mean she couldn't enjoy it in the moment.

Her fingertips traced the inked words that ran across his chest. 'What does this mean?'

He shifted a little, flicking a glance at his chest, then focussing his attention back on the stars overhead. *'Amor fati,'* he said the words quietly.

'Yes. I love...' she translated with a small frown.

'It's Nietzsche,' he said. 'It means to love one's fate.' He turned towards her, scanning her face as if to read her reaction.

She was contemplative. 'Your fate, as in your role as Sheikh?'

His smile was dismissive. 'Partly, yes. All of it. My parents' death, the duty that put upon me. There was a time when I felt that what was required of me might cripple me. I was only young—fifteen, or sixteen—and I remember riding out here and lying just like this. Well...' a smile lifted his lips at the corners '...not quite like this—there was no woman.'

She smiled back, but didn't say anything; she didn't want him to stop speaking.

'I lay here and looked at the stars and felt as though the sky was falling down on me, suffocating me with its vastness. How could I—a boy completely alone in the world, with no parents, no siblings, only paid advisors—possibly be what was best for the country?'

'It was an enormous responsibility to bear at such a young age,' she said quietly.

'I felt that way *then,*' he responded quietly. 'I now realise that this responsibility was a gift. What a great thing, to be able to lead my people, to rule a country such as this.' He waved his hands towards the sand dunes that rolled away from these ruins.

'Amor fati,' she said simply.

'Yes. I lay here and realised that I was being self-indulgent. There was no sense wondering if I could be Sheikh. I was. And so I had to be.'

'If it makes any difference, you strike me as a natural at this.'

'Oh?'

She nodded. 'The night we met, before I knew who you were, I knew, somehow, *what* you were.'

'And what is that?'

'A ruler.' Her smile was slow to form. 'You have a natural authority that can't help but convey itself.'

He laughed gruffly. 'I'm used to being obeyed.'

'It's more than that. It's the way you move, the way you speak. I think that your fate chose you.'

'We could also say your uncle chose my fate.'

Her eyes flashed to his and pain sliced through her—brief and sharp. He saw it and shook his head by way of apology. 'I shouldn't have said that.'

'No.' She bit down on her lip. 'But you're right.' Her fingers chased the tattoo, running over the inky black lines. 'He was—is—an extremist. He always has been. He felt my parents were too moderate, that an all-out offensive was called for. He believed that only by destroying Ishkana could Taquul truly prosper. He wanted the war brought to an end once and for all—by any means necessary.'

'He wanted genocide,' Amir said quietly, but with a ruthless undercurrent to the words. 'And it is best if we do not discuss Johar.' The name was said with disgust.

She nodded. He was right. There was nothing she could ever say that would pardon her uncle's sins; nor did she want to. She judged him as harshly as Amir did.

'I am sorry,' she said quietly.

That drew his gaze, and the look in the depths of his

obsidian eyes did something funny to her tummy—tying it in a bundle of knots.

'It was not your fault, Johara.'

He said her name quietly, without a hint of the anger he felt for Johar.

She expelled a soft breath. 'I mean that I'm sorry you had to go through that. The grief…'

He pressed a finger to her nipple and drew an imaginary circle around it. She could barely concentrate. His touch was sending little arrows of need darting beneath her skin.

'Why did you send for me tonight?'

He lowered his mouth, pressing a kiss to the flesh just above her nipple. She shivered.

'I shouldn't have.' He lifted his head to smile. 'I told myself—after the library—that I would stay away from you. But then I saw you looking at me and I knew you felt the inevitability of this.' He lifted a finger, tracing her cheek. 'I knew that if I sent for you and you came, it would be because you didn't care about how forbidden and impossible this is.' He brought his mouth to hers. 'I sent for you because I found myself unable to resist.'

She moaned as he kissed her, her hands seeking his body once more, a new hunger growing inside her. She gave herself to the power of that, falling back against the cool granite of the tower as their bodies became one once more.

'It's best if I leave you at the West Gate.'

They hadn't spoken since leaving the ruins. It was as though each step of the powerful horse brought them closer and closer to the palace and the reality that awaited them. Out there, in the wildness of the desert, nothing had seemed impossible, but the constraints of who they were grew more apparent as the palace loomed into sight.

'Where will you go?'

'I'll take him to the stable yard.'

'You're afraid of being seen with me?'

She felt his harsh intake of breath. 'We discussed this. What we just did has to be kept secret.'

'I know.' She swept her eyes downwards, studying the horse's thick mane, wondering at the cloying sense of tears.

'There are a thousand reasons we cannot let anyone know what we're doing.' He brought the horse to a step and leaned forward, pressing a hand to the side of her face, drawing her to look at him.

His teeth clenched as he saw the raw emotion on her features.

'Johara…'

'I know. The war. The peace treaty. I'm a Qadir, you're a Haddad.'

'Yes,' he said, gently though, leaning forward and pressing his forehead to hers. 'But it's so much more than that. You are supposed to be marrying Paris. What would the press make of an affair with me while you are all but engaged?'

'I'm not engaged,' she said stiffly.

'In the media's eyes—and I believe your brother's eyes—you are. Your reputation would be damaged beyond repair.'

'This isn't the eighteen hundreds, Amir. No one expects a sacrificial virgin at the altar.'

'No, but you are a princess and people expect *you* to be perfect.'

She pulled away from him, jerking her face in the opposite direction.

'And I suppose you have similar concerns,' she said darkly.

Amir didn't pretend to misunderstand. 'One day I will marry. At present, my kingdom has no heir. But there is no one who would be hurt by our affair.'

'Paris and I are *not* a couple.'

Amir compressed his lips. 'As I said, I believe, in the eyes of your brother, your union is a *fait accompli*.'

'So what I want doesn't matter?'

'It matters. To me, it matters a great deal. I cannot speak on your brother's behalf.'

So measured! So reasonable! She wanted to scream.

And yet, he was right—she'd already felt the pain of being the press's latest object of fascination. For months she'd been hounded after her break up with Matthew. Anyone who'd known either of them had been pressed to give a 'tell all' interview. Private photographs had been found and shared in the articles. The invasion had been unbearable. It had been the catalyst for her departure to America.

Regardless of Paris, having an affair with the Sheikh of Ishkana would be huge news. Her people would hate it. Her brother might never forgive her.

She turned back to face him, regretting the concern she saw on his features, because she'd put it there with her silly reactions.

'You're right.' She nodded firmly. 'I'll go in the West Gate.'

His eyes lingered on her face a moment longer, as if he was reassuring himself before pulling on the reins, starting the horse back on the path.

At the gate, he paused in the midst of a row of pomegranate trees.

'Your schedule is busy tomorrow.'

'I know.'

'I won't see you until the afternoon.'

'At the tour of the *masjid*?'

'Yes, I'll be there too. But we won't be alone.' He cupped her face. 'Tomorrow night, meet me in the forest. Do you remember the way?'

She nodded. 'I think so.'

'Good. Just come to the edges of it. I'll be waiting.'

'What time?'

He thought of his own schedule, and knew he would clear whatever he needed to be available. 'I'll be there from seven. Come when you can.'

Her heart was speeding. Seven o'clock felt like a lifetime away.

He climbed off the horse then reached up and took her hips in his powerful hands, lifting her easily off the back of the stallion. He held her close, and everything that was primal and instinctive stirred to life inside her.

'As soon as you can,' he said with a smile, but there was a darkness to that—the overpowering need shifting through them.

'I will.'

He kissed her—a light touch of his lips to hers—but it wasn't enough for Johara. She needed more—she didn't want to leave him. She lifted up, wrapping her arms around his neck, deepening the kiss, her body melded to his, and he made a thick noise in his throat as he held her tight to his body, kissing her back with the same hunger before pulling apart, wrenching himself free, breaking what was already becoming something neither could easily control.

They stared at one another for several seconds before a noise had her breaking away from him, moving quickly to the palace wall and pressing against it. He watched her for several beats before swinging onto his horse, pressing himself low to the neck and riding away.

Johara watched him go, her heart racing, her cheeks hurting from the ridiculous smile she couldn't shake.

CHAPTER NINE

It was an hour into the tour of the *masjid* that Amir began to suspect Johara was a far better actor than he.

She was listening with all of her attention as the *allamah* showed them through the historic place of worship. It was Amir who was struggling to concentrate. He found his eyes straying to Johara when he too should have been listening. He found that he sought her out every few moments, trying to get her to look at him, wanting to see something in her eyes.

What?

Why did he need to look at her so badly?

To know that she didn't regret it.

He compressed his lips and looked away, turning his attention to a piece of art he knew well—a seven-hundred-year-old tapestry weaved from bright and beautiful threads. He moved towards it, as if fascinated by the detail, when in fact he just needed some breathing space.

There was no denying their chemistry; that was clear and mutual. But the danger for them both was real and undeniable. Shouldn't he be protecting her from that by fighting what he felt? For her sake, shouldn't he be stronger?

He closed his eyes, knowing he couldn't. They'd started on this path now and it wasn't in his power to stop.

And yet he could see danger on both sides. He had to

at least protect her from discovery. If they could keep this thing secret then when the time came for her to leave, she could continue with her life with no ramifications.

That was what he owed her.

And what about your people? a voice in his head demanded. What would they feel if they knew he'd been intimate with the Princess of Taquul?

He glanced towards her and something in his chest tightened. Yes, she was the Princess of Taquul, but she was so much more. To him, she was simply Johara, but to his people, was it possible she would continue to represent a threat? A reminder of past hatred and violence?

The peace was too important to risk.

Secrecy had to be ensured.

He vowed not to look at her again.

'You're cross with me?' Johara murmured, flicking him an inquiring glance as they walked side by side through the enormous room that led to the large timber doors. It was just the four of them and the *allamah* and Ahmed had moved further ahead.

He jerked his attention to her. 'No.' He looked away again. 'Why would you say that?'

'You're so serious. And trying so hard not to look at me.'

He kept his focus directly ahead. 'To avoid suspicion.'

Her laugh was soft. 'Where's the fun in that?'

And before he could know what she intended, she moved a step closer, her hand brushing against his.

He glared at her. 'Johara.' His voice held a warning.

Her smile was pure teasing. 'Relax. I'm not going to give the game away.' She brushed his hand again. 'But remember, it *is* a game. Try to have a little fun.'

Ahmed turned a moment later. Johara kept walking, no

sign of their conversation on her face. 'A crowd has gathered outside. Would you prefer a back entrance?'

Johara looked towards Amir. 'The purpose of my being here is to be seen,' she reminded him. 'We should show a united front.'

He hesitated for some unknown reason, and then nodded. 'Yes. Fine.'

Johara was effortless. He watched as she moved down the stairs, a smile on her face that disguised how she might have felt at being in the heartland of Ishkana so soon after the war had ended. If she held any anger towards his people, she hid it completely.

A woman was calling to her. He watched as she moved closer, but too close! Why didn't she stay back a little? He made a motion to Ahmed, who caught it and signalled to a security guard to intervene, to put some more space between the Princess and the crowd.

But it was too late.

A projectile left the hand of a man near the front of the group. Amir stood frozen to the spot as whatever it was sailed through the air, heading straight for Johara. He swore, began to run, but there wasn't time.

When he reached her, it had hit her square in the chest. The smell was unmistakable. Coffee. Warm, dark coffee was spreading over her white clothing, soaking the fabric, revealing the outline of her breasts. Fury slashed him.

The man was already running but Amir was quick. He reached into the crowd and grabbed him by the collar, pulling him towards through the rope line.

'Your Highness.' Johara's voice was urgent. 'I'm fine. It doesn't matter.'

But Amir barely heard her. He was not a violent man but as he held this person in his grip, he found his other hand forming a fist, and he badly wanted to use it.

'We will take him away,' Ahmed said, moving between Amir and the culprit. The man, to his credit, had the sense to look terrified.

'If you are going to act in this manner, at least stand and face your consequences. Coward,' Amir said angrily, but Ahmed was already pulling the man away, and two security guards had intervened to move Johara into the back of a waiting car.

He followed behind, sliding into the empty seat. Only once they started moving did he turn to her. Her skin was pale, her fingertips were shaking slightly but she was otherwise unharmed.

If there weren't two guards sitting opposite them in the limousine he would have reached across and put a hand over hers. Hell, he would have pulled her onto his lap and kissed her until she forgot anything about such an assault.

'I apologise, Your Highness.'

Her eyes met and held his. 'It wasn't your fault.' She reminded him of what he'd said the night before.

'I assure you, the man will be punished—'

'Don't do that either.' She sighed. 'You said it yourself. You can tell people we are at peace but you can't make them feel it in their hearts. Why should he be punished for doing something that six months ago he would have been lauded for?'

Amir ground his teeth. 'For the simple reason I have said it is wrong.'

She laughed. 'You are powerful, but not that powerful.'

'You are here as my guest,' he muttered. 'And your safety is my complete responsibility.'

'And?' She fixed him with a level gaze. 'I'm safe, aren't I?'

'It could have been—'

She shook her head. 'It wasn't.' She looked down her front. 'At worst, I'm embarrassed.'

Her phone began to vibrate. She reached into her pocket and pulled it out. Her brother's face stared back at her. She looked at Amir; it was obvious that he'd seen the screen.

She angled away from him a little.

'Mal? This isn't a good…' She frowned. 'That was quick. Yes, I'm fine.'

She was conscious of Amir stiffening in the car beside her.

'As I was just saying to His Majesty Sheikh Amir, it was only a cup of coffee.'

'I don't care.' Malik's voice showed the strength of his feelings. 'What the hell were you doing standing so close to a crowd of wild Ishkani—?'

She glowered at the window. 'How do you know where I was standing?'

'It's already on YouTube.'

'Geez,' she said again, with the shake of her head. 'Thank you, Internet.'

'I want you to come back here.'

Her heart stammered. She looked at Amir unconsciously. 'Nonsense. Because of a bit of coffee?'

'It could have been a bomb. A gun.'

'It wasn't. That wasn't the point the man wanted to make. He's angry. There's anger on both sides. We can't deny people their right to feel those things.'

'Nor should you suffer because of it,' Malik said firmly.

'I'm not suffering.'

'But it—'

'Stop!' She looked at Amir but addressed Malik. 'An inch is as good as a mile, right? It was a coffee. I believe it was a spontaneous act from a man who's suffered through the war. That's all. There's no sense making a mountain out of it.' Her PR mind was spinning over what had happened. 'In fact, if anything, we should make light—include a visit to a coffee house in tomorrow's schedule or something. Show that we have a sense of humour. And under no circumstances will I accept there being any consequences for this man.' She glared at Amir.

'But he—'

She interrupted Malik, waving a hand through the air so the collection of delicate bracelets she wore jangled prettily. 'Yes, yes, he threw a warm coffee cup at me. My clothes will be ruined, and an embarrassing clip is now on the Internet, but so what? Do you know what will happen if we respond too strongly to this?'

Amir was leaning forward a little, captivated by her, wanting to hear what she said—aware that her perspective was one he needed to have.

'We will make the thousands of people who feel that same anger in their hearts want to rise in defence of this poor man. Let's treat his actions with kindness and compassion. No one will expect that, and it will make the forgiveness all the more powerful.'

Amir's eyes drifted to the security guards. They were well trained, not looking at Johara or Amir, but he could see the shift in their faces, the obvious surprise and admiration.

'Now calm down.' She was speaking to her brother but her eyes were on Amir again, and he knew the words were meant for him, too. 'Put your feelings aside, and your concerns for me. I'm fine. Let's speak no more of this.'

'It is unforgivable.'

Ahmed nodded. 'I'm aware of this. I'll have the police bring charges immediately; he should pay for this.'

Amir was tempted. So tempted. But Johara's words and wisdom were impossible to ignore. He expelled a breath.

'No.' He frowned. 'Have him brought to me here.' Amir thought a moment longer. 'I want to speak to him.'

'To...speak to him?'

Amir flicked his gaze to Ahmed. 'Her Highness has advocated mercy. I'm interested to see if the man deserves such kindness. Bring him here.'

'Your parents were right.'

It was the first thing he said to her when she arrived at the forest, several hours later, a little after seven. They were the words he'd been aching to speak but couldn't until they were alone. Instead, he'd gone back to ignoring her in the limousine, as befitted their perceived relationship.

He drew her towards him, clasping his hands behind her back, his eyes running over her features possessively.

'About what?' The question was breathless. He held her tight.

'You have a gift with people.'

She lowered her lashes, as if embarrassed by the praise.

'I mean it.' He caught her chin, lifting her eyes to his. Something shifted through him, something powerful and elemental. He kissed her; he couldn't help it. 'Were you hurt?'

She shook her head. 'It was just coffee.'

'Hot coffee, and a plastic cup.'

'Yes,' she said, lifting her shoulders. And then, because it was just the two of them, and they were alone, he saw her mask drop, just a fraction. 'I was surprised, and I suppose my feelings were hurt. I was too confident. Everything on this trip has been so easy to date. Your people have been overwhelmingly welcoming, given the circumstances...'

'They've also been accusatory and frosty,' he remarked, pulling away from her, taking her hand and guiding her deeper into the forest.

Her smile was enigmatic. 'Well, yes, at times. But of course they see things from their perspective. Here, I'm the bad guy. In Taquul, that's you.' She lifted her shoulders. 'It's just a matter of perspective.'

'More wisdom.' He squeezed her hand. They moved quickly, both impatient to get to wherever they were going, to be alone.

'I thought you were going to hit him.'

'I wanted to.' He looked down at her.

'I'm glad you didn't.'

'I saw him this afternoon.'

'The man who threw the coffee?' Her brows lifted.

'Yes. Ahmed brought him here, at my request.'

He could feel concern emanating from her in waves. 'Why?'

'To see if you were right.'

'And was I?'

'Yes.'

She expelled a breath. 'People don't generally lash out without cause.'

'No.' He held a vine aloft, waiting for Johara to walk ahead of him. 'His twin brother died in the war. Right at the end.'

Johara's eyes closed in sympathy. 'So recently?'

'Yes.'

'And if peace had been agreed months earlier…'

'He wouldn't have died.' Amir nodded crisply. 'That's why this matters so much. We have to make this work.'

'You will.' She stopped walking to look at him. 'I know Mal is as committed to this as you are. How can peace efforts fail if you're both determined to have this succeed?'

He didn't need to answer. They both knew there were many things that could unravel the fragile accord. Their relationship was at the top of that list for him. If today had shown him anything it was how close to the surface his people's hostility was.

But he'd looked into the eyes of a man who'd lost so much, who was grieving, and instead of bringing the wrath of his position down on him, he'd spent thirty minutes talking with him. Amir understood grief; he knew it first-hand. He'd listened to the other man and when it became apparent that there had been difficulties accessing his brother's estate—a task he had undertaken for the widow and children—Amir had personally called the parliamentarian who oversaw such matters to ensure it moved smoothly going forward.

Johara had been, in every way, correct. Her wisdom was enviable, so too her grace under literal fire. She would have made an excellent queen.

The thought rocked him to the core. He stopped walking for a second, his eyes fixed straight ahead. They were nearing the edge of the forest, where it gave way to the end of the river. Here, there was a small lake, surrounded on all sides by rock. It was private, held by the palace, the last watercourse between here and the desert.

'What is it, Amir?'

He shook his head, clearing the thought. Johara was intelligent and worldly, but she was certainly not a candidate for the position of his wife. The very idea sent panic along his spine. Anything approaching that would certainly lead to all-out war. Besides, she was the opposite of what he wanted in a wife. When he married, it would be to a woman who was…what? Why couldn't he see that future now? He frowned. Because he was here with Johara—it would be the epitome of rudeness to be thinking of some hypothetical future wife when his lover was at his side.

'I was thinking of Paris,' he substituted, for lack of anything else to say.

'Really?' She frowned. 'Why?'

He began to walk again, forcing a smile to his face. 'I was wondering why your brother is so keen for you to marry him.'

'They've been friends a long time,' she said simply.

'And?'

She laughed. 'Yes, I suppose that's not really an answer.' She tilted her head to the side, considering the question. 'He's a nice guy.'

'The only nice guy in Taquul?'

She flashed him a withering look; he lifted her hand and pressed a kiss to her fingertips.

'Neither of those responses is particularly enlightening.'

'I know,' she sighed. 'Mal is very protective of me.'

Amir didn't want to answer that. He knew that if he said what he felt—that he was glad—she would become defensive. *I don't need him to protect me!* Yet an ancient fibre that ran through Amir liked the idea of someone playing that role in Johara's life, even though he knew she was right—she didn't need it.

'For any reason?' he said instead, and as soon as he'd asked the question, he knew there was more to it.

Her lips pursed, her eyes skittered away. 'You've probably read about it.'

'About what?'

Another sigh. 'Come on, Amir. It was a long time ago.'

'I'm not protecting your feelings, *inti qamar*. I have no idea what you mean.' She looked at him, the term of endearment slipping easily into the sentence. It was what he'd called her in the maze. My moon. Appropriate tonight, when it was glowing overhead, beautiful and enchanting.

'Oh.' She frowned. 'I was with someone before. I was younger, and completely unguarded. I thought I'd fallen head over heels in love with the guy—so why hide how I felt, right?'

He ignored the prickle of something like jealousy shifting through him. 'Go on.'

Johara nodded. 'We dated for just over a year. It ended badly. The papers got a *lot* of mileage out of it.'

Another burst of emotion, this time one of darkness. 'Newspapers will do that.'

But her expression showed she was lost in thought. 'It was truly terrible. I was twenty-one, and I'd been so sheltered. Worse than that, I honestly thought I loved him. I trusted him.'

Amir's chest tightened. 'He wasn't trustworthy?'

Her laugh lacked humour. 'Not even a little.'

He waited, but not patiently.

'Oh, he didn't cheat on me or anything. But I found out, about six months after our break up, that he'd been selling stories to the gutter press. So many little lies and falsehoods: that we'd had a threesome in Rome—a lie—that I'd secretly fallen pregnant—another lie! All for money!' She shook her head bitterly. 'I would have paid him off, if I'd known money was his motivation.'

Amir reached above them and snapped a twig with more force than was necessary.

'Except I think he also wanted to hurt me, and, honestly, I think he liked the limelight. When he was my boyfriend, he was followed around by paparazzi, blogs did articles on him.' She shook her head. 'Italian *Vogue* used him as a cover model. But once we broke up, he must have begun to feel irrelevant.'

Amir swore under his breath. 'What a poor excuse for a man.'

She laughed. 'That's pretty much what Mal said.'

'Your brother knew about this?'

'He's the one who discovered the truth.' Her brow furrowed. 'He had the stories investigated.'

'How did he act?'

'He paid Matthew to shut him up.' She grimaced. 'Last I heard, he's living in Australia somewhere.'

'Good riddance.'

'Yeah.' She pressed her teeth to her lower lip. 'So for Malik, he doesn't ever want me to get hurt like that again. And Paris is a great guy, and a good friend of his. Malik trusts him implicitly.'

Something inside Amir bristled. 'But that doesn't mean you should marry him.'

'No,' she agreed softly. 'And yet…'

Amir held his breath.

'This is something we shouldn't discuss.'

He forced himself to sound normal. 'Why not?'

'Because we're sleeping together.'

'And we're both aware that's where this ends. I'm not harbouring a secret desire to marry you,' he said, trying to make it sound as though the very idea was ridiculous.

'I know.' Her voice was quiet. Wounded? Now he felt like a jackass. 'I guess I feel like there's the whole duty thing. Paris is from a great family. Our marriage makes sense. I like him. I don't know if I'd ever trust my own judgement again, when it comes to men, let alone trusting someone *else* after Matthew. Maybe Paris isn't…'

Amir had changed his mind. He couldn't listen to her talk about the prospect of marrying someone else without wanting to burn the world down. He hadn't expected to feel so possessive of her, but he did. He couldn't fight that, or deny it.

'You are a passionate woman, Johara. If you marry, it should be because your passions are aroused, because your heart is caught, and because you know—beyond a doubt—

that the man deserves you. Not because he's nice and your brother thinks he's suitable.'

Her lips parted, her eyes lifting to his. 'And is that how you'll choose a wife?'

He shook his head. 'It's different.'

'Why?'

'Because I'm Sheikh. I don't have the luxury of marrying a woman I choose for any reason other than her suitability to rule at my side.'

They stood there on the edge of the forest, so close, eyes locked, hearts beating in unison, the conversation troubling to both for reasons they couldn't fathom.

Distraction came in the form of one of the *juniya* birds. It flew close to Johara's head, drawing her attention, and she followed it beyond the last tree, her eyes catching the water for the first time. She gasped, shaking her head. Stars shone overhead, bathing the still water in little dots of silver.

'What is this place?'

He saw it through her eyes—the large stones that formed walls, creating the feeling of a fortress, the calm water on the edge of the desert, enormous trees that decorated the circumference but left space for the stars to shine.

'My swimming pool.' He grinned, willingly pushing their conversation aside as he pulled on her hand. 'Are you game?'

She flicked a nervous look at him. 'I don't have a bathing costume...'

He drew her closer, pressing his nose to hers. 'Didn't you hear me? This is private...'

Awareness dawned and she laughed, reaching for the bottom of her shirt. 'I see.'

He stepped back as she discarded her clothes, stripping down to her underwear, then removing that scrap of lace, so she was completely naked. He made a growling noise low in his throat, possession firing through him. She took a step forward, her eyes asking a question he answered with a nod. Her fingers caught the fabric of his clothes, lifting them from his body, more slowly than she had her own, so that he wanted to take over, to strip himself naked and pull her against him.

He didn't.

He stood and he waited, his body being stirred to a fever pitch of desire he could barely handle.

Slowly, painstakingly slowly, she undressed him, her fingers grazing his flesh as she went. Her eyes were huge in the moonlight, dark pools every bit as mesmerising as the water beyond them.

'It's beautiful here.' Her voice was thick; he could only jerk his head in agreement.

Her lips moved forward, pressing against his tattoo, and as she did so she whispered the words, *'Amor fati'*. They reached inside him, wrapping around his heart, his soul, the essence of his being.

He loved his fate. He'd worked to love it, when it had been, at times, the last thing he wanted. His fate was not this woman; she was an aberration, a temporary pleasure—a guilty pleasure. One he found himself utterly powerless to resist.

CHAPTER TEN

'HOW LONG DID you live in New York?'

Johara ran her fingertips over the water. It was sublime. She'd lost track of how long they'd been here. An hour? Less? More?

'Almost four years.'

His brows drew together.

'You're surprised?'

He laughed. 'Are you a mind-reader now?'

She pressed her face closer to his. 'Yours is easy to read.'

'Oh?'

'For me, at least.'

'Ah.' His grin sparked butterflies in her bloodstream.

'I should have thought your brother would object.'

She smiled indulgently. 'Mal didn't like the idea at first.'

She felt Amir stiffen at Johara's use of the diminutive of Malik's name. 'But you changed his mind?'

'We came to a compromise.'

Her smile became harder to keep in place. Her eyes shifted away from Amir's.

'And it was?'

'That I should go. For a time.'

Amir's features darkened. 'For a time? You mean until it suited him to have you come back?'

She wanted to defend Malik but, in truth, the terms

they'd struck—terms which had, at the time, seemed reasonable—now infuriated her. 'More or less.' She lifted her shoulders. 'I'm a princess of Taquul. My place is in my country.'

'Where do you want to be?'

Her eyes widened. No one had asked her that before.

'Let's pretend you're not a princess,' he said quietly. 'Where would you choose to make your life?'

Johara's heart turned over in her chest. The first answer that sprang to her mind was ludicrous. Too fanciful to say, much less give credit to. She'd spent five days in Ishkana, and it was a country that would never accept or welcome her. Why should she feel such an immense bond to this place? Her eyes ran over Amir's face without her meaning them to. The answer was right in front of her. *Wherever you are.*

Stricken, she tried to smile and pulled away from him in the water, swimming towards the edge. He came after her.

'You can't answer?'

Oh, she could answer, but the answer would terrify both of them. She bit down on her lip, and strove for a light tone of voice.

'I am what I am, Amir. I'm Johara Qadir, Princess of Taquul, and while I loved everything about New York, I always knew it was temporary. I knew that, one day, he'd ask me to return home and assume the responsibilities that have been mine since birth.'

But Amir was frustrated by that; she could read it in the terse lines of his face.

'Don't pretend that if you had a sister it would be any different,' she teased, surprised she could sound so light when her heart was splintering and cracking.

He frowned. 'I cannot say what it would be like,' he

agreed. 'I understand that he wants you back in Taquul. But marrying Paris is part of the agreement, isn't it?'

She dropped her gaze to the water. Tiny ripples moved from her fingertips towards the water's edge. She watched their progress, thinking of how like life that was—a small action could have such far-reaching consequences. 'Yes.' Her eyes swept shut. 'It's what my brother intends for me to do.'

'And what you want? Does it matter?'

'I can say no,' she murmured, meeting his eyes and wishing she hadn't when a feeling of pain and betrayal lanced her. 'He won't force me. If he tried, I'd leave, and I'd leave for good,' she promised. 'The decision is mine.'

Amir pulled her closer, into his arms, staring down at her for several long beats. The sky was silent; even the juniya were quiet in that moment.

'And there was no one in New York?'

Her breath snagged in her throat. 'On the contrary, Manhattan is heavily populated.'

He didn't laugh. His thumb smudged her lower lip, his eyes probing hers. 'You didn't meet anyone that made you want to stay?'

She shook her head. 'There were children. The most beautiful children. I fell in love with each and every one I worked with. I had friends—have friends. But no, there was no man.'

'I find that impossible to believe.'

'Why?'

'Because you're—'

She held her breath, waiting, needing him to finish the sentence.

But he shook his head, a tight smile gripping his lips. 'Four years is a long time.'

She exhaled slowly. 'It is,' she agreed. 'But Matthew

messed me up pretty good.' She lay backwards in the water, and he caught her legs, wrapping them around his waist, holding her there as she floated, staring up at the sky. There was such safety in his hold on her. She felt—whole. Complete. Content. But not for long, because the realisation of those sentiments brought with it a crippling wave of concern.

'Part of what I loved about meeting you was the anonymity. I felt such a connection with you, and all the better because you had no idea I was Johara Qadir.'

'No.' For a moment his voice broke through the serenity of the moment. She remembered his reaction that night, his assurance that if he'd known he would never have acted on those feelings. And none of this would have happened.

'You couldn't sell the story of what we'd done. You couldn't hurt me.'

Silence followed those words, so she began to regret them, and wish she hadn't revealed so much of herself.

But slowly, his hands curled around her back and lifted her from the water, bringing her body against his. His eyes latched to hers.

'I never want to hurt you.'

She swallowed, her throat thick with emotions. 'I know.'

Staring at him, bathed in moonlight, Johara felt as though every moment of her soul were shifting into alignment. Everything she'd ever been and whatever she was to become were resonating right there; she was her truest, purest form of self in his arms.

'I hate that a man treated you like that.'

'Yes.' She tried to sound crisp and businesslike, but the truth was it still hurt. Not Matthew's deeds so much as her own naivety and quickness to trust. She'd gone against her brother's wishes, she'd ignored his warnings, and she'd paid the price.

'I want to show you something tomorrow.'

The change of subject surprised her. She lifted a single brow, waiting for him to continue.

'The gallery, here in the palace. Will you come and see it with me?'

Her stomach looped. 'I'd like to,' she said, truthfully. 'But my schedule is already jam-packed.'

'Your schedule has been revised.'

She stared at him in surprise. 'Revised why?'

'In light of the security concerns today…'

'That was an angry man with a coffee,' she corrected, shaking her head. 'You had no business interfering with the arrangements my state department made.'

'Your safety is my priority.' He lowered his voice. 'As it is theirs—they were also anxious we limit your exposure to uncontrollable elements.'

'You mean people?'

He smiled, but she wasn't amused. Frustration shifted through her.

'Amir, I'm here to do a job. I want to do it.'

'And you can,' he promised. 'The higher profile events are still there. Your schedule has been curtailed, that is all.' He ran his eyes over her face slowly. 'But if you disagree, then have it reinstated.' He lifted his broad shoulders, but he might as well have been pulling on a string that ran right to her heart. She felt it ping and twinge. 'I trust your judgement.'

The string pulled again. Her heart hurt.

I trust your judgement. No one had ever said that to her before.

She lifted a palm to his cheek. 'Thank you for caring.'

His eyes widened and she saw something like shock in the depths of his eyes before he muted it, assuming an expression that was ironic. 'You're my guest in Ishkana. It's my job to care.'

Boundaries. How insistent he'd been on those boundaries, right from the start. He was insisting on them now, just not in so many words.

'I'll defer to you,' she said. 'On this matter only.'

He laughed, shaking his head. 'Heaven forbid you defer on anything else.'

Her own smile came naturally, but she knew what was at the root of her capitulation. A lighter schedule meant she could sneak more time with him. Her time in Taquul was almost at an end. They had to make the most of the days they had left.

'Your Majesty.' Ahmed's expression showed worry. 'It's four in the morning. Where have you been?'

Amir hadn't expected to be discovered returning to the palace. He stared at Ahmed, a frown on his face, wondering for a moment what he should say before realising he didn't have to say anything. He answered to no one.

'Did you want something?'

Ahmed continued to stare at Amir. His hair was wet, and, while he'd pulled his pants on, he'd left his robe off for the walk back to the palace. He had it thrown over one arm now. He'd been too distracted to dress.

'If you're going to insist on monopolising me, then I shall have to think of a form of payback.'

'Oh? What do you have in mind?'

She'd straddled him, taking him deep within her, and leaned over him so her dark hair teased his shoulders. 'What if I told you I have no intention of wearing underwear tomorrow, Amir?'

A smile flicked at his lips as the memory seared his

blood. Desire whipped him. It was practically daylight, and still he found he couldn't wait to see her again.

'Yes, sir. There's been an intelligence report. A band of vigilantes is forming in the foothills.'

Amir heard the words with a heavy heart, the statement jolting him back to the present, regretfully pushing all thoughts of Johara and her promise from his mind. 'Well, that didn't take long.'

'No, sir.' Ahmed's voice was similarly weighted.

'Damn it.' Amir dragged a hand through his hair. 'Give me twenty minutes then meet me in my office. Have Zeb join us,' he said, referring to the head of the security agency.

'Yes, sir.'

'Your hair is like a bird's nest,' Athena chastised with a smile. 'What in the world happened?'

Johara smiled, remembering every detail of the night before. 'I went swimming.' The words emerged before she could catch them. Her eyes met Athena's in the mirror. 'Alone. Last night. I found a stream and it was so hot, and no one was around…'

Athena stared at Johara as though she were losing her mind. 'Your Highness…'

Johara sighed, reaching up and putting a hand on Athena's. 'It's fine. No one saw me.'

She could see the fight being waged inside Athena. Their relationship was strange. While they were friends, it was a friendship that existed in a particular way. Athena would never overstep what she considered to be her place, despite the fact Johara often wished she would.

'What is it, Thena?' She pronounced her friend's name 'Thayna', as she always did when she wanted to set aside their professional roles and be simply two women who'd known each other a long time.

Athena's smile, though, showed the conversation was at an end. 'I was just thinking how to style it. A bun will hide the mess.'

'These are your parents?' She stopped walking, staring at the beautifully executed portrait, her eyes lingering on every detail.

'Yes.' At her side, Amir was very still. 'Painted the year of their marriage.'

'She's beautiful.' And she was. The artist had captured something in his mother's features that made Johara feel a tug to the other woman. She shifted her gaze to Amir's, conscious that servants surrounded them so keeping a discreet distance and a cool look pinned to her face. 'You have her eyes.'

He returned her look but it was futile. It didn't matter how cool either of them attempted to appear, heat sparked from him to her, making her fingertips tingle with an impulse to reach out and touch. She ached to drag her teeth across his collarbone, to flick her tongue in the indentation of his clavicle, to run her fingertips up his sides until he grabbed her and pinned her to the wall…

Her cheeks flushed, and she knew he recognised it because his attention shifted lower in her face and a mocking smile crept over his mouth—mocking himself or her, she didn't know.

She turned away from him, moving a little further down the hallway, her gaze sliding across the next painting—another couple. 'My grandparents,' he supplied. The next had her feet stilling, to study it properly.

'It's you.'

It jolted him—the painting had been done when he was only a small boy. 'How can you tell?'

'Your eyes,' she said seriously. 'And your smile.'

Ahmed had moved closer without either of them realising, and caught her observation, a small frown on his face. 'I beg your pardon, Your Majesty.' He addressed Amir alone.

'What is it?' Amir's impatience was obvious.

'There's an update, on the matter we discussed this morning. Zeb has the information. He's waiting in your office.'

Amir's brow creased in consternation but he nodded, turning back to Johara. 'I have to deal with this.'

Disappointment crested inside her. Perhaps Amir sensed it because he lowered his voice, though Ahmed stood at his elbow. 'I won't be long.'

It was too obvious. Heat sparked in Johara's cheeks. She looked away, nodding with what she hoped appeared disinterest. 'It's no bother, Your Majesty. I have plenty here with which to occupy myself.'

Amir didn't stay a moment longer than necessary. He turned on his heel and stalked down the corridor. Johara watched until he'd turned a corner, before realising that Ahmed was still there, his eyes intent on her face.

She forced a polite smile. 'The artwork here is first class.'

'Yes, madam.'

Frosty. Disapproving. She turned away from him, telling herself she didn't care. She continued to tour the gallery, each painting deserving far more attention than she gave it. She couldn't focus on anything other than Amir.

'My mother used to play the piano,' Amir said quietly. 'She was very good. When I was a child, I would listen to her for hours.'

Johara reached for another grape, grateful that they were—finally—alone. It had taken a heck of a lot of logistics but they'd managed to find a way to give all of their servants the slip, so that they could now sit, just the two of them, in his beautiful private hall that he'd brought her to the first morning she'd arrived. The morning he'd asked if she was pregnant. How much had happened since then!

'Do you play?'

He shook his head. 'No. I think her musicality escaped me.'

'Music can be taught,' she pointed out.

'The techniques can be, but not the passion and the instinct.'

Johara smiled. 'Remind me never to play if you're in attendance.'

'You play piano?'

'Yes.' She reached for another grape, but before she could pluck it from the vine he caught it and held it to her mouth instead, his eyes probing hers as he pushed it between her lips. Passion and desire were like flames, licking at the soles of her feet.

'Strangely, it was one of the things I excelled at.'

'Your dyslexia didn't make it difficult for you to read music?'

'Impossible.' She laughed. 'But I hear something and can play it.'

'I'm impressed.'

'Don't be.'

He lifted another grape to her mouth.

'It's just the way my brain is wired.'

'I want to hear you play.'

She leaned closer, pressing a kiss to the tip of his nose. 'And yet, I just said I won't play for you.'

'And what if I ordered you to?' His voice was mock-demanding.

She laughed. 'You and what army?'

He moved closer, grabbing her wrists, pinning them above her head as he used his body to press her backwards. 'Haven't you heard? I'm King of all I survey.'

'Including me?' she asked, breathless, lying on her back with Amir on top of her, the weight of him so pleasing, so addictive.

'Definitely you.'

'Ah, but I'm not one of your subjects,' she reminded him. 'I'm the enemy.'

He stared at her, his look serious. 'Not my enemy.'

It was strangely uplifting, but she didn't want to analyse the meaning behind his statement, because it would surely lead to disappointment. She kept her voice amused.

'My allegiance has to be earned.'

He smiled lazily, releasing one hand while keeping her wrists pinned easily in the other. He traced a line down her body, over her breasts, finding the peaks of her nipples and circling them before running his hand lower, and lower still, to capture the fabric at the bottom of the long dress she wore.

'I can think of one way to ensure loyalty.'

'Oh?'

'Let me see, first, if you are a lady of honour.'

She laughed. 'A what?'

'If you are true to your word.'

'Oh!' Heat stained her cheeks. She held her breath as his fingers crept up the satiny skin of her inner thigh and found what he was looking for—nakedness. She had gone without underpants for him. And she'd hoped he'd remembered her parting statement, and that the thought had driven him as wild as it had her.

His answer was everything she'd hoped for.

'Well?' she asked huskily.

'Just as promised.' He spoke with reverence. Their eyes met and something shifted inside her heart.

His dark head dipped down, his tongue stirring her to a fever pitch of longing, making her ache for him, reminding her of the maze, of everything they'd shared together since, of everything they were. Pleasure, passion, power; her blood was exploding with needs, her pulse too fast to be contained. She pushed up, needing him, wanting more than he could offer, craving the satisfaction she knew it was within his grasp to give. His mouth moved faster and she shattered, her fingertips driving through his hair, her mouth capable of shaping only two syllables: *Am* and *Ir*. Over and over and over she cried his name, as though it were an invocation that could ward off what they both knew was coming.

But she refused to think of the future, about what would happen in two days' time, when her tour was at an end and the flight took her back over the mountains to Taquul, and the future that was waiting for her.

She couldn't think about that. Not when there was this pleasure to be relished and enjoyed.

He knew they needed to move, to leave this sanctuary. He was Sheikh and, despite the fact he answered to no one, he couldn't simply disappear for hours at a time without arousing suspicion. His absence would be noticed. So too, he imagined, would hers.

But the weight of her head on his chest was so pleasant. Just for a little while longer, he wanted to keep the doors to this room shut, to lie as they were: naked on the scatter pillows, the heady fragrance of trees and flowers and the sound of flowing water creating their own world and atmosphere. It was a *masjid* first and foremost and here he felt that he was worshipping Johara as she deserved to be worshipped.

'Will you come to my room tonight?'

The question surprised him—he hadn't intended to ask it, but he didn't regret it.

'Sure.' Her voice, though, was teasing. 'I'll just let your guards know I'm popping in for a quick roll in your bed. That won't raise any eyebrows whatsoever.'

He laughed, shifting so he could see her face. 'There's a secret way.'

She met his gaze. 'Into your room?'

'Yes.'

'Why?' And then, realisation dawned. 'For exactly this purpose.'

Another laugh. 'Yes.'

'So you…sneak lovers in…regularly?'

He heard her hurt and wondered at his body's response to it. He wanted to draw her into his arms and tell her she had nothing to be jealous of. He'd never been with a woman like her. He doubted he ever would be again.

'No, Johara. Never.'

'Oh. Then why…?'

'Because my room has been the Sheikh's room for many hundreds of years.' He lifted his broad shoulders. 'And whichever palace concubine my predecessors decided to amuse themselves with would arrive via a secret tunnel.'

Her jaw dropped. 'You're not serious.'

Her innocence made it impossible not to smile. 'Perfectly.'

'But…'

'But?'

'Well, it's a security risk, for one,' she huffed.

'It is not a corridor anyone knows about.'

'Want to bet?'

He arched a brow, waiting for her to continue.

'It seems to me like the kind of thing your enemies would pay a lot of money to learn about.'

'The palace is guarded like a fortress.'

'I know that.'

'It's safe.'

'I know that too.' She gnawed on her lower lip, her eyes clouded, but after a moment she sighed, surrendering despite her first response. 'Well? How do I find it?'

CHAPTER ELEVEN

'THIS PLACE IS...'

She looked around, wishing she didn't find the room so incredibly sumptuous and sensual. 'I mean...'

His smile was sardonic. 'Yes?' But he knew how she felt. Shirtless, wearing only a pair of slim-fitting black trousers, he prowled towards her, capitalising on the overwhelm a space such as this had given her.

The carpets were a deep red in colour, the furnishing a similar colour, velvet, with gold details. There were chairs but in the middle of the space, making it very obvious exactly what the room was to be used for, was the most enormous bed Johara had seen. It could easily accommodate ten people.

Her mouth felt dry as she stepped towards it, studying it with a curiosity she couldn't resist.

'What's that?' She ran her finger over an ornate brass hook that hung in the centre of the bed's head.

'For handcuffs.'

She spun around to face him, oddly guilty. 'Handcuffs?' The question squeaked out of her.

He prowled closer, and the nearer he got, the faster her pulse went. She bit down on her lip as he grabbed her wrists, rubbing his thumb over them. 'Or rope. Or silk. Whatever your preference.'

Her eyes moved back to the bed, as desire ran the length of her spine.

'Does it tempt you?'

She shivered quite openly now, lifting her eyes to his, uncertainty in their depths. Yes, she wanted to say. It tempted her—a lot. But only with him! It was a fantasy she'd never had before—never even thought to have. But with Amir, the idea of being tied up and made love to was, perhaps, the most intoxicating thing she'd ever contemplated.

So she clung to outrage instead, because she was aware of how dangerous her supplication had become, how completely she'd surrendered to Amir and his ways.

'I just can't believe there's a place like this in your palace. A harem!'

His smile showed he knew exactly how she felt, and why she was intent on denying it.

'It hasn't been used since my great-grandfather's reign.'

She looked away, her eyes betraying her and straying to the hook once more, her nipples straining against the silk fabric of her bra.

She was fighting a losing battle.

'So what do you do when you're dating a woman?' she prompted, needing to focus on something other than this overtly sexual room, and the hook that would accommodate handcuffs just perfectly.

He tilted his head, waiting for her to continue. 'Are you asking if I bring women here?' he prompted, gesturing to the bed.

'God, no.' She shook her head urgently, not wanting *that* image in her mind. 'I just meant…do you date, publicly? Can women come to your room?'

'I can do whatever I want,' he said gently. 'I'm Sheikh.' He pressed a finger to her chin, lifting her face to his. 'It is for you that we must be secret about this—and for the sake of the peace treaty.'

She nodded. 'So if I were just some woman you'd met, you'd have me delivered to your room whenever it suited?'

His laugh was little more than a growl. 'You make it sound so archaic. So one-sided. If you were just a woman I'd met,' he corrected, 'I would invite you for dinner. We would share a meal and then I would ask you if you wanted to come to my room. The choice would be—as it is now—yours.'

Her heart turned over in her chest. She had the suspicion she was being combative and she didn't know why. Something was needling her, making her frustrated and wanting to lash out.

'I'm sorry,' she said truthfully, lifting her fingers to his chest and pressing them there. 'I don't know why I'm acting like this. I just didn't expect this room to be so—'

'Confronting?' he suggested. Then, 'Unpalatable.'

She shook her head, not meeting his eyes. 'Palatable,' she corrected, so quietly it was barely a whisper.

In response, he pulled her hard against him, and before she could draw breath he was kissing her as though everything they cared for in this life depended on it. Her body moulded to his like it was designed to fit—two pieces carved from the same marble. She felt his heart racing in time with hers, thudding where hers was frantic, a baritone to her soprano.

Time and space swirled away, concepts far in the distance, as he stooped down and lifted her easily, kissing her as he cradled her against his chest, carrying her through this room and into a corridor that was wide but dimly lit. She felt safe. She felt whole.

She relaxed completely, a beautiful heaviness spreading through her limbs. When they entered his room, she spared it only a cursory glimpse, and took in barely any of the details. It was similar to the suite she'd been provided with, but larger and more elaborate. It was also quite spartan. Where hers was filled with luxurious touches, his had been pared back. The mosaics on the floor were beautiful, but there was no art here. Just white walls, giving the windows all the ability to shine, with their view of the desert. Or, as it was now, of the night sky beyond.

He placed her gently onto the bed then stood, looking at her, his eyes showing a thousand and one things even when he said nothing.

Johara smiled and reached for him—her instincts driving her—and he came, joining her in the bed, sweeping her into his arms once more and kissing her until breathing became an absolute afterthought.

'You don't have to do this, sir.'

'I want to.' Twelve-year-old Amir fixed his parents' servant with a look from the depths of his soul. It was a look of purpose and determination. It was a look that hid the pain tearing him into a thousand little pieces.

'I have identified their bodies, for security purposes,' Ahmed reminded Amir softly, putting a hand on Amir's shoulder. His touch was kindly meant; it was then Amir remembered Ahmed had children of his own, not too far apart in age from Amir.

'I want to see them.'

He spoke with a steely resonance, and it gripped his heart. There was much uncertainty. In the hours since his parents' death, he'd had to grapple with the change in his circumstances, the expectations upon him. He felt deeply but showed nothing. He was a leader. People looked to him.

'Amir,' Ahmed sighed. 'No child should have to see this.'

He drew himself to his full height. 'I said I want to see them.'

It was enough. Even Ahmed wouldn't argue with the Sheikh of Ishkana—for long.

'Yes, sir.' He sighed wearily, hesitated a moment then turned. 'This way.'

The corridor was dimly lit but muffled noise was everywhere. The palace had woken. The country had woken. News had spread like wildfire.

They were dead.

At the door to the tomb where their bodies had been brought to lie, Amir allowed himself the briefest moment of hesitation, to steel himself, and then stepped inside.

Three people were within. Lifelong servants. People who felt his parents' loss as keenly as he, who grieved with the same strength he did.

'Leave me,' he commanded, his eyes falling to his father's face first. He didn't look to see that he'd been obeyed. He knew that he had been. Only Ahmed remained, impervious perhaps to the Sheikh's commands, or perhaps knowing that, despite the appearance of strength, a twelve-year-old boy could not look upon his parents' crumpled bodies and feel nothing.

He kneeled beside his father, taking his hand, holding it, pressing his face to it, praying for strength and guidance. He moved to his mother next, and it was the sight of her that made a thick sob roll through his chest.

She looked asleep. Beautiful. Peaceful. He put his hands on either side of her face, as though willing her to wake up, but she didn't.

It was the worst thing he'd had to do, but seeing his parents like that became the cornerstone of his being.

The war had killed them. Taquul had killed them. The Qadirs...

* * *

He woke with a start, his heart heavy, a strange sense of claustrophobia and grief pressing against him, before realising he wasn't alone.

He pushed the sheets back, staring at Johara in complete confusion. It took him a second to remember who she was, and then it all came flooding back to him—their affair, their intimacy, the way he'd started to think of her and smile at the strangest of times.

What the hell was he doing? His parents' visage was so fresh in his mind, the hatred he'd felt that night—and here he was, with a Qadir…

No. Not a Qadir. Johara.

Her name was like an incantation. It relaxed him, pulling him back to the present, reminding him of everything they'd shared in the past week.

She was a Qadir, but she was so much more than that. When he looked at her, he no longer saw her family, her place in the Taquul royal lineage, her birthright; when he said her name he saw only her, not the uncle for whom she'd been named, the uncle who had orchestrated his parents' murder.

But guilt followed that realisation. He'd promised his parents' dead bodies he would never forget. He'd promised them he would hate the enemy for ever, and here he was, seeking comfort in Johara's arms, craving her in a way he should have been fighting against.

He moved to the windows, the ancient desert a sight that comforted him and anchored him, reminding him who he was. He breathed in its acrid air, letting it permeate his lungs. He was a Haddad. He was of this country, this kingdom, he served the people of Ishkana and nothing would change that.

What he and Johara were doing was… He turned towards

the bed, her sleeping body making him frown. He couldn't describe how he felt about her, and this. He knew only that there was a greater danger here than he'd ever imagined.

A knock sounded at the door—loud and imperative. Amir saw that it disturbed Johara and winced, crossing to the door quickly, grabbing shorts as he went and pulling them on. With one quick look over his shoulder, he pulled it inwards. Ahmed stood there, but he was not alone. Zeb, and several guards, were at his back.

Amir pulled the door shut behind himself, shielding his bed and lover from view before consulting his wristwatch. It was almost four. Only something serious would have brought anyone—particularly this contingent of men—to his room at this hour.

'What is it?'

Ahmed nodded. 'There's been an attack.'

Amir tensed. 'Where?'

'In the *malani* provinces.'

His eyes swept shut. Anger sparked inside him. 'How many?'

'Two confirmed dead so far.'

He swore. 'Insurgents?'

Ahmed looked towards Zeb. 'Taquul insurgents,' he said quietly. 'They set off a bomb outside a nightclub.'

Many times in his life had he been told news such as this. He braced for the inevitable information. 'How bad?'

'It's an emerging situation. The damage is being assessed.'

'Whose bomb?'

'That's not clear,' Zeb murmured. 'It has the markings of a state device, though the timing…'

'Yes.' Unconsciously, he looked over his shoulder. It was impossible to believe anyone in Malik's military would be foolish enough to launch an attack while Johara was deep in Ishkana.

'What scale are we talking?'

Ahmed winced. 'It's bad, sir. A building's collapsed.'

Amir swore.

'I've put the border forces on alert.'

Amir stiffened. It was protocol. Zeb had done the right thing, and yet the familiarity of all this hit him like a stone in the gut. Just like that, he could see the peace evaporating.

'We need more information.'

'Sir?' Ahmed's brows were furrowed.

'Was this the act of a rogue military commander, or the insurgents in the mountain ranges looking to profit from ongoing unease between our people, or a state-sanctioned skirmish in disputed land? We need to understand what the hell happened and why, before we respond.'

'But you will have to respond,' Zeb insisted. 'We don't have all the details yet but this was a vicious peace-time attack. Your people will expect—'

'My people want peace,' Amir said quietly, thinking of the sadness he'd seen in the eyes of the man who'd thrown coffee at Johara. 'Not a knee-jerk retaliation that springs us back into the war.'

Silence met the statement.

'The Princess—' Zeb's expression was uneasy. He looked to Ahmed before continuing. 'She would be a good bargaining chip. To ensure Malik apologises, takes responsibility…'

Amir felt a surge of disgust and then rage. 'Even if he had nothing to do with it?'

'I find it hard to believe an attack of this kind could occur without his involvement.'

'This is what we will discover. But in the meantime Her Highness remains our honoured guest. No one is to speak to her of this, to touch her, to even think of using her in any way. Understood?'

Zeb frowned. 'It is my job to advise you on the best military strategies...'

'Fine. You've advised me.'

'The death toll could be in the hundreds. You must act, sir. I have the eleventh division mobilised. They could retake one of our strongholds in the mountains—'

'No.' He shook his head, then in a tone designed to placate, 'It's too soon.'

'Too soon? The destruction. The inevitable death count—'

'We are no longer at war.'

'What is this if not an act of war?' Zeb pushed with obvious impatience.

Amir fixed him with a stare that was designed to strike fear into the other man. It worked. Contrition overtook his expression. While Amir allowed—and appreciated—a lot of latitude from his advisors, he remained the ultimate power holder.

'We don't have enough information to know yet.'

'But if it was state-sanctioned?'

Amir considered that. He had met with Malik and seen in his eyes the same desire for peace that lived in Amir's heart. They both wanted this, for their people. 'We'll discuss that if we come to it.'

'And you'll respond accordingly?'

Amir compressed his lips, not inclined to answer that without having more of an idea as to the circumstances of the attack.

'The Princess should be held until we know,' Zeb pushed. 'Detain her, show our people that we're not feeding our enemies cake and wine...'

'She is not the enemy,' Amir said cuttingly. 'And I have already told you—no one is to bring her into this.'

'She is in it, though,' Ahmed said gently. 'Her presence alone requires some kind of action.'

Ahmed's words reached inside Amir and shook him, forced him to see clearly the tenuousness of Johara's place here in the kingdom. He had come to know her, beyond the fact she was a Qadir and a princess of Taquul, but why should he expect his people to feel as he did? She could easily become a focus for anger and revenge. His gut rolled with a burst of nausea; his skin felt hot and cold all over.

He turned back to the men. 'I want a meeting in the tactical rooms. Fifteen minutes. Discover what you can in the meantime. I need answers. And I want to speak to Malik Qadir. Arrange that as soon as possible, Zeb.' His eyes met Ahmed's. Something passed between them. Understanding. Agreement. 'Let me be clear here—my goal is to maintain the peace.' He softened his tone. 'For too long we have answered violence with violence; I understand your instincts now are to do the same. But that will only perpetuate what we've always known. The fight for peace will be won with diplomacy, not military force.'

He paused, knowing what he had to do and hating the necessity of it. But for her safety…to prevent anything ever happening to her as had happened to his parents? An image of his mother's face filled his mind, as she'd been the last time he'd seen her, in the tombs beneath the palace. Fear hardened into resolve. Johara would be protected at all costs.

'Johara Qadir will leave the country immediately.' He faced Zeb. 'Her safe passage is the most important job you will have tonight, Zeb. If anything happens to her—'

'I know. It will inevitably renew the war.'

Amir waited until they were gone before pushing the door to his room open. Johara was awake now, looking at him, her eyes huge and hair tousled. He wasn't sure what she'd heard, but it was clear she knew something was amiss.

She stood as he walked towards the bed, her nakedness taking his breath away even then.

'Something's wrong?'

He contemplated not telling her. He contemplated saying nothing, but she deserved to know. Besides, her brother would undoubtedly contact her imminently.

'Yes.'

'What is it?'

He ground his teeth together, moving towards her. 'There was an attack. A Taquul bomb in one of the northern towns.'

Her features showed surprise and then sorrow. 'You said this would happen.'

'Yes, but I had hoped…' He shook his head. He hadn't, really. He'd known that peace was a Sisyphean task, yet still he'd pushed for it, worked towards it, knowing his people deserved at least a chance. He still believed that. For their sake, he had to quell this, ensure it didn't form the beginning of more conflict. But the attitude of his chief military advisor showed what a battle he was waging—even within his own government.

'Was anyone hurt?'

'Yes.'

'Killed?'

'The exact number is unknown but we expect the count to be high.' She dipped her head forward, and he knew she felt as he did—sorrow. Futility. Anger.

'You have to go.'

She nodded, looking around for her clothes. 'Yes. I shouldn't have fallen asleep. What can I do?'

He stared at her, committing everything about her to memory. He could never see her again. These last few days had been something he could never put into words, but it had to end. She wasn't simply a woman with whom he could enjoy a no-strings affair. He wanted her too selfishly. In another day or two, he wouldn't be able to relinquish her. It had to be now. To his people, and his government, she would always be the enemy. He was putting her at risk every minute he kept her here.

'How can I help?'

Her words were some kind of balm. No one had offered him help—and so simply—all his life. But he pushed the offer aside. 'You misunderstand, Johara. You need to leave Ishkana. I have arranged your transport. You are to leave now, in the dead of night, before the country has awoken to this news.'

Her mouth dropped open.

'That's… No.'

Another surprise. People didn't say 'no' to him. 'You misunderstand me again. I'm not asking you to leave.'

Her eyes narrowed. 'You're ordering me?'

He expelled a sigh, moving across the room and pulling out some clothes. He understood her resentment of that—all her life she'd been ordered around and yet she deserved so much better. He didn't want to be just another person who sought to control her. 'I'm telling you what is going to happen. You cannot be here if war breaks out. The risk to you is too great.'

'War won't break out. My brother and you will work together to prevent that from happening.'

'We don't know yet that this bomb wasn't detonated with your brother's permission.'

She gasped. 'You can't seriously think—'

He shook his head. 'No.' He frowned. 'But war with Taquul is familiar.'

'All the more reason for us to challenge that assumption.'

He shook his head with frustration. Why wouldn't she understand? 'There are powerful members of my government already demanding retribution.'

'You can't do that.'

He ground his teeth together. 'I have to do what is best for my country.'

'And that's peace. We both know that.'

'Yes, Johara, but peace may not be possible.'

She shook her head. 'I refuse to believe that. Let me stay here with you, standing by your side showing that we are committed to a peaceful outcome.'

The image she created was vibrant but impossible. Zeb's response had shown him that. *Detain her.* A fierce reaction resonated along his spine. 'Your place is in Taquul with your people.'

Her eyes sparked with anger. 'Can't you see that's what's wrong with all this? *Your* people. *My* people. They're all damned people, living side by side. Isn't this peace about breaking down barriers, Amir? Wasn't that the purpose of my being here?'

His heart had kicked up a notch. He dragged trousers over his boxers without looking away from her. 'This changes things.'

'It doesn't have to.' She moved towards him with urgency. 'You said, from the outset, there would be difficulties. This is one of them. Are you truly intending to fall at the first hurdle?'

'No.' He reached for a shirt. 'But having you here complicates matters. You have to leave.'

'Why? For whom does it complicate anything?'

'You represent something my people have been taught to hate, and also fear.'

'Me?' She dug her fingers into the space between her breasts; his gut twisted at her look of obvious disbelief. 'I'm just one woman, a woman who's here with an open heart and mind, wanting to improve relations. Your people will see that—just don't push me away. Let me stay. Show your citizens that you and I are both invested in the peace process, that we believe it will succeed…'

'And what if Malik and I cannot agree on this? What if war is inevitable? You think my military will not expect me to keep you as a prisoner?'

She gasped. 'You would never do that.'

'No.' He dragged a hand through his hair, frowning. 'Of course I wouldn't, and that's the problem. You compromise me. This, what we've been doing, has made me forget.' He softened his tone, moving closer. 'But I can't forget.' He lifted a hand to her cheek, touching her for what he knew would be the last time. 'We created a perfect void, you and I. A magical space removed from anything and anyone else. But nothing about this works when the world intrudes. The reality of who we are and what our countries require of us is there, banging at the door. Wake up and hear it, Johara. This has to end and you need to leave.'

He felt her shiver, her body trembling against his hand. 'You're wrong.'

He took a step back. 'This was wrong. I thought we could separate what we were doing from the circumstances of who we are, but I never will. We stand on the brink of war once more. Your people. My people. You, and me. You are a Qadir.'

She shook her head, tears filling her eyes, so he felt pain throb low in his gut. He angled his face away for a moment, unable to see her cry.

'Is that all I am to you?'

He closed his heart against her hurt. 'No. But it's the part of you I have to focus on.'

Silence hung between them, heavy and accusatory. He fixed her with a determined gaze.

'I promise that I will protect you with my dying breath but even that isn't enough to guarantee your safety. I have forbidden my military commander from using you as a pawn in this, but I cannot control this to my satisfaction. You are at risk every minute you remain here, Jo.' The diminutive of her name slipped out in his need to convince her.

'I'm not afraid,' she insisted, her eyes showing fierceness.

'You should be.' He blinked and saw his parents' bodies. His blood turned to ice. 'I will not have your death on my conscience.'

'Then let me absolve you of that. I'm choosing to stay—this isn't your responsibility.'

But she would always be his responsibility. It was inevitable. He didn't want the burden of protecting her; he couldn't lose her because of his selfish desire to have her at his side.

Johara brushed a hand through her dark hair, drawing his attention to her face. 'I won't leave; not now. My visit is scheduled to end tomorrow. Let me stay until then, keep to my schedule. Please, Amir. We cannot capitulate to what's likely to be a few rogues. Why can't you see that? It's exactly what they want! Surely this attack was designed in the hope of disturbing the peace—'

He held a hand in the air to silence her, his blood slamming through his body. 'And what better way to disturb the peace than to harm you? You think that even if you stayed I would ever allow you to keep to your schedule? To leave the palace when the mood is like this? No, Johara.' He refused to soften even when faced with her obvious hurt. 'The night we met, I thought you idealistic. But you are also naïve. You have been sheltered, to some extent, from the ravages of this war. You do not understand the lengths men will go to—'

'How dare you?' She glared at him down the length of her nose. 'How dare you speak to me as though I am—' she stopped abruptly, her face filled with torment '—

stupid?' she finished on a sob, pressing her palms to her eyes.

He stood perfectly still, because if he moved, even a little bit, he knew he would crumble altogether. He wanted to cross to her and pull her to him, to wrap his arms around her and hold her tight, to kiss her until this all faded away into nothingness. To tell her that whoever had told her she was stupid because of her dyslexia was mad, because she was the smartest, most courageous person he'd ever known. But he would not weaken. She needed him to be strong; his country needed him to be strong.

Her eyes narrowed, her lower lip trembling, but when she spoke it was in a tone that was pure steel. 'You think you're the only one who's watched his country suffer at the hands of the enemy? I know what we've done to each other! I've lived it, too! That's why we need to stop it. Work together—'

'As your brother and I will do,' he said, determined to turn her away. 'If this was a rogue attack from the mountain people then we will work together to—reason with them and understand them, just as you urged me to understand the man who threw coffee at you. They have played their part in this war and perhaps they have motives we don't comprehend. You've made me see that, Jo. You've changed how I view conflict, people, war. You've changed me.' The admission cost him. It emerged thick and throaty, dark with his emotions.

He paused, bracing himself for what he needed her to know. 'You cannot remain. You are a liability.' He knew he had to be firm, harsh, to get her to see sense. Feeling as though he were dropping off the edge of a cliff, he spun away from her. 'And you're a distraction I don't want, Johara. I need you to go now.'

CHAPTER TWELVE

'YOU'RE A DISTRACTION I don't want, Johara. I need you to go now.'

She stared at his back, his intractable words beating her in the chest. Her eyes swept shut; she struggled to breathe. Hearing these things at any time would have been difficult, but naked in his room, she felt vulnerable and exposed, disbelieving too, as though what he was saying went against everything they'd become.

'The fate of my country hangs in the balance. Of course I can't just run away from that.' She looked around for her clothes, and finally saw them discarded near the foot of the bed. She stalked towards them, scooping them up and pulling her pants on quickly. Her fingers shook, making it difficult to clasp her bra into place. 'And you don't know me at all if you think I'm the kind of person who would quit at the first roadblock.'

'Then do what you must in the bounds of Taquul but you will leave Ishkana, and leave now, before the kingdom awakes to this news.'

'And they'll think I've deserted them! They'll think my opinion of the peace is fragile when it's not! I believe in this peace as much as I believe in this—what you and I share.'

His eyes closed for a moment, as though he was physically rejecting that sentiment. 'They will be far more concerned with whether or not the war is about to break out again.'

'You're making a mistake.' She knew that to be the case. Every cell in her body was screaming at her in violent protest. Leaving was wrong. Not just Ishkana, but Amir. All week she'd braced herself for the necessity of that, and she'd known it would be hard, but, seeing him with the weight of the world on his shoulders, she finally understood what had been happening to them. Ever since that night in the maze.

She lifted a hand to her mouth, smothering a gasp and turning her back on him while she analysed her head, her heart, everything she was feeling.

It was a secret affair, one they'd agreed would have clear-cut boundaries, but Johara's heart…it hadn't realised. Not really. She'd fallen in love with him, with all of herself. The desert sky was still an inky black, the stars overhead sparkling, though now it was with a look of mischief. They'd known what they were doing in the maze, contriving for these two people to see one another and give into that cataclysmic desire. Qadirs and Haddads, unbeknownst, hidden, lovers.

At the very edge of the horizon, where sand met sky, whispers of purple were radiating like flames, promising the break of a new day. Soon it would spread, licking upwards, covering the heavens in colour, and then it would begin. How they acted on this day would determine so much.

She spun back to face Amir. His back was still turned. The sight of him like that, closed off to her, sparked a thousand emotions in her gut. Something inside her snapped, but underneath it all was the wonderment of her realisation.

'What if I stayed?' she said quietly, moving towards him, circumnavigating his frame so they were toe to toe, eyes clashing.

'I won't allow it, and nor will your brother.'

Anger exploded in her gut. 'Neither of you can control me,' she said fiercely.

'This isn't about control. It's about your safety.'

'You're saying you can't keep me safe until this is over?' she challenged him, so close she could feel the exhalations as he worked to control his temper.

'I'm saying your safety would become all I could think of,' he contradicted, putting his hands on her shoulders. 'And I need to focus on *this*—the country—with all of my attention. In Taquul, you will be safe.'

'Maybe I don't just want to be safe, trapped in Taquul, dull yet protected,' she responded. 'Maybe I'd rather be at risk here with you, than anywhere else in the world.'

The words were thrown like a gauntlet. They stared at each other, the meaning behind her statement impossible to miss.

She waited, needing him to speak, but he didn't, and so she asked, quietly, her voice just a whisper, 'Do you really want me to leave, Amir?' She pressed her hand to his chest, feeling the thudding of his heart, wondering if it was beating for her.

'I *need* it.'

She shook her head, pain beginning to spread through her. Why couldn't he see what was right in front of him?

'I'm not afraid.' She tilted her chin defiantly. 'You overreacted earlier this week, when the man threw a coffee cup at me, and you're overreacting now. I'm not made of glass.'

'Overreacting? Did you not hear me, Jo? I've just had the chief of my military agency telling me to *detain you*.' A shiver ran down her spine at the ugliness of that—how quickly people could turn! 'If it turns out that this attack had *any degree* of government assistance then those calls will become louder. Here in Ishkana, to almost all of my people, you *are* the enemy.'

Stricken and pale, she trembled. His eyes swept over her, spreading nothing. No warmth. She felt cold to the core of her being.

'You will leave this morning, instead of tomorrow afternoon. Understood?'

'No!' She shook her head in a last-ditch effort to make him see things as she did—or had. She couldn't deny the kernel of fear that was spreading through her. But she had to be brave—more was at stake now. If he knew how she felt and what she wanted, would it make a difference?

'You're the one who doesn't understand. I don't want to leave now. I don't want to leave tomorrow. I want to stay here in Ishkana with you, for the rest of my life, however long that might be. Anything else is unacceptable to me.' She pressed her hands to her hips, adopting a stance that was pure courage and strength when inside she was trembling like a leaf.

His expression was impossible to interpret. Dark eyes met and held hers, and he said nothing for so long that her stance began to weaken, one hand dropping to her side, a feeling of loss spreading through her.

'It's impossible.'

'There would be difficulties,' she corrected. 'But what we have is worth fighting for.'

'If things were different,' he said quietly, his hands lifting to catch her face, cradling her cheeks as he held her so he could see everything that crossed her expression, 'I might want that too.'

It was both the bursting of light and hope within her and the breaking apart of it too. 'Things don't need to be different. I'm here with you now. Does it make any sense for me to be elsewhere?'

His eyes swept shut. 'There's no future for us, *inti qamar*. We've always known that.'

Her heart was in pain. 'Don't you see what I'm trying to tell you?'

He moved a finger to her lips. 'Don't say it.' His Adam's apple jerked as he swallowed. 'Please don't say it. I don't wish to hurt you by not answering with what you would hope to hear in return.' He padded his thumb over her lower lip.

'So then say it,' she whispered. 'I know you feel it.'

'You're wrong.' He shook his head. 'I fought this. I fought you.' He had. When she'd first come to Ishkana he'd tried so hard to stop any of this from happening. 'I should have fought harder.' He stepped back from her, and again she had the sense that he was ending the conversation, making an arbitrary decision that there was no more to say.

It violated everything she felt and wanted. She stamped her foot as he crossed to the door. He was leaving.

'I love you, Amir.' He stopped walking and stood completely still. 'I have fallen so completely in love with you, and not just you—this damned country of yours. I want to stay here with you as your wife, to live my life at your side. Whatever the risks, I want to be here with you.' His back was ramrod straight. 'I love you.'

She felt as though she were paused mid-air, waiting to have a parachute pulled or to drop like a dead weight towards earth. She didn't move. She waited, her lungs burning with the force of breathing, her arms strangely heavy.

'Loving me is—'

She held her breath.

'I don't want your love.'

She flinched.

'I will never return it.' His eyes bore into hers, the seriousness of what he was saying eclipsed by a look that showed her he meant every horrible word he said.

'Then what exactly have we been doing?'

He clamped his lips together, his jaw pressing firm. 'Not falling in love.'

She shook her head; she couldn't believe it. 'I have been.' She swallowed past a wave of bitterness. 'And nothing you say will make me change my mind on that.'

His response was to walk away from her, across the room. At the door, he turned to face her. 'Forget about me, Johara. Go home to Taquul, live your life. Be happy. Please.'

The helicopter lifted from the palace, and he watched it take off into the dawn sky. With one call he could have it summoned back to the palace. A word to a servant and the pilot would respond, bringing the helicopter—and its passenger—back to him. *I want to stay here with you as your wife.*

It was impossible.

If this morning's outbreak of violence had demonstrated anything it was that the people of Taquul and Ishkana would never tolerate anything of the sort. *Detain the Princess.*

If he weren't Sheikh? And she weren't a princess?

No. He wouldn't lose himself in hypotheticals. He was Sheikh Amir Haddad of Ishkana and his allegiance was—and always would be—to his country.

He wouldn't think of her again.

'It makes sense, Jo.'

She sat very still, listening to her brother, her eyes focussed on the spectacular view framed through the windows of this room. Desert sand, the crispest white, spread before them, meeting a sky that was a blisteringly bright blue.

It was just as it had been from the ruins.

So much of Taquul was like Ishkana.

'You must be able to see how right this is. It's what our parents wanted, it's what I want, what he wants. I think deep down it's even what you want.'

'Well,' she couldn't help drawling her response, 'I'm glad you've given what I want *some* thought, seeing as I'd be the one marrying him.'

'You used to like Paris,' Malik said with a shake of his head, coming to sit beside her. The smell of his tea reached her nostrils.

'I still like Paris,' she agreed. 'I consider him a friend. But I don't intend to marry him.'

Malik sighed. 'What's got into you?'

She turned to face him, her eyes clear. 'What do you mean?'

'You've been…different…since you got back from Ishkana.'

Got back. Returned. Came 'home'. All perfectly calm ways to describe the fact she felt as though a rocket had blasted her world into pieces.

'I felt the same way about this before I left. I have never intended to marry Paris. Not really.' She sighed. 'I can see the sense of it. I can tell it's what you want, and yes, I can see why. But I won't marry him.'

'He cares for you.'

I love you. He hadn't said anything back. Did that mean he didn't love her? Or that he *couldn't* love her?

It didn't matter. Four weeks had passed. Four weeks. With effort, work and a lot of the reason, sympathy and diplomacy Johara had advocated for, peace was being forged, and it was strengthening with every day that passed. Life was normal again. Except it wasn't. In the middle of her chest there was an enormous black hole. She went through the motions each day, imitating the woman she'd once been. But while her body had returned to Taquul, her heart and soul had remained behind in Ishkana. She doubted the two would ever reunite.

'I can't marry him,' she said, more strenuously.

'Why not?'

Why not? The truth was screaming through her. She stood uneasily, jerkily, moving to the window. The maze was around the corner. If she leaned forward, she'd be able to see just a hint of its verdant walls. She closed her eyes, nausea rising inside her.

'I *am* different.' The words were barely a whisper. She heard the rustle of clothing as her brother came to stand behind her. 'Something happened in Ishkana and it's changed me. I might have been more malleable once. I might even have agreed to this, to please you, and because yes, I can see that it makes a sort of sense. But not now. I can't. Please don't ask me again.'

'What happened, Jo?' There was urgency in his question. 'Did someone hurt you?' She heard the fear beneath the statement. Why couldn't they stop worrying about her? As though she were so fragile, and couldn't look after herself.

'I was treated as an honoured guest,' she assured him. 'No one hurt me.'

And because the words had been pressing down on her like an awful weight for a month now, she said them aloud, needing to speak them to make them real, and to understand them better. 'I fell in love.' She angled her face towards her brother's. 'I fell in love in Ishkana. The idea of marrying Paris—or anyone—makes my blood run cold. Please don't ask it of me.'

'Fell in love?' he repeated, frowning, as though this was an entirely foreign concept. 'With whom?'

Was there any sense in lying? She bit down on her lip, searching for what she should say or do.

But Malik swore, shook his head. 'No. Not him.'

'Yes.' She twisted her fingers at her side, seeing her brother's shock and wishing she hadn't been the instrument of it, and also not caring, because inside she'd grown numb and cold.

'Johara, you cannot be serious.'

She bit down on her lip. 'I love him.'

'This man is—he is—'

'What is he?' she challenged defiantly, anger coursing through her veins. 'The war is over.'

'But the sentiments are not.' He sighed angrily. 'We were at war a long time. You might be ready to forget that but our people won't. There's been too much loss. Too much hurt. It's going to take time and you, a princess of Taquul, cannot simply do as you wish.'

'Of course I can.' She held his gaze levelly, her expression firm. 'I refuse to be bound by a war that has ended, by a war that was started a century ago. I refuse to hate a man I hadn't even met until a few weeks ago. I love him—and you cannot, will not, change my mind or my heart.'

Malik glared at her with a mix of outrage and disbelief. 'I forbid it. I forbid any of this. You will marry Paris and that's the end of it.' He stared at her for several more seconds then turned, stalking towards the door. He slammed it behind him; she didn't so much as flinch.

Amir told himself he wouldn't ask about her. This day wasn't about Johara. It wasn't about him. This was an event marking six months of hard-fought-for peace, a meeting with Malik Qadir, to show the world that the two leaders were intent on progressing matters. It hadn't been smooth sailing, but each little outbreak had been quickly quelled. All-out war had been avoided.

'Let me stand by your side. Let them see us united.'

He heard her voice often. Her promises. Her offer. Her desire.

'I love you.'

He wouldn't ask about her.

Within minutes, this would be over. A handshake in front of the media, and then they'd slip into their separate cars, go in separate directions, lead separate lives. Because they were Qadir and Haddad and that was what they did.

Malik had her eyes.

Amir felt as though he'd been punched in the gut. But hadn't it been that way since she'd left?

The documents were signed—more trade agreements, a relaxation on sanctions, the beginning of an economic alliance that would strengthen both countries. The business was concluded.

'Leave us.' Amir surveyed the room, encompassing Taquul and Ishkana aides in his directive.

Malik gave a single nod to show his agreement.

There was the scraping of chairs, the sound of feet against tiles, the noise as the door opened to the corridor beyond, and then they were alone; silence fell once more.

'The agreement is in order.' Malik's voice was firm. 'Our people will benefit from this.'

Amir nodded. He wouldn't ask about her.

'And it is timely too,' Malik said, standing, extending his hand to bring the meeting to an end.

If he was going to ask, it would need to be now. *How is she?* The words ran through his head, demanding an answer. He needed to know as he needed to breathe. Nothing more—just *how is she*? Was she happy?

So much of his own happiness depended on that.

'My attention can now be given over to the details of my sister's marriage.' Malik said the words simply, without any hint of malice. He couldn't have known that his statement was an instrument of intense pain to Amir. He kept his face neutral, but his body was tense, like a snake ready to strike.

'Marriage?'

'Yes.' Simple, with a smile. No ulterior motive. 'You met her fiancé, Paris.'

Amir nodded, standing, his chest constricting. 'Yes, of course. When is the wedding to take place?'

'Next week.' He held his hand out for Amir to shake. Amir stared at Malik's hand for several seconds, a frown on his face. He wanted to say so much! He wanted to ask questions, to know everything.

But he didn't have any right to ask.

'Wish…her well from me.'

A week came and went. Amir kept busy. He worked twenty-hour days, involving himself in every single ministerial portfolio. Very little went on that concerned his people of which he was not aware. He reviewed education initiatives, went through medical funding with a fine-tooth comb, oversaw high-level military meetings, and all the while he refused to pay attention to the days that were passing. He wouldn't think about Johara.

He didn't deserve to think of her.

She had offered herself to him—her heart, her love, her service to his country—she had given him everything she had to give and he had told her to go. He'd told her to have a happy life. And that was what she was doing—with Paris.

He couldn't think about what she would have looked like on her wedding day; would she have smiled as she walked down the aisle? Was she nervous? Excited? Was she truly happy?

He couldn't think about what would happen after. Man and wife, the life they'd lead. He couldn't think about her being kissed by another man, touched by him. He couldn't think about any of it.

He'd made his decision, and even as he'd told her to leave he'd known he would regret it. He'd expected this. He owed it to both of them to hold the course.

This was for the best.

'Did they ever tell you how they met?'

Amir frowned, lifting his gaze from the wedding portrait of his parents, a decoration that had sat on his desk for so long he barely looked at it any more, focussing on Ahmed. The older man had been leaving, their meeting concluded. In fact, Amir had thought he had already left.

'No.' Amir shook his head. 'They didn't.'

'I'm not surprised.' Ahmed's smile showed affection, but something else—strain. His eyes swept over Amir.

'I was only twelve when they died. It wasn't something we'd discussed.'

'It was the night your father's engagement was supposed to be announced.'

Amir frowned. 'They hadn't met before?'

'No.' Ahmed moved to the photo, picking it up off the desk and looking at it thoughtfully. 'She was a guest at the party, the cousin of a diplomat. Your father bumped into her—spilled a drink on her skirt, if I remember correctly—and the rest was history.'

'You're saying he was supposed to marry someone else until that night?'

'I'm saying within half an hour of meeting your mother

he insisted the engagement agreement be set aside. They were inseparable.' Ahmed sighed.

Amir held his hand out, and Ahmed put the photo in it. The happiness in his parents' eyes was palpable. Through the veil of time he could feel the joy that had been captured in this moment.

'I know how happy they were,' Amir agreed.

'Yes. They were happy.' Ahmed frowned, sighed heavily once more, so Amir looked towards the older man with a frown, wondering what was on his mind. 'I often think about that. Would they have changed anything if they'd known what would happen?'

Amir stiffened in his seat, replacing the photo on the edge of his desk with care. 'It's impossible to know.'

'No.' Ahmed's smile was wistful. 'It's not. I believe that even if they'd been told on their wedding day what fate awaited them, they would not have shied away from it. Not when it brought you, and the time they had together.'

Amir's chest felt tight.

'I'm sorry, Your Majesty. At my age, the brain tends to become reflective.'

Ahmed moved towards the door. Before he could open it, Amir said, 'My mother paid a high price for that happiness.'

Ahmed frowned. 'I think if she was here she'd say it was worth it.'

Amir often dreamed of his parents. That they were drowning, or on fire, or falling from a cliff, and in every dream he reached for them, his fingertips brushing the cotton of his mother's clothes, or the ends of her hair, grabbing without holding, so close but ultimately ineffectual.

He knew what was at the root of the dreams: a disbelief that he hadn't been able to save them. A desire to go back to that night and do something, anything, that would change the twist of fate that had taken them from him.

His powerlessness had sat about his shoulders for a long time, and he'd never really accepted it.

This dream was different. Johara, in a maze. Not like the maze in Taquul, this had white walls, and as she ran through it the corridors became narrower and narrower, so that he could never reach her. Whenever he got close, she'd slip away again, disappearing no matter how hard he looked.

He woke with a start, his breath rushed, his forehead covered in perspiration.

She's getting married.

'I love you.'

'I want to stay here with you.'

He swore. Anger flooded his body. He ached for her. He felt her everywhere he looked, but she was gone.

He hadn't been able to catch her; he'd failed her.

CHAPTER THIRTEEN

BEING BACK IN Manhattan was a balm. It was temporary, but it was enough. She stifled a yawn with the back of her hand, glad the evening—the launch of a new therapy space and classroom funded by her charity—had been a success. And for a brief moment, as she'd walked through the room and smiled and spoken to the assembled guests, she'd almost felt like herself again.

Almost.

It was impossible to forget. It was impossible to feel whole when so much of herself was locked away in a space she couldn't access. She'd stopped counting the days since she'd left Ishkana. When it had passed ninety, she'd known: it was too long. He wasn't going to change his mind—he was glad she'd left. He'd forgotten about her. He'd drawn boundaries for their relationship and he was sticking to them with a determination that was innate to him.

Day by day she'd concentrated on Taquul, on taking on a role there, on seeming as though she were fine and focussed on a life that no longer held any appeal for her. She didn't speak about Ishkana or Amir, not even with her brother, and Malik never asked. At least he'd dropped the matter of her marrying Paris—for now. She went through the motions, day in, day out, breathing, eating, sleeping, smiling, when inside she felt as though she were withering and dying.

She used to try not to think of Amir but that was ludicrous—like trying to stop one's heart from beating. It was something she did reflexively so now she didn't even bother to fight it. She accepted that he would always be a part of her, even when he wasn't. She accepted that she would always look for him, think of him, reach for him—and that she'd never again see him or touch him.

Pain was her constant companion, but so what? She could live with it; she would live with it, because even pain was a reminder of him. And in the meantime, she could still make something of her life. She would always know that he was missing, but she refused to be cowed by that. In time, she'd grow strong again.

Perhaps she was already strong? She'd refused Malik's attempts to organise her marriage. She'd come to New York when he'd clearly wished her to stay. She was carving out the best life she could. And one day, she'd be happy again. Never complete, but content.

She had to be. There had been too much loss, grief, sadness and death for her to waste her life. She wouldn't allow herself to indulge in misery.

Her car pulled to a stop outside the prestigious high rise she called home while in the States, her security guard coming to open her door. She ignored the overt presence of guards flanking the door—the apartment was home to many celebrities and powerful politicians; such security measures were normal. Her guards walked her through the lobby. She barely noticed them.

Almost home now, she let the mask slip for a moment, allowing herself to feel her loneliness and solitude without judgement. The elevator doors pinged open and she stepped inside. One of her guards went with her, as was protocol, but before the doors closed another man entered. Unmistakably, he was of a security detail, but not hers.

A second later, the walls seemed to be closing in on her as a second man entered the elevator. Johara couldn't breathe. Her eyes had stars in them. She pressed her back to the wall of the elevator, sure she was seeing things, or that she'd passed out and conjured Amir from the relics of her soul, because he couldn't possibly be right in front of her, inside the elevator, here in Manhattan?

His dark eyes glowed with intent, his face a forbidding mask that made her knees tremble and her stomach tighten. She opened her mouth to ask him something—to ask if it was really him—but she couldn't. No words would form.

'I'd like a meeting with Her Highness.' He addressed his comment to her guard.

Her stomach flipped.

The guard looked to her. She could see his doubts—the peace was new. He didn't want to offend this powerful sheikh, but nor could he consent to this highly improper request.

She had to say something. A thousand questions flooded her. Anger, too. What was he doing here? Why had he come? It had been too long. Too long! Didn't he see how she'd changed? Couldn't he tell that inside, behind the beautiful dress and the make-up and the hair, she was like a cut flower left in the sun too long? She angled her face away from his. In the circumstances, his handsome appearance was an insult. How dared he look so good? So virile? So strong and healthy, as though he hadn't missed a moment's sleep since she left?

'I'm tired,' she said—the words ringing with honesty because they were accurate. She was exhausted.

'Yes.' It was quiet. Sympathetic. He *could* see what she

hid from the rest of the world. He could see inside her heart and recognise its brokenness.

She swallowed, hurting so much more now that he was here. The elevator doors closed but the carriage didn't move. Not until Amir reached across and pressed a button.

'This is important.'

Resistance fired through her. What she'd said to him, the night she'd left, had been important too. He hadn't listened. He'd made up his own mind and nothing she'd said could change it. She'd told him she loved him and he'd turned his back on her as though she meant nothing.

'I'm tired,' she said again, shaking her head. Her guard moved closer, as though to protect her. Amir stiffened and waved away his own guard. Most people wouldn't have noticed, but she was attuned to every movement he made. She saw the tiny shift of his body, the strengthening of every muscle he possessed.

His gaze bore into hers; she knew he registered everything she felt, and she didn't try to hide it. She returned his stare unflinchingly, because she wanted him to feel what he'd done to her. It was petty but necessary.

A muscle jerked in his jaw and a moment later he nodded, a look of acceptance on his features. 'Tomorrow, then.'

Her stomach squeezed. Tomorrow felt like a year away. She'd never sleep if she knew he wanted to speak to her. What could he possibly have to say?

It had been too long.

She bit down on her lip and damn it! Tears filled her eyes. She blinked rapidly, clearing them as best she could.

'We don't have any business together, Your Majesty.' The words were shaky. 'If it's a state concern, there are more appropriate channels—'

'It isn't.'

She had to press her back to the wall, needing its support.

The elevator stopped moving and Amir's guard stepped out, keeping one hand pressed to hold the doors open.

'This is a private matter.' His eyes didn't leave her face. 'This level is my apartment. Here is the key to my room. I'll stay until five p.m. tomorrow. If you find you would like to hear what I have to say, then come to me. Any time, Johara. I will wait.'

She stared at the key as though it were a poisonous snake, her fingertips twitching, her heart aching, her brain hurting.

'It's your decision,' he said quietly, and the gentleness of the promise had her reaching for the key.

She didn't say anything. She didn't promise anything. She couldn't. She felt blindsided, utterly and completely.

He turned and swept out of the elevator, but he was still there, even as the doors closed and it crested one level higher. She could smell him. She could feel him. Just knowing he was in the same building was filling her body with an ancient pounding of a drum, or the rolling in of the sea, waves crashing against her, making her throb with awareness, need, hurt, pain, love, and everything in between.

At three in the morning, she gave up trying to sleep. She pushed out of bed and walked towards the window, staring out at the glistening lights of New York. Even at this hour, the city exuded a vibrancy she'd always found intoxicating. But not now.

She barely saw the lights. All she could think about was Amir. Was he staring out at the same view? Thinking about her? Why was he here?

This is a private matter.

What could that mean?

Her heart slammed into her ribs—hard—then she turned

back to the bed, looking at the table beside it. His key sat there, staring right back at her.

Her heart flipped.

What was she doing?

Instead of standing here asking an empty bedroom why he was there and what he wanted, she could go down and demand he tell her. That made more sense.

Before she could second-guess herself, she grabbed her silken robe and wrapped it around herself, cinching it at the waist, then reached for the key. There was no risk of being seen by a nosy guest or paparazzi; she had the whole level of the building.

At his door, she hesitated for the briefest moment. She lifted a hand to knock, then shook her head, pressing the key to the door, pushing it inwards as she heard the buzz.

It was immediately obvious that he wasn't asleep. The lounge area was dimly lit. He sat in an armchair, elbows pressed to his knees, face looking straight ahead. The moment she entered, he stood, his body tense, his expression dark.

He wasn't surprised though. He'd been waiting for her. The realisation made her stomach clench.

'Why are you here?' It was the question she most desperately needed an answer to.

'To see you.'

It was the answer she wanted and yet it wasn't. It gave her so little.

She moved deeper into the apartment, the similarities to hers in its layout disorientating at first.

'Why?'

More was needed. More information. More everything.

'Please, sit down.'

She eyed the armchair warily, shaking her head. She felt better standing.

'Would you like a drink?'

She made a groaning noise of impatience. 'Amir, tell me…'

He nodded. He understood. He crossed to her, but didn't touch her. She could sense the care he took with that, keeping himself far enough away that there was no risk of their fingers brushing by mistake.

'I came to New York because it was the easiest way to see you.'

She frowned.

'Your brother would not send you back to Ishkana.'

She swallowed.

'You invited me?'

'No. But after he lied about your marriage to Paris, I read between the lines. You told him about us.'

Her jaw dropped. 'He what?'

'He told me you were to be married. At first I believed it to be true.'

She shook her head. 'He was wrong to do that. I never agreed. I would never agree.'

'I know.' His tone was gentle, calming. But she didn't feel calm. Frustration slammed through her.

'You told him about us, and he doesn't approve.'

She ground her teeth together. 'Whether he does or doesn't is beside the point. Malik has nothing to do with us.'

He studied her for several long seconds.

'He's your brother,' Amir said quietly.

'Yes. But I'm a big girl and this is my life. I make my own decisions.'

'I wanted to see you,' Malik said quietly. 'But arranging a visit to Taquul and coinciding our schedules proved difficult. Particularly without alerting anyone to the purpose of my visit.'

'Yes, I understand that.' She frowned.

'When I heard you were coming to New York, I followed.'

I followed. Such sweet words; she couldn't let them go to her head.

'Why?'

His smile was a ghost on his face. His eyes traced a line from the corner of her eye to the edge of her lips and she felt almost as though he were touching her. She trembled.

'Before you left Ishkana, I should have explained everything better. Only I didn't understand myself then. I couldn't see why I acted as I did. It took losing you, missing you, hearing that you were to marry someone else and knowing myself to be at the lowest ebb of my life only to pass through sheer euphoria at the discovery that you were not married. It took all these things for me to understand myself. I couldn't explain to you that night, because I didn't know.'

She swayed a little, her knees unsteady.

'I didn't ever decide to push you away. I never consciously made that decision, but it's what I've been doing all my life, or since my parents died at least. I have many people that consider me a friend yet I do not rely on anyone. Not because I don't trust them but because I don't trust life.' His smile was hollow. 'I lost my parents and I have been permanently bracing to experience that grief all over again. Until I met you, I shielded myself the only way I knew how—I made sure I never cared about anyone enough to truly feel their absence.'

Her stomach felt as though it had dropped right to the ground outside. Sadness welled up inside her. 'That sounds very lonely.'

'Loneliness is not the worst thing.' He brushed her sympathy aside. 'But you made it impossible to not care. I tried so hard not to love you, and yet you became a part of me.' He stopped talking abruptly, the words surprising both of them. 'Losing you would have been almost the worst thing that could happen to me—feeling that pain again would have been crippling. But so much worse if it were my fault. When you told me you wanted to stay with me, as my wife, I wanted to hold you so close and never let you go—but what if? What if something happened to you, and all because of my selfishness?'

Her heart was splintering apart for him. His fears were so understandable, but all this heartbreak…

'And I'm a Qadir,' she said quietly, trying to hold onto a hint of the bitterness that had been their stock in trade for generations.

He returned her stare unflinchingly. 'You're the woman I love.'

Her breath caught.

'And I am still half terrified that my love will ruin you, but I have realised something very important in the long months since you left the palace.'

She waited, impatient, desperate.

'You were right that night. This should have been your decision. You know what the risks are to our marriage, and you know that it will change many things for you, including, perhaps, your relationship with your brother. But these are your choices to make, not mine. I pushed you away, as I push everyone away, because that seemed better than taking this gamble. Yet it isn't mine to take.'

His voice was deep, gravelled.

'Only let me assure you that if you wish to make your life with me, I will do everything within my power to keep you safe and make you happy.'

She was silent. Dumbfounded.

'I know I hurt you.' Now, finally, he touched her. The lightest brush of his fingertips to hers. 'It was something I swore I wouldn't do yet in trying to protect you that's exactly what happened.'

She tilted her face away, tears stinging her eyes. 'You did hurt me,' she agreed softly. 'You pushed me away at a time when you could have used my support. You made me irrelevant. You're not the first person to do that, but it hurt the worst with you because I expected so much more.'

He groaned. 'I acted on instinct.'

She bit down on her lip, nodding. 'And I went home, and I waited, and I thought of you, and I have missed you every single day and you've been nowhere. It was as though it never happened. And now you're asking me to forget, and feel as I did then?' Her heart was battered and mangled and yet it was also bursting. Her defiant speech felt good to throw at him, but it wasn't really how she felt. She watched her words hit their mark, the pain in his face, the apology she felt in his eyes.

'I came here knowing you might not want what you did then. But still I had to explain. I didn't ask you to leave because I didn't love you. I loved you too much to have you stay. And I love you now, too much to fight you. Just know that you will always be my reason for being, Johara. Whether you're with me or not, everything I do will be for you.'

He lifted her hand to his lips and kissed it lightly, and she tilted her head back to his, facing him. 'I love you.'

He offered the words so simply, and they pushed inside her, shaking her out of the state she was in. This was really happening. He was standing in front of her pouring his heart out and she was holding onto the anger she'd felt. Was she doing exactly the same thing he had? Pushing him away because she was scared of being hurt again?

Maybe love always brought with it a sense of danger—and the gamble made the pay-off so much sweeter.

'So what are you saying?' she asked quietly, surprised her voice sounded so level when her insides were going haywire.

'Is that not obvious?'

She shook her head. 'I think I need you to say it.'

He nodded, his Adam's apple shifting as he swallowed. 'I wish I could go back to that night and change everything I said and did. I wish I had pulled you into my arms, thanked you for what you were offering and walked hand in hand with you to deal with the problems that faced *us*. Not me. *Us*. About *our* countries.' Her lips parted as she drew in a shaky breath.

'But I cannot go back in time, and I cannot change what I did then. So I am promising you my heart, and my future, and everything I can share with you. I am asking you to marry me, if you can find it in your heart to forgive me. I am asking you to be not just my wife, and the mother of my children, but a ruler at my side. You are brilliant and brave and your instincts are incredible. I would be lucky to have you as my wife, and Ishkana would be blessed to have you as its Queen. I'm asking you to look beyond the past to the future that we could have. And in exchange I promise that I will never again fail you. I will never again fail to see your strength and courage, to understand what you are capable of.'

Tears fell unchecked down her cheeks now. He caught one with the pad of his thumb, then another, wiping her face clean.

'Don't cry.' The words were gruff. 'Please.'

She laughed, though, a half-sob, a sign of how broken and fixed she felt all at once.

'Damn it, Amir, I wanted to hate you,' she said, stamping her foot. 'I have missed you so much.'

'I know.' He groaned, pulling her towards him, holding her close to his body. 'That is mutual.'

She listened to his heart and knew that it was beating for her, just as it always had. She stayed there with her head pressed to his chest, listening, believing, adjusting to the reality she was living, to the happiness that was within reach. They both had to be brave, but the alternative was too miserable to contemplate.

She blinked up at him, smiling. 'Let's go home, Amir.'

He made a growling sound of relief, pleasure, delight, and then he swooped his lips down to kiss her. 'Yes, *inti qamar*. Let us go home.'

'You can't be serious.'

Amir couldn't take his eyes off Johara. Through the glass of his bedroom, he watched her sleeping and felt as though nothing and no one could ever hurt him. She was here, in Ishkana, where she belonged. Seven months ago he'd pushed her away, believing the best thing he could do for her was arrange safe passage to Taquul. How wrong he'd been. And how fortunate he was that her heart was so forgiving…

'We flew back a few hours ago.' Behind him, the sun was beginning to break into the sky. 'It's all agreed.'

'You cannot marry her. I forbid it.'

'Your lack of consent will hurt Jo, Malik, but it will do nothing to change our plans.'

Silence met his pronouncement. If the past had taught them anything it was that neither wanted to risk another outbreak of violence. They both knew the cost too well. Malik might be furious, but he would not threaten military action.

'You must have kidnapped her. Taken her against her will.'

Amir straightened at the very suggestion. 'I will never, in my life, do *anything* against your sister's will. She came here because we are in love, Malik, as you are well aware.' The gentle rebuke sat between them. It was the reason, after all, that Malik had lied about an impending marriage to Paris.

'Love,' Malik spat with disbelief. 'She is a princess of Taquul. Her place is here.'

'Her place,' Amir corrected with a smile that came from deep within his heart, 'is wherever she wants it to be.'

Inside, Johara caught the statement through the open door, her eyes blinking open. She listened, her breath in a state of suspension as the man she intended to spend the rest of her life with spoke to—she could only presume—her brother.

'I insist on speaking to her.'

'Yes, of course,' Amir agreed. 'She is still asleep, but I have no doubt she will wish to speak to you about this. The purpose for my call is simple—I wanted to alert you to the state of affairs and to caution you against saying or doing anything to upset her.'

'Is that a threat?'

'A threat? No. It's a promise. If you push her away, you will lose her completely, Malik. She has chosen where she wants to be, and with whom.' He sighed. 'I love your sister. I plan to make her very happy by giving her everything she could ever want—and we both know that is for us to be, if not exactly friends, capable of existing harmoniously.'

Silence met this statement.

'She and I are to marry. She will carry my children, the heirs to Ishkana. They will be your nieces and nephews. Can you think of anyone who will benefit from continued estrangement?'

* * *

Inside the bedroom, Johara smiled, her eyes fluttering closed. She was exactly where she wanted to be and, with all her heart, she knew that the decision she'd made had been the right one. The only one she could ever make. Her heart, the skies, fate and future had guided her here—it was where she was meant to be.

EPILOGUE

AMIR HAD BEEN WRONG. He had believed his people, and the people of Taquul, would revolt at the very idea of a union between himself and Johara. He had braced for that, and prepared Johara for the inevitable splashback.

There had been none.

Nothing but euphoric delight and anticipation. Every detail of their union was discussed at length. He could not turn on the television without catching some talk-show host speculating about which tiara she would wear down the aisle, and whether the jewel for her ring would be of Taquul or Ishkana.

Billboards were pasted across the city with a smiling photo of Johara, welcoming her to Ishkana. Despite the pain his people had felt—or perhaps because of it—they welcomed her, knowing that lasting peace was truly at hand. With this marriage, the war became impossible. Their union bonded the countries in a way no peace treaty alone ever could. They were family now. His children would be a mix of them, and of their countries, and he had every intention of their being raised in the light of both countries and cultures.

Separation was not the way forward. Unity was. Just as Johara had said.

In the end, she wore a tiara that had belonged to her

mother, and a wedding ring that had been his mother's. Her dress was made of spider's silk, lace and beads, and when she walked towards him, he felt as though it were just him and her, and no one else in the world. When she walked towards him, he felt as though he might be about to soar into the heavens.

She smiled at him and he felt a thousand and one things—gladness, love, pleasure, relief, and a small part of him felt sorrow that his parents would never know her. But in a way, their happiness would be a part of this, because through their example he'd finally understood that being fearless was a necessity to love.

A year after their wedding, to the day, they were blessed with the birth of a son. Two years later, twin daughters followed. And for all the years into the future they'd hoped for, peace, happiness and prosperity favoured not only Amir and Johara, but the people of their kingdoms as well.

There was, as it turned out, never a story with less woe than that of Amir and his Jo.

* * * * *

MILLS & BOON

Coming next month

CLAIMING HIS BOLLYWOOD CINDERELLA
Tara Pammi

The scent of her hit him first. A subtle blend of jasmine and her that he'd remember for the rest of his life. And equate with honesty and irreverence and passion and laughter. There was a joy about this woman, despite her insecurities and vulnerabilities, that he found almost magical.

The mask she wore was black satin with elaborate gold threading at the edges and was woven tightly into her hair, leaving just enough of her beautiful dark brown eyes visible. The bridge of her small nose was revealed as was the slice of her cheekbones. For a few seconds, Vikram had the overwhelming urge to tear it off. He wanted to see her face. Not because he wanted to find out her identity.

He wanted to see her face because he wanted to know this woman. He wanted to know everything about her. He wanted… With a rueful shake of his head, he pushed away the urge. It was more than clear that men had only ever disappointed her. He was damned if he was going to be counted as one of them. He wanted to be different in her memory.

When she remembered him after tonight, he wanted her to smile. He wanted her to crave more of him. Just as he would crave more of her. He knew this before their lips even touched. And he would find a way to discover her identity. He was just as sure of that too.

Her mouth was completely uncovered. Her lipstick was

mostly gone leaving a faint pink smudge that he wanted to lick away with his tongue.

She held the edge of her silk dress with one hand and as she'd lifted it to move, he got a flash of a thigh. Soft and smooth and silky. It was like receiving a jolt of electricity, with every inch he discovered of this woman. The dress swooped low in the front, baring the upper curves of her breasts in a tantalizing display.

And then there she was, within touching distance. Sitting with her legs folded beneath her, looking straight into his eyes. One arm held the sofa while the other smoothed repeatedly over the slight curve of her belly. She was nervous and he found it both endearing and incredibly arousing. She wanted to please herself. And him. And he'd never wanted more for a woman to discover pleasure with him.

Her warm breath hit him somewhere between his mouth and jaw in silky strokes that resonated with his heartbeat. This close, he could see the tiny scar on the other corner of her mouth.

"Are you going to do anything?" she asked after a couple of seconds, sounding completely put out.

He wanted to laugh and tug that pouty lower lip with his teeth. Instead he forced himself to take a breath. He was never going to smell jasmine and not think of her ever again. "It's your kiss, darling. You take it."

Continue reading

CLAIMING HIS BOLLYWOOD CINDERELLA

Tara Pammi

Available next month

www.millsandboon.co.uk

COMING SOON!

We really hope you enjoyed reading this book. If you're looking for more romance, be sure to head to the shops when new books are available on

Thursday 15th October

To see which titles are coming soon, please visit

millsandboon.co.uk/nextmonth